How Blind
Is
Love…
Really?

A Novel
By Kae Brown

My Father's Child Publishing
Union, NJ

Peace
and
blessings

Kae Brown
05

Published and distributed by My Father's Child Publishing
P.O. Box 364, Vauxhall, NJ, 07088
www.myfatherschildpublishing.com

Edited by Walida Edwards, Keisha Ray, and Blair Bailey.

Cover created- started by Teka, finished by Deneen of Deesignz.
www.deesignz.com

Back cover photo by Blair Bailey.

Publisher's Note
This book is a work of fiction. Names, characters, places, and
incidents are either the product of the author's imagination or are used
fictitiously, and any resemblance to actual persons, living or dead,
business establishments, events, or locales is entirely coincidental.

ISBN 0-9764710-0-0

First Print February 2004

DEDICATION

This book is dedicated to those that have passed on but had a major impact in and on my life while they were here. Nanny Brown '86, Serena Slade '91, Daddy (William Brown) '93, Grandma Mary Bailey '95, Brenda Sister Charles '95, Eric Hines '96, Dwight Giddens '97, Tanya Mickens '98, Aunt Lois Bailey '99, Aunt Sameerah Mickens '99, Grandma Pearl Curry '02, Al Kabir Sorey '03, Renee Dobson '03 and Che Broadus '04.

I know your up in heaven, shining down on me. Watching closely over, what God has made me to be. And if I remain faithful, to my Father up above. We will be together soon once again in love.

I love and miss you all
KAE

CHAPTER 1
HOW?

I woke up dizzy. I strained to look around. This space was the size of a breadbox. My head ached. There was dried blood on my left hand. I lifted my blood stained hand to my right eye.

"Ouch!" It was nearly swollen shut. I braced myself and sat up on the edge of the cot that I was occupying. My bones cracked. It was dark and damp. I closed my good eye. I gently dropped my face into my hands. Slowly, I shook my head from left to right.

"*How did I get here?*" I remembered being in the mess hall eating what I considered to be "mess." Better yet, I was staring at it. To me, this place was named perfectly.

It brought me back to when I was six years old. One morning, I was sitting at our white kitchen table across from my mother. My lovely mother drank black coffee and read the Star Ledger newspaper, while I stared at my oatmeal as if it were pig slop. Up and down I bought the spoon from my Strawberry Shortcake bowl to my mouth. Each time I let the slop spill back into the bowl. I could not muster up the courage to eat it. She looked at me over the top of her paper.

"Eat that food Diamond. Don't play with it!" I sat there unmoved. She sipped her coffee.

"Diamond, there are starving kids in China, now eat!" Once again I sat there like a mime. My mother slammed the paper down.

"Diamond, do you know how blessed you are to have that food?" I dropped the spoon back into the bowl and pushed it towards her.

"Well you eat it then. You need a blessing more then me." She reached across the table. *Whap!* She popped me square in the middle of my mouth. I was such a smart mouth little kid. I just looked at her with the evil eye. You see, I have thick shapely eyebrows like my dad. I could shoot you a look to kill by scrunching down my forehead and making my eyebrows into the same shape as a lowercase m. She raised her hand again.

"Sab Ma!" I slid my bowl back towards me and ate a spoonful. I held my nose as I swallowed. Hmm, it wasn't that bad. I straighten up because my dad was not there to protect me at the time. As usual, he was out working hard so me nor my mother wanted for anything.

All that kept echoing in my head was, "Eat your food, don't play with it," and *Smush!* The female C.O. (Corrections Officer) mushed my face in my plate. I jumped up. I breathed out like a raging bull. I was a grown woman, damn it, not a little kid and this big burly bitch named Jackson was not my mother. She smirked.

"I told you to eat your food and not play with it!" I picked up the tray with both hands.

"Bitch you eat it!" Then I mushed the tray in her face. Why did I do that? Every guard in the place jumped on me like I was some type of wild, ferocious animal. I was choked, kicked, maced, and punched. You name it, they did it. Then they threw me in the hole for a month. Ooh so that's how I got here, but I know you are wondering how I got here "*here.*" The place that houses the hole, the big house, the joint, in laymen's terms, jail? Well, let me see, where should I begin? Hmmm... Since I got a month to be in here, I might as well start from the very beginning.

I already told you about the pig slop filled morning. After breakfast, I was sitting on my front steps playing jacks when a moving truck pulled up. The driver was a very tall dark-skinned male with a full beard; the passenger was a pretty fair skinned lady with long hair. They got out, looked up at the brick front house and smiled. A station wagon with South Carolina plates then pulled up onto Russell Street directly behind the moving truck. A big mouth big butt lady jumped out screaming, "Mitch you need to slow the hell down, driving all fast trying to leave somebody. You trying to get me lost in this bullshit town?" I just shot her a look. My grown butt was getting ready to stand up and say, "*You live in a bullshit town!*" But, as I stood up to place my hands on my imagination, for you slow ones, my young undeveloped hips, my mother appeared in the screen door.

"Diamond, sit ya grown ass down cause I know you was fixing to say something smart." My mother knew me like the back of her hand because I was going to do just that, say something smart. At that time a teenage boy climbed out of the front seat of the station wagon.

"Ma you just jealous we can't afford to move in this bullshit town." She looked at him and rolled her eyes.

"Boy! No I am not jealous." Me and my mom looked at each other and laughed as if to say, "*Ooh she a nut.*" Then 3 kids emerged from the back of the wagon. One boy was about eleven or twelve. He walked up to the new house real cool. He rubbed his hands together.

"Yeah dig our new pad!" The 2 kids who looked about my age jumped up and down screaming, "Yaaaaaaaaa!" I rolled my eyes and said aloud, "Ooh God! Would you calm down already? You getting ready to get on my last nerve." My mom adjusted the vent windows on the screen door. She sucked her teeth.

"What damn nerves Diamond? You ain't got no nerves! Be nice...Look, a new playmate for you. Now maybe you can stop playing with all the boys in the neighborhood. We need more little girls around here and look, one is moving right across the street from us." I looked at my mother and mentally said, "*Get a grip. I am too old to have playmates.*" What did she think I was still five years old? She was such a wreck. Well they began to move their stuff in and I kept playing with my jacks. At that time Danny and David from next door came over and sat on my stairs. They were very good at just inviting themselves somewhere they were not invited. I looked at them both from head to toe.

"Hello! Isn't that what you say when you step up on somebody's property." David replied, "Shut up Diamond. You're always talking smart. But what up anyway? Who dat over there?" I rolled my eyes.

"How the hell am I suppose to know?" My mother yelled from inside the front screened in porch, "Diamond Crescent is that you out there cussing like you grown?" I was busted. I didn't know she was still squatting being nosey.

"No Mommy!" We all covered our mouths and snickered. David was eight and Danny was seven. They were brothers that looked alike but acted opposite. David then saw the little girl come out and stood up to get a better view.

"Dag D, she pretty even though she young. Why you don't look like that?" I snapped, "If you think she so pretty then why don't you go sit on her steps!" He began creeping down the stairs.

"Maybe I will! Come on Danny." Danny's shy butt looked like he saw a ghost as his eyes opened up wide.

"No way man! I ain't even going over there! Did you see the size of that man?!" Me and David laughed because Danny was so scary. He was cool though. These 2 were my best friends. We did everything together. Including busting each other's chops. My mother then appeared in the screen door once again. This time with juice and home made chocolate chip cookies. The boys looked at my mom and said in unison, "We love you Auntie Ann!" David added, "You're the best mom in the whole wide world." She smiled and winked at him.

"Oh yeah? Maybe I should call your mom and tell her you said so." They both cried out, "Nooooo! Don't do that." You see their mom and my mom were best friends since they were kids. My parents were both of their Godparents and their parents were mine. I smacked away on a cookie with crumbs on my face.

"Yeah Ma! Call Auntie Debra and tell her since they

so tough." They both sucked their teeth at me, but continued to eat and drink. I loved my Auntie Debra and I loved the fact that they lived right next door.

My Godfather a.k.a. Uncle David, on the other hand, had gotten married to someone else and bought a humungous house in West Orange, NJ. It had 6 bedrooms and a built in swimming pool. He had two more kids, who were both boys as well. The kicker? He had a white wife. A perky, white, valley girl wife. Aunt Debra called her 'Snowflake.' Uncle David's other kids with 'Snowflake' where Damien who was three and Demond who was one. He still came and picked me up to do things because I was his only daughter. I loved my Uncle David even though he wasn't shit. You see my parents and Godparents are straight out of a movie. My mother and Aunt Debra are best friends and so are my father and Uncle David. The only difference between my dad and my uncle is, my Uncle David still wanted to be a player. Still after two kids with Aunt Debra and she said she was tired. They had been together since she was seventeen, never married, and then ten years later he messed around and got this 'Snowflake' trick pregnant and my aunt put him out. So 3 years later she was still single saying, "Men ain't shit," and she was gonna raise her sons better then that. She was always telling me, "Girl why a man gonna buy the cow if he gets the milk for free?! D, don't be no fool, you hear?"

I would just smile and say, "O.K. Auntie." Then think, *ooooowwwww Uncle David be stealing milk from the store and Auntie Debra acting crazy cause we ain't got no where to keep a cow around here.* So, back to the new family. The little girl dropped a box trying to help and broke something. The little boy was running around acting crazy. So I saw the father grab the boy by his right hand and the girl by her left hand and began to walk towards us. He marched them right up to the front of my steps.

"Hi, I'm Mitch and these are my precious twins, Starr Angel and Samir Ali." They both whined out, "Daaaaadddddd." He leaned down towards them and whispered, "What?" They looked up at him and gave him the wide-eyed 'you know better' look.

"Ooh I'm sorry. This is Starr and Sam." He then whispered to them, "Is that better?" They both shook their heads wildly up and down. He stood back up straight and looked back at us.

"We are new to this neighborhood and I thought you looked about their age so I wanted to bring them over and introduce them. Starr and Sam say hi."

"Hi," they both replied as one and looked down like they were ooh so shy. By this time you know nosey Ann a.k.a. my mother appeared in that screen door once again.

"Hi. How are you?" She walked out the screen door and down the stairs with her hand extended shaking Mitch's hand. He smiled broadly, exposing his white teeth.

"I am Ann and these are my three children, Diamond, David, and Danny." He smiled broadly.

"Diamond. What a pretty name for a pretty little girl. And David and Danny look at those muscles. Are you two body builders?" David blurted out, "You know... We try." I looked down and blushed.

"Thank you." My mother playfully mushed me in the back of my head.

"Girl please! You know you ain't even shy." I stood up and did the black girl's trait. I rolled my neck and my eyes.

"I am too shy!" She pointed her thumb back at me.

"Mitch see how shy she is." They both laughed. She leaned down and squeezed the twin's cheeks.

"And what are these little darlings names?" David cut in, "Ma this is Starr and Sam." He acted like he knew them for years. Mitch inquired about our ages.

"How old are your children Ann?" She smiled at us.

"Well actually these two knuckleheads are my Godsons who live right next door. David is eight and Danny is seven. My only child is Diamond and she is six."

He exclaimed, "Well Starr and Sam are six too." She slapped my knee.

"See Diamond I told you, you would have a new playmate." I just looked at her. She crossed her arms over her chest.

"Well I was waiting for my husband to come home so we could have a proper greeting. As a matter of fact I know you probably will be tired after all this moving and won't feel like cooking, so why don't you and the whole family come over for a little barbeque?" My mother loved to cook anything that was considered soul food, well any food.

"No we don't want to impose upon your family." His muscular arm was in reach. She tapped him.

"Don't be silly! You guys are coming and that is that." He laughed at my mom.

"O.K. don't twist my arm." She leaned in towards Mitch.

"Why don't you let the kids stay over here for now because I know they get in the way."

"Who you telling!" They started laughing together. He looked both ways and started back across the street.

"Thanks again." He told Starr and Sam to behave and listen to Mrs., "What is your last name?" She waved her hand.

"Ooh they can call me Auntie Ann. Everybody does."

"O.K. listen to Mrs. Auntie Ann." She laughed once again. He was not that funny and I will tell daddy when he gets home just how much she thinks he is funny then she can hahahaha laugh at that. Mitch crossed back across the street and my mother ran in the house to start cooking. Sam and Starr were both cute as they could be. They were caramel colored with little round faces and they both had dimples. Mr. Mouth a.k.a. David started the conversation.

"Where you guys from?"

"South Carolina," they replied in unison.

"Dag that's far. Why you move to Jersey?" Starr fiddled with her fingers.

"My dad's job transferred him here so we will be living here from now on." Samir added,"He works in New

York as a stock broker but everyone told him to live in Jersey and commute so here we are in Foxhall, New Jersey." I cleared my throat.

"Ahem, it is Vauxhall! Please get it right." Sam looked down at his feet.

"Sorry." I rolled my neck.

"It's alright but don't let it happen again." David got angry at me chumping Sam.

"Shut up Diamond!" I jumped up from my stairs.

"You shut up." He waved his hand at me.

"Anyway, don't mind her. She's a witch." I sat back down.

"Just like your mother." He glared at me with a scowling face.

"Good! I'm telling her." I sucked my teeth.

"Good! I don't care! Tell, tell you smell!"

"Whatever Diamond!" David then ignored me and started talking about what we did for fun, where we went to school, and what we watched on TV. Me and Danny just sat there. I began to play with my jacks again and Starr asked, "Can I play with you?" I handed her the ball.

"I don't care." She bounced the ball and picked up one jack. She looked at me.

"After this, do you wanna play Candyland?" David frowned up his face.

"That is for girls. Let's play hide and go seek."

David reached over with his hand and tagged me.

"Ah-ha, ah-ah, Diamond, you're it again, ah-ha!"

I whined, "Aww man. I'm always it!" Starr placed the jacks and ball in my plastic baggy.

"I will be it for you Diamond." I smiled at her.

"O.k. thanks." We all hid and I guess from the twin vibe she found her brother first. The rest of us reached the home base, which were my steps. I yelled in, "Mom can you bring us something to drink we thirsty!" She yelled out, "I only got two hands Diamond and both of 'em working so come in here and help get everybody something to drink."

I moaned, "Aaawww man!" Starr volunteered to

help me and picked up the empty pitcher from the porch. I jumped up so happy to finally have a helpful new friend.

"Thanks!" I smiled at her. We went inside the kitchen and we got the cups and mom brought a fresh pitcher of cherry red Kool Aid outside to the porch.

"Here y'all go and don't bug me no more." She smiled as she began to re enter the house.

"I am getting everything ready for this evening O.k.?" I gulped down my juice and reached for more.

"O.k. Ma." Once she walked all the way back in the house, I wiped my mouth with the back of my hand.

"Dag, don't bother her when she's cooking. She will cut your head off and put it in the pot too." We all laughed. Next thing I know my dad was pulling up in his 1981 gold Mercedes Benz that he got brand new the year before. I was jumping up and down on my steps screaming, "Daddy, Daddy!" I ran down the stairs and waited for him to pull into the drive way and get out. I jumped in his arms. I mean I was daddies one and only little girl. He kissed my forehead.

"Hey my little Diamond. What's cooking good looking?" I always laughed when my dad said that to me. My mother came out to get the groceries daddy had brought home. She had called him at his office and gave him a list to pick up. It was like 8 bags full of stuff. He put me down and waved towards the stairs.

"Everyone come get a bag." All the other kids jumped off the steps. We grabbed a bag each and marched them in the kitchen. Then we heard the music every kid loves to hear. I screamed, "Ice cream truck!" We all ran outside like we had money and stopped the truck. I screamed louder towards the house, "Daddy we want ice cream... pleeeaaassse?" My mother came to the screen door.

"No! Not before dinner," and she walked back in. My dad snuck outside. He put his finger to his mouth.

"Shh!" He brought us the ice cream anyway. He whispered, "Now sit on the steps and quietly eat your ice cream." My mother screamed from inside the house,

"Danny did you buy them ice cream anyway?!" My dad walked up the stairs and in the screen door.

"No baby, you said no and no means no." He turned and winked at us through the screen door. I knew my mother wouldn't catch us because she was in the kitchen cooking and she doesn't stop cooking for no one. Starr licked her vanilla ice cream with sprinkles that ran down her hand.

"Your dad is cool." I chewed on my sprinkles.

"I know," and I smiled. After we finished our ice cream we sat on the stairs and talked about our favorite TV shows and stuff like that. It was 6:30 and my mom came out. She looked at Samir.

"Go tell your family whenever they're ready." My mom watched him cross the street and no more then 15 minutes later the whole family was coming. At the same time David ran next door and got his mom to come too. My mom had gotten so busy she forgot to call Aunt Debra and tell her to come over. Aunt Debra came switching over and walked up to me.

"Who is my favorite daughter?" I jumped up in her arms and gave her a hug and a kiss.

"I am your only daughter." She held me in her arms and with her right hand she pulled at one of my braids.

"Your hair looks so pretty D." My mom had just corn rowed it in a style with a million beads. Since my hair was pretty long, like past my shoulders all I could do was swing it. I swung it.

"Thank you." My mom and dad were standing in the door. My mom sucked her teeth.

"Oh brother Diamond. You are going to break your neck if you keep swinging that mess." Her and my dad came out the screen door onto the stairs. I gave Aunt Debra another kiss on her cheek. She scrunched up her face.

"Girl your mouth is sticky. What were you eating some ice cream or candy?" My mother looked at me and noticed the white ring the vanilla ice cream left around my mouth and screamed, "Danny why you be trying to play me for a fool all the time?" He covered his mouth hiding his laugh.

"What?!" She raised her right eyebrow.

"I got your what. I said no ice cream and you bought it anyway. No wonder Diamond doesn't respect my authority." He playfully punched Aunt Debra in her arm.

"Damn Debra you talk to much." Debra scrunched up her face and rubbed her arm. My dad was laughing but my mother wasn't. The new family was walking over so he reached around my mother and hugged her from behind.

"Don't act up we got company coming." He smacked her on the butt. That always made her smile. My mom started walking towards the back of the house.

"Everyone come in the backyard so we can all get acquainted." It was about 7:15 and we were all in the back chowing down and listening to my mother's favorite songs over and over again. One song was Candi Staton's Victim and the other was Diana Ross's The Boss. Let me give you a run down of who was there incase your lost. It was me, my mom and dad, Aunt Debra, David and Danny, the new family whose last name was Mitchell. It was Mitch, yes his name is Mitch Mitchell and I still laugh when I think about it, Krystal, his wife and the kids mother, the twins Starr and Sam, their older brother Shareef who was 12, Mitch's youngest sister Michelle and her 16 year old son Michael. Michelle and Michael lived in the Prince Street Projects in Newark, NJ. That is why earlier she had said, "Moving to this bullshit town" cause she was just jealous that she lived in the hood and we lived in the suburbs (the fake suburbs). Michelle and Michael had flown down to South Carolina to help them drive back and move their stuff in. My mother had made hamburgers, hotdogs, ribs, potato salad, baked beans, salad, corn on the cob, and she baked a chocolate cake and made cookies and rice krispie treats for the kids.

I was so grown and always in grown ups conversation so I got all the scoop. Mitch moved here for a better job with his family so the kids thought. But after a few beers you know people start to volunteer a little T.M.I (*Too Much Information*). I mean he did move here for that, but he had a little innocent affair what ever an "innocent affair" is, cheating is cheating right? Anyway after the affair was said and done the lady became a stalker so they moved. Krystal said she didn't want to catch a body what ever that meant at the time. Now that I'm older, I know she meant kill that chic for messing with her husband. Krystal did hair so she was going to set up the basement into a shop of her own. Michelle was one of those think she can do it all. She chomped on her corn on the cob as the butter ran down her hand.

"When the shop opens I will work in there." Her comment went ignored. For now she was working as a nurses aid in University Hospital in Newark. My mom use to work in a law firm but when she had me she stopped working. First of all my dad didn't want her to work and second he owned a laundry mat, a liquor store, and a beauty salon. At that time my dad told Krystal, "I have an empty chair in my hair shop if you're interested." She wiped her hands and mouth on her napkin.

"Yes I would be." She smiled, "I found a new job all with in 1 day of moving to a new place." Michelle sucked her teeth at my father not offering her a chair. He just sucked down his third Budweiser. Now back to Michelle. She was a single mother who let her son Michael say and do what he wanted. Her philosophy was she would not hold him back from his right of freedom of speech. She let him curse and say whatever he felt like saying. Like I said earlier, she was a nut. All and all we had a good night their first night in town. Our new neighbors kept kidding saying they could get use to this to treatment. Aunt Debra butted right on in saying, "Don't! This is just a little neighborly hospitality and shit for today but tomorrow we will act like we don't know ya!" All the adults laughed. Us kids continued to play in the yard. When all was said and done for the evening it was nearly 11 PM. Luckily it was Friday night. All that time me and Starr sat together and talked.

The boys began to get tight. Shareef and Michael talked and kept their distance because they thought they were too old for us. As the adults cleaned up, I blurted out to my dad, "Ooooowwwww Daddy (I always asked my dad cause he didn't tell me no) can Starr spend the night?" He tossed some trash in the garbage.

"I don't care. It is up to Starr's Mommy and Daddy." I tugged on Mitch's shirt.

"Ooooowwwww Starr's Mommy and Daddy, can Starr spend the night?" They looked at each other and Mitch replied, "It 's O.K. but we don't want to intrude." My dad popped the top on another beer.

"No it's not an intrusion. I'm just glad Diamond finally got another girl to play with." Then Danny and David were jealous and David (Mouth Almighty) said, "No fair Ma. Can Sam spend the night with us?" She stretched.

"Boy you know I don't care." So it was all set. Starr was staying with me and Sam was staying with the boys. I grabbed Starr by the wrist.

"Come on Starr, we going to my room." She kissed her mom and dad bye. I was half way up the back steps and my mom cleared her throat.

"Miss Diamond did you forget something?" I kept going.

"No." My dad cleared his throat.

"Excuse me Diamond. I think you did forget something." I turned at the top of the deck.

"Oooooh nice to meet everybody, thank you for coming." He shook his head.

"No little miss smarty pants. Where is my kiss good night?" I smacked my forehead.

"Oooooh." I ran down the deck and over to my dad. I kissed him. I adored my dad and in my eyes he could do no wrong. I hugged him tight.

"Love you," and I bolted passed my mother and tagged her.

"Your it." My mom jumped up, chased me and

grabbed me.

"Gotcha!" She kissed me like 100 times. I wiped my face and frowned.

"Ooh Mom, you're so embarrassing." She put me down.

"Spell it?" All the adults laughed. Me and Starr continued to my room. Starr looked around in sheer amazement.

"Your room is great." I had posters up with a pink canapé bed, a pink and white dresser, just pink everything. When I think back now it was just sickening. I was so grown with a pink TV and a pink phone. I handed her some P.J.'s. She was about my size and I gave her my favorite pair to make her feel welcomed. It was a pink and white night shirt with a unicorn on it with sparkles and glitter everywhere. Starr put it on and modeled it in the full-length mirror on the back of my door.

"This is so *perty*." She had a little country twang in her voice. She was such a sweetheart. We sat up all night. While I brushed her long hair that reached to the middle of her back, we talked about boys, school, marriage, and having children, like we were grown.

We fell asleep when the sun was coming up. My mom let us sleep late. We woke up at like 12 and missed all our Saturday morning cartoons. It was the beginning of August. We had about 3 weeks left before school started. Those 3 weeks we became inseparable. I completely forgot about my original best friends, David and Danny. Starr forgot about her twin. Over those 3 weeks, their house got set up, Mitch and Krystal started their new jobs, and Michelle and Michael went back to the hood. My mom continued to cook and bake and Aunt Debra, well she was still Aunt Debra.

She worked as a branch manager in a bank. She hated her ex but he did take care of her and the boys. My daddy wanted another baby at this time but I wanted to be an only child. He was trying to get me to understand that he would still love me the same but I wasn't trying to hear all that. It was all about me and only me. My mom was already pregnant when my dad was trying to convince me, but she miscarried the baby at 3 months. She decided she didn't want anymore and got her tubes tide so she didn't have to go through the pain of losing a child again. I always wonder if I would have had a brother or a sister but if you read on you will find out that I gained a sister.

CHAPTER 2
SCHOOL STARTS

O.K., so now it is the first day of school and me and Starr were in the same 1st grade class (yippee). I introduced her and Sam to everybody and everybody loved them. As the years went by, me and Starr still remained best friends. We would tell outsiders that we were sisters. The summer before the 5th grade we pricked our fingers and made our sisterhood official. We became blood sisters. I had taken the role on as being her sister seriously. I wouldn't let anyone do anything to her. Even though they had been in Jersey almost 5 years, she was a still a sweet southern girl at heart. I was a rough and tough northern girl so I had to protect her from the wolves up here. She was so sweet that some people couldn't stand it because they thought it was fake. I can remember in the 5th grade, our last year of Washington elementary school. Starr accidentally hit this girl, Cheryl, in the mouth with a basketball in gym class. Cheryl's mouth started bleeding. Starr was so upset she offered to walk Cheryl to the nurse, but Cheryl screamed, "No! You did this on purpose and I am going to get you!" So that is when I stepped in.

"Winch, she didn't do it on purpose and if you even think about getting her I will get you!" Everyone in class howled, "Oooooooooooooooowwwwwww!" Cheryl snapped her fingers in my direction.

"Ooh yeah? I will take both of y'all on." At that time the teacher intervened and told everyone to be quiet and for Cheryl to go to the nurse. I whispered, "We will see after school tough girl." Starr looked at me worried with a tear in her eye. She sniffled.

"I never had a fight before. I have never even had an enemy, you know that." I put my hands on my hips.

"And you won't have a fight today! You're my sister and I will protect you. Remember that. Don't worry, you know I am not a stranger to fighting. Now stop worrying about that. Lets play ball!" I bounced Starr the ball and we began to play again as if nothing happened. See, having my two God brothers around kept me tough from a young age. Around our neighborhood we would be fighting all the time. Plus the fact that my father thought he was "*Ali*" didn't make matters any better. But, where Starr was from and even in Jersey everybody loved her so she told the truth when she said no one ever hated her before. It was O.k. by me 'cause people had hated me before. This would not be my first or last fight. So at 3 o'clock you know everybody was all souped up for a fight. Me and Starr walked out of the school. Cheryl was standing there with her friend and guess what she did? She said, "What up Starr? What up Diamond? I was just mad earlier I don't even want to fight."

Starr smiled and gave her a hug. I just looked at her like she was crazy. I pointed my finger in her face.

"Yo, you owe my sister an apology." She stepped back.

"What?!"

"I didn't stu stu stu stutter. You heard me. You tried to diss her in front of the class and I can't go for that so apologize." She rolled her eyes and apologized, and if I were her, I would have apologized too.

Anyway, after that, her and Starr became cool, but I wasn't feeling her. She was a punk and I didn't need her down on my team. Her nickname was 'Pumpkin Pie' cause she was shaped like a pumpkin, but from that day on I started calling her "Punk-in" Pie cause she was the biggest "Punk-in" our school. Starr said I was mean and needed to give people a chance. I told her ain't nothing happening cause if I can't trust a person with my back then I don't need them. So, that was 5th grade year. We graduated from elementary school and headed to 6th grade. Now around our way, 6th grade was one school for all the 6th graders called Central Six or C-6. This was the year of our first school dance. Starr went with Danny and I went with Samir. This was the night of both of our first kisses. I was so fresh I kissed Sam and he said, "Yuck!" Danny kissed Starr and she blushed. Anyway, 6th grade was cool no major drama to report but when we left there it was time for the semi big time, junior high school. For the first time in all the years that me and Starr had been friends we were not in all the same classes. I was pissed and she was sad. I marched right into the principal's office my first day and asked why we were not in the same classes. The principal, Ms. Hines was not at her desk but the vice principal Mr. Bell was. He looked over the top of his glasses and cleared his throat.

"Listen young lady. That is just how it goes and from the way you carry yourself I guess I will be seeing you in this office quite frequently." I just smiled and backed out of the office.

"No Sir, not me." And with that said and done, I left quietly. Dag, it was only my first day and I didn't want him calling my mother. She told me to always remember, "You go to school to learn, not teach." At least we had the same lunch to catch up on gossip. Our first day there was difficult. This was the first time we would really switch classes. Our junior high was 7th, 8th, and 9th grade. The 9th graders would smack our books out of our hands, send us the wrong way in the halls, give us wedgies, etc. It was their way of welcoming us, nice huh? Well we now were 11 going on 12 and my body was blossoming a little to fast. I skipped a training bra and went straight into a "B" cup. Yuck I hated having "boobies," as I would call them. Starr still had on her t-shirt. She wanted boobies bad so she had her mom get her some training bras even though she had nothing to train. Of course the 9th graders would be looking at my breasts making me sick. In the junior high, it was the first time me and Starr had real boyfriends. Can you guess who my first boyfriend was? Samir, of course. He was so sweet, and Starr hated it because he would hang around us and it was no more just me and her. So she decided to get her a boyfriend. It wasn't nobody but Danny. We would all walk to school together, walk home together, go to the movies and just hang out. We were the four musketeers. These were the first guys we played catch a girl get a girl with. You know that game where the girls get a head start and the guys chase the girls. Whoever they catch, they suppose to get them, meaning have sex with them but to us it just meant get free feels. Like grabbing boodies and French kissing. It was dumb that us four played together 'cause of course Samir wasn't going after Starr and Danny wasn't coming after me. One day, my dad stood in the kitchen doorway and watched me pour a bowl of Fruit Loops.

"Diamond, I notice you're slowing down on your love for me and giving it all to Samir." I turned my back and went in the fridge to get out the milk.

"Ooh Daddy, I am not! I promise I will always love you." I placed the bowl on the table and walked over and kissed my dad on the cheek. I extended my empty palm.

"Now can I have some money please?" He went in his wallet and got out a twenty-dollar bill. He slammed it in my hand.

"You need to get a job." I hugged him.

"Ooh Daddy!" I think my dad was a little jealous of Samir. Before he left the kitchen he added, "You young D, but not to young to know that guys ain't shit, so be careful."

"Ooh Dad. It ain't like we getting married." At the time of this particular father daughter talk Starr called me on my phone, which went with me wherever I went in the house. My mother always joked and said I should get a phone attached to my ear. But anyway, I excused myself from the rest of this talk. I was saved by the bell. I held onto my cordless as me and my bowl of cereal went up the stairs to my room.

"Hey sis, what's up?"

"Guess what?"

"What?"

"I got my period." I choked on a spoonful of Fruit Loops.

"What? How?"

"What do you mean how? It just came D." I was scared then, I didn't want my period. I know you get cramps and be sick and gotta wear a thick pad like a diaper. I finished my cereal and went over to see my best friend to comfort her. She looked older, more mature. I felt like a kid. Sam over heard what happened and told Danny. Danny said, "Gross" and wouldn't come over. He stayed away from Starr that day like she was contagious. She was hurt by him acting up. So, the next day I made a special trip to his house to tell him off. He said he was sorry and went over and apologized to Starr. I had so much juice on my block it was ridiculous.

Well at the turn of the next school year Starr got some boobies and I got my period and my mother just had to tell my father. And on that very day he wanted to have a serious heart to heart talk with me. Here I am cramped up and sick and he wants to kick it. I was laid up in the bed holding a hot water bottle on my stomach and he barges in my room. He flopped down on the foot of my bed and tapped my foot.

"Look Diamond your body is changing and that means now you can have a baby." I rolled over, covered my face with my pillow and moaned.

"Ooh boy Daddy. Ain't nobody having no babies." He yanked the pillow off my face.

"I didn't say you were, but your body is capable now to produce one D. I was a boy once and they usually have one thing on their minds. S-e-x!" I was grossed out at my dad talking about sex. I rolled over to face him and turned my lip up in disgust.

"D, don't look at me like that. I was a boy once. They will tell you 'I love you', and 'I want you and need you', and he will get you pregnant and be gone and you will be stuck with a baby and he will still be doing his thing. I told you about these streets D. Did I ever lie to you?" I shook my head.

"No daddy." He then cupped his hands behind his head and leaned back on the wall that my bed was pushed up against.

"D, I think you're old enough to know the story of me and your mother. We met when I was eighteen and your mother was fifteen." He chuckled as he rolled his eyes up in his head.

"Yeah your mother was a cutie and she lied about her age saying she was seventeen. She was shaped like you so I thought she was telling the truth. You see Diamond I was living the fast life; I was out in the streets, getting that fast money. Do you know what I mean?" I sat up and shoved a pillow behind my head as I leaned on the headboard.

"Yeah, I guess." My dad sat up straight.

"No D. I don't want you to guess I want you to know, so I will tell you. I was selling drugs. Me and your Uncle David were partners and both got caught up. At age twenty I got sentenced to 3 years in prison. I had money stacked up and I kept it stashed. That is when I found out your mom had lied cause she was only seventeen at the time I got locked up and couldn't get in the jail with out an adult cause you had to be 18 to come in the jail alone." He began to rub his hands together.

"So D, I was stuck. I had one of my friends on the streets dealing for me and your mom, she remained loyal to me and she went to college. I don't know how she got in with all the days she cut school to be with me. I thought she just was chilling at home all day and she was suppose to have her tale in school, but her grandmother raised her after her parents died in a car crash and she couldn't do nothing with her so she ran wild. D if you ever..." I put my hand up to bring him back to the current story at hand.

"Dad please finish the story, gees." He jokingly

smacked my foot.

"Anyway, I ended up only doing 18 months and came right back out doing the same thing again, being locked up made me wiser and I knew I had to get in and get out, but come out on top." He stood up and paced back and forth.

"D, I was almost twenty two years old and decided to buy a laundry mat. I figured, hey people always need clean clothes. My laundry mat was making good money but I was still thirsty for more dough. I made my drug operation bigger to make more money quick. I kept your mom away from all that; she was a lady and my lady at that so I didn't want her getting caught up. I made her keep going to college to get that education. She graduated from 2 year college a year later in May and found out she was pregnant with you that October of 1975." He stopped pacing and leaned on my dresser.

"I put your mom through so much shit. I cheated and got caught, and even beat her up one time." I sat up and screamed, "What?! You put your hands on my mother?" He ran over to me and covered my mouth.

"Shh! Girl I don't want the whole neighbor hood to know." At that moment as he pulled back from me, I looked at my father as a different person. He leaned back on the dresser and I sat up swinging my legs over my bed.

"I would never let a man put his hands on me no matter what! I would like to see a nigga try." He laughed and shook his head.

"D, you so much like me it is ridiculous. Now can I finish my story?" I extended my left hand towards him.

"Proceed." He crossed his arms across his chest.

"When I found out that your mom was pregnant, that was the best thing that ever happened to me. I knew I had to get out of the game before the game got me 'cause I did not want to raise my child from a jail cell so, I got smart. I started investing my money and making it work for me. When your mom was 3 months, I married her before she started showing and people would be talking." I shot my dad a look with my lip upturned once again.

"Ill! You had sex before marriage." He immediately turned a beet red color and began to adjust his collar and clear his throat.

"Well um, yeah missy, I did. So don't follow in my footsteps. I hope you wait." I looked down at the floor.

"I will." He reached over and lifted my chin to look at him.

"I will be proud of you if you do, but if you don't, just come talk to me." I thought, yeah right talk to my dad about me, his little girl, "*Knocking boots*", yeah right, I don't think so. I just smiled and nodded. He sat back down on the bed.

"D, when your mom was 6 months pregnant my dad died and left me (my dad was his only child) his liquor store that he owned for years."

Now, this was weird 'cause my dad's mom died from liver damage from drinking when he was 12. All of these things helped my dad get out of the game quicker. On June 12th, 1976, my mom had me, a beautiful baby girl by the name of Diamond Crescent Staple. My dad continued, "I bought this very house a month before you were born as a surprise to your mother. I had it fully furnished behind her back. I got everything finalized the 3 days she was in the hospital and when I bought y'all home I pulled up to this house, not back to our apartment we shared in the hood, in the projects in Newark." He extended his legs out and placed his hands on his knees.

"Your mom worked for a law firm full time. I told her she didn't have to work anymore. Just stay home and raise my daughter." I laughed.

"Your daughter dad? Wasn't I both of y'all daughter?" He pointed at me and smiled.

"Yeah I guess... but D, I want to talk about the hitting thing again. The first time I put my hands on your mother was my last. I caught her talking to another guy and got jealous. I walked up to her in the Five and Dime store that we had back in the day and smacked her. I didn't let her explain that the guy was a classmate. Once I smacked

her she ran off crying and broke up with me for a while." He
rubbed his forehead reminiscing.

"I thought I had lost her forever but after a little
smooth talk and a lot of begging, I was back with her." I
frowned my face and he playfully mushed me in my temple.

"D, I want to explain everything to you so you
understand. Ever since you were born, I was done with the
drug game 'cause I wanted to see my baby girl grow up. D,
most of my friends started getting high off their own
stashes and are still turned out on drugs today, if they
haven't died or been killed yet. The only friend I still got is
your Uncle David who was in the game with me but went a
different route after he came home from jail. Him and Debra
both went to college and he started doing investments.
(Who you think invested my daddy's money?) Your Uncle
David bought the house next door when David and Danny
were already born." The difference between Daddy and
Uncle David was he still wanted to have his cake and eat it
too. The boys didn't make Uncle David want to do right at
all. He kept telling my dad that he loved Aunt Debra but he
wasn't ready for marriage and my dad said, "But you ready
to play house plus you got 2 kids?" My dad said he told him,
"Man, do right by your family," but Uncle David wouldn't
listen. He got that slut from his office pregnant and left Aunt
Debra for her. My dad stood up again and walked to the
door.

"See Diamond, I know you love your Uncle David
but he is a prime example of how nigga's ain't shit." I
started to respect my father in a new way. We were talking
like adults and as he was leaving my room he added,
"When we kicking it D, express yourself. If you gotta cuss,
then cuss, don't get ridiculous with the shit, but I want you
to feel like you can come to me for anything and tell me
anything O.k.?" I stuck my two thumbs in the air.

"Cool Dad." He turned the doorknob.

"D, do me a favor? Don't tell anyone about our talk,
especially your mother, and don't cuss in front of your
mother. She's not cool like me!" I smiled and waved my

hand.

　　"O.k. Daddy." He opened the door to leave.

　　"No matter what you still my little girl and if Sam breaks your heart I will break his legs."

　　I playfully threw my pillow at him, "Ooh Daddy," and laughed. Once he left my room I called my best friend to let her know I was a woman now too.

CHAPTER 3
GROWING PAINS

O.k. it was June 11th 1989. 1 day until my thirteenth birthday. I was having my party a day early. My parents were giving me a big blow out in the yard. This would be our first grown up party. I went to my daddy's shop and let Krystal do my hair. Ooh yeah, she liked working in my dad's shop so much she never left to start her own shop in the basement of their house. Me and Starr got our hair done the same way. French rolls and crimps with color spray in between the crimps. We were styling. We got our nails and feet done at Krystal's nail salon up the street from my dad's shop. (No relation to Krystal the twin's mother.) I had on my brand new birthday gifts from my dad which were big bamboo name earrings, a name plate and a matching nameplate bracelet. All with diamonds, I mean, that is my name. My mother was pissed off that my dad bought me all this stuff and she got on my father. As they bought condiments out of the house my dad said, "Look Ann get off my back. You only become a teen once. That is my daughter and she deserves all that stuff." My mother rolled her eyes. She was just jealous. She began to slam the Heinz mustard and ketchup on the food table while my dad ignored her attitude and made sure the charcoal was hot on the grill. The first to arrive to my bash was of course my sister Starr. We wore matching outfits and hair do's. We wore spray painted shirts that said K.A.B.'s for life on the front and our real names then AKA our nicknames on the back. Starr's nickname was dimples because of her dimples and my nickname was D-Rock. K.A.B.'s stood for kool ass bitches but we told our parents it stood for kool and brave. It was a crew of us in the K.A.B.'s. We all had the same shirts made.

My next guest was Samir. He came over and handed his gift to me. He got me a pair of pink Reeboks and a white t-shirt spray painted with pink and purple writing that said Diamond and Samir forever. It shined with rhinestones all over it. It was fat (nice). I loved it. I was so excited and couldn't wait to wear it. It was my favorite gift. I kissed Samir on the cheek. My father came over, looked at the shirt and cleared his throat.

"So Sam, you gonna be with my daughter forever huh? So when is the wedding?" Sam placed his arm around me.

"Yes I am going to marry her when I graduate from college and play pro basketball or get a fat job so I can support her and she don't have to work. She can just cook and clean and watch the babies." I pushed his arm off my shoulder.

"Excuse me? I don't need a man to take care of me, and I'm damn sure not sitting home cooking and cleaning. And what babies are you talking about? I want to work so if you ever try some funny shit I can be out with no worries." My mother was standing behind me and tapped my shoulder.

"Did you just curse?" I looked at my dad with '*help me*' eyes. He walked up close to my mom's face.

"Ooh Ann she just slipped up. She will never do it again, right Diamond?" I shook my head up and down.

"Yes daddy." She turned her back and began to fix the food table again.

"You see you let her get away with murder." She was going on and on moving and slamming stuff on the table. My dad looked at me, Sam and Starr and made a face behind her back. He moved his hand up and down like a mouth and was mouthing blah blah blah blah. She turned around and caught him and placed her hands on her hips.

"You saying I am a nag Danny? You trying to say I talk too much?" He hugged her from behind and kissed her on her cheek.

"No that is not what I am saying, but it is her

birthday party today so let her live, get on her tomorrow, please?" She snatched away from him and stomped up the back stairs to the deck and went in the house.

"That is exactly what I will do." She slammed the sliding glass doors shut. My dad placed his hands around my throat and playfully choked me.

"See Diamond, you always getting me in trouble." I knocked his hands down from around my throat and looked him in his eyes.

"You a man. Handle that." He walked back over to the grill.

"You too much girl. I know how you my daughter." We all laughed. My party was scheduled to start at 4 o'clock. It was going to be a cook out/party. My Dee Jay's D-Nice and Dre arrived at 3 o'clock to set up. By 4:45 my back yard was packed. It was all the people from my junior high and the other junior high.

It was 2 junior high schools in my town, Kawameeh and Burnet. We went to Kawameeh and the girls from that school called themselves the 'Kawameeh cuties.' We called the girls from Burnet the 'Burnet boodies." We used the word boodie in our everyday vocabulary. Everything was boodie to us. Instead of using corney, ugly or wack, we used boodie. My mother said I used that word too much because every other word out my mouth was 'he's boodie' or 'she's boodie' or 'school is boodie' or 'that's boodie.' Everything was boodie. Anyway the Burnet girls called us 'corny Kawameeh' and themselves 'beautiful Burnet." It was all in fun 'cause a lot of us were friends even though we went to different junior high schools. It was mad (a lot of) people at my party. It was suppose to be only mostly 8th graders but word travels fast when it is a party. I didn't discriminate against the 7th and 9th graders that showed up. Even high school kids came to party and it was all-good. My party was the jump off of the summer. A lot of guys I didn't know, cause they lived in Union not Vauxhall.

Real quick explanation about Union/Vauxhall. Vauxhall was a section of Union, a black section, of a mostly white town. Not many blacks lived in Union at that time but the few that did would come out to Vauxhall when they could. So the guys I didn't know from the other junior high were trying to talk to me asking if I had a man. When I would say, "Yes" they would say, "So, I don't care." The kicker is Sam got mad at me. He grabbed my arm.

"Diamond, what's going on? If you wasn't so pretty I wouldn't have to go through this." I snatched my arm away.

"Excuse me Samir. What does that mean?" He backed away from me.

"You know what it means. I am leaving Diamond." I waved my hand at him.

"Fine. Leave!" He started marching out of my backyard. Then in my mind I said *bump that!* I followed him yelling, "Samir, come back here!" We were having our first fight. He kept heading out the yard towards the street.

"No I won't come there. Go back in the back and entertain your guests. You steady flirting with every guy you can, so don't let me stop you." I quickened my pace.

"What do you want me to do Samir Ali?" That is what I called him when he was making me mad.

"Do you want me to be rude to my guests? Better yet, why don't I just put everybody out so the Dee Jay can spin records for just me and you." Tears formed in my eyes. I screamed, "This is my day and you are trying to ruin it!" He stepped onto the curb.

"No. You're ruining it for yourself cause ain't nobody tell you to follow me." I flailed my arms around.

"You know what Samir? Lets just call it quits!" He looked me dead in my eyes.

"I couldn't have said it better myself. I don't know what I ever saw in you, you not even that pretty. I know I can do better." I didn't know Starr was behind me. She pushed passed me.

"Samir you better take that back!" He sucked his teeth.

"No and mind your business!" She got up in his

face.

"No this is my business. You better take what you said back right now!" He got closer in her face and their noses almost touched.

"And if I don't Starr?" She moved back a little and lifted her cup of juice.

"I am warning you Samir. Take it back! Take it back right now or else!" I interrupted and put my arm around Starr.

"Starr he don't have to take it back. It's O.k. Lets go party." At that time Danny came out to the front. The Dee Jay was playing Da Butt by E.U.

"Come on Starr my song is playing and I want to see you *doing da but, owww, sexy sexy!*" I dropped my arm from her shoulder and she shot him a look.

"So go dance ain't nobody stopping you." He screamed, "Ill! Who put a bug up your ass!?" She waved her hand up and down towards him.

"Not now Danny, not now! Anyway Samir Ali take it back!" He put his hand in her face.

"No!" What happened next was a shock to us all cause Starr took her cup of juice and threw it in her twin's face. He lunged at her but Danny jumped between them to hold Samir back. Sam screamed, "I am going to kill you Starr Angel!" She dropped the cup and put her dukes up.

"I'd like to see that." Danny struggled to hold Sam. Starr just waved her hand towards Sam and picked up the cup.

"Come on sis. You don't need him." She pulled a tissue from her pocket and wiped my face.

"And I don't need him either. Danny its over." We walked back to enjoy the party. By that time the Dee Jay was playing Soul 2 Soul's Back to Life. Danny came in the backyard and grabbed Starr by the arm. He dragged her back to the front of the house. I gave them 5 minutes then went out there to make sure he wasn't killing my best friend. When I got up there they were sitting on the steps smooching so I left them alone. I went back to my party and put on a façade like I was O.k.

When the party was over I had given out my number 3 times. I found out later that 2 of the boys were friends. That was Hass and Dogg. They were from Elizabeth and I don't know who told them to come to the party. Me and Hass danced on one side of the yard and exchanged numbers. Then I went to get something to drink and I met Dogg. The third boy I met, his name was Shawn but everybody called him Red. He had just moved to Union so I was the first to give him my number, but not the last. Word travels fast when you break up. I had my own phone line and never had any guys call me besides Samir, Danny, and David. I didn't care now cause Samir treated me bad and I didn't want him back. At almost midnight everyone was finally leaving. I was exhausted and the adults cleaned up. That was my mom, dad, Aunt Debra, Uncle David, (of course he came but by himself it was not that type party, Snowflake wasn't invited) Mitch, Krystal, and even Aunt Michelle. I had grown to love her ghetto butt over the years. My dad still didn't let her work in the shop. I had gotten so much stuff for my birthday. It was my responsibility to take my gifts to my room. My Uncle David got me a big Gund teddy bear and put a diamond tennis bracelet on the arm. My mother was pissed cause she hated Uncle David with a passion. He really wanted to gain my mothers acceptance back but he could forget it. When I was finally ready to get in the bed I checked my messages. Samir left 3 saying the same thing.

"Please call me D, I miss you." I was laughing cause we only broke up a few hours ago. My phone rang and it was Starr. "Happy birthday! It is after midnight so I wanted to be the first to tell you happy birthday aaannnd my brother is near tears, he apologized to me and wants to talk to you. I wouldn't if I was you but if you want to..." I cut her off.

"O.k." He got on the phone.

"D, I'm sorry." I fluffed the pillows on my bed.

"Its O.k."

"So we back together?" I sat up straight on my bed.

"No it is not that simple." His temper flared.

"Bump you then!" After that, I heard the dial tone. Starr called me back.

"Bump him D, he is so boodie. We will find you somebody new downtown Newark when we go pick up your b day gift I got you tomorrow."

"Goodnight Sis."

"Good night." I knelt down and said my prayers thanking God for everything. I went to sleep and dreamed about Samir. I don't remember exactly what about, but I know it was about him. He always called me in the morning but that morning, my phone didn't ring. Starr called me to set a time so we could go downtown after church. Starr wanted me to have my gift on my actual born day. We all went to the same church, which was Bethel A.M.E so it hurt me not to sit next to Sam like we usually do and write notes back and forth the whole service. We would use up all the free space on the church bulletin. He wouldn't even look at me. After church, I changed my clothes and put on the shirt and sneakers Samir bought me with some white shorty shorts. I missed him so much already.

I rang Starr's doorbell. Sam opened the door, when he saw it was me, he closed it right back. I rang the bell again. Starr opened the door and gave me a hug. She sang "Happy birthday to you," the Stevie Wonder version. Y'all know, the black people's way. We went downtown and got my gift, which was the name anklet to go with my name chain, bracelet, and earrings. Starr had gone with my dad to pick out my gifts from him a month prior and she laid away my gift. It was small but it was cute and I adored it. She also had gotten a picture we took at the roller skating rink blown up and at the bottom it had printed, "Just me and my sis." She had done extra work around the house for 6 months to save up to get me something nice for my 13th birthday. She was such a good friend and sister. On the bus ride home, I could tell she felt bad for me. She slung her arm around my neck.

"Maybe I should break up with Danny and get our friendship back to what it was. Just me and you." I smiled at her.

"No, please don't hurt my brother's feelings." She removed her arm and shrugged.

"O.k. Whatever you want." I knew this was my best friend and always would be. When we got home from downtown, me and Starr walked to the Union Market. The Union Market was a big flee market that people hung out in. At the market we walked around and bugged out with some of our friends. We met some guys from Irvington named Moni, Dashon, and Derrick and exchanged numbers. Before we left I got some cotton candy and we walked up the street. Once I got in and checked my messages all 3 guys I met had called. Hass left a message saying, "Yo dis Hass. I had fun at your party. Call me." Dogg's message said, "Your party was all that. This Dogg, hit me up." The third guy I met, Red, said, "Peace and blessings Diamond. Beep me when you get in." Yuck, that was a turn off. They could have at least waited a few days to not look so anxious. I just wanted Samir and only Samir to call me. I didn't want to be bothered so I didn't return any of the calls. I went out and sat on my steps. Sam was sitting on his. We just sat and stared at each other for like an hour straight until my dad came out and called Sam over. My dad stood up.

"Samir yesterday you were marrying my daughter and today you hate her. What's going on with that?" Samir kicked at a pebble.

"I don't know ask her." I looked at my manicure.

"I don't know ask him." My dad let out a slight chuckle, "Well D, if y'all not an item why you wearing that shirt." I shrugged my shoulders.

"I didn't have anything else to wear." They both looked at each other and laughed at me. I couldn't help but laugh as well cause I had so far from nothing else to wear it was ridiculous. My dad started up the stairs to enter the house.

"Good, since everybody is laughing why don't I leave you 2 alone." As the screen door closed behind my dad, me and Sam just stared straight ahead. He made the first move when he slightly turned to face me and touched my leg.

"D, I'm soooo sorry pllleeeaaaaaasssseee forgive me?! I want you to be my wife some day. I don't want to fight, I just got jealous. I don't like guys looking at you but I can't stop that. You didn't do anything wrong you was just being you." I leaned in and kissed him. "Mmwwahh" he smiled and I knew we were back together again. We went in my house and cut my birthday cake, well my second one, I was so spoiled it was a shame. As time went on, we were soon in the 9th grade; We were the big timers of the school. Sam and I and Danny and Starr stayed together. We were all happy doing well. We had our little differences here and there but besides that everything was good. On October 31st the twin's birthday, they had a Halloween party at their house which Dee Jay Pookie spun the music for. He only played club so we were getting down to hits like Like This and I'll Beat That Bitch With a Bat. If you not from Jersey you might not know what songs I'm talking about but real Jersey folks do. We love club music in this state. Starr got matching gifts from her dad like mine and Samir got clothes and money. I bought him some timberlands and my sis a locket with our picture in it. It was dark and spooky the way they had their basement set up. Samir was a vampire and I was a princess. That was the night I got my first hickey on my neck. Thank God it was fall. I could wear turtlenecks to camouflage the love bites with out my mother bugging out. Let me just say that the remedy combing the hickey or putting tooth paste or ice on it didn't work for me. When I would be in my room I would stare at it and smile, "*Yeah I'm a woman now*," little did I know then that it was gonna take a lot more to be a woman then some little hickey on my neck. For the rest of that year, things were good. Good up until we approached the summer before high school.

CHAPTER 4
BREAKING UP IS HARD 2 DO

The summer before our 10th grade year me and Starr wanted to be the shit for high school. We went shopping at the mall and killed our parent's charge cards. We still had the same taste in clothing so we had a lot of things similar. Over the past few years we both began to blossom. I was a little thicker than Starr; she had more backyard then anybody. She never did get much breasts, but she made up for it in the butt. Me I was blessed with both. I guess that is how my mom snatched up my dad since I was supposedly shaped just like her with this hourglass I have. My dad wanted me to wear loose jeans and long shirts (*Negative*) but I was rocking just the opposite, tight jeans and belly tops. He was not pleased and told me on the regular, he did not want to kill Samir. Something in the air that summer made everyone's feelings change. Sam said he didn't want to break up but he needed his space. His space he needed was named Shakira. I was in denial for almost the whole summer until one Saturday, a week before school was set to start, me and Starr caught him all hugged up on her down the school a.k.a. the playground around the corner from my house. He was playing me out in public and I wasn't haven't it. I did the dummy move and ripped them apart. Then me and Starr jumped her. All the kids in the playground egged it on instead of breaking it up. I was steady asking her, "Bitch did you have enough yet?" Samir was just standing there cheesing (smiling hard) reciting, "That's my girl." He got a big kick out of the whole thing. Starr just followed my lead. I knew I would have to fight Shakira again cause

38

supposedly she wasn't no punk, but whatever, I didn't care, she could bring it on. I would just have to watch my back. After the fight me and Starr walked away with just 1 broken nail each. We had both broken the same pointer fingernail and laughed at the coincidence. Then when we were out of everyone's view I cried. My best friend hugged me.

"Fuck him! You don't need him." I was trying to get myself together before I walked in the house. You know how mothers are. I couldn't get in the door before my mother wanted to play 21 questions.

"Diamond what's wrong? What Samir do? Were you crying? What happened to your nail? Were you fighting?" My answers were, "Nothing, nothing, no, nothing, no." She just left me alone and I proceeded to my room. I laid on my bed and looked at the ceiling. I had so much stuff in my room that reminded me of Samir that it was sickening. I got up and began to remove all of his items. I took down our pictures together that trimmed the whole border of my mirror. I took the teddy bears he got me and threw them on the floor. I opened my draws and got out all his football, baseball, and basketball jerseys out. I ran down stairs to the kitchen pantry and yanked a big black garbage bag from the Hefty trash bag box. My mother was in the kitchen drinking tea and reading the paper. She looked at me. I looked at her and smiled. I ran back up to my room and stuffed all his stuff in that bag. I still had that rhinestone shirt from when I was thirteen in my draw. It was faded from me wearing it so much and had lost most of the rhinestones but I still loved to wear it to bed. I ran to my desk drawer and yanked out my scissors. I cut it in half and placed it in the bag as well. He had bought me a bracelet for our 3rd anniversary and a chain with his number on it. Number "3", I put that in the bag as well. All the letters and poems he wrote me, the movie stubs, all that sentimental stuff all went in the trash bag as well because to me it was all trash. I even had his pictures transferred to iron on's and ironed them onto my pillowcases. They came off as well. I knew my mom knew something had happened but she didn't press me on it. As I was packing the bag, I heard my dad come in the front door. I dragged the bag downstairs into the kitchen. My dad looked at me and then at the bag with the teddy bears sticking out of it.

"Hey Diamond. Do you want to talk about something?" I smiled to fight back the tears.

"No." He bent over and reached into the fridge.

"Well I just want to remind you that I am always here for you and I'd hate to kill Samir 'cause I don't want to go back to jail." My mother slammed her paper down and shot him a look of death. He turned with an apple in his hand.

"What?! Whatcha looking at Ann? Come on now, she knows I did time before, she's not a baby. I keep it real with my daughter." My mother slowly shook her head from left to right.

"Well you don't need to tell her everything Dan. You just don't think do you?" He rinsed his apple off in the sink.

"What the fuck are you talking about? I don't want my daughter to be all fucking sheltered and gullible about the streets Ann. They ain't no fucking joke and I can tell her what the fuck I want to tell her about my life. I want her to know jail ain't no place for nobody to be, and if I keep her informed she won't be there." That's funny huh? Cause that's where I am now, in jail. My mother jumped up and her chair fell over.

"I don't know who the fuck you cursing at or yelling at. I ain't your child, Diamond is and I don't give 2 shits from a rats ass what you share with your daughter, I really don't." He walked up on her like he wanted to hit her.

"Ann you act like you new to this shit. Like cause you live in these so called suburbs that the fucking hood ain't right around the corner. I want my daughter to know that nigga's ain't shit." My mom pushed passed him.

"Y'all sure ain't, you sorry bastard!" She left the kitchen and ran up the stairs. When she got up the stairs to her room, she slammed the door as hard as she possibly could. By this time I had tears streaming down my face. I mean, I had heard my parents argue before but never like that. They had started to grow apart and I could feel it. My dad had been hanging out in the streets more and with Uncle David at that. My mom would be mad but just not say anything to him. See, me and my mom were complete opposites. She was what I would call a punk. Not me I don't back down from no one or bite my tongue at no time. My dad came over to me and hugged me.

"Sorry Dad. I didn't mean to make you argue, honest I didn't. Please don't leave us dad, I can't stay with her by myself." My dad pushed me back and laughed while looking in my eyes.

"Who said I was leaving? I ain't going no where. This my damn house, if anyone gotta go, she going, and I ain't letting that happen cause she cook to damn good." I smiled. He used his thumbs to wipe away my tears.

"Now get out of here girl and go handle your business." I smiled.

"O.k." I dragged the bag into the dining room and left it in the corner. I ran up the stairs 2 at a time to my room to call Samir. He answered on the 1st ring.

"Yeah, who dis?"

"Samir it's Diamond."

"D, we need to talk."

"Yeah Samir, we do."

"How fast can you come over?"

"Well I can come right now, but come outside, I am not coming in."

"O.k." We hung up. I went to the bathroom to wash my face and put Visine in my eyes to get the red out. I then barged in my mother's room with out knocking. She was lying down with her eyes closed resting. I walked over to her bed and tapped her shoulder.

"Ma I'm sorry." She opened her eyes.

"For what?" I sat down on the side of her.

"For making you and Daddy argue." She let a faint smile grace her lips. She sighed.

"Diamond, it is not your fault. Me and your father

are just going through it right now. We have different views on parenting and we clash sometimes but we will be alright." At that time my dad walked in.

"You better be alright Ann. I hate to fuck you up." He mounted over my mother and pinned my mother down and started tickling her. My mother was laughing hard.

"Stop Dan! D, get him!" I jumped up from the edge of the bed.

"Nope Mom. You on your own. You gotta handle that." I traipsed towards the door. My dad whispered to my mother, "I'm sorry baby."

"Me too boo," and then they were kissing before I could get the door closed. Yuck, I didn't want to think about what was coming next. So I hurried down the stairs and ran in the dining room and dragged the bag out by the front door to talk to Samir. I opened the door and he was standing there looking good I might add but I wasn't going to give in. He had on a blue Yankee's fitted cap, blue jean shorts and a white fitted tank top which in New Jersey we call wife beaters. He was showing off his nice body, um um um, sorry y'all I caught a flash back. Anyway, I wanted to kiss him and the way he was looking my young body wanted to do more then kiss. Yes, I was still a virgin but for that split second I wanted to give my virginity to Samir. But then I snapped out of it realizing why we were standing here. He broke my daze by opening his mouth.

"What up? Can I come in?" I sighed.

"No I will come out." You see being that Samir had been in my life so long he was allowed to just come to my house whenever he wanted. It was vice versa at his house for me. That is why my dad said he would hate to have to kill Samir cause he knew we was close. He was scared we were having sex especially when we would be in my room with the door half closed, but we wasn't. Anyway Sam tried to push past me.

"Man I'm coming in!" I blocked the doorway.

"No you're not." We tussled in the door and fell back over the garbage bag. He landed on top of me and the bag.

"What's in the bag?" I tried to push him off of me.

"All of your belongings Samir." He kept me pinned down.

"What do you mean? You gonna let that little episode break us up?" I didn't answer him.

"Diamond you gonna let that hoe break us up?" I shouted,

"No you gonna let her break us up!" He got up and straightened his clothes.

"I see, any excuse to break up with me huh? You could have just broke up with me Diamond, don't play games. If you don't want me, just say it." I jumped up and pointed my finger in his face.

"Ooh noooo nigga! Don't even try to guilt trip me. You was cheating and got caught and I am not going to put up with it at all, I am too pretty..." He cut me off by grabbing my hand and holding it.

"No you wrong about that." I yanked my hand back.

"What?!" He grabbed it back and kissed it.

"You're not pretty Diamond, you're beautiful and I love you. Damn D, I made a mistake, please don't push me away like this, we put almost 4 years into this and now you wanna just throw it all away in this trash bag and hand it to me and say bye? I know you don't cause I'm not gonna let you. Man bump that lets go outside so we can talk." He yanked me by my arm and he pulled me outside. I was trying to resist but he wouldn't let me. We ended up down my front stairs and on the side of my house. Then he kissed me but I wouldn't kiss him back. He tried to kiss me again pushing me up against the house and I still wouldn't give in. All that time I never looked him in his eyes. I kept my head hung low to block the tears. I tried to turn away once again. I was unsuccessful.

"Look at me D, look at me! Do you think I would hurt you intentionally? D, I didn't know what I wanted that is why I needed space. I know we going to high school next week and I don't want to lose you to no upper classman. Me and the boys were sitting around kicking it on Midtown Miller.

(Midtown was where we hung out at sometimes. It was a street called Miller Street and we nicknamed it Midtown Miller because it was in the center of our town.) Charles said he saw you talking to some older cat. So I wanted to try to end it with you before you ended it with me. That's when the crew hooked me up with Shakira." My tears of sadness turned to tears of madness.

"Charles said what?! First of all you gonna let your crew dictate our relationship? Second of all they could have at least hooked you up with something better then that shit and third, Samir you so fucking gullible cause Charles has been trying to talk to me on the down low for over a year now. I never told you because that was your boy and I didn't want to start no trouble so I just ignored him and dissed him off." O.k. pause Charles and them were Samir's boys (a few to name were Black, Hood, Ab, Buddah, Wali, Rallo, Q-tip, Kay-Kay (the boy) and Mal.) Some of them were jealous because they couldn't keep a girl. They all wanted to cheat, plus a lot of them were already having sex and was pressuring Sam to get at me. Me and Sam had talked about having sex and were going to, on a few occasions, but something always ruined it. Like my parents coming home or his parents coming home, my period or I would just get scared and change my mind. I mean I loved Samir so I would give him anything. O.k. back to the story, so after I said that Samir's eyes looked like he was seeing fire. I think he was seeing red as they say. He backed up off me and began to walk down the driveway toward the front of the house. I yelled, "Samir where are you going?!" He punched his right fist into his left hand.

"I gotta go handle something I'll be back." I ran down behind him.

"No Samir we need to finish this now! Samir if you keep walking then you are walking away from any chance of us getting back together." He ran in the direction towards the school.

"I gotta take my chances D. I'll be back." That was it; I couldn't be but so bothered. Me, Starr and some of our other girls (Keisha, Akira, Shannon, Bookey, Shorty, Te and Kim) were going skating. We were going deep cause the fight had gotten around and I knew it might be trouble. It was 6:30 and Krystal's nail salon closed at 7:30 and I needed my nail fixed. I mean since I was available now I had to make myself look presentable. I ran across the street, got Starr and she was thinking the same thing. On our way walking to the nail salon we talked about our relationships.

"Yo sis, I don't want Danny anymore. I want something new and exciting so I'm going to end it with him and chill for the end of the summer, wait the week out for high school to start and meet me an older guy."

"I can't lie, I still want Samir back but after him running off that is the last straw." She quickened her pace.

"You know D, maybe you should meet somebody new. I mean we just beat up this girl and didn't do anything to my brother." I cut her off and put the palm of my hand in her face.

"First of all Starr I can't help how I feel and the only reason I hit her is because she's a phony bitch trying to play me out. She knows that's my man and she speaks to me all the time and always ask me 'how you and Samir doing?' I never thought about that before, but damn she just asked me Tuesday how we were, so even if he lied and said we broke up, she calls herself my peeps, she should have said ain't nothing between us happening cause D is my peeps. Feel me?"

"I feel you on that and I know how phony she is, that is why I tried to crack that bitch skull but how can you let him go unpunished? Fuck that, he's not innocent, lets jump him. He did you wrong so we should make him pay, don't let him get away with that shit. I would never let a nigga pull a fast one over on me. Naw he gotta pay no matter what, even if he is my brother, you mean more to me then he does, so you know I will definitely help you lay his ass out." I didn't say anything else to Starr. I just let her talk. She didn't love Danny like I loved Samir that is why it was nothing for her to cut him off. I didn't want to argue with her I just kindly changed the subject.

"Um hum your right, so anyway what you wearing skating?" She turned her lip up.

"I don't think I want to go." So I left it at that. I was going; I didn't care if Starr didn't want to. She knew we had beef but if she wanted to stay home over this petty disagreement we just had, more power to her. When my nail was done I waited for her to finish. On our way walking home, she act like she was mad at me for something I had no control over, "love", you can't help who you love, it just don't happen like that. We all know love is blind but the question we should ask ourselves is how blind is love... really? Does it blind us just enough to let us play the fool for a while or does it keep us blinded forever? When we rounded our block Starr finally had something to say.

"I decided to go skating to watch your back." I dug in my pocketbook for my house keys.

"You shouldn't feel obligated to go skating for me. I could hold my own." She looked for her house keys as well.

"Fine. Then I won't go but when Shakira and her crew approach what you gonna do?"

"What I gotta do!" She turned on her heels.

"O.k. then fine!" She walked in her house and I went in mine. The bag was moved to the den and Samir was sitting on the couch with my dad watching TV. Better yet, looking through it because he wasn't paying any attention to the TV. Once I saw Samir I got an even bigger attitude. I started up the stairs. "Hey Dad." Sam jumped up and ran to the stairs.

"D, wait, I need to talk to you." I turned on the 4th stair up.

"About what? What do you want Samir? Tell me what the fuck you want? Matter of fact I don't care what you want Sam, get out of my house! I don't want to see you no more! Get out of my house! Get the fuck out!" He waved his hand.

"You know what I will get out D. You not worth what

I just went through. When you grow up call me."

I screamed, "Bitch I am damn near grown and I don't care what you went through, it can't be worse then what you put me through now get out!" My mother was in her room and snatched her door open.

"Diamond Crescent Staple! Watch your mouth and show Samir some respect in this house. You will show any guest in here respect do you understand? You don't need to be cursing like you grown, if you want him to leave, ask him, you don't demand shit up in here. You getting a little beside yourself here lately and you are not grown so just remember that! You keep on and you won't be skating or nothing else, do you understand me?" I looked down at the step I stood on.

"Yes Ma." He looked at me and shook his head. He went back in the den and said bye to my dad, grabbed that bag full of stuff I gave him and said to my dad, "I will see you later. She don't want to talk now and I can't take her talking to me like that and I don't want her and Ma to get into it. Oh boy, now I know she is extra mad at me since she just got yelled at." My dad said, "I will talk to her for you, and you know Diamond don't pay Ann no attention. None! So cut it out! And if Ann gets too out of control I will handle her. You go home and put that hand on ice Tyson." Samir laughed. "Aw now Big D don't start." They both laughed. I was still standing on the stairs. When Sam walked out, he looked at me one more time. I rolled my eyes and I mouthed, "Fuck you bitch!" He shook his head again and walked out. I wanted to say. Sam what happened? But I couldn't. My pride was standing in the way. As soon as that door closed all I heard was "Diamond!" I went down the stairs and in the den and sat next to my dad. He looked at me.

"Do you wanna talk?" I jumped up.

"No, I wanna get ready for skating." He picked up the remote and checked the time on the TV.

"Well it is only 7:20. I know you like to get there at 8:30 so can we talk for a minute?" I flopped back down and put my hands under my chin and my elbows on my knees.

"O.k. Dad. Shoot." He turned the TV off.

"Can I ask you what happened between you and Samir?" I sat up straight.

"I don't want to talk about it."

"O.k., can I ask why you were fighting today?" I twiddled my thumbs.

"Don't want to talk about it." He looked at me over the top of his glasses.

"Well maybe you don't want to go skating until you do." I sucked my teeth.

"Come on Dad. You acting like Ann up there, all in my business. You told me before I don't have to share everything with you. I don't want to share that." He took his glasses off.

"I think you do and I'm not acting like nobody up there, she is still your mother so respect her as such or you might not be going skating at all." I sighed and dropped my shoulders.

"O.k. I see how y'all do. Samir must be the man up in here." He touched my shoulder.

"It's nothing like that Diamond but I'm concerned." I sat back.

"Yeah O.k., it don't matter." I then thought bump it and told him everything up to when Samir ran off. My dad sipped his soda.

"Did you ever stop to think why he ran off?" I swung my hair off my shoulder.

"No and I don't care why. All I know is we were talking and he jetted." My dad clapped his hands and rubbed them together.

"Let me tell you something about respect. If another man tried to kick dirt on you to get at your girl it is disrespectful and you gotta do what you gotta do to gain your respect back. That guy Charles that tried to talk to you caught a bad one today. Sam ran off earlier to find him and when he did he asked him straight out did you try to talk to my girl? And Charles laughed at him and said hell no who wants that so and so..." I placed my hand up like a stop sign to stop the story.

"Wait what is so and so, did he call me a bitch?" My dad smacked my hand down.

"That is not important, let me finish. Anyway, words where exchanged and he invited Charles to shoot the one (a.k.a. fair fight in New Jersey terms) and Charles said, 'igght' and Samir knocked him out. Then he came here to apologize to you but you came in getting on him. He was already hyped up from the fight and he didn't want to get into it with you so that's why he left. See I knew me teaching him boxing skills would pay off one day." He smiled like Sam was his son. I snapped my fingers to bring him back to the current conversation.

"I can understand what happened but he could have at least told me where he was running off too." My dad flicked the TV back on.

"If he did would you have let him go? And if so would you have let him go alone?" I laughed.

"You right Dad cause I would have wild out on Charles too. Anyway, Samir could have done better then just running off." My dad shrugged his shoulders.

"You right, but when your emotions get the best of you, you do what you gotta do. Well, it is almost 7:45 and if I am taking you skating you better hurry up, shower and get dressed." I did just that. I checked my messages and Starr had called twice once apologizing and the second one saying what time we leaving for skating cause it was going to be on.

CHAPTER 5
ALL SKATE

So me and Starr went skating and met our other girls there. It was 9 of us total, me, Starr, Shannon, Bookey, Shorty, Kim, Keisha, Akira, Te, and Kia. Kia was a last minute add to the group because her mother use to be bugging and not wanting her to go skating with us, but she got out that night. Everybody knew what was up for the night. We were all dressed cute but not too cute just in case anything popped off. I couldn't get in Skate 22 good when my girl Keisha approached me.

"Shakira here. She was telling Darnell she gonna fuck you up after the rink was over and you know me. I was laughing at her dumb ass like yeah ight wait till Diamond get here." I dropped my skates down.

"Well I'm here now and we don't gotta wait till the rink is over we can do this now." Keisha shrugged her shoulders and recited her favorite saying.

"Whatever is whatever." So I proceeded into the rink to get a locker and put my skates on. I sat on a stool right next to Shakira to change into my skates. She didn't open her mouth. I guess the bitch had lockjaw. She just looked all around like she didn't see me cause she was scared stiff. I really thought she was supposed to be one of the tough ones. She was disappointing me. I began to skate ignoring this simple bitch with all the mouth. There were mad cuties in the rink that night. I mean they was probably always there but I was just so big on Samir I couldn't see them. It felt like guys could see I was single cause 3 guys pushed up and 2 (Pop and Khaliq) out of the 3 were cute so they're the 2 that got the number. I mean me and Sam were finito! I couldn't live in a funk forever I had to get on with my life. Anyway, me and my crew were skating and that is when bitches started acting up. We were skating

50

and they were skating (they meaning our rivals). They were bumping us and we were bumping them. It was like a big game to all of us. You know Shakira punk ass was not bumping me. The big bitch she was with kept bumping me but my motto is "the bigger they are the harder they fall." I wasn't scared. Plus Starr's favorite line was, "she ain't that big! I'll take the big one!" I know y'all surprised right? Sweet little non-fighting peacemaker Starr wanting to take the big one. I had rubbed off on her. So one by one we all got off the big rink to take our skates off and go to the small rink to dance. Let me explain. It was 2 rinks, one big rink and one small rink and we used the small one to get our party on. It was more like a dance floor cause nobody came to the back on the small rink with skates on. Just sneakers or boots or whatever, ready to move your body. The bumping continued on the dance floor. I looked out the side of my eye and saw Samir leaning on the side of the small rink/dance floor and my heart dropped. He was leaning up against the rink wall facing the dance floor with his baseball cap pulled down low over his eyes. He had on a pair of jean shorts, a t-shirt, and some construction style timberland boots looking good. He had his gold gucci link chain on with the bracelet to match. He just stared directly at me making me feel uncomfortable. I felt like a kid who was acting up and their parents were watching them. I suddenly got a nervous feeling in my stomach wondering if Samir had seen me give my number out. I mean yeah we were broken up but it was still the same day and I didn't want to seem like I didn't care that we had just broke up. Plus Samir wasn't wrapped too tight so I was shook. While I was in my thinking zone, I saw a fist fly out of nowhere from the big bitch. I ducked it quick and my reaction was to swing. I swung on some chic I didn't even know and that did it. It was a big brawl between her girls and my girls. Security rushed the back and broke it up. The security guards were so big. They were snatching us up like rag dolls. Somebody had got a hit off on me cause my face was hurting, my back was sore, and my acrylic nails were all cracked and bleeding. I remember when I was a little girl my great grandmother (my mother's grandmother) use to say to me before she died, "Fighting is a hard job cause you can't quit when you want too!" She was right. Starr had 4 scratches on her left cheek. She was jumping all around saying, "I'm gonna kill one of these bitches." We kindly got escorted out of the rink with our stuff to the outside. All of us. The one bouncer said, "We don't care if you kill each other, just do it outside of our establishment."

When we were outside I was ready for round two. I yelled out, "Yo Shakira, lets me and you get the one and end it today. Me and you only, so this shit don't have to carry over into school next week, bitch lets do this." Shakira waved her hand towards me.

"No! I don't feel like fighting you no more." I handed my pocketbook to Starr.

"Well I'm getting ready to swing on you so if you don't fight back that is on you but I am about to handle my business." I walked out into the empty part of the parking lot preparing myself. Sam and a few of his boys had come outside. Samir yelled my name.

"Diamond come here!" I turned towards him.

"Ill! No! Get out of here." I cracked my knuckles.

"Shakira I'm waiting bitch." Her friends were gessing (taunting) her up to fight me saying things like, "She ain't tough Kira, fuck her up. She got to much mouth." And my friends were playing her friends out saying, "Shakira kick D ass?! hahaha that's a joke. If our girl D got to much mouth she got the skills to back it." See everyone knew my dad didn't just teach Sam how to box. He taught me too and I was good with mines. So Shakira got hyped up and began to walk towards me.

"Bitch I'm coming!" I began to shadow box.

"Don't talk about it, be about it!" She was putting her skates down and Samir came running over first and grabbed my arms.

"You not fighting no more!" He turned around and looked at Shakira approaching.

"This shit is over. I don't want you, I want my girl, I know I fucked up but that's over now don't call me or come around me, just bounce!" She screamed, "I don't want you either Samir!" I tried to get out of Samir's grip.

"Yeah right bitch you want my man! You trying to be my best buddy wanting my man the whole time. Smiling in my face, all the time you wanted to take my place." Starr yelled out, "Backstabber!" I turned and smiled at her, that was my sister-girl.

"O.k., I still want the fair one though, move Samir. Get off me." He held me tighter.

"No I won't move." I tried to swing on her over him and she moved back. He grabbed me up at the collar.

"What I tell you? What I just say? You not fighting Diamond and that is that." Hood chimed in, "Enough! why don't y'all stop all this petty fighting shit and leave it alone. Shakira was obviously scared."

She cut in, "Shut up Hood. I ain't scared of her and nobody else."

"Whatever bitch you fucking scared. Now shut your mouth, I'm trying to save you from an ass whipping." All the guys started laughing. She said, "Yeah ight, Diamond if you want a piece of me come and get it." I became irate.

"What?! What?!" I tried to lunge at her again and Samir yoked me up at the back of shirt this time.

"Diamond you ain't fighting and that is that. What don't you understand about you ain't fighting?" I just looked at her with a scowled face.

"This shit ain't over I'm gonna see you. And don't try to start no shit in school where you know it will get broken up at. Once I hit you with that first punch, it will be ended and we will both get suspended. We can handle our business outside school walls at a later date." She walked towards her friends.

"No handle it now cause if you don't then it is over. I am not gonna be fighting over no man, I'm to cute for all of that." Ab yelled out before I could respond.

"Ill Bitch! No you not!" She was a cornball girl. Kinda

short, kinda fat, kinda black, and kinda wack! Bald headed bitch. I looked in Sam's eyes and begged, "Please Sam let me go please." He looked in my eyes.

"D, what part of no don't you understand? She got the lump upside her head and you got the man, let it go D, for me? Ight let it go." I freed myself from his grip.

"O.k. Sam, whatever." He grabbed my wrist.

"Come on, we need to talk. Lets walk home." It was only 10:15 and my dad wasn't coming to get us until 11:30. So, I called him from a payphone and told him someone was fighting and the rink had let out early, (I didn't tell him it was me who was fighting, are you crazy?) and we were going to walk home. That was going to be a nice half hour walk because Skate 22 was in Union. After I placed the payphone back in the cradle Sam blocked me.

"O.k. D come on." As I pushed past him in the rink parking lot I walked directly to Starr and grabbed my Gucci tote from her.

"O.k. Starr come on." As she started to walk in sync with me Samir whispered, "I kinda wanted to be alone with you." I turned and shouted, "For what Samir?! I'm not your girl no more. That stuff I said, it was just talk. I came with Starr and I am leaving with her, now you either walking home with us or we walking alone it don't matter but make your choice quick cause I'm ready to go." He pushed between me and Starr to walk in front of us.

"O.k. D fine. Lets just go." I just smiled to myself, what I say goes. I looked Samir up and down, I might take him back, I don't know yet. Me and Starr pushed right back passed Samir to be in the front. When we first started walking it was quiet. Me and Starr stayed side by side and Samir walked behind us. He kept stepping on my heels on purpose so I could turn around and say, "Stop Samir" and he would say, "Make me." I would turn back around and smile and Starr would look at me and give me a half of smile. We were getting ready to go in, but decided to walk up to Joe's Pizzeria for a slice. My fingers were killing me from my nails being broken down. I had forgotten about the pain in the heat of the moment but they were throbbing reminding me of what had just went down. Once in the pizza stand the twins sat at the counter while I rounded the hall to the ladies room. I soaked my hands in cold water to bring the throbbing down and get the blood off my hands. I came out and Starr and Samir were arguing about me. As I approached their backs all I heard was Starr say, "If you hurt my sister again I will take your heart out." And he said, "Shut up! I ain't gonna hurt her. Mind your business!" She sucked her teeth.

"Diamond is my business and don't you forget it." I came over and tapped both of them on their shoulder.

"Excuse me can I interrupt for a minute?" They both looked at me. They saved me a seat in between them. I sat down and put my left arm around Samir and my right arm around Starr and yelled, "Group hug!" and pulled them in close and made them bump heads. They both said, "Ouch!" and playfully hit me on the arm. I rubbed both arms.

"Ouch! For real that hurt. Dag, somebody else already tried to jump me today now I'm getting tag teamed by the twins. What da deal with that?" We all laughed and ate our pizza. When we were done, guess who came strolling in. Charles and 2 of his cousins from down Little Bricks in Newark. He approached Samir.

"So what up nigga?" Samir turned to him on his stool.

"What up?" Charles backed up to get space between him and Samir.

"So let's get the fair one now nigga!" Sam jumped up from the stool.

"You got the fair one earlier when I put your wimpy ass to sleep." Charles paced around nervously.

"You snuck me!" Sam waved his hand.

"Bullshit nigga! Face reality, you got knocked out." Charles threw up his fists in the air.

"So let's fight again." I stood up at that time to block Samir. I grabbed him by his collar.

"Sam you not fighting again. If I can't fight, then you can't fight!" Charles punched his fist into his hand.

"So Samir you need your little bitch to protect you?" I turned on my heels to face Charles.

"Bitch?" I turned back to Samir and patted his shoulder.

"Fuck him up boo." Frank, the owner of the pizza parlor yelled, "Take it outside!" Starr threw money on the counter and we hoped up and ran outside. When they got out to the parking lot Samir was whooping Charles ass again and his cousins tried to jump Samir. I had my handy dandy mace and I maced the 2 of them in their face. They were both coughing and gagging while they wiped their eyes from the burning.

"Ooh shit! That shit burns. We gonna get you bitch." With my mace still in tow ready to flow I shrugged my shoulders.

"I don't think so!" Samir finished Charles off. The owner's son's Joey and Pouch came out and yelled, "That's it. Either leave or were calling the police!" We left there and continued running home with Sam still stepping on my heels. Once we got a safe distance away from the pizza stand, I turned around and put him in a headlock.

"Say sorry D, you are the queen of the earth! Say you and Starr are the most beautiful girls in the world. Sis give him straight body shots!"

"Gladly!" She began to playfully jab him in the sides. I finally let him go and me and Starr held each other for support. He bent over with his hands on his side to catch his breath. He spit.

"O.k. Bet! Payback is a bitch and when I catch you alone it is on!" He straightened up and began to walk with us again.

"Starr don't go to sleep tonight." We were all laughing and acting up. We finally reached home at almost midnight. Once in front of my house I started up the stairs.

"Good night y'all!"

"Good night Sis!"

"Bye Diamond." Once in the house, my dad was sleeping/watching TV in the den. I tapped on the wall.

"What's up Pop? I'm home." I ran up to my room to answer my ringing phone before Ann woke up.

"Yeah it's me." Samir cleared his throat.

"D, could you please come outside cause I have something I want to say to you." I played with his emotions.

"Uuuuuummm lets see? No, not coming out." He begged, "Pppllleeeaaassseee D, don't play I'm serious." I yawned aloud.

"I am too Samir. I'm tired." His voice dropped down to a near whisper.

"O.k. D." I let out a hearty laugh.

"Sike Sam stop crying! Meet me on my steps." I couldn't get down the stairs good and he was sitting on my steps. I opened the screen door and jumped back.

"Damn how you get here so fast?" He smiled and held his cordless phone up. He had been sitting on my steps the whole time. I sat down next to him on the opposite side of my steps.

"Why you so far away Diamond?" I extended my legs.

"Sam what's up? Lets cut to the chase, what do you wanna talk about?" He reached over to touch my leg.

"Us." I removed his hand from my leg as if he had the cooties.

"There is no us anymore." He scooted over closer to me.

"Ooh I see you gave some nigga your number in the rink and now you wanna act stink?" We both had to laugh at his corny rhyme. I became fidgety.

"No that's not it at all. I gave him a fake number anyway." (I lied.)

"Well I wanna be with you. Did your dad tell you what happened earlier?" I lied again, "No." A puzzled look crept across his face.

"He didn't?! He said he was gonna talk to you... Wait yes he did cause you knew about it at the pizza parlor just now." I looked him in his face.

"Sike! He told me, but since when is my dad your mouth Samir? I mean he did tell me some stuff but this is between you and me, so if you have something to say then you need to say it." He reached over and took my hand in his.

"O.k. you right. What do you want to know?" I adjusted my body to face Samir directly.

"O.k. Why is it O.k. for you to creep with Shakira..."He yanked my arm.

"I wasn't creeping." I pulled my arm back.

"Yeah you're right. You wasn't creeping you was doing it in public view playing me out." My temperature started to rise again. He pulled my hand back and softly caressed it.

"D can we please not argue about this again? I was wrong and I admitted it, I'm sorry." I gave him a side mouth smile.

"O.k. Samir but why couldn't I fight her for disrespecting me but you could go fight Charles for disrespecting you? It is all the same thing isn't it?" He exhaled.

"No, I'm a man and you are a woman. It is not lady like for you to be in the streets fighting and carrying on. You to cute for all that." I pulled my hand back and jumped up.

"Ooh, so I get it. It is real manly like for you to be in the streets fighting huh?!" He scratched his head.

"It is better then females fighting and besides all that I didn't want to fight him. I asked him a question, he got smart and it was on, but you don't see me chasing him down to fight again, do you? That was him coming at me to fight just now, so I had to handle mines. Now that's through and you already fought Shakira twice what's the point to keep fighting her? I mean enough is enough already." I sat back down away from him on the stairs.

"O.k. Daddy (sarcastically.) Is that what you wanted to talk about?" He rubbed my thigh.

"No, you know what I want to talk about." I shook

my head.

"No I don't. Not, if you don't tell me." He curled his right pointer finger in and out.

"Move closer to me so I can tell you." I slid over slightly.

"So what up?" He leaned directly into my ear.

"D, you know I love you right?" I moved back a little.

"Yeah I guess." He ran his fingers through my hair.

"I want you back D. I want you to be my girl again like we were. No space, no friends just us." I frowned and slid back across the step.

"Sam, I know you apologized for what happened but I just can't over look that. I need time to think and see what I want to do." His voice elevated as he adjusted his fitted Yankees cap.

"D, you know what you want to do. Stop playing around. You want me and I want you. Damn D you getting me heated (stressed.)" He took off his tank top. Now just in case I didn't tell you or if I did and you weren't paying attention, Samir had a banging (nice) body. He was cut up in all the right places. He had a nice strong back and he knew that his body was my weakness. So once I saw his rock hard chest and washboard stomach I jumped up to go in the house.

"Look Sam I gotta go." He pulled the bottom of my shorts to pull me back down. He got close to my face with his face and looked me dead in my eyes. It looked like he had a tear in his eye. He had turned his fitted baseball cap around with the rim in the back and he looked so sincere. He licked his juicy pink lips.

"Can I just look at you for a minute?"

"Yeah. 1,2,3..." He jumped up and flung his arms around.

"Damn D, be serious for once." I got defensive and jumped up too.

"I am serious Samir. Give me some time O.k.?... Please?" He began to walk down the stairs.

"O.k. D but don't wait too long." I placed my hands

on my now developed hips.

"Why Sam? Why not wait too long? You shopping around for something new already?" He turned around on the bottom step.

"No D nothing like that. I just can't live with out you. Good night." He walked down that last step with his head hung low. I wanted to call him back but I couldn't. I flopped back down on my steps and watched him walk across the street. When he got to his stairs he sat and we just sat and stared at each other. I remember when I use to love living across the street from Samir, but at that moment I wish he lived somewhere else. I finally made the first move to go in the house. As I walked in the door I heard my dad scramble back to the den. I yelled out, "Dag nosey. Good night!" He laughed knowing he was caught.

"Good night pumpkin." I went up stairs to my bedroom and put my nightclothes on. I looked out the window and Sam was still sitting there. I began to cry because I felt bad for Samir, but I felt even worse about what he did to me. I felt bad that I didn't take him back but I felt even worse because I couldn't take him back. I just laid and cried until I cried myself to sleep. It was just 1 week before high school started and I was all depressed and in a funk. I tried my best not to talk to Samir during that time period. I know you're saying, "How do you avoid someone who lives across the street from you?" Very carefully. He called me the first few days like every 10 minutes and I would look at my caller ID and never pick up. After those few days he called like every few hours and after that like once or twice a day and the weekend before school started he didn't call at all. I did slip up and talk to him a few times over that time frame but as soon as he talked that us shit I said I had to go. The weekend before school started me and Starr did our final school shopping. In the mall while looking in Macy's she started in on me and Sam's relationship.

"Yo D, what you going to do with my brother?" I picked up a size 10 Guess jeans.

"What do you mean?" She took the jeans out of my hands to inspect them.

"Well you keep leading him on. Are you going to take him back or what?" Livingston Mall's halls echoed as my voice escalated.

"Why Starr? I'm not sure what I want to do. It has only been 2 weeks." She spoke even louder as she spun around a rack of matching guess tops.

"Well how long do you need? How long you gonna keep my brother on hold like he some slouch nigga? You know chics throwing themselves at Samir and he be saying, no me and my girl just having problems right now, we gonna work it out." My eyebrows went up in shock.

"Well damn Starr whose side are you on? Those chics or mine? I don't know what I want to do with your brother. What do you want me to do? I love your brother and you know I do but he hurt me. I am too young for all this drama." She reached out and placed her arm around me.

"I know D, but so is my brother, so I am just saying let him go if you don't want him. School starts Wednesday and it is mad cats in the High. We can just get one of them." I just turned and held up a medium shirt to my front.

"You know Starr, I don't want no guy right now." She playfully looked me up and down 3 times.

"Ooh, so you want a women? You gay now?" I mushed her in her head. We both laughed. Starr always knew how to make me laugh. Well it was Saturday and everyone was going to a back to school jam at the Multi Center in town. The Multi Center was directly across the street from the Union Market. I didn't want to go but Starr did. Her and Danny didn't want each other anymore. They were both done there. She begged me to go. Even though I really didn't want too she was my best friend and this was one of those things that best friends did for each other even though they didn't want too. The party was going to start at 7 and end at 12. Starr called me after we got from the mall.

"Samir is going to walk us to the party." I smiled to

myself.

"O.k." That was a good thing because I was ready to talk to him and was going to take him back. We were meeting outside at 7:30, and when 7:30 rolled around Starr came out alone.

"Samir don't want to go since you're going." I was crushed.

"What? Why?" She placed her Liz Claiborne purse over her neck and stuck her right arm through the strap were it sat between her breasts and the purse part rested on the side of her.

"He said he tired of you playing him. So... Who needs him. Lets just go." I knew he was in the basement so I started to walk towards the back of her house.

"Hold up Starr I want to talk to him." She looked down at her Swatch watch.

"O.k. hurry I am going to walk to the corner store and get some gum. I will be right back O.k. No more then 5 minutes Diamond!" I waved at my friend.

"That's all I need." I waltzed right to the back of the house like I always did, in the backdoor, and down the stairs to the basement. Sam was sitting in the recliner chilling in his gray Polo sweat pants and a white wife beater. They supposedly call them wife beaters because when Italian guys get locked up for beating up their wives they have them on. I don't know how true it is but, we crazy up here in Jersey ain't we? Anyway, he was watching some game like always and didn't acknowledge my presence.

"Come on Samir. Me and Starr are ready." He flicked the TV channel.

"I told Starr I'm not going. You don't need me to walk with y'all. You'll be safe." I shifted my weight from one leg to the other.

"I know, but I want you to walk us." He remained unmoved.

"Why Diamond? Why you want me to walk you? You're a big girl now. You can hold your own in the streets." He never once looked at me; He kept his eyes glued to the

TV set. I was fed up with him ignoring me. I walked over and stood in front of the TV. You know he wasn't having that. He stretched his neck to look around me at the TV.

"Can you please move Diamond? I'm trying to watch this." I spread my legs and arms out to cover the whole TV.

"Ooh is what is on that TV more important then me?" He squirmed around to try to see the TV.

"No, but I want to see this Diamond, so move." I placed one hand on my hip and pointed my left finger at him.

"But what if I wanted your undivided attention?" He sat silent. I licked my lips.

"Ooh, I know how to get it." What I did next I didn't plan or expect to do but I did it anyway. I had on a sleeveless white blouse and I unbuttoned the top 3 buttons. I seductively toyed with my cleavage.

"Do I have your attention now?" He just stared with his mouth open.

"I guess that means no." Then, I unbuttoned the shirt all the way and let it fall back so he could see my young perky breasts, with my bra on of course. I began to walk towards him slowly.

"Where are your parents?" He sat up straight.

"They went out since they knew we were going out." I stopped in my tracks.

"Where is your brother?" He stood up.

"At his girl's house." I pushed my blouse back and placed my hands on my hips to keep it back.

"Ooh O.k. So do I have your undivided attention now?" He began to walk towards me.

"Yeah you got it." I dropped my hands and closed my shirt.

"Wait! Ooh shoot! Your sister was walking to the store and coming right back. We can't do this now. I gotta go to the party with her." He stopped walking towards me.

"Do what now D?" My fingers trembled as I tried to button my shirt quickly.

"'It' Sam." I blushed while I buttoned the bottom button. He came closer and placed his hands on my shoulders.

"Huh?... Wait! Ooooooh 'It!' You want to have sex D?" I just looked at him and then down to the floor feeling embarrassed. I secretly knew what I was doing though cause I knew Starr was coming back. It wasn't going down but I like to pretend. He slid his arms from my shoulders to my waist and hugged me tight. He breathed in the scent of my hair.

"D I don't ever want to be with out you." I returned his hug.

"Me either Sam." He pushed me back and grabbed my face in his large hands. We kissed and Starr came running down the stairs screaming, "Damn Diamond I said 5 minutes. Can you count?" Me and Sam still hugging just looked at her and smiled. She stopped dead in her tracks.

"Ill! Was y'all just kissing?" I looked from Samir to Starr.

"What if we were?" She covered her mouth.

"Then I am going to be sick." I stuck my tongue out at her.

"O.k. Then we weren't." I winked at Samir. She wrinkled up her nose.

"Yeah right!" We all laughed. Starr tapped her watch.

"Can we go now D?" I looked at Samir.

"Yes we can as soon as my man gets dressed." We smiled at each other as he ran up the stairs to go get dressed. Starr yelled behind him, "Hurry up Sam. Nobody wants to wait on you all day." He stopped on the top step of the basement stairs.

"Come on sis give me 5 minutes." She rolled her eyes.

"That's all you get!" He continued all the way up to the second floor of their house. We both flopped down on the couch. She turned to me.

"You O.k. now? Y'all back together I see." I smiled.

"Yes Starr we are." She jumped up to get the remote and turned to MTV.

"I know y'all going to be together forever. We gonna be old and gray and y'all still gonna be together and I will be on like husband number 5. You know I am going to live to be like 150!" I snatched the remote from her to turn up my video. It was L.L. Cool J's Around The Way Girl and you know me and Starr were.

"Yeah you probably will." We then laughed together and the phone rang. It was next to me on the end table so I reached over and picked it up like I had done so many times in the past.

"Hello Starr and Samir's line." A female voice bellowed out, "Hey Starr let me speak to Samir please?" I sat up straight.

"Who's calling?" The female voice let out a little laugh.

"Starr it's me, Yah-Yah. What other chic is calling Samir?" The hairs on my neck stood up at attention.

"Ooh I didn't recognize your voice Yah-Yah what's up?" I emphasized Yah-Yah for Starr. I then turned and looked at Starr who was all into the video and not paying attention to me. I grabbed the remote and turned off the TV so she could hear my convo. Yah-Yah was very familiar with me thinking I was Starr.

"Nothing much, you sound different you gotta cold?"

"No but I sound different because this ain't Starr this Samir's girlfriend Diamond." Starr's face had the 'oh shoot' look. I focused my attention back to the phone call.

"Oh really? Since when?" I answered with an attitude.

"Since 4 years ago." Starr tapped my hand.

"D who's that?" As if she didn't hear me say Yah-Yah before. So I pulled the phone away from my ear and screamed, "Yah-Yah Starr, its Yah-Yah!" She heard me loud and clear and she turned her head. I got offended by Starr turning away. I placed my ear back to the phone.

"Yah-Yah please hold." I placed my hand over the

mouthpiece.

"Starr, look at me." She turned slow and kept her eyes down.

"Yeah?" I bent down to look her in her eyes.

"Who is Yah-Yah Starr?" She began to fidget in her seat.

"Look D. You gotta take that up with Samir. I don't have nothing to do with that." I put the phone down on the couch between us.

"Ooh yes you do because this chic act like you and her is fly." She picked up the phone.

"Look D let me handle this." Her hand shook as the phone reached her ear.

"Hello. Yah-Yah? Hey, this Starr. My brother will call you back O.k.? (Pause) No no don't worry. He will call you right back O.k. bye." I jumped up and screamed, "Starr what do you mean by telling her don't worry?" She patted the spot next to her for me to sit down.

"Look Diamond that is why I kept asking you what you were going to do with my brother. Yah-Yah is just his friend but she does like him. She is Shareef's (their older brother) girlfriend's younger sister. She been trying to get with Samir for a minute and when you wouldn't speak to him he just started speaking to her on the phone. He told her he still loved you but he didn't think you were going to take him back and maybe he should move on. So he backed off from you and was talking to her. I told her don't worry because she was scared Samir would be mad that she called and you answered." I paced back and forth heated!

"Well she should be scared! And now I will call him down here to call her back and tell her bye and don't call here no more." I yelled up from the basement to the second floor.

"Samir sweetheart could you come down here for a minute?!" He yelled back, "Yeah hold up here I come I'm ready to go." I tapped my left foot impatiently and crossed my arms over my chest.

"No, can you come right now Sam. It's important." Samir came running down the 2 flights of stairs and I smiled at him.

"Sam do you love me?" He smiled back.

"Yeah why? Is that a trick question?" He then had this confused look on his face. I extended my arms around his waist.

"Would you do anything for me?" He kissed me on the forehead.

"What you want from me girl?" I let my smile fade, walked over, grabbed the phone and shook it in his direction.

"Samir Yah-Yah called." His face dropped.

"What's the matter Samir? I just want you to call her and tell her it is over between y'all and don't call here anymore." He shook his head.

"No D. I can't do that." My arms shot up like rockets over my head. I screamed,

"What!?" He remained calm.

"I can't do that because first of all there is nothing between us. We're just friends that talk on the phone, that's all." I placed a hand on my hip and rolled my neck around.

"Well could you end that friendship then?" He was adamant about his decision. He picked up his house keys from the end table.

"No D I won't. I like talking to her as a friend." I got mad then.

"Ooh I see, keep her as a back up just in case huh?" He sighed.

"No Diamond, please don't start and don't put shit in the game. You don't have no right to tell me who I can and can't be friends with. I don't pick your friends for you and you shouldn't have answered my phone." Why did he say that? I screamed on him.

"Ooh I see, we back together but you can do what you want and I have to just accept that right? It's cool Sam don't call Miss Yah-Yah back. I don't care but can we just go to the party?" Starr sat quietly the whole time. I snatched up my small Fendi bag and grinded my teeth together.

"Come on y'all lets go." I was furious. I started walking up the stairs and they were behind me trying to whisper. I turned around and shot them both a look to kill.

"It is impolite to whisper." Their faces looked like little kids that got caught with their hands in the cookie jar. We walked to the party in complete silence. When we got there we just went in to see what was going on. It was a party for high school kids and kids going to the high that Wednesday after Labor Day. I was pissed on the inside but I didn't let it show. The first place I went was the ladies room and Starr followed me. Once inside the bathroom she checked the stalls for legs.

"D, I didn't want to say this in front of Sam but what about Pop and Khaliq that you met at the rink a few weeks ago? They call you and you talk to them on the phone." I looked at my lip gloss in the mirror.

"First of all, no I only talk to Khaliq on the phone because come to find out Pop and Khaliq are brothers. I didn't know that when they got my number at the rink. I forgot to tell you I found out they both had the same father. They claim their father is Dominican but they mad (crazy). They black as me. Since I met Khaliq first, I talked to him but I was going to tell him to stop calling me tomorrow cause me and Sam had gotten back together. But we can be friends like him and Yah-Yah are friends. Anything he can do I can do better." I smiled at myself in the mirror while I fixed my hair. I had gotten a wrap and I loved to comb my hair after a wrap. It laid so flat and pretty. Starr blew a kiss at herself in the mirror.

"O.k. D I just don't want y'all to do stuff to hurt each other anymore. I don't like being in the middle. I was going to tell you about Yah-Yah but I didn't know how too." I flashed Starr a phony 32 teeth smile.

"Don't worry about it Starr. It's over and done with. It's all good." She put her hair behind her ear.

"Well for the record, I didn't tell him about the skating rink guys either so y'all are even." I put my arm around her.

"O.k. Starr I don't want to talk about it no more O.k.? Lets just go party." I shot her another phony smile to shut her up. We walked out of the ladies room and into the party. The music was bumping and this cute guy grabbed Starr's arm. He must have been about sixteen or seventeen. He was tall and light brown with curly hair. She smiled hard and mumbled to me, "D don't leave me O.k.?" I shrugged.

"O.k." He began whispering things in her ear and she was giggling. I couldn't take it so I walked away. As I walked away I noticed it was the boy Shawn a.k.a Red I met at my 13th birthday party. I had never spoke to him and never told Starr about him so I didn't say that I knew him. The code is if your girl use to talk to him, then you don't. But since I never talked to him, it was cool. She screamed behind me, "D, where you going?!" I pointed to some empty chairs and she nodded up and down. I went and sat down. It was a couple next to me kissing and groping each other. I was so ready to go but I knew Starr wanted to be there. I just sat there and thought about how Starr didn't tell me about that Yah-Yah bitch. I know that Sam is her brother but damn I am her sister and best friend that should have counted for something but it was all-good. This ugly guy sat down next to me and rubbed his hands together like he hit the jackpot.

"What's up sweetie? What's a cutie like you doing sitting here all alone?" I rolled my eyes with much attitude attached.

"Nothing much." He leaned in towards my ear.

"Well you gotta name cutie?" I rolled my eyes again and crossed my legs and my arms over my chest.

"Yeah I do." We sat there for a few seconds in silence and he exclaimed, "Well?" I snapped back, "Well what?!" (By this time I was very annoyed.) He licked his big black and pink discolored lips.

"What's your name?" I breathed out so he could hear it.

"Well you didn't ask me what my name was you

asked me did I have one so I said yeah I do but if you must know it, it's Diamond." He leaned back in his chair laughing and grabbing his family jewels.

"That was cute and that is a cute name for a cute girl. Bye the way I'm Nadir." I thought, *who cares*! He was getting on my nerves and his breathe was kicking. He didn't take hints well.

"Do you gotta man Diamond?" I looked out the side of my eye at him up and down.

"Yeah I do." He thought he was saying something cute by saying, "So what's your man got to do with me?" I just looked at him like he was stupid. Not only didn't he take hints well, he didn't take them at all. He placed his hairy black arm on the top of my chair. I inched up so he wouldn't touch me.

"Well you going to the High this year?" I mumbled, "Yeah." He squinted his eyes indicating that he needed bifocal glasses.

"Are you new around here. I have never seen you?" I frowned up my face tired of playing 21 questions with him.

"No! I have lived her all my life and I am going into the 10th grade." He covered his mouth.

"Whoa! Ooh snap! I don't want to be robbing the cradle." I had had all I could take so he got dissed.

"Ill! Nobody asked you to sit here and talk and how old are you anyway?" He rubbed his hands together again.

"I'm 19 but I will be in 12th grade. I stayed back twice." So, he was dumb and ugly. Sarcastically I replied, "Ooh wow! You are sooo much older than me and so much smarter too." He pinched my cheek and I slapped his hand down.

"I like you. Is your man here?" I swung my hair off my shoulders.

"Yeah he's..." I looked up to see if I saw him and he was talking to this tall Puerto Rican chic with long curly/kinky hair and bright red lipstick on. They were deep in conversation and I didn't like it. I just calmed myself down. I exhaled and decided I was going to gradually stroll past them. The guy snapped his brown nails in my face.

"Hello? You still in there?" I looked at him with my lip turned up in disgust. He raised his eyebrow obviously thinking we would have more dialogue.

"You were saying?" I jumped up out of my seat.

"I was saying I gotta go!" I briskly walked away. I began to walk through the party and I walked right passed this bitch and my man. Samir was so into his conversation he didn't even see me. I walked out of the party room and down the hallway to go outside. I got by the door and my other girls from the rink and a few others from school was yelling, "Hey Diamond come here!" I turned back around and me and Sam locked eyes because he was standing by the door that led into the party. I guess it was dark and he didn't notice me walk pass him but out in the hallway in the light, he noticed. The girl looked at me and this bitch had the nerve to take her hand and lightly push Samir's face back towards her. I just looked with my mouth open. He said something to her and she frowned. He walked towards me and I walked towards the girls that called me. I forced out a smile.

"What up ladies?" Sam walked up behind me and wrapped his arms around my waist.

"Hey y'all what up?" They all said in one shape or form, "Hey Samir." He looked at them and pointed at the top of my head.

"Could I borrow her for a minute?" One girl from school, Kesha H., that didn't know the drama said, "Yeah Samir, take her. She is your girl." He smiled and so did they but I didn't. He hugged me from behind and I tried to pull away. The Puerto Rican girl walked away from the entrance and into the party. We leaned up against the hallway walls. He softly touched the tip of my nose.

"You having fun?" I sighed.

"Yeah its O.k." I really wanted to tell him to go fuck himself but I kept my cool. He grabbed my hands.

"You want to dance?" I grabbed them back.

"No I need some air but you can go dance though."

"No, I want to be with you. Can I go with you outside to get some air?" I shrugged my shoulders and walked out the door. I sat on an empty bench by the Multi Center. He sat next to me and stared at me. I stared straight ahead. He put his arm around me.

"D, what's wrong?" I strengthened up a fake smile and looked at him.

"Nothing Sam." I turned back straight. He leaned in towards my ear.

"You want to go back to my house and finish what we started? My parents staying in Atlantic City until tomorrow." I frowned.

"No Sam I don't." He exhaled and sat with his legs apart and his forearms on his thighs.

"D that girl I was talking too was Yah-Yah." I pretended I didn't hear what he just said because I didn't want to hear it.

"Huh Samir?" He sat back up straight.

"You heard me. That was Yah-Yah. I wanted to introduce y'all but I thought you would act out." I lied.

"No I wouldn't have Samir and it's O.k. That is your friend. You can be friends with whoever you want to be." He said matter of fact-ly.

"You right D. I can but I want my friends to be your friends. I mean yeah Yah-Yah likes me but I like you and I chose you. She is just cool to talk too, O.k.?" I looked down at my freshly painted nails.

"Fine Sam." He took my hand in his.

"Can I introduce you two?" I pulled my hand back.

"I don't think that is a good idea. I might hook off on her." He sighed.

"I knew it D. Why? Why you want to hit her?" I fought back tears and cleared my throat.

"Because she all in your face trying to play me out and you all in her face and it looks disrespectful to me. Everybody asking me ooh I didn't know you and Sam broke up?" (Yeah I was lying). He furrowed his eyebrows.

"Who said that?" I was annoyed at this time and

threw my hands in the air.

"Come on now that's not important. Who cares who asked. Just know folks is asking and they could pick up on the vibe between y'all." He thought aloud.

"You know you right, she was kinda all over me. I kept telling her I wasn't leaving you and she finally said 'O.k. I wont pursue you no more but the minute she mess up again I am sliding up in that spot and not leaving for no one.'" I jumped up and paced back and forth in front of him.

"What?! When I mess up again?! You the one that messed up Samir." Sam grabbed my arm and pulled me back down.

"D calm down. Who am I sitting here with? I don't want her or I would be with her right?... Right?" I rolled my eyes.

"Right. Yeah right, whatever Samir." He started tickling me.

"Say I"m right." I couldn't help but laugh. I was laughing so hard I felt like I was going to throw up.

"You're right! You're right!" He continued to tickle me.

"Say I'm always right." I laughed harder.

"Yeah right!" He pulled his bottom lip in and tickled me some more. I was cracking up laughing putting up the time out sign.

"You always right." I was squirming around so much and ended up with my head in his lap looking into his big brown eyes. He mouthed, "I'm sorry." I mouthed, "I know." He pushed my hair back off my face.

"No D seriously. I'm sorry for all this. Can we get passed it and it be just us again?" I placed my index finger to my temple.

"Hmmm?" He put his hand under my armpit to tickle me again. I answered him quickly.

"O.k. yes Sam. We won't talk about that past stuff anymore O.k.?" He gave me a big sloppy kiss on my cheek.

"O.k. and you the only friend I need. I told her not to call me anymore." I couldn't help but smile. I reached up from his lap and pinched his cheek.

"You such a good little slave doing what Master Diamond tells you." I jumped up to run and he playfully ragged me back.

"What you say? You must want some more tickling." I forced my arms down to keep from Samir tickling me.

"No Samir I don't... Please I will do anything." He let me go and looked me in my eyes.

"Ooh really." I got serious and looked him in the face.

"Really?" He stood up and extended his hand.

"O.k. My house now." I placed my hand in his and he pulled me up from the bench.

"Fine lets go." And we were off.

CHAPTER 6
LOSING IT

Me and Samir walked briskly back to his house. We got half way home and I stopped and smacked my forehead.

"Waaaiiittt! We forgot about Starr." He snapped his fingers once.

"Ooh shoot. Let me go back and get her. No, um let me tell her you were ready to go and I will come back for her." I unclipped my beeper from my hip to check the time.

"No Sam. It is already 10 and that will only give us 2 hours." He smiled and rubbed his hands together.

"You need more time then that?" I blushed and looked down. He grabbed me around my waist.

"Sike Boo. O.k. lets just go back." I kissed him on his cheek.

"Sam we have plenty of time for sex." He reached for my hand.

"You right D, but I was ready." We walked back to the party with our fingers intertwined and found Starr. She was still talking to the same guy from earlier. She was sitting damn near on his lap. As she saw us approaching she waved us over.

"Hey y'all where y'all been?" Sam stared and then pointed at the mystery man.

"Outside talking. Who dis?" Starr flicked her hair behind her ear and pointed in our direction.

"Diamond and Samir, I want you to meet Shawn." We both said in unison, "Hi" but Sam's face was looking like bye. She linked her arm through Shawn's.

"Shawn is going to walk me to Sage Diner after the party. After that I will be home O.k. you guys?" Sam looked at me and smiled basically smiling to say ooh it is on. He then looked at Shawn.

"Yo fam, take care of my sister ight?" Shawn threw

up the peace sign.

"Yeah man you got it." Sam grabbed my hand and yanked me towards the door.

"Let's go D." So once again we began to walk to his house. This usual 10 minute walk felt like 2 minutes, we got there so quick. We snuck around back incase my parents or Aunt Debra were in the window and went to the basement. Once downstairs I sat down on the couch while he paced the floor.

"You want something to drink?" I shook my head, "Yes." He ran upstairs and got me a cup of juice. I swallowed hard at the lump growing in my throat. He ran back down the stairs like lightning and handed it to me. I held the cup tight with both hands.

"Thank you Samir." Then I took a small sip. He put his arm around me and kissed my neck. I jumped and spilled the juice on the floor. He got up and got a towel from the basement bathroom and wiped up the juice. He pried the cup out of my hands.

"Are you O.k.?" I was shaking because I was so nervous.

"Yeah I'm O.k." He grabbed my hand in his.

"We don't have to do this you know. D, I can wait." I placed my hands on his shoulders and looked him in his sincere eyes.

"No Sam. I want to do this for you." He leaned over and kissed me real soft. It sent tingles through my body and my panties got wet as the rain forest. I never felt this sensation come over me before. Sam ran his warm tongue over my neck and into my ear. I was so nervous I didn't know what to do. I just sat there like a statue. Samir was a virgin like me but he had an older brother to clue him in. They would watch porno's and stuff like that so Sam had more of an idea what to do then me. He ran his gentle hands over my throbbing breasts and unbuttoned my shirt. He tried to unhook my bra but couldn't get it. I laughed and covered my mouth like Ms. Celie from the Color Purple. He whispered directly in my ear with his warm Big Red breath.

"Ooh that's funny?" I snickered.

"Yes. It is." He kissed me again. This time hard and sexual. It felt so good I took my bra off for Samir. I could see a bulge growing in his shorts and I got scared all over again. He licked my erect nipples and then began to suck on them. I think he tried to pull milk out of them he was sucking so hard. I pushed his head off of me.

"Ouch Samir!" He ran his thumbs over my sore nipples.

"Sorry D." He then laid me down on the sofa and got on top of me. He used his knee to push my legs apart so our bodies laid in sync. We were tongue kissing and it was feeling so good. He sucked on my neck and I sucked on his. He traced the edge of my ear with his tongue.

"Diamond take your shorts off." He got up to allow me to sit up. I did what he said. I stood up and dropped my shorts. I sat back down. He pushed my back to force me to stand up again.

"Uh, your underwear too Diamond." I was nervous but I slid them down my thighs and let them drop to my feet. I stepped out of them and sat back down next to Samir. He used his hands to pry my legs apart. He rubbed my vaginal hairs and then rubbed my clitoris. Next he stuck his middle finger inside me. It hurt a little bit and I arched my back. He removed his finger and leaned over to peck my lips.

"D, it is tight and wet just like it should be." I draped my arms over his shoulders and around his neck.

"How do you know how it should be?" He kissed me again.

"Cause I do." He pushed my arms off and jumped up to slip out of his shorts. It was pitch black in the basement and I couldn't see much of anything. He began to push me back on the couch.

"D you sure you want to do this?" I shook my head back and forth feverously. He stopped in mid air and straightened up.

"It's O.k. D. You don't have to, we can slow down." He handed me my underwear and my shorts. He searched in the dark for my bra and top. Once I had all my articles of clothing, I dressed quickly. I felt bad for changing my mind, so after I was dressed I was getting up to leave. Samir yanked me down by the top of my shorts.

"D, where you going?" He leaned in towards me and we started kissing again as if we were having a sword fight with our tongues. He ended up back on top of me with his manhood swelling again. He went to unbutton my shirt and we heard the basement door open. The light flicked on. We quickly sat up and tried to act like we were talking. I didn't know who it was so I turned my head just incase it was one of his parents. It was his older brother Shareef coming down stairs with a girl that was not his girlfriend. He jumped back.

"Ooh shit lil' bro I didn't know you were down here. Who that with you?" I twirled my neck back around to face Shareef and the tramp he was with.

"What Shareef? Who else would it be?" I thought, Shareef probably thought it was Yah-Yah and got scared. He laughed nervously.

"D, I was just joking. What y'all doing?" I rolled my eyes and sucked my teeth.

"Dag Shareef, me and your brother is just talking, is that O.k.?" He cleared his throat.

"Since that's all y'all doing can y'all talk in the living room or in Sam's room or somewhere else? I need the basement for a while." He looked over his shoulder and smiled at the girl. She smiled back looking down trying to act shy. Whatever bitch is what I felt like saying to her. I know Shareef bought her down to the basement just incase their parents came home. Then he would have more time and places to hide that chic. So, me and Sam went and sat on the steps outside. He placed his arm around my shoulder.

"How do you feel?" I leaned into his chest, which felt like a rock.

"O.k. Sam, I'm sorry we couldn't do it today." In my mind I was saying yes! He looked sympathetic and ran his fingers through my hair.

"It's cool D. We have time for that but I am glad we are back together." I rested my head on his shoulder.

"Me too Sam, me too." I thought, I love him. We just sat in silence and watched the stars waiting for Starr to come home. Sam looked at his watch.

"It is 12:15 do you want to walk to the diner and get something to eat?" I shrugged.

"I don't care." In my mind I knew he wasn't hungry he wanted to check up on Starr. We walked to the Sage Diner hand in hand and it was packed. We spotted Starr and Shawn in a booth and decided to invade what little privacy they had in a place that crowded. We scooted them in towards the walls of the booth and sat on the outside. Sam rubbed his hands together.

"I will be right back. I gotta go to the bathroom and wash my hands, they sticky." He winked at me and smiled. I felt my face get red cause he was trying to say they were sticky from, you know, playing with my privates. I just looked down at the ceramic table and kept my eyes glued there. Starr didn't pay any attention to the comment cause she was to busy huffing and puffing.

"What are you doing here Diamond?" I traced the pattern on the table.

"He wanted to walk down here and get something to eat." She got testy and threw her arms in the air.

"Well could y'all get y'all own booth." I got testy right back. I looked at her and turned my upper lip up.

"Ill! We sure will." I said it in a joking way. She calmed down and patted my hand.

"Sis you know I don't mean it like that but you know." I smiled.

"Yeah I do. It's cool." Sam came back and flopped down. Shawn started the convo.

"So are y'all ready for high school?" I danced around a little in my seat.

"Yes!" Sam stared at me and didn't answer. The waitress came over to take orders. When she got to me and asked what would I be having I responded,

"Nothing for us were not staying." Sam whipped his neck around and shot me a look. He pointed at me.

"What? You not hungry?" I stood up and extended my hand toward him.

"No and I am ready to go, so can we?" I winked at Starr.

"Bye Shawn. Nice to meet you." Sam ignored my hand and kept sitting there. I grabbed his arm to pull him out the booth. Sam looked at his watch and looked at Starr. She rolled her eyes at him as to say, nigga please you ain't Daddy. Of course when we got outside we got into it.

"What do you mean by we not having anything we leaving? I wanted to check that cat out." I rolled my eyes in the air and waved my hand at Samir.

"Ooh Sam please. They just met let them get to know each other first before we have a family gathering. Her and Danny are through so you can stop trying to look out for your boy." He huffed and puffed.

"It ain't even like that. Danny was doing his thing in the back of the party with some chic. He with her now at her crib." I began to walk towards our block.

"So! She must be a whore if he over there now and they just met." He laughed. I placed my hands on my hips.

"It's all good. Starr got her a winner there. He is a cutie." He looked at me like I was stupid for saying that Shawn was cute. So he walked in front of me. I just sighed and walked behind him. When we got to our block he slowed up so we could walk together. He looked me up and down with sex in his eyes.

"You going in the house?" I yawned and stretched.

"Yeah Samir I'm tired and it is almost 1. I will see you tomorrow for church?" He swiftly kissed me on my lips.

"O.k." He sat on his steps. I got my keys out and went in the house. I couldn't wait to get in the bed and that is exactly what I did.

CHAPTER 7
SCHOOL DAYS

Well it was 6 AM, Wednesday morning and my drill sergeant mom woke me up for my first day of Union High School. She cooked a big breakfast for me, Sam, Starr, David and Danny who came over at like 6:45 AM to eat. We had pancakes, eggs, bacon, biscuits, you name it, she cooked it. I told you she loved to cook. Sam gobbled down 2 pieces of bacon at a time.

"Ma you cooking every morning for us?" My mother scrubbed a pan in the sink.

"Hell no boy. I am just cooking for your first day of high school. Aren't you guys excited?" We all grumbled so she could get her answer. She was more excited then any of us. I did have butterflies in my stomach but I didn't want to let in on that to anyone. Starr and Shawn were still kicking it, so he was walking with us to school. Once Shawn rang my bell, we headed out the door to leave. Sam pulled me back in the screen door. He looked around and whispered directly in my ear.

"Yo, it is something about this Shawn cat that I don't like." I just rolled my eyes.

"He is all right to me Sam. Stop being so p-noid (paranoid)!" Danny had a new girlfriend, Gina and she was an airhead. That was the one he was all up on at the party. They just met that weekend and now they were a couple. How dumb. Him and Starr couldn't stand each other. They didn't even speak. At breakfast that morning they were like total strangers. I didn't want me and Sam to end up like that. David was souped up for us to come to the 'High' because he thought he knew it all and we would need his help getting around. Yeah, like he was the only other kid in the whole school, huh. He was in the 12th grade this year.

Danny dumb ass was supposed to be in 11th but remember he stayed back. Dumb ass. Anyway me, Sam, Starr, and Shawn walked to school together, while David rode with his brother. He knows he was bothered that Shawn and Starr were walking together. Anyway, we got there and it was a mad house with people all over the place. Me and Starr tried to walk with confidence like we knew our way around. Our schedules had been mailed to us a week before, and we only had the same gym class together, not even lunch. I mean we were popular so we had a lot of friends but I hated being apart from Starr because school would be boring. I had first lunch and she had second lunch. We would see each other coming in and out of the cafeteria and in that 4 minutes we had to pass to the next class we would try to squeeze in any events that had happened thus far that day. Then we would say goodbye and pass the notes we had wrote each other in previous periods which were usually about a bunch of nothing. All she use to ask me in her notes were, "Did you see all the cuties in school?" I would write back to her, "You are becoming boy crazy." Of course, guess who was in my first period class? Shakira punk ass and guess who was in my 4th period class? Shakira punk ass. She didn't say nothing to me and I didn't say nothing to her and she better had kept it that way before she got beat up again. Gym wasn't until 6th period and guess who was in me and Starr class? No not Shakira punk ass, Yah-Yah's big bird looking ass. I had to keep my cool because as soon as I saw her my temper flared. I didn't want to get suspended on the first day. She was looking real corny with some no name jeans on and bright red lipsticks smeared across her perched lips. She was such a cornball. I was laughing inside saying, if Samir ever plays me for her then he would be playing himself cause she is boodie! Anyway me and Starr were sitting next to each other on the bleachers and she came up to where we were sitting.

"Hey Starr!" Starr looked at me and back at her.

"What up." She said it real soft and real quick. Yah-

Yah placed her hands on her hips and cocked her head to the side.

"So Starr, what up with you?" Starr leaned back and placed her elbows on the bleacher behind us.

"Nothing much." She dropped her hands from her waist.

"How's your parents?" Starr sighed.

"They ight." Yah-Yah then pushed my hot button with her next question.

"How's your brother?" That is when I took over the convo.

"Samir is just fine. Thanks for asking." She squinted her eyes and chuckled.

"Ooh thanks for telling me but I wasn't talking to you." That's when I stood up on the bottom bleacher just incase something was about to pop off.

"Yeah but I was talking to you." She backed up as to give herself room. She slowly turned her head from left then to the right and then looked directly at me.

"Who you getting smart with?!" I looked to my left and then to my right and then looked directly at her. I added in my pointer finger that I extended towards her.

"Bitch, ain't nobody talking but me and you!" She threw her hands up in the air.

"Bitch?! I got your bitch!" And with that, she started walking away. I cupped my hands around my mouth like a megaphone.

"Like I said bitch, I'm talking to you. Your best bet is to walk away cause you don't want none of this." As I pointed at myself she turned around and looked me up and down.

"Whatever! I'm too old for this childish shit. Little girl you need to grow up." I jumped off the bottom bleacher to the shiny hardwood gym floor.

"Whatever bitch! I got your little girl right here in my fist you dumb ugly corny Puerto Rican ho. You want my man but-cha can't have him. Rice and beans eating bitch!" She directed her back towards me and did a half twirl with her hand.

"Yeah ight! Whatever!" I screamed even louder.

"Yeah I know it's yeah ight, whatever cause you scared." She just waved her hand as to say whatever and kept walking away. Starr looked at me and shook her head. Thank God the 4 classes that had gym at the same time, were all just sitting on the bleachers chilling the first day or I would have been out of there for 3 days for sure on suspension. The teachers couldn't hear all that over the commotion in the crowded noise-filled gym. I took my seat back on the bleachers and Starr was looking at me grinning and shaking her head. I couldn't help but smirk a bit.

"What?! Why you looking at me and shaking your head?" She burst out laughing.

"Cause your ass is crazy girl." I laughed at her comment and playfully balled my fists up.

"I know, and don't you forget it!" We laughed our asses off and just chilled for the rest of the class period. It was a few cuties in our class. Nothing for me to leave Samir over, maybe creep but not leave him, I'm messing with you. Me, Shakira, and Samir had 7th period English together. Our teacher was cool as hell. His name was Mr. Murphy. When we first got into to class we were all talking. He walked in and smiled at the class.

"Settle down class, I'm Mr. Murphy and welcome to Union High School. I want to start by asking do I have any volunteers to tell me what they did this summer?" A few hands shot up but this big mouth kid Jason blurted out of turn from the back of the class.

"Some of us spent our summer fighting." Me and Samir both turned around in our seats and looked at him. He thought he was a comedian but I was going to have the last laugh. So I raised my hand high. The teacher smiled and pointed at me.

"And some of us spent our summer learning what ACNE was!" Jason's face had broken out bad. Everyone turned and looked at him and laughed. The teacher couldn't help but chuckle.

"O.k. class settle down. Let's see if I can play Sherlock Holmes for a minute." He walked over to my desk and stood in front of me.

"From the looks of things you are the fighter for the summer. Do you care to share?" I sunk down in my seat a bit.

"No, I'd rather not." He patted my desk.

"That's O.k., anyone else care to share?" No one raised their hand. So he looked around at all the students and pointed at Samir.

"You sir, what did you do this summer?" Jason didn't get enough the first time around. He blurted out a second time.

"He was the reason for all the fighting." Samir pushed back from his desk and jumped up so fast his chair fell back.

"Yo Jason, why don't round 2 of the fighting begin now?" Jason got embarrassed because he knew Samir would have beat that ass.

"Come on Samir man, you know I was just playing." Sam remained standing and bent down to pick up his chair.

"That's what I thought." The class began to howl and hiss. Mr. Murphy intervened and raised his hands in the air.

"Settle down class please." He walked over to Samir and patted his shoulder.

"Please take your seat." Mr. Murphy then walked back to his desk and slightly leaned on it almost sitting on it. He rubbed his face.

"O.k. let me put my detective hat back on. You 2 date and had a little problem over the summer. A few fights were had but now everything is O.k." I sat up tall and looked dead at Shakira.

"You bet it is, this is my man and I ain't giving him up for no chic!" She looked straight ahead rolling her eyes. He scooted up on the desk completely.

"O.k. Miss so since everything is O.k... Excuse, me sir in the back? It is over so let's not bring it up again."

Jason shook his head yes. He looked around at the class one last time.

"Since everyone is so shy I will share my summer with you." The rest sounded like blah blah blah blah because I was not listening. I was doodling Samir and Diamond all over my notebook. Then, I reached over and got his notebook and did the same thing to his. The bell rang and for homework we had to write an essay about our summers since we didn't want to do it in class. Well, that was my first day of high school. It wasn't all people cracked it up to be. Through the school year me and Yah-Yah continued to get into it. We never completely came to blows cause she was a scaredy cat. One thing I knew was that she was giving it up to guys and since me and Samir had only made it a few bases and still hadn't bought it home yet, she had an advantage over me. Samir went out for the basketball team and of course he made it. He was one of the star players and of course other girls started really wanting my man. I am the jealous type, that's me, and I didn't want my man talking to no other chics, but he did anyway cause he was just nice like that. In the hall all you would hear was, "Hey Samir!" and he would respond with out looking, "Hey what up" and then keep stepping. I knew bitches was trifling and saying what up to see what was up, like would he creep out on me. Me and Sam was good but I knew if I wanted to keep him I would have to start having sex soon. We were both still virgins and he told me he would wait until I was ready but I didn't want nobody else throwing it at my man and he wouldn't be able to resist, so I put operation, "give Samir some" into effect. I tried in my basement, my bedroom, his basement, his bedroom, the living room, you name it and I tried to have sex with him there. I even went in the bathroom with him cause I knew his pants were down but he would say the same thing every time.

"No Diamond you're not ready. You just worried I'm gonna do it to someone else, but D stop worrying, I wont cheat on you, I promise, you have my word O.k.?" I said,

"O.k." but wasn't thinking about what he was saying. I was going to give it to him. I laid off for a few weeks and after that we were in his basement and I tried again. We were almost there but we heard his parent's car pull up in the driveway. He was patting his privates through his pants saying, "go down boy go down" and I had to laugh. We were supposed to be studying for an English test but we started studying each other. I knew Sam wanted me bad, but was acting like it was no big deal. The rest of the school year we never got to it. We just did heavy making out. The place that was made for a penis always had his fingers in it and that was fine for me and for him. Starr had kept seeing Shawn but Shawn was seeing her and many others so she decided to play his game. She began to just talk to mad guys. She didn't care whether they knew each other or not. Shawn didn't like that so he tried to get Starr on a girlfriend level but she wasn't having that. She liked being single and able to date whom ever she wanted. In the mean time David told me Starr had filled out nicely and wanted a shot at her. We were sitting in my room just shooting the breeze and I threw my pillow at him.

"Hell no! Your brother Danny, do you remember him? He use to go with her." He shrugged his shoulders.

"So, he said he don't want her and besides that is young stuff we're older now. I don't need your approval anyway I am going to push up, if my brother don't care why should you?"

"Cause I do David. Don't do that." He tossed the pillow back at my head.

"Why you acting up D? She's a virgin too. I would tear that ass up." I took my pillow and hit him over the head. I screamed at the top of my lungs.

"Don't talk about my sister like that David or I will kill you!" He tooted his lips up and to the side.

"Ooh like you and Sam ain't slapping naked bodies." I scrunched up my face.

"We're not!" He leaned back slightly shocked.

"Word?! I thought y'all would have been slapping

bodies by now." I hit him with the pillow again over and over again about 5 times.

"Ill David! Stop being so nasty." He laughed and snatched the pillow from me.

"O.k. O.k. I wont push up on her. I will just floss around her and make her push up on me. When she sees the size of my..." I cut him off and pointed at my door.

"Good bye David! Bye get out!" He laughed harder.

"I was going to say the size of my brain D. How smart I am! You need to get your mind out the gutter." I put up the sign for sure with my fingers.

"Sure Dave. Sure. Whatever, get out." He strutted to the door like a peacock.

"Fine I'm gone, but I'm still going to give it to Starr good." I threw the pillow at him as he dodged out the door. When I heard the front door open and close, I laughed to myself at my God brother, thinking, Starr would never want him so he better get out of here. I reached over on my nightstand and picked up my phone. I called Starr to let her in on me and Dave's little convo. After I told her what he said she didn't respond how I wanted her too.

"Yo D, what up with him? I'm down. I wouldn't mind kicking it." I got an instant attitude.

"Starr uh hello?! You use to go with his brother." She sucked her teeth.

"Come on D! We were young then, it meant nothing. You and Sam the only ones still holding on." I sucked my teeth back at her.

"So if Dave said O.k. Starr come over right now so I can hit that you would go?" She sucked her teeth harder.

"Hell no! What I look like? But I will get a free meal or movie date or something. Shit, we got to eat to live." I was aggravated by this time.

"O.k. fine. I'm out of it. Y'all do what you want to do."

"Well D I won't put nothing between us ever and you know that so if you don't want me to then I won't." I laid back on my bed.

"Starr you gotta do what you feel is real." I heard her

switch the phone around.

"You right, but I don't want to do something that may be wrong but I just don't see it." I gave an example to her that popped in my head.

"O.k. That is like me breaking up with Samir and then talking to your older brother Shareef." she replied,

"That would be fucked up."

"Exactly Starr, now you getting it."

"Ooh I kinda feel you, but it don't matter cause I ain't messing with Dave like that anyway. I was just messing with you. And the difference between you and Samir and me and Danny is y'all are in love and we never were." I let out a trivial laugh.

"Well beware. He is on the prowl and he said he is gonna get you to want him." She cut in. "What?! Yeah ight! I would like to see that." We laughed at him because he thought he was so dope. He made me sick, brother or not. The 10th grade was done and it was the summer again when some more drama came.

CHAPTER 8
BECOMING A WOMAN- SO I THOUGHT

David was graduating and going away to school at Syracuse in NY to play basketball and not be so far away from his family. By the way he never did get with Starr, he tried to get her to notice him but she played him. So he found another cup of coffee to dip his spoon in. Some chic that nobody liked but she is pointless to my story so forget her. Anyway, one sticky, hot Friday night David had a big graduation/congratulations/good luck/going away party and I told Samir that night that I had had enough. I was ready. I had a sure proof plan all mapped out and I was going to follow through with it. The next morning we got up bright and early. We decided to catch a cab to one of the motels out by the highway. For those of you in Jersey, we went to Route 22, to Clinton Manor. Since this was my idea I was using my b day money to pay for everything. We told our parents we were spending the day together doing things like going downtown, out to eat, to the movies, bowling, skating. All that so our whole day would be covered. The day before I had went and bought condoms and a cute bra and panties set. I mean I had just turned 16, I felt it was time. We got to the motel and I went into the front desk alone to get a room. We didn't want the front desk asking us anything or looking at us funny. When I asked for a room the clerk popped on her chewing gum and looked at me over her thick glasses.

"For over night or a short stay?" I flung my hair over my shoulder.

"What is a short stay?" She scratched her dry red hair.

90

"4 hours. For people to handle their business and go." She looked me up and down as if she knew that I only needed a short stay. My face flushed and I must have looked white. I clutched my nameplate.

"Ooh my gosh (like I wasn't there for that). No give me a room for over night." I knew we weren't staying that long but still I had to be safe. She dangled the key from her fat pork sausage-looking finger. I snatched the key and headed out of the lobby. Our room was on the outside and up the stairs. I was so nervous but you couldn't tell by my face. I walked with confidence like I was experienced at this. When we got in the room we closed the drapes nice and tight to get it really dark in the room. We turned the TV on and flopped on the queen size bed and watched Saturday morning cartoons. By this time we were hungry. There was an I.H.O.P. (International House of Pancakes) right across the road. We crossed the highway to get something to eat. We ate and bugged out like we didn't come to handle something. But I thought, I came to handle something and damn it, I am going to handle it. We went back to our room and laid on the bed side-by-side and fell asleep. Unbelievable. I woke up about 1:30 PM and Samir was still knocked out. I tip toed in the bathroom to rinse my mouth out and freshen up the kitty cat. When I came out he was curled up like a baby, so I laid back down next to him and tickled him until he woke up. He woke up cranky whining, "Stop" and rubbed his eyes. Once he looked around he covered his mouth and laughed.

"Ooh snap! I was knocked out and I didn't know where I was at. My bad D." He rolled over and we laid facing each other. We just stared at each other. He rubbed my hair and I smiled. I leaned in and kissed him and then moved back. He leaned in and kissed me and then moved back. I pushed him back so he was laying flat on his back and mounted on top of him. We then began to kiss passionately. I took his shirt off him and kissed his chest. It was hard like a rock, um um um that was my man. I licked the cracks and crevices that made up his chests and his abs. He took my shirt off and lightly traced over my bra.

"Nice bra Diamond." It was all lace and completely see through. I took it off and he kissed my breasts softly. It sent tingles through my body. I was tired of playing around with this so I unbuttoned his jeans and I could see a bulge already. So I purposely slowed down and undid his zipper really slow at the speed of a snails pace. He looked down at my hands and then up at me.

"D do you need some help." I smiled.

"No Sam I'm good." So he started to undo my pants and moved like a jack rabbit. We both stood up and stepped out of our jeans. We laid back down and began kissing again. We were under the covers and he slid his boxers off and I did the same with my bikini style underwear. O.k. now we were both buck naked under the covers. The condoms! They were in my bag allllll the way across the room. I didn't want him looking at me completely naked and he didn't want me looking at him. So as I kissed him I paused between each kiss to say.

"Sam you gotta get the condoms out of my bag." He looked over at the bag.

"No you get 'em." I rolled over with my back towards him.

"Well it don't matter to me. I will just go back to sleep." He huffed and puffed.

"O.k., O.k. D!" He grabbed the comforter off the bed and wrapped it around him and went and got the condoms. When he came back his soldier was down but we started kissing again and it didn't take long for it to rise again. He placed the condom on and began to play with my wet spot to get it wetter. I couldn't believe we were finally going to do this. He climbed on top of me and tried to enter me. He tried to force it directly in with out working it in slowly. I screamed, "Ouch Sam! That hurts." He kissed my forehead.

"Sorry D, are you sure you want to do this?" I began to tremble.

"Positive go again." So he went nice and easy and

it was a force getting it in. It hurt so bad but I was going to brave it out for him. He worked it all the way in and at the first pump it slipped out. I wanted to say, "O.k. that's enough we tried," but he looked so pleased so I whispered, "Put it back in Samir" and he smiled and said, "O.k." It hurt so bad tears rolled down my face. He licked my tears away.

"Are you O.k. baby?" I tried to smile but wanted to cry.

"Yes Sam. I'm just happy, that's all." I was really just hurt. In my mind I was saying, never again, he could forget it. He moved in and out slowly while he looked in my face.

"How does it feel D?" I lowered my eyes.

"Fine. How does it feel for you?" He stuttered, "Uuuh uuhh" I raised my eyes to meet his.

"Huh Sam what are you saying?" He was still stuttering, "Uuuhh uhhh" as his eyes rolled in his eyes. I got scared cause he couldn't talk and I was pounding on his chest.

"Sam what's wrong? What is it?" He kept going faster and faster.

"Uuuuuuuuuuuhhhhhhhh." He had bust his first nut (ejaculated) inside of a vagina and not outside in his hand. After he finished looking like he was having a convulsion he was breathing like he ran a marathon and collapsed on me.

"I love you Diamond." He sat there for a minute and then pulled out. He sat up on the edge of the bed and reached over and put his t-shirt on and went in the bathroom. I put mines on and rushed in the bathroom when he came out. I tried to pee but it was hurting. It finally came out and when I wiped myself I was bleeding. I was scared, hurt and confused. I put a cold rag down yonder to soothe it. At the age of 16, I had had my cherry bust. After all those cheers we use to sing as kids talking about, "The devil made me do it" and "In and out my cherry tree" it was finally done. I was in there like 15 minutes and Sam softly knocked on the door.

"D baby, are you O.k.?" I wiped my tears that formed in my eyes.

"Yes Samir I'm fine. I will be out in a minute." I got up and looked in the mirror. I thought, ooh my God I'm not a virgin anymore. I wanted to cry myself a river, but I didn't. I walked out slowly and peeped around the bathroom door. He put the remote down and looked at me.

"You sure you O.k.?" I smiled and kept my eyes glued to the TV.

"Fine Samir. What's on TV?" He watched me as I approached the bed next to him.

"Once Bitten is on HBO." I crawled in bed beside him and I fell asleep again. He was watching some sports show when I woke up and it was only like 3:30. I was scared he was going to ask me to do it again and low and behold he did. He leaned in and kissed my face.

"D do you want to make love again? I promise I will be gentle." I smiled.

"O.k." came out loud but inside I screamed, hell no! But it was a little better the 2nd time and a whole lot better the 3rd time. By then it was 7 PM so we decided to get washed up and catch a cab to Fuddruckers to eat and then home. We got in at like 10 and my dad was sitting in the den. I tried to sneak past but he called me out.

"Did you have fun D?" I smiled and kept walking.

"Yeah Dad. I'm just tired from beating Samir in bowling. I am going to go up to bed."

"O.k. But are you to old to give your dad a kiss goodnight?" I thought in my mind, ooh shoot he knows. I ran into the den quick.

"O.k. Dad but it will cost you." He laughed. I went over and tried to kiss him quick so he wouldn't see the hickeys Samir put on my neck. He pulled me in for a hug.

"Good night Diamond but keep the windows closed tight." I walk towards the doorway.

"Why?" He picked up the remote.

"Because from the looks of your neck the vampires are out." He was making a joke about all the hickeys on my neck. I waved my hand.

"Ooh Dad good night!" I went upstairs to call my

best friend. I called Starr and who answered? Samir. I felt a wave of embarrassment come over me.

"Let me speak to my sister please."

"Why? Can't wait to tell her huh?" I got more embarrassed from his comment.

"No Samir I just want to speak to her is all." So she got on the phone and I told her everything that happened blow by blow. She made a gagging noise.

"I am sick to my stomach thinking about you and my brother. I know I am next but I don't want to lose my virginity to Shawn because he has been around."

"Well sis don't rush it." One day towards the end of the summer Starr was sitting on her steps when Danny walked by. He stopped dead in his tracks in front of her. He slowly rubbed his hands together and licked his deep pink lips.

"Hey sexy." She let a crooked grin creep across her lips.

"What up?" He pointed towards the stairs.

"Can I sit down?" She shrugged her shoulders real cutesy.

"I don't care." He sat down and leaned back on his elbows. They started talking about miscellaneous things and then he blew her a kiss and she invited him in. No one was home because her parents and older brother were out and Samir was at my house. We were having a Block Buster night. So, her and Danny crept in her house and guess what? She gave it up to him, her first love. She called me immediately after it was over and Samir answered my cordless.

"Hello. (Pause.) D it is the nut from across the street. She said it is important."

So I snatched the phone and all I heard was, "There is none left!" I was concentrating on, The Silence of the Lambs and just blurted out, "None what?"

She screamed, "Virgins."

I screamed louder, "What?!" Sam hit pause on the VCR and faced me.

"D what happened?"

"Nothing, she is watching a Lifetime movie and telling me what happened." I readjusted the phone to the ear farthest away from Samir.

"O.k. Starr. Go ahead." She told me everything. She told me how it hurt and she just wanted to get it over with so she did. She said she didn't care about Danny's girl because she didn't like her anyway. I laughed cause I didn't like her ass either. I was glad and hoped they got back together, but Starr didn't because she still didn't want to be tied down. My phone clicked and when I clicked over it was Danny calling asking me to talk to Starr because he really wanted her back. Sam was getting pissed because he said this was our time together and he was telling me to stop playing matchmaker and hang up the phone. So I told Danny I would try but I couldn't make any promises and I would call him back. I clicked back over to Starr and told her that her brother was bugging so I would call her back. I hung up to make Samir happy. Once I clicked off, I looked into Samir's eyes.

"There. You happy?" He hit the play button on the remote.

"Very." I had in my head, I have got to get Starr and Danny back together. They did start talking again but nothing more then that for the rest of the summer. In September Danny broke up with his girl because he claims she was getting on his nerves. In October Starr was at Danny's house and they were trying to work it out. They were sitting in the living room talking when the phone rang. Starr answered and it was Gina, Danny's ex-girl. Gina sucked her teeth picking up on Starr's voice.

"Could you put Danny on the phone?" Starr rolled her eyes and handed him the phone. I heard the phone conversation went something like this: Gina said to him, "I am glad you moved on so quickly but I just wanted to tell you I am about 4 weeks pregnant and I am keeping it." He nervously dropped the phone and Starr picked it up and handed it to him. Pissed he asked, "What do you mean?"

"What do you mean what do I mean?" He tried to whisper into the receiver.

"I thought you were on the pill."

"I was before but I stopped. When you asked me before if I took the pill, all you said was did I take the pill and I told you yes. You never asked me when did I take it, and at that time I wasn't taking it. So congratulations Daddy." He paced the floor.

"Look I'm not ready to be a father and you not ready to be a mother." Starr stood up to put on her green, white and yellow Nautica jacket.

"Danny I'm leaving. You need to handle that. Call me later." He grabbed her by the waist of her Express jeans.

"Wait Starr. Please don't leave." She dropped her jacket.

"O.k. I will be in the kitchen getting something to eat." He blew her a kiss.

"O.k. Boo. Looking good in those jeans!" Gina cleared her throat.

"Excuse me Danny! Hate to break up your little love affair but I was talking. Ooh that is your boo now? Well you so phony Danny cause you told me you hated her." He sucked his teeth.

"Well we're working on our problems." She laughed to herself.

"Well she is playing you." His tone of voice changed.

"Look, shut the fuck up about Starr and tell me when you wanna get this abortion cause you're not keeping this baby." She exclaimed, "Ooh yes I am. I have names picked out and everything. I am ready to be a mother." He tried to reason with her.

"Look Gina you can have a baby. Just not mine. Get an abortion now and get pregnant by someone you with. We're not even together. Why you wanna have a baby by me? How do I even know it is mine?" She started crying.

"I love you Danny. How could you say that to me?"

"Ooh boy. Well I don't love you. Make sense Gina, why have a baby by me? I don't want it. I won't help you with it. I won't watch it, love it or none of that so think about it." By this time she was crying uncontrollably. She was yelling, "Fuck you Danny! I don't need you to help me with my baby. I can do it all on my own. You ain't shit but what comes around goes around."

"Whatever bitch!" And he hung up on her. Now pause, what my brother did was real messed up. If you make a mistake you have to own up to it. Back to the story at hand, he calls Starr back into the living room. She sits next to him and he rubs her thigh.

"Hey baby!" She flung his hand off.

"Cut the crap Danny. What's going on?" He looked down at the floor.

"Gina says she is pregnant but I don't think it is mine." Starr snatched his face up.

"Hold up Danny. Gina is a lot of things but hoe is not one of them and you know she was faithful to you. So what you gonna do?" He rubbed his throbbing temples.

"I don't know. I don't want no kids now at all. Especially not by her. She don't want an abortion but I gotta do what I gotta do to make her see that that will be the best thing for all of us." Starr stood up and reached for her jacket.

"Look I'm gonna leave now and back out of your life for a minute." He cut her off.

"No! Starr please that is not what I need right now. I need you by my side not away from me." She placed her jacket on and zipped it up.

"Look I can't deal with this drama Danny. I will be right here for you but please just let me go until you know exactly what the deal will be." He stood up and blocked Starr.

"Well I know I don't want her or that baby."

"Well whether you want it or not if she decides to have it, that baby will be your responsibility and you gotta do right by your child. Don't trip Danny. Don't do your unborn seed the way you claim your dad did you." He leaned in and kissed her forehead.

"Yeah Starr, you're right." He hugged her tight, then walked her to the door. As soon as she left he called me and told me everything that happened. And when she got in she called and told me what happened. She was really hurt even though she didn't show it to him because she was really starting to feel him again. She told me she was glad she didn't give back into him and be his girl again. I knew what I needed to do. I needed to talk to Gina.

CHAPTER 9
THAT'S JUST MY BABY DADDY

O.k. so I couldn't stand Gina and I only spoke to her because she was my brother's girl. She picked up that I didn't like her because she would always ask Danny why she don't like me and he would say she likes you she's just not social. He was lying. I didn't like her ass. She was conceited and she was an airhead and she thought the world revolved around her and it didn't. Anyway, I called Miss Gina and the convo went like this:

"Hello, can I speak to Gina?"

"Yeah this Gina and who this?"

"This is Diamond, how are you?"

"Fine Diamond. How can I help you?"

"I just wanted to talk to you about the situation at hand."

"That is?"

"That is that your pregnant by my brother and I know he is being a dick and you need a friend now so I am trying to be one to you."

"Look Diamond, you don't like me and I know this and I'm not that fond of you, so cut the crap and tell me what you want."

"Listen I know you're mad at Danny right now and you think you paying him back for breaking up with you and you're not. We are only juniors in high school and he works a part time job so were do you think you will get money

100

from?"

"First of all my family has money so I don't need his money, second I can do it all alone, I'm not asking him for shit."

"Well if you don't want him for shit why you call him and tell him?"

"Cause he has a right to know."

"Well I know you didn't make that baby alone but why you lie and say you were taking birth control pills? That is fucked up and now you are trying to trap my brother but guess what? You going to be the one that is trapped because he is still going away to college but you will be stuck here and you will struggle. He won't because he is still going to be free and you will be tied down and he won't care."

"Well I don't care; I'm having this baby. So he can't weasel his way out of this one and if he don't want to be bothered with his own flesh and blood fuck him."

"Look Gina this is not getting us anywhere, can me and Danny come over so we can talk civilized?"

"Y'all can come over and say what you want but I am keeping this baby."

"O.k. Gina. I will call him and we will come over. Give us about an hour."

"Whatever" and she hung up. I was so pissed at Danny I couldn't see straight. I felt like I was his damn mother, and speaking of mothers, Aunt Debra was going to hit the roof if she found out. So I called Danny and told him we needed to go to Gina's house to talk. When we met up outside, he was all excited like I was going over there to fight her. I had to bust that bubble real quick.

"Calm your ass down. We're going over there to talk, and that's it. Danny you better be nice to her, act like you still like her or something like that and maybe she will change her mind. Apologize a lot no matter what she says or does." He cracked his knuckles as we took that walk 'down the bottom' in Vauxhall.

"Look sis I'll try but you know how I get." I yanked

the top of the back of his shirt.

"Well today you better get it right and be nice. I'm not playing Danny, she is trying to keep this baby." He looked down and kicked a pebble on the sidewalk.

"I know." Then I blacked out on him. I screamed and flailed my arms around like I was in the damn Matrix.

"What happened to all the condoms your mother gave you?! Are you trying to die for some pussy?" He put his right hand up like he was being sworn in at court and I was the judge.

"I swear to God D, she trapped me because the 1 day I went over to her house, I didn't bring no condoms cause she said before I came she was on her period. So she started trying to get at me and I said naw shorty you bleeding and she said ooh it went off already and I said well I ain't got no condoms and she said you can pull out and I said no that's O.k. but why you ain't never get on the pill? She said I did get on the pill and I said ooh O.k. then I guess this once it is O.k. and she said yeah and then I broke her back..." I rolled my eyes up so far in my head I could see my brain. I reached over and covered his nasty mouth.

"Spare me the details! Please!" He laughed and pushed my hand off his mouth.

"So you see I did make a mistake D and when I tried to pull out she grabbed me tight and I busted inside of her." I punched my left fist into my right palm.

"I should kick her in her stomach for playing you, but I'm not even going that route." He pointed his index finger at me.

"Naw sis you should." I sucked my teeth.

"Hell no Danny! What if someone did that to me?" His forehead scrunched up almost connecting his eyebrows with his nose.

"I would kill 'em!" I twisted up my lips to the side.

"O.k. then." So we walked to Gina's house. I stepped up on her stairs and as I extended my finger to ring the bell she swung the door open and let us in. We followed her into her den. She sat in the recliner and folded her legs underneath her, while we sat on the couch. We sat there watching TV with out a word being said, so I elbowed Danny and he greeted her.

"Hey Gina, how you doing?" She rolled her eyes and flicked the TV channels with the remote.

"Fine." It was such a cold response, I saw frost when it came out of her mouth. He talked soft and leaned over and rubbed her knee.

"Baby I'm sorry for all the mean stuff I said, but you hurt me." She adjusted her body and let her legs come from under her. She sat up straight with tears in her eyes.

"Well you hurt me. You just dumped me for Starr like I meant nothing to you." He licked his lips and whispered, "No baby. I didn't dump you for Starr cause me and Starr are just friends. We're not together. I broke up with you because I didn't feel the same about you no more Gina and I didn't want to cheat on you (which let me tell all of y'all was a bunch of bullshit but anyway) so I did the right thing." She cried and wiped her nose on her hand. (Yuck!)

"Well Dan I still feel the same way about you. I love you Dan. What happened to us that made you not want me anymore?" He sat back and shrugged his shoulders.

"I don't know. You just started getting on my nerves." She leaned in to him and grabbed his hand.

"Tell me what I was doing wrong and I will change." He pushed her hands off.

"You were always nagging me. Playing me too close. Accusing me of something when I wasn't doing nothing." She threw her body on the floor and knelt in front of him like he was God Almighty!

"Well I can change if you give me another chance. I swear I can, just try me Dan, please?! What can I do?" He looked at me and so did she. He cleared his throat.

"D I think we can work this out on our own. I'll walk you to the door." She smiled.

"Danny I will be in my room. Bye Diamond. Thanks for stopping by." He walked me to the door and in a hush tone I whispered, "Danny don't fuck her. She will think you want the baby, I'm telling you." He ushered me out the door.

"I'm not, I'm not. I'm just gonna let her suck my..." I placed my hand up like a stop sign.

"Ill! Stop thinking about sex. If you sleep with her she will think you guys are back together." He looked back over his shoulder at her going up the stairs. She waved and he smiled. He turned back to me and whispered in my ear.

"Maybe I will have to get back with her to get her to get an abortion." I threw my hands up.

"Look do what you gotta do but don't put your hands or your dick on her or in her." He playfully punched me in my arm and pushed me completely out the door.

"O.k., O.k. bye get out already." I turned around on the stoop.

"Ill! Don't act stupid." He kissed me on my cheek.

"Sike Sis. You know I love you." I playfully wiped it off.

"Just remember what I said." I walked down her block, Tuxedo Place to Vauxhall Road. I was on my way home from concerning myself with his problems, but little did I know that once I turned onto Russell Street, I had problems of my own awaiting my arrival.

CHAPTER 10
THROW YOUR GUNS IN THE AIR

I took longer strides once I hit my block and worried that he would fuck up, and knew he was going to be a father. I got home at about 6:30 PM. I had been bothered with that mess all day. I hadn't spoken to Samir and I missed my man and wanted him bad at the time. So I decided not to call him, I just went over there. His mom and dad went to the City to a company party for his dad's job. Shareef was back at Delaware State College being a 5th year senior and Starr was out with Shawn. Yes, she was still talking to him but she refused to have sex with him cause he was having sex with to many other chics. Anyway, I went to the back door of the Mitchell's like I always did and it was open as usual. I just let myself in as usual. I heard the TV on down stairs in the rec room so I decided to sneak up on him and surprise him. I went down stairs and heard moaning. When I got to the bottom of the carpeted stairs my jaw dropped and I got the surprise. Samir and Yah-Yah. Yeah, you heard me. She was on her knees and his pants were down around his ankles. She was so busy going to work sucking his dick like it was the neck bone from Grama's collard greens, they didn't even hear me come down the stairs. I tried to go back up as quietly as I came down, but I tripped up the top step. Samir yelled, "Who dat?" I didn't answer him. I just kept going and I heard his footsteps running after me to see who was in his house. I went straight out the back door and ran down the driveway. He was running after me yelling my name like there was a fire.

"Diamond! Diamond! Come here. Where you going?" He tackled me on my front lawn to stop me. As he stood up, he extended his hand to help me up.

"D it's not what it looks like." I just sat on my front lawn looking up at him.

"Ooh yeah Samir? It looked like you were getting your dick sucked." I finally stood up to my feet without his help. I wiped the blades of grass off my pants. I was disgusted and sickened. I looked down at his unzipped jeans.

"Fix your pants Samir. I'm sure you have red lipstick all around your dick." Then, he said the words all females love to hear.

"Who told you to come over with out calling?" I screamed, "WHAT!!!" I want you to understand how loud I said 'WHAT.' The whole tri state area must have heard me say 'WHAT.' He tried to clean it up and cleared his throat and stuttered over his words.

"I uh, mean you uh said you was gonna um call before you ur uh came over." I was too weak and hurt to argue. I spoke softly to avoid choking out a tear or two.

"You know what Samir... your right. I should have called first. I'm sorry call me later when your company leaves." His right eyebrow shot up like it was in a stick up.

"Huh?!" I know he was expecting me to act crazy but I shocked him. He fixed his face back to normal status and rubbed his hands together.

"I mean O.k. I will and we will talk about this like 2 civilized people in a minute. O.k? Diamond baby, I love you." He tried to kiss me on my lips, but I turned my head and he still got my cheek. See, I didn't have the energy right then because I was dressed too cute for all that. I had on some Ann Klein khaki's with a brown and beige Gap v-neck sweater along with my brown Nine West tie up ankle shoe boots. I went in the house, put on my gray Polo sweat pants, a white Hanes t-shirt and my construction style timberlands minus the leather around the top. Remember those were the style then. I wouldn't be caught dead in those N.F.L.'s now. (No, not the National Football League, but No Fuckin' Leather!) But anyway, I listened to some Onyx, off their hottest CD ever, Bacdafucup.

"Its time to get live live live like a wire. I set a whole stage on fire!" and "Throw your guns in the air buck buck like you don't care!" and once I heard that I got souped! I sat on my porch hiding out waiting for this bitch and behold like 5 minutes later they came out the back door and down the driveway. He didn't even begin to walk her home. He walked her to the end of the driveway. She tried to hug him but he pulled away. He started walking back up the driveway and she began to walk down the street and that was my cue. I walked out of my house real calm and I bolted across the street towards her like a bolt of lightning and hooked the mess out of her. She lost her balance and fell back and screamed for Samir.

Sam came down the driveway to see what happened and yelled, "D stop!" She was trying to fight back but I had her pinned down to the ground punching her in her face and choking her around her throat. I was trying to kill that bitch, so with me she had no wins.

She grabbed my shoulder length hair and I yelled, "Bitch you better get off my hair," and choked her harder. Sam came running over and pulled me up off her. He put me in a half nelson. You know what that is right? Where a person interlocks there arm underneath yours and pushes them upward so you can't move. Any-who, He was struggling to hold me.

"D would you calm down and stop." While he was holding me this bitch tried to run up on me. Since I didn't have use of my arms, all I could do was kick my feet up and at her. I kicked her square in the mouth. Blood shot out of everywhere. She looked like a scene from Michael Jackson's, Thriller, with all her teeth bleeding and her clothes and hair disheveled. She held her mouth and spit out blood.

"Diamond, I'm going to kill you!" I tried to get out of his hold by moving up in down in a monkey like movement.

"Samir get the fuck off me! Let me go." I screamed in her direction, "Bitch kill me now!" He put a tighter grip on me extending the half nelson to a full nelson.

"No Diamond. Not until you calm down." I was in pain because the full nelson does a job on your back so I stood still. She was still standing their bleeding and crying. I don't know if more tears or more blood were shed from this dumb bitch. Samir finally let me go and jumped in front of me when she tried to run up again. The bitch tried to charge me like I was the red flag a matador waves around and she was a bull. He pushed her back with his free hand because he was pushing me back with the other. He was twisted around like a pretzel trying to keep us apart. He pointed down the street towards Yah-Yah's route to walk home.

"Yah-Yah go head now. Go home!" I was still trying to get at her from around Samir and I finally did. I grabbed her long hair and tried to snatch that bitch bald. She was crying while holding her roots.

"Samir please help me. Get her off my hair!" I got a good grip on it while she held it tighter and closer to the roots. Sam pulled me by my waist.

"D stop!" He finally got me off of her, but not with out me having a hand full of her hair in my fist. She was all fucked up and I didn't care. She ran down the street towards Hilton Ave. She was screaming like a wild woman.

"Watch your back Diamond" I spat on the sidewalk.

"No bitch you watch it!" I looked at Samir and shook my head from left to right in shock. I hocked up a good amount of phlegm in my mouth. He tried to say something and as he talked I spit it in his face. Ill, some of the spit landed directly in his mouth and some hung from his nose. He grabbed my arm and twisted it behind my back.

"Why you do that D?!" With his free arm he used his t-shirt to wipe his face. I screamed, "Because I hate you Samir Ali! And I swear to God and on my Grandparents grave, I never want to see you again! Get the hell off me before we be out here scrapping (fighting in other words) next!" He grabbed me by my collar and pulled my face into his.

"No I wont get off you. We need to talk." He picked me up and put me over his shoulder. I was kicking and screaming like I was being raped.

"Help me! Somebody help me!" He covered my mouth with his hand and I bit it. He snatched his hand back from my teeth and shook it around.

"Ouch! You dumb..." He kept carrying me in the house. I think he wanted to call me a dumb bitch but he voted against that. I am so glad for his sake he did. When we got inside he put me down cause he knew I wouldn't wild out in his parents house. We were in the kitchen and he pulled out a chair from underneath the table and demanded me to sit. I bolted for the back door.

"Fuck you! I'm leaving!" I got to the door and began to open it. He grabbed me and slammed the door shut. Then he shoved me down in the chair he had invited me to sit in before. He sat next to me.

"Look D. I'm sorry you had to see that, but you did. I can't sugar coat what happened but I can explain. Yah-Yah came over here unexpected and rang my bell. She was crying saying her boyfriend had smacked her and she needed a friend to talk too." I bit on my bottom lip like it was a piece of steak.

"So why the fuck she come here? When did you become her best friend?" He got smart with me at that point.

"Is you gonna talk or listen?" I kicked him in his shin.

"You sorry son of a bitch! I didn't just get caught cheating, you did." He rubbed his shin and breathed out like I was getting on his nerves. So I stood up.

"Since I'm such a bother, I'll leave." He snatched me right back down. He grabbed me by my shoulders and looked me in my eyes.

"D, you're not a bother. Look...let me finish... Anyway, she was telling me all about her man Q and this and that and that and this and I was sitting on the couch and she was sitting in the recliner. So she moved over next to me on the couch saying 'Diamond sure is lucky to have a man like you' and I said 'she sure is' and she said 'no I'm serious, I wish me and you could have made it work' and I told her 'well we can't I love my girl' and she said 'I know you do' and she tried to kiss me and I said 'whoa don't do that Yah-Yah' and she said 'well I have to admit I have wanted to kiss you since we first met, please one kiss Sam and I will leave' and I said 'no I'm going to have to ask you to leave'(now you know by this time the steam is coming from my nose and my mouth has completely twisted to one side listening to Samir act like he was some type of saint) so she said 'O.k. O.k. I'm sorry what we watching on TV?' and I said to her 'nothing. If you feeling better cause I would hate for Diamond to come or call and you be here' and she said 'O.k. I'll go but I want to give you one thing' and she started unbuckling my pants and started sucking my dick. D it felt so good I just couldn't stop her and she said let me pull these down for you and I let her. I'm saying my mind was in a fog cause that must have been when you came down stairs. I swear D, I never meant to hurt you." I wiped away the streams of tears that saturated my cheeks.

"Well Samir Ali once again you did. Every freaking time you do just that. Hurt me. And I can't take it no more Sam. I just can't. I think we will be better off as friends." He screamed and pointed in my face.

"No got damn it! We're staying together." He took both hands and began to shake me, like I was chocolate milk with the chocolate settled in the bottom.

"Do you hear me Diamond? Huh, do you?" I smacked his hands off me before I had shaken child's syndrome.

"Yeah, I hear you talking, but you better settle for a friendship cause in a minute we will be enemies. Get off me Samir." He grabbed me again and wrapped his strong arms around my delicate neck.

"No. I want my girl. I want to keep my girl!" Here came more tears. If I added all of them together, there would never be a water shortage. I was trying not to cry, but I couldn't help it. He kissed me in my ear.

"D don't do this not now. D please. I made a mistake." I swung my arms around to free myself.

"Sam you made a mistake again. How many

fucking mistakes do you need to make?! Get a bitch pregnant on me? No, no better yet go out and get married?! What Sam?! What?!" I was crying hysterically now. He was hugging me over and over again. I was screaming,

"Get off me Sam. Get off. I want to go home. Let me go." He held me tighter, locking the muscles in his arms making it almost impossible for me to remove him from me.

"No Diamond, no! Not until you accept my apology." I used my hand to wipe the slob away from my mouth.

"I do Sam. I swear I do but I want to go home, let me go home Sam." He gradually rubbed his nose on my cheek from left to right and then in a small circular motion.

"No! Not until you say your mine and I'm yours." I cried uncontrollably, stumbling over my words.

"I I I c.c.c.ann't... say that Sam..ir. P.p.p.lease let m.ee go. Please!" He shook his head, now with his own tears streaming down his face.

"D I hate to see you upset like this. Please stop baby. Please!" I grabbed him by his collar and looked him dead in his eyeballs.

"Stop hurting me then and you won't have to see me like this! But you know what, you wont have that chance again Samir. It is over from here on out. You're a free man and I'm a free woman." He jumped up and turned the kitchen table over. The basket of fruit on the table went all over the place. I had never seen Samir act like that before. He was pacing back and forth punching his hand in his fist.

"You can't! I wont let you! I won't! I will chase every nigga away that even try to talk to you. I swear to God D. Play if you want too." I didn't say anything. I just stood up and straightened my clothes. I walked to the back door to go out. He came up behind me and breathed down my neck.

"Where do you think you going?" I turned around to be face to chest since he was taller then me. I looked up at him sternly. By this time the tears turned to anger.

"Look you fucking nut, you can't hold me hostage here. I'm leaving." He put his palms up on the door, on both sides of me to lock me in.

"No you're not." I jabbed my pointer finger in his chest 3 times.

"Yes... I... am!" He grabbed my finger and slightly bent it back.

"Over my dead body." I flinched from the pain and yanked my finger from his grasp.

"O.k. then if that's how you want it." I pushed passed him and grabbed a knife out of the wooden block on the linoleum counters. My hand was physically shaking as I flashed it in his direction.

"Sam now lets be reasonable. Please don't push me over the edge to stab your ass up in here, cause you know I'll do it!" He just had to test the waters. Just like a kid with a hot stove. You tell them don't touch it, but they do anyway. What happens? They get burned. His eyes squinted up into tiny slits on his face.

"You wouldn't dare!" Ooh yeah? Well, I charged him. He grabbed my arms and we struggled. I aimed downward and threw the knife and it stabbed into his foot. He let me go and pulled the knife out the top of his foot. He checked his foot. Blood was soaking through his white sweat sock. He kept repeating the same phrase.

"I can't believe you just did that. I can't believe you just did that." My eyes opened to the size of golf balls and I saw more and more blood drain from his foot. I was so scared I called my parents. Thank God they were home. My mom played 21 questions, while I screamed and cried asking what should I do. She instructed me to wrap a thick towel around his foot and help him out the house. Once outside, my father was behind the wheel and my mother opened the front car door for Samir to get in. My dad broke the sound barrier getting Samir to Overlook Hospital in Summit. His parents were called and they met us at the hospital.

CHAPTER 11
THE AFTER MATH

Samir had to get 16 stitches in his foot. That meant no basketball when the season started in a few weeks. He would have to wait at least 6 weeks to play and he was pissed. That was good for his dumb cheating ass. Neither one of us told our parents what really happened that night. We just said that we were playing a little too much and it got out of control. When we left the hospital, we all went back to Samir's house. Our parent's bright idea was, that I was to help Samir until his foot got better. That meant after school if he needed anything, get it for him or if he needed his books from school bring them. Basically, wait on him hand and foot when nobody else was home. We were sitting in the kitchen at the table that his father had turned back over. His father made a joke that I didn't think was too funny.

"You guys can really be like a married couple now." I crossed my hands over my chest.

"No I can't miss work." My dad grabbed a beer that Krystal handed him.

"Sure you can. I am the boss and since you thought it was fun and games to play with a knife, you will have to pay the consequences." I sat up straight and escalated my voice.

"Yeah, but if Samir... Never mind." My dad took a swig.

"Yeah, but if Samir what D?" I sighed and my shoulders slumped.

"Nothing Daddy. I will do it. Happily." My mind told a different story. *I will torture his cheating ass.* See me, Starr, Danny and Samir all worked for my dad in one of his businesses. Me and Starr worked in the hair salon shampooing heads and sweeping up. Samir worked in the laundry mat over seeing it and Danny worked in the stock room of the liquor store. So now I had to miss out on 4 to 6 weeks pay to take care of Samir's trifling ass in the afternoons after school. I would have just disobeyed my dad and not did it, but I wanted my car when I turned 17 in less then 8 months. So, I had to do what my dad said. At that moment I wanted to scream out, he cheated and its over! but I just leaned over on my mom's shoulder.

"No there is no married couple here. We're not even together no more. We needed a break. A permanent one." Our parents looked at each other and Krystal cocked her head to the side to look into my eyes.

"So D, you 2 not a couple anymore? I didn't know that." I sat up and rubbed my sweaty hands on my pants.

"Its O.k. me and Sam are O.k. wit it. We still friends right Samir?" He shook his head with his mouth tight. My dad crumbled up his empty beer can and reached for another.

"Damn Diamond did you even apologize to Samir yet for damn near cutting his foot off?" Sam smiled but I didn't. I gritted my teeth.

"Sorry." Sam was sitting at the bar counter in his kitchen with his foot propped up on one of the stools.

"That's O.k. boo." I wanted to hook off on him (punch him in his face in other words) but, instead I let him know something.

"My name is Diamond not Boo." I guess our parents picked up on the bad vibe and Mitch said jokingly, "Ooh my God D. You don't love my son no more. I guess the wedding is off." Everyone thought it was a big joke, but me and Samir. I stood up and yawned.

"Yep it's off. Listen, can I go home now Mommy. I'm really tired." I had a tear in my eye. My mother reached for my hand and rubbed it lightly.

"What's wrong baby?" I cleared the spit forming in the back of my throat.

"Nothing Ma. I just gotta get out of here." She gently released my hand.

"O.k. D. Go on home. I will see you in a bit." As I was leaving I heard my mom say to them, "She is probably just upset about hurting Samir." I stopped at the door with my hand on the knob. I was a minuscule second from marching back into the kitchen, but decided to keep going. I wanted to say, no that is not it at all Mom. I am upset about him hurting me but I voted against it. By the time I was outside I was crying a river, damn the streams from earlier. I dashed across the street, unlocked my door and ran straight up to my room. I laid on my bed and cried some more. I reached over and made sure my ringer was off and kicked my Tims off. I noticed they had dried blood on them. I wondered if it was from Yah-Yah or Samir? Whosever it was, Sam was going to pay for it. I fell asleep in my clothes and slept all night and half the day. Starr came over and woke me up. She was standing over me, shaking me to wake up as if I needed to be shaken again.

"D what happened?" I turned my back to her.

"Nothing. Me and Sam were playing and we got carried away." I pulled the covers over my face and she yanked them back.

"D go brush your teeth, get rid of that morning dragon breath and come back and tell me the truth." I moaned and groaned.

"That is the truth." I pulled the covers back over my head. She pulled them off again, this time stripping the covers all the way back like a drill sergeant. She reached over me and threw all my pillows on the floor.

"O.k. I will try this again... Diamond what happened last night? I thought best friends shared everything but men right?" By that time I had started tearing again. She sat on the edge of my bed and hugged me. She was tearing too and didn't even know what had happened. I began to confess the whole situation to my best friend. She was fuming by the time I finished the story.

"You should have dropped the knife on his dick and then seen if Yah-Yah would have sucked it then." I had to laugh at that. She always knew how to make me laugh. I had to make her vow not to say anything. She vowed, "I promise" and then asked me what happened with Danny and Gina. I had completely forgot about him and Gina. I picked up the phone and heard the pause in the dial tone signaling that I had messages. I dialed the Voicemail center and it said 20 new messages.

Danny had left close to 10 messages and Samir had left almost another 10 saying he was sorry and he could hear in my voice that I was serious but, he said and I quote, "I was serious too D, and it is me and you and no one else." He was scaring me a little bit playing this nut case role. The other few messages were from Starr wanting to be nosey, but since I didn't call her back fast enough, there she was getting the info out of me face to face. So I called Danny and he said he was going to jump in the shower and then he was coming over. So I told Starr to leave until he left then I would call her when he left to let her in on everything. She agreed and left. He came over and told me what happened. He closed my room door to keep out Nosey a.k.a Ann.

"I talked her into getting an abortion but I have to be with her and promise her that it is only her." He asked me if I could tell Starr the deal and ask her to wait for a minute for him. I shook my head.

"O.k. when is she going to get the abortion?" He looked at my door to make sure no one was coming.

"Next week. Her Aunt is going to take her." I smiled.

"Cool. That is a relief." He wrinkled up his forehead like he was my father.

"Where were you at when I was calling missy?" I stretched.

"Sleep." I didn't feel like talking about Samir no more so I refrained from telling him. He would find out soon enough since him and Samir were like, best friends. That Monday back in school, I saw Yah-Yah and I was prepared to fight if I had too but that bitch had lock jaw and didn't say shit and neither did I cause I had said all I needed to say. Her lip was busted and her eye was swollen. She had a knot that resembled a breast on her head. I laughed at that. So for the next 4 weeks I took care of Samir as planned. I would fix him a snack and make sure he was comfortable after school. He had decided to stay in the basement because it was fewer steps and a full bathroom down there. He was on crutches and he wanted to be babied, but I was not the one. For the few minutes I was over there everyday he just talked about us and I just let him talk. I would be thinking about how soon I would be driving and get out of this town to meet guys. I mean, we took the bus Downtown Newark and went to the Rink and met out of town guys, but when I got my license and car me and Starr and few other girls would be chilling. Anyway, I knew deep in my heart I still loved Samir but I couldn't take him back. I have to confess one day, the twin's birthday, he had got to my soft spot and we did kiss but as soon as I realized what was going on I jetted. During those 4 weeks I started talking to this guy Quan, let me tell you about him.

CHAPTER 12
QUAN AKA Q

Quan played on the basketball team right along side Samir but do you think I cared? If you said, "hell no" you are right. Samir crippled ass couldn't play anyway. Quan was so sweet and caring. So different from Samir. He was a quiet cutie. You know the strong silent type. He was a senior and told me that since I came to the high he liked me. The way we started talking was like this. I was in the school library after school checking out books for Samir's Social Studies report. I had a lot of books in my hand, and on my way out he accidentally bumped into me and made me drop all the books. I was so damn mad because I didn't want to do shit for Samir and I kept thinking, this damn klutz making me drop all this shit. He kept apologizing while he helped me pick up all the books. I snatched 2 out of his hands.

"It is O.k. Just forget about it." He read my facial expression and noticed I was mad. He apologized again.

"I really am sorry Diamond. I didn't mean to get you mad." I dusted off the books which had gotten dusty from that dirty ass library floor.

"It is O.k. trust me. I'm not mad at you. I'm mad at Samir for not being able to come get his own damn books." He looked at the ground and noticed we missed a book. He picked it up and extended his arm towards me.

"You such a good girlfriend coming to get..." I yanked the book from his grasp, and raised my right eyebrow.

"I am not his girlfriend. I'm just doing this to be nice because I'm the reason he is on crutches." He let out a small laugh.

"Yeah I know. He told the team y'all was playing and it happened by accident." I rolled my eyes and gathered the books in my arms.

"Yeah O.k. Q. Whatever HE said." I began to walk towards the library doors and he walked along side me.

"I am sorry to hear y'all broke up." I stopped dead in my tracks and looked around for one book that was missing.

"Yeah well I'm not." He followed my gaze and noticed the book had slid across the floor under a table. He ran over, picked it up and smiled as he walked towards me. I grabbed the last book out of his hands and headed out the library. He cleared his throat as I was placing my foot into the school hallway.

"Excuse me. Uh Diamond?" I turned around with a major attitude.

"What?" He looked down at his swamp type Timberlands.

"Can I call you tonight?" He looked so nervous and cute and I was being such a bitch. I placed the books on my hip like I was caring a two-year-old toddler.

"Why?" He looked up at me and then back down again.

"Because I'm digging you." My arms got tired and I walked back towards him and placed the books on the table.

"Yeah?! Well I thought you were Samir's boy?" He traced the cover of the top book with his finger.

"We O.k., but just on the team. That is all." I shrugged my shoulders.

"O.k. then." I opened my small black Liz Clairborne purse, reached in and got my favorite Bic pen, grabbed his hand and wrote my number inside his palm. I let his hand go.

"Q don't waste my time O.k.?" He stared at his hand as if he had Janet Jackson's autograph in it.

"Ooh I won't. I promise." I threw my pen back in my bag and headed back out of the library, while he walked further back into the library. As I was coming out and smiling to myself, Yah-Yah and her friend, Sharonda, approached me.

"So what you want to do now Putah (bitch in Spanish)?" Now mind you, I had all these books in my hands. I was already in enough trouble at home for stabbing Samir and I didn't want to have to get suspended on top of that, but you know me by now. I had to handle my B.I. A.K.A business. I braced myself for a fight. I dropped the pile of books on the hallway floor.

"First of all bitch, don't ever fucking approach me like you 'bout it." Sharonda looked me up and down.

"You neither bitch. What y'all want to do?" So Sharonda mushed me and I lost my balance. I tripped over the stack of books and almost fell. Yah-Yah tried to punch me but missed and I lunged at her. I started pulling her hair and Sharonda was pulling mine saying, "Get the fuck of my friend!" So, I let go of Yah-Yah and gave Sharonda the business (fought her instead). I boxed that bitch like she was a man but she wasn't ready for me. She was blocking her face and I was hitting her with body shots. These punk bitches didn't know, I floated like a butterfly and stung like a bee. Yah-Yah just stood there and the hallway monitors came and broke it up. Maria grabbed Sharonda while John grabbed me. Greg, the coolest hall monitor, looked at Yah-Yah and shook his head. Marie, the mean one, had to make the public announcement we all knew was coming.

"You two are going to the office." She was talking about me and Sharonda. Yah-Yah just stood there frozen. Sharonda threw her hands in the air.

"Yah-Yah?!" Yah-Yah just flung her hair back and looked at Sharonda like she was nuts.

"What?! It is no need for both of us to get in trouble Sharonda." I laughed in Sharonda's face. So me and this bitch I barely knew got suspended for 3 days and Yah-Yah got off. I wasn't punished since I was defending myself. You know word travels fast and Quan called that night. The first thing he asked? "What happened?" I gave him a brief over view and said I didn't want to talk about it. So we talked about other things. The next day when Starr went to school she walked right up to Yah-Yah before first period and punched her in the face. They got suspended for 3 days as well. Starr didn't get punished either cause she lied and said Yah-Yah started with her. Once we got back to school those 2 dizzy bitches, Yah-Yah and Sharonda, started beefing since it was Yah-Yah's beef and she didn't help when I was beating her ass. After that first night me and Quan spoke we spoke every night after that. I liked talking to him. For 2 weeks straight we would talk late and fall asleep on the phone every night. I was really feeling him in a matter of 2 weeks. I was scared to let him come over so we just kicked it on the phone. My 4th week taking care of Samir he begged me to take him back. I still refused. I handed him his afternoon snack. "Please move on. I love you and always will but our life together is over. We can begin our friendship if you want." He snatched the plate of cookies.

"Fine D. You do what you want, see who you want. I don't care." I winked at him.

"Thanks for your permission; I think I will take you up on that." He bit into the cookie then waved the half eaten cookie in my direction while he spoke with is mouth full.

"Yeah and I will kill that nigga D, so just try me O.k.?" I sucked my teeth as I went up the stairs.

"Sam whatever." It was 7:30 and his dad was coming in and I was going out. This was my last day with Samir. Thank God. I ran home and called Q. It was Friday night and he asked could we go the movies. I felt my stomach do flip flops thinking about Samir's threat.

"O.k. but pick me up from the corner of my block.

Springfield Ave and Russell St." He agreed. I got dressed and when I came downstairs fresh dressed like a million bucks with my beige riding pants on, tall brown riding boots and long brown sweater. My dad looked me up and down.

"Where you going?" I danced around the den.

"To the movies with a friend." He snatched his reading glasses off.

"What damn friend?" I laughed at his fake anger.

"A friend from school." He put the paper down.

"I didn't meet this friend from school, so who is it?" I sighed.

"Come on Dad. That's not important. We just cool from school, that all." He picked his paper back up.

"O.k. You better not let Samir find out." I got an attitude and yelled, "Whatever." He pulled rank then to show me whose boss.

"Be home by 12." I buttoned up my brown sailor type wool coat and mumbled, "Yeah whatever," (Under my breathe of course) and I left. Q was sitting at the corner waiting for me. He looked so cute. He was tall and brown skin with dimples and a little peach fuzz on his face. He had bedroom light brown eyes. His hair had waves for days and they were spinning nigga they were spinning like Chris Rock always says. I got in and kissed him on the cheek. He jumped.

"What was that for?" I smiled and unbuttoned the top button on my coat.

"That's how I greet my friends." He returned my smile. We went to the movies in Perth Amboy and saw, The Bodyguard. After we went to Union Square Diner on 22 in Union. We were both quiet. I know why I was quiet because I didn't feel right being out with someone else besides Samir. He picked up on it and reached across the table to touch my hand.

"Thinking about Samir huh?" I picked up the empty straw paper and folded it into origami.

"No." He nudged my hand for me to look up at him.

"Come on now. Tell me the truth." I looked up at him

and smiled.

"O.k. yeah a little." He sat back in the booth.

"Maybe you should reconsider?" I tucked my hair behind my ear.

"Reconsider what?" He tapped on the table like a drum.

"Y'all being together. By the way you never told me why you guys broke up." I took a sip of my water with lemon.

"I never told you cause it is none of your business." He put both his hands up towards me.

"Well I'm sorry to get in your business but you know what the rumor is don't you? That Samir cheated on you with Yah-Yah." Tears swelled up in my eyes. I was so freaking emotional back then. He pulled napkins from the dispenser and handed them to me.

"Look D I'm sorry. I didn't mean too..." I dabbed at my eyes.

"No Q its O.k. You wanna talk about it then lets do just that, talk about it." So I told Q the whole story and he just looked at me and shook his head. Our waitress, Janelle bought the food to our table. I had the chicken and shrimp fajitas.

"D if you were mines I would never do you like that." I began to put my fajitas together minus the guacamole.

"Well that's what they all say." He put salt and pepper on his french fries.

"D I'm different." I bit into my fajita. Um Um good.

"Ooh boy please you only 17. Wait until you go to college and get a little older. You will change your tune." He stood firm on his answer as he bit into his medium well cheeseburger.

"No D, I don't think so, I seen my dad cheat on my mom and I know how hurt she was. She always told me since I was little don't ever do that to a woman. Treat her how you want to be treated. If you want to cheat break up with her but don't forget, be truthful at all times." I wiped my mouth with my napkin.

"Your mom sounds like a smart woman." He smiled as he popped a fry in his mouth.

"She's cute too." I smiled. He was making me feel better. He looked at his watch.

"Well let me get you home cause it is like 11:30." I got the rest of my food to go.

"O.k." When we got to the corner of my block he stopped. I reached over and rubbed his knee.

"Can you take me to my door please?" He got souped up and shifted his stick shift bubble back civic into 1st gear.

"Sure." We pulled up in front of my house.

"Would you like to come in and meet my parents?" His eyes darted to the clock on the radio.

"It's a little late D. That would be disrespectful. Can I come by tomorrow and meet them?" A nice big smile invaded my lips.

"Sure!" I leaned over and kissed him good night on his cheek. He blushed a little and smiled showing his dimples.

"Call me when you get home." He let the car roll back a bit.

"Yeah no doubt." I got out and went up my stairs. He actually waited for me to get in and turn on the porch light. He called me when he got in and we talked until we fell asleep once again.

CHAPTER 13
NO MORE DADDY'S LITTLE GIRL

The next morning I got up and cleaned my room, got dressed, and flat ironed my hair. I went down stairs and of course my mother was cooking breakfast. She cooked like it was Sunday morning before church when it was only Saturday. We had started slacking on church, only going once in a blue. I think that was a part of my downfall. As soon as I hit the kitchen my parents stared at me. My mom smiled over the frying pan.

"So how was your date last night?" I grabbed a piece of bacon from the plate.

"Fine. Quan is coming over today to meet you guys and chill with me for a little while O.k.?" My mom turned off the fire from the last batch of bacon.

"That's fine but I hope you cleaned that dirty room if you having company." My dad hadn't had much to say until then.

"Why her room gotta be clean; he is not going in it." I laughed like it was a joke but he wasn't smiling. He kept reading the paper and talked from behind it.

"I'm serious Diamond; you don't need all them boys in your room." I pushed the down button on the toaster and sat down at the table.

"First of all Dad all what boys?! Face it, me and

125

Samir is over. It has been a whole month. I have moved on, can you?" He rattled the paper around to look at me over the corner.

"I don't care who you date Diamond Crescent. You just won't be a tramp in my house." I had no idea where that came from. Maybe some neighbor hood gossip I don't know but I wasn't going to stand for it. That's the only thing about living in a small town, folks is so nosey and everybody knows everybody. I stood up angrily.

"A tramp? What the hell are you talking about? I'm not even having sex (and technically I wasn't at the moment) and now I'm a tramp? Dad you need to check yourself. It is mad girls my age having babies and being disrespectful, drinking and doing drugs, but not me. Yeah I know I am not a perfect angel but I come damn close." My mother poured her a cup of coffee.

"O.k. Diamond that's enough. Watch your mouth and sit down so we can talk." She came to the table to get the sugar.

"Dan what is your problem? We all love Samir in here but for whatever reason her and Sam are not together anymore." My toast popped up. I buttered my light toast.

"You think Samir is so great? Why don't you go over there and ask him why we broke up." I ran to the wall and grabbed the cordless phone.

"Better yet Dad, call him." He looked at me like I had lost the little bit of sense I did have.

"I'm not calling him. That is none of my business." I threw my toast on a plate and piled bacon on top of it.

"Exactly! So I can date who I want and I am going to date Quan but he don't ever have to come here." My mom stood up to check me.

"Hold on D, you are getting besides yourself. Watch your tone and your mouth when you are talking to your father, but besides all that this is your house and that room upstairs, that is your room. Please bring him over to meet us and he can go in your room. I said so." My father was silent and I was too. I didn't know what was happening to me and my dad but I was scared we wouldn't be the same. I know I wasn't daddy's little girl like he wanted me to be anymore but I was growing up. I poured me some O.J. and snatched up my bacon sandwich.

"I am going to my room if you need me." After I left I heard my mom and dad get into it.

"You owe your daughter an apology Dan. What is wrong with you? You have a good daughter. She pretty much do what we say and don't give us much trouble. She got a smart mouth but what teenager doesn't?"

"I don't know what came over me Ann. I just want to protect her from the harm a guy can cause. I know Samir hurt her but I don't know how and in my eyes she will always be my little girl, but if she ever talk to me like that again I will knock her block off." I heard the kitchen water running. I guess my mother was washing dishes.

"Well Dan that is not the way and she is not a little girl anymore you need to get over that, and how can Samir be in her room all day everyday and this other guy she meets has to sit up under us. We always said we wanted to have an open relationship with her and be flexible so she don't have to be sneaking in the streets. If she brings her friends here at least we know where she is."

"Damn Ann you're right, I was wrong, but if she ever talk to me like that again..." She finished his statement.

"I know, I know, you will knock her block off. You getting old and she might give you a run for your money. Now nigga go talk to your daughter incase she's in her room plotting to kill your ass." He laughed.

"Yeah you're right I'm going, and Ann, I am not old, I look good for a 25 year old man." She cracked up.

"Sheeeeiiitttt! 25 my ass." And they both laughed. I heard him coming upstairs. I was sitting on my bed writing in my journal. Anytime things didn't go my way, I wrote in my journal so you know it was filled with shit about Samir. My dad knocked.

"D can I come in?" I kept writing.

"Sure. This is your house you can do whatever you

want." He came in and leaned on my dresser.

"D that's not fair. I'm sorry about what happened. I was just trying to protect my little Diamond. Can you forgive dear old dad?" I kept my nose in my journal.

"Yeah." I never looked up. He put his hand on my shoulder.

"Are you sure?" I quickly looked up and glanced at him and then back down.

"Yep." He put his hand under my chin to raise my head up to look at him.

"You don't sound too sure." I sighed and let my shoulders hunch.

"Dad, (a tear fell from my eye) I'm not a little girl anymore. I'm going to be 17 in a minute. I'm not saying I'm grown but I'm damn near it. You just played me downstairs. We supposed to be cool but I guess that was all fake huh?" He sat down on my bed next to me.

"No D its not, we are friends and I want you to come to me with anything." I pushed my journal closed.

"Well the first time I do come to you with something other then Samir you blow up at me." He put his arm around me.

"I'm sorry for that D, bring Quan over and I will behave I promise, but you know I gotta be a father some what. Just like I did with Samir." I sighed.

"Ooh boy third degree?" He smiled.

"And you know this." I got up and gave my dad a hug and looked at him.

"Now can you get out?" He laughed while he scooted up from the bed.

"You don't want to duke it out do you?" I started shadow boxing.

"No Dad I don't want to hurt your old butt." He fell back.

"Ooh that was cold, I just told your mother, I'm not old, and uh D, if you ever talk to me the way you did downstairs again, I will knock your block off." I turned up my lip.

"Sure Dad. Sure you will." In all the years of my life he gave me one spanking and felt so bad the next day he bought me a brand new bike. I wanted spankings more often. He left and I called Quan. I was so happy to hear his his sexy voice, "What time are you coming over?"

"Whenever you want beautiful."

"Right about now would be good."

"Let me get dressed and call you when I'm on my way."

"O.k. but hurry up."

"O.k., O.k." And we hung up. I checked my messages and Samir had called. He said could I call him because it was important. I called him and Starr answered.

"Ooh my best friend can't call me no more. She end it with my brother and me too." I laughed.

"Starr never that. Don't play me. Guess what? Me and Q went to the movies last night."

"Did you have a good time?"

"Yeah he's so sweet and cute. I like him a lot." She dropped her voice to a whisper.

"Well you better not let my nutty brother find out." I laughed.

"You better not let him find out." She giggled.

"I won't, I swear. So anyway what up with y'all." I smiled into the phone.

"Nothing much yet, he's coming over in a little while." She sighed.

"Ooh boy if Samir see his car it will be all over."

"I know. I'm going to tell him to pull in my yard." She laughed.

"That's a good idea."

"Well I will give you all the details when he leaves today. Lets hang out this evening Starr. You been on so many dates and I miss you."

"Me too it's a date for later, don't stand me up girl."

"I won't. Bye" We hung up and I completely forgot I called for Samir. I called right back and Starr picked up.

"Girl let me speak to your brother."

"For what?" I sucked my teeth.

"Dag nosey! None ya!"

"Hold on... Samir telephone!" He picked up the other line.

"Hello." I talked nicely to him.

"Hey Sam."

"Hey D. How was your date last night?" My heart sunk.

"What are you talking about?"

"Ooh you dumb now D? With Q. He coming over today right? He parking in your yard right? So I can't see his car right?" I gritted my teeth.

"Let me speak to your sister Samir." He let out a devilish laugh.

"She didn't tell me. Next time tell her to make sure no one else picks up when the phone rings."

"So you listened to my phone convo?"

"Yeah Diamond pretty much I did." I sucked my teeth.

"I hate you Samir!" And with that, I hung up. My phone rang but I didn't pick it up or look at the caller ID. I knew it was that damn Samir. I was pissed off. It rang again and again and I didn't answer it. I went downstairs to get some more bacon. That was my weakness. I was so aggravated I forgot about Quan. When I came back upstairs Quan had left 3 messages. That was him calling those times not Samir. The first message he said, "D I'm ready to come. I guess you not in your room. Call me." The 2nd message, "Diamond, what are you doing? I beeped you. Call me." The 3rd message, "Diamond I guess you left out, I'm going to be here waiting. Call me." I called him and I didn't get an answer. I kept calling and like the 4th time I called a lady answered and it sounded like she was sleep. She answered the phone obviously annoyed.

"Hello!" I swallowed hard.

"Hello. Sorry to wake you ma'am but is Quan home?" She sucked her teeth.

"No he is not. Who is this?" I barely squeezed out.

"Diamond." She changed her tone to sound nicer.

"Ooh hello Diamond. Q went to the corner to shoot hoops. He said to beep him when you called."

"O.k. ma'am thank you very much good bye." I hung up. I beeped Q like 15 times and he called back out of breath.

"Are you O.k.?"

"Yeah are you still coming?"

"Yes, I was waiting for you forever."

"Sorry."

"That's O.k. Let me run home and shower again."

"It's O.k. if you're sweaty. I want to see you now." He laughed at my impatience.

"O.k. D but I gotta go home first and handle that. I will be quick I promise." I sighed.

"Well O.k. but hurry." He laughed again.

"O.k. I will, but the longer you hold me on this pay phone the longer it will take."

"O.k. Well don't call just come."

"O.k. bye" We hung up. I couldn't believe Samir. My phone was clicking while I was talking to Quan and I didn't click over. It was Samir who had left a message saying what time is lover boy coming over. I'm waiting for him. I had had enough. I marched across the street and rang the bell. Krystal opened the door.

"Hey Diamond. Starr is upstairs in her room." I closed the door behind me.

"Hey Ma. I'm not here to see her, I'm here to see Samir, is he down stairs?" She sighed.

"You know it. Watching some sports, I don't know." She smiled like I was there for a social visit. If she only knew. I knocked on the basement door.

"Samir can I come down there?"

"Who dat?"

"Samir it's me."

"Who me?" He was doing that silly shit to get on my nerves so I flung the door open.

"Diamond Samir."

"Let me think about it." I was taking deep breaths trying not to act out.

"Well I'm coming down anyway." I closed the door behind me so no one could hear our convo just incase it turned into an argument. His foot was just about healed up but he had it propped up on a pillow while he laid back on the couch. I turned the TV off and flung his foot down on the floor.

"Ouch girl watch my foot." I sat down next to him.

"Look Samir leave me alone O.k.?" He looked at me.

"I'm not bothering you."

"Well leave Q alone." He crossed his hands behind his head.

"I'm not bothering him. I don't care if you date him. I don't give a fuck D. Earlier I was just fucking with you, I found me someone new too, and would you mind leaving, she's on her way over." At that moment I was heart broken but don't ask me why. I don't know what happened next but I blurted out, "Who is she Samir?" He smirked.

"Why?" I sucked my teeth with attitude.

"Sam I am not playing with you. Who is the bitch?" He unfolded his hands from behind his head.

"Why she gotta be all that? Huh?" I exhaled.

"Well no girl better not dare walk up in here cause I will be sitting here waiting for her." He leaned up and pushed my back a tad bit.

"No seriously D you gotta go." I knocked his hand off me.

"Ooh she comes before me?" He leaned in close to my face.

"Does Q come before me?" I thought, ooh my God Q, he will be at my house and I'm here. I knew deep down inside I had to leave but I didn't want no girl coming to see Samir.

"What Samir?" He leaned into my ear.

"You putting Q before me?" Here I went crying again. I whimpered like a puppy.

"No Samir." He rubbed my shoulders.

"Well call him. Tell him don't come." He handed me the phone and I started to dial Q's number but I couldn't do it. I wiped my eyes.

"Samir you cheated on me. You hurt me Samir." He kissed on my neck.

"Diamond I know and I am soooo sorry for that. You know I love you and I need you." He grabbed my face.

"Look at me D," tears were streaming down my face. He kissed my left cheek and I didn't stop him. He kissed my right cheek and I didn't stop him, and then we kissed. I mean a real long deep tongue touching the tonsils kiss. When we stopped I fell back in his arms.

"What about your company?" He rubbed my cheek with his thumb.

"Fuck her. What about yours?" I pulled away and jumped up.

"Samir I gotta go." He got mad and blacked on me.

"Ooh so you gonna be up in here all on me and now go be with some other nigga?" I backed up towards the stairs.

"No Samir. See me and Q are just friends, he actually wants me to give you another chance." He rubbed his hands together.

"Smart man."

"I am going to go talk to him." He looked at the clock on the wall.

"What time will you be back?" I went to the basement bathroom.

"Later Sam." While in the john I washed my face. I waved bye to him and ran up the stairs and out the house. I said bye to Krystal on the way out. She yelled behind my back.

"Bye Diamond come back soon." When I was leaving I saw Q's car parked outside my house. Shoot he had beaten me. I hurried and ran across the street. Poor Q, my dad probably giving him the 3rd degree.

CHAPTER 14
MEET THE PARENTS

I bust in the door and smiled when I saw Q. He was sitting at the kitchen table with my mother listening to her recipe for 'Ann's rock 'em, sock 'em, then drop 'em chocolate cake. I panted like a dog from running across the street.

"Hello y'all." He flashed that million-dollar smile with those perfect white teeth. Crest white strips weren't even invented yet, but looking at his teeth you would have thought he used them everyday.

"Hey D. Your mom was telling me how she makes this chocolate cake so moist." He was sitting there enjoying a nice big piece of it. He licked the chocolate off the fork and I was turned on.

"I'm uh so sorry Q but I..." My mom turned towards me from her Fry Daddy which she was frying chicken in.

"Yeah I was telling Quan how I sent you to the store for me." I looked puzzled.

"They didn't have any baking soda at the corner store D?" I gradually shook my head from left to right.

"No Ma." She picked up the fork and removed some chicken.

"I guess I gotta go to Pathmark or Shoprite." I was late with the story, but I had realized that my mom had covered for me. I smiled to myself, my mom really is cool.

"Well you met my mom. Where is Daddy at Ma?"

She wiped her hands on her apron.

"He went to play ball with the guys but he said to tell you he hopes to get back in time to meet Quan." Quan walked his plate to the sink and began to wash it.

"I am looking forward to meeting him." I walked up next to him and shut the water off.

"Q you don't have to wash that. O.k. thanks Mom. We are going up to my room now." She smiled at us together.

"Yeah O.k., Quan would you like to stay for dinner?" I turned and shot her a look because I didn't want him to stay for dinner. I wanted to be with Samir. I know I was being dumb but call it what you want to call it. Love makes you do dumb things. He ripped a paper towel off from the roll to dry his hands.

"Sure. If that cake is any indication of how you cook..." She stuck a fried wing in his face.

"It sure is sir and here is a piece of fried chicken to show you." He bit into it and frowned up his face. A look of worry crept across her pretty, young face.

"What? What's wrong with it?" He licked his fingers.

"Sike it's real good." She playfully took her gold hoop earrings off as if she was getting ready to fight.

"Diamond you better get your friend O.k." I tugged on his arm.

"Yeah I will. Come on Q I can't hold Mamma Ann back. She don't play when it comes to her cooking." We all laughed. Quan followed me upstairs to my room. I closed the door tight and plopped down on the bed and laid back.

"What do you want to do?" He looked around my room examining the pictures on the wall. He noticed Monopoly on my shelf. He pointed to it like it was the Christmas star or something like that.

"Lets play that." I was so happy because I loved Monopoly and nobody ever wanted to play with me. I hopped up and pulled it from the shelf. We played and after our game, which I won, because I was the banker and of course I was cheating, we were in the middle of watching my favorite classic movie, Beat Street, when my dad knocked on the door.

"Come in." Quan was sitting on the floor and jumped up. I continued to sit on my bed. He shook my dad's hand firmly.

"Nice to meet you Mr. Staple." My dad tightened his grip on Quan's hand trying to intimidate him.

"Yeah you too son. So you like my daughter?" I moaned.

"Ooh boy Dad, it was nice seeing you but can we finish watching this?" He put his hands up towards me.

"O.k., O.k. D; I am not going to embarrass you." I snickered and looked at my dad up and down.

"Dad with those little gym shorts on you already did." My dad pulled at his small shorts.

"Ooh Diamond, I'm gonna pay you back for that one." He couldn't help but laugh cause the shorts were young. They were so young that if they were human they wouldn't even be out of diapers. He slowly backed out of my room.

"Nice meeting you Quan. See you at dinner." I guess Ann told him Quan was staying. He left and tried to be slick. He pushed my door open wide. I kindly got up and shut it back. Q's eyes opened wide.

"D open the door." I fell back on my bed and hugged my pillow.

"Why?" He shrugged his shoulders.

"I don't want your dad to think nothing." I sighed and waved my hand at Q.

"Ooh boy please." He adjusted his self back in his spot on the floor.

"No D for real. Open it please." I sighed out loud.

"Ooh brother..." I got up and opened the door. I came back and sat on the edge of the bed and whispered in his ear.

"But how we supposed to do it with the door open?" He jumped damn near out of his skin.

"What?!" I pinched his cute little cheek.

"Damn Q I was just joking." He snatched one of the many pillows from my bed and laid on it.

"Your father will never have me for dinner and since your mom can cook I know she knows just how to prepare me. Y'all will be having 'Al La Quan' for dinner." I laughed at him and my phone rang. I was so busy laughing I didn't look at my caller ID. I snatched up the phone.

"Hello." It was Samir.

"Hey D. I see Mr. lover boy still there." I fidgeted around.

"Yeah."

"Well what happened? I thought you were coming back?" I coughed.

"Uh huh yeah." He yelled, "Diamond don't play with me! Do you want me to come over there?" I got paranoid.

"Nnnnnnnooooooooo!" He gave me an ultimatum.

"O.k. then, you got a half hour to get him out of there or I will be there." I was shook (scared). I mumbled into the phone.

"I can't do that."

"Why not? You need some help?" I pulled the collar away from neck. It was getting a tad bit hot around it.

"No... Wait... Just stop O.k.?"

"Say my name Diamond since y'all are just friends."

"Naw. I can't do that."

"Why not? You scared?"

"No. Of course not. Of what?"

"Well let me tell you something, the only reason he is talking to you is because the girl he was putting time in with was Yah-Yah and he was real big on her and she dissed him and told him she wanted to get at me and plus he knows about our little incident so now he mad at me (when Sam said her name I saw fire)." I screamed at the top of my lungs, "Bye Samir!" And I hung up on him. I thought back to that day and remembered Samir saying her man Q but I didn't pay it any attention. Quan looked at me.

"I kinda figured that was him. Are you O.k.?" I scowled at him.

"Fine are you O.k.?" He looked confused and reached up and touched my leg.

"Yes why you ask me that?" I pushed his hand off me, jumped up and paced back in forth in front of him.

"Let me ask you something. Were you messing with Yah-Yah?" He stood up with me.

"A while ago, yes I was why?" I leaned on my dresser and crossed my arms over my chest.

"Well this is real convenient then huh?" He looked even more confused as he looked me in my eyes.

"I don't know what you mean?" I made it real simple for him. I leaned up and in his face while using my hands to accent what I was saying.

"She played you for Samir so now you want to get back at her for dissing you and you want to get back at him because she sucked his dick and you using me for the bait huh?" He watched my hands as they flew all around and caught one in mid air and held it.

"No Diamond that is not it at all. I really like you and I always have but you were with Samir, but now you're not so that is why I wanted to talk to you." I breathed out heavy and rolled my eyes. I pulled my hand back from his loose grasp.

"Bull shit Q, you ain't no better then Samir. And I can remember Samir saying that Yah-Yah said you put your hands on her." He stepped back a few steps and pointed at his self.

"Me? I would never put my hands on that girl. She is a liar." I turned side ways to not face him.

"I don't care cause you would never put your hands on me." He stepped up in my face and palmed my face like a basketball with his gentle hands.

"You're right I wouldn't and I never put my hands on her or any other female, that is not my style." I sighed and pushed his arms away.

"You know, it don't matter, I would like it if you would just leave now." I turned my head and waited for him to leave. He reached down to the floor to pick up his beeper and car keys.

"If that's what you want Diamond." I sat on my bed and waited for him to exit. He then sat next to me on my bed.

"Let me just say this, I know Sam told you that but can't you see what he is doing? He is trying to hate on our friendship D. I'm not trying to push you no where you don't want to be. If you don't want to be no more than friends I am cool with that and if at any time you want more I am cool with that as well but Samir is just mad, that's all, but it is all good and if you want me to still leave I will." I turned my head to look at him and he rubbed my face softly.

"But I would much more like it if you wanted me to stay." My mind was swimming. I didn't know what I wanted. I jumped up.

"Excuse me for a minute." I went into the bathroom. I sat on the edge of the tub and my mind was going a mile a minute. Samir, Quan, Samir, Quan, Samir, Quan? I couldn't take it. I looked in the mirror, get your self-together girl. I was in the hall going back to my room and my mother called me to come to dinner. I walked in my room and Quan was standing up ready to leave.

"If you don't want me to stay then I won't but I did really want some of Mamma Ann's cooking." He smiled then I smiled. I looked at him.

"You can stay Quan." He began to get his stroll on in front of me.

"Thanks; the last one to the table is a rotten egg." so I pushed him out of the way and bolted in front of him. I ran down the stairs blocking him from getting in front of me and beat him to the table. Q was fun and I did like him. We sat down and ate dinner. We had fried chicken, collard greens, potato salad, candied yams, and macaroni and cheese. Hungry yet? Shit I am. Anyway, my father asked Q what he wanted to do with his life and so on and so forth. I just sat quietly staring at Quan noticing how handsome and sexy he was. How he put the fork to his mouth. Um he took my mind of Samir, way off. My mother asked him about his family and he told her he considered himself an only child because his father cheated on his mother and he has 2 brothers and a sister from him but he was in this with his mother who was a nurse who worked all crazy shifts and he tried to behave and not put more stress on her then she already had. My mother being her nice self told him she would fix a plate for him to take home to his mother because she sound like she needed it. His beeper went off at that time and he never asked to use the phone. So after dinner we had sweet potato pie for dessert and talked some more. When we were done my mom began to clear the dishes.

"Diamond I will do your dishes for you since you have company." I jumped up happy to hear that. I hated doing the dishes.

"Thanks Mom. Q come by more often." He picked up his plate.

"Mrs. Staple I don't mind doing the dishes." She smiled at him like she wanted him.

"No thanks but that was nice of you to offer." We went back to my room and his beeper went off again.

"Do you want to use my phone?" He kept his eyes glued on the TV.

"No I'm good." I was pissed because I wanted to know who was beeping him. I know he's not my man but still I'm nosey. Either way like 20 minutes later it went off again. He jumped up.

"Look D I gotta go." I whined.

"Why Q?" He clipped his beeper to his blue and yellow Nautica sweat pants.

"My mom keeps beeping me." I picked up my cordless and extended it towards him.

"So call her back." He smirked as he swung his keys around his index finger.

"Ooh D you don't trust me?" No I don't, but I played it off.

"It's not that I just wanted you to stay." He walked to my room door.

"D I have been here all day and I don't want to wear out my welcome, but let's just see when you invite me back. Can you walk me to my car please?" I kept lying on my bed.

"I'm not the man, you are. You will be safe." He laughed then pulled me up by my arm.

"O.k. then can you walk me to the door?" I stood up and stretched poking my butt and chest outward.

"I think I can handle that." When we got out the door and onto the porch the beeper went off again. I grabbed Quan's hand.

"Q I'm taking a chance with you, please don't hurt me." He touched my hair.

"I would never..." I cut him off by closing my eyes and slowly raising my hand.

"Never say never and I didn't ask you what you would never do, please Q I'm serious with this." He grabbed my face in his hands.

"And I'm serious too Diamond. I would never hurt you at all. Yo, this last month has been all that. I hope we can take it further. I want to make you mine if you will let me, if you won't and just want to be friends that's fine too but I just want you in my life either way." I cocked my head to the side.

"O.k. Q I understand all that but..." He put his finger over my mouth to "Shh!" me and then he kissed me. It was soft, slow and sweet. He looked at me after we finished kissing.

"I hope that was O.k. to do." I licked my lips to taste more of his sweet saliva in my mouth. His breathe tasted like straight Winterfresh gum.

"Yes it was but next time ask first." He pecked my lips again quickly.

"I'm use to just taking what is mine or at least one day gonna be mine." I smiled and put my hands on my hips.

"Yeah ight nigga." He smiled flashing them deep dimples making my heart melt. He then left with the plate in his hand and I watched him pull off.

CHAPTER 15
LET'S TALK

After he pulled completely off out of my view I walked across the street to deal with Samir. Ooh I had forgotten about my girl talk date with Starr. I darted across the street and Mitch answered the door.

"Look what the wind blew in." I playfully hit his arm.

"Hey Pop is my sister upstairs?"

"Yep in her room on the phone, where else?" I laughed.

"Thanks." I went up to Starr's room. I knocked.

"Come in!" Her dad was right. She was laid back talking on the phone with Danny. I snatched the phone from her ear.

"Let me say hi to my brother."

"Hey what up Danny?"

"You tell me what up with Quan at your house all day." I sucked my teeth.

"Ooh Danny shut up. We just friends."

"Since when?" I got an instant attitude.

"Since... Mind your business."

"D do me a favor please? I want Starr back bad as hell. I finally got rid of Gina." I whispered,

"I'm telling you, you went about that whole situation all fucked up Danny. You wait till the girl has the abortion, wait the 2 -3 weeks for her to heal and then dump her again. She looks like she's getting a little heavy too."

"I guess from eating everything she can see from stressing over me. Damn my dick must be all that." I sucked my teeth harder.

"Ill! Don't talk to me like that. I don't want to hear about that." He played me out.

"Ooh boy bye Diamond put my boo on the phone." I screamed, "Ill! Starr take the phone before I smack him." She took the phone and told him she would call him later. So then me and Starr started playing catch up and both talked a mile a minute. We act like it had been years but it had only been like 2 weeks since we had a good deep talk. We still knew everything just not details. She told me all about her many dates and I told her about everything even what had happened earlier with Samir.

"Well D I know you love my brother and I hate it. I can't figure out why you still love his trifling ass." I shook my head.

"Me either sis, me either." Next Krystal was knocking at the door.

"Diamond you're wanted in the basement." I looked at Starr who had her lip turned up so high it looked like it was going to stay that way.

"Ill! Ma tell Samir she is here to see me not him, so he better get out of here." Her mother opened the door.

"O.k. I will tell him but he will be coming up here in a minute for Diamond." Starr got mad at her mother.

"Ooh no he's not." Krystal playfully hit her daughter bare foot.

"Ooh Starr don't be so mean to your brother." Starr screamed, "Ma whatever!" Her mother was so nice and passive and all 3 of them (Shareef, Starr, and Samir) ran right over her. Starr waved her hand at her mother.

"O.k. Bye Ma." She sighed.

"Starr you don't have to be so rude." Starr rolled her eyes.

"O.k. Sorry Ma but get out O.k.? Is that better?" Her mother walked out the room.

"I don't know what happened to my sweet little girl?" Starr rolled her eyes around in her head like they were disco balls.

"Well I don't know either. Bye." Her mother left. Starr was real flip at her mouth. Not bad as me but I had rubbed off on her. Anyway, after me and Starr talked I went to the basement to see Samir.

"Yes Sam how can I help you?" He patted the spot next to him.

"How was your date?" I flopped down next to him but on the opposite side of the couch.

"How was yours?"

"I told her don't come cause I thought you were coming back." I exclaimed,

"Well you never told me who she was." He replied with a smirk.

"It's not important." I thought, she's probably imaginary, a figment of his imagination.

"Well Samir I'm here. What do you want from me? Blood?" He slid down closer to me.

"No D, I just want a fair shot at you, I'm not trying to compete with Quan, you're my girl not his." I yelled,

"Samir!" He rubbed my thigh.

"Well you know what I mean. Look at all the good times we had together D. I'm sorry for acting crazy the last month but I was thinking it was the medicine that had me bugging. All I know is I love you and I am sorry for all I put you through. Do you forgive me?" I smiled just as dumb as I wanted to be.

"Yes Sam I do." I kissed him. Inside my head I was feeling dumb but in my heart I was feeling love. I could hear Starr in my head saying don't be stupid for my brother. I was being stupid but ooh well. I left after that and went home. Me and Sam didn't say anymore and we were not back together from that. I wanted to work on a friendship and not rush back into anything. Quan's mother called while I was across the street and left a message thanking me and my family for the plate of food and she also said that she couldn't wait to meet me. So I called her back to say she was more than welcome. She was nice and laid back and she said she wanted to take me to dinner on Tuesday evening if that was O.k. I said, "That's fine with me." Quan called me that night but I didn't pick up because I was so confused on what I wanted to do with him and Samir. The next day in school Q walked me to my first class and I was staring at him thinking about that damn beeper going off so much and him saying it was his mother. *Horse shit!* But I couldn't prove it so I let it slide. He put his arm around me and tickled my neck.

"I called you last night, were you sleeping or cheating on me?" I got defensive and shrugged his arm off me.

"I was sleep! We don't go together so why you giving me the 3rd degree?" He looked disappointed and confused at my reaction.

"I'm not...I I I just missed talking to you last night that's all." I turned my back towards him.

"Well you survived." I went into my classroom and sat at my desk. He just looked at me like I was crazy. My next class Samir came and walked me too. I just allowed both of them to walk me to my classes to keep the peace. I knew I would have to keep both of them on the low from each other or it would be something. I knew Samir was going to start practicing again and I didn't want it to be nothing between them but of course, I was wrong.

CHAPTER 16
BASKETBALL SEASON

Tuesday at the close of basketball practice, 2 of the guys asked Quan if he wanted to grab something to eat afterwards. He shot a lay up.

"No I can't cause me, Diamond, and my mother going out to eat." Now he said this loud enough for Samir to hear and why he do that? Sam dribbled his basketball over to where Q was.

"What you say man?" Q looked Sam up and down.

"I wasn't talking to you fam." Sam placed the ball on his hip balancing it with his right arm.

"Well I was talking to you. I tried to be nice and let y'all be friends but you taking shit far asking my girl to dinner with you and your moms. She not going no where with y'all." Q used the towel hanging around his neck to wipe sweat from his brow.

"Ooh yeah? Well I would like to know this, you and what army plan on stopping us?" Sam started laughing. See that is what the nut did when he was getting real mad. He dribbled the ball and began to walk away.

"O.k. Q. You got that." Q threw the ball up again trying to perfect his lay up.

"Ight then." While Q's back was turned Sam took the basketball he had and hit Q in the back of the head. Q turned around and charged him and the other teammates

146

including Danny broke it up. The coach made them stay after practice so they could straighten the altercation out. Coach Charles told them both the same thing.

"Anymore break outs like that and you are both off the team!" Q needed to be on the team to get his scholarship to Georgetown and Sam needed to be on the team because playing basketball was his life. They shook hands and agreed to end it, but Sam pulled Q into him during the handshake.

"I will see you nigga. This shit ain't over." Q squeezed Sam's hand harder.

"You on nigga." They released grips and went their own separate ways. Q came to get me heated at what happened. When I got in the car he told me the whole story and proceeded to diss Samir. "That fag ass nigga this" and "that punk mother fucker that." I closed my eyes, raised my left hand, and cocked my head to the side.

"First of all, that stupid shit is between y'all and second of all don't disrespect Samir in front of me. I don't play that. I wouldn't let him do that to you, so don't do it to him. He was wrong, but fuck that, don't talk bad about him in front of me." Q slammed on the breaks and I flew forward. Should have been wearing my seatbelt.

"You know what D? You need to make up your mind right now and decided who you want to be with. I'm not gonna be fighting this cat all the time and you choose him over me and I'm playing myself." He was pissing me off so I hit him with a low below.

"Yeah like you did with Yah-Yah right? Played yourself." He shifted his car into first and pulled off again.

"D you know you real young acting. You need to grow the fuck up acting like I did you dirty. He's the one that cheated on you, not me so don't take your fucking attitude out on me." He continued to drive like that was that, but for me it wasn't.

"First of fucking all nigga, I don't know who you think you talking too and second of all since you want to point fingers I'm not the one that broke your heart by sucking another man's dick she did, so don't be acting like a fucking nut case with me cause I am not the one! You know what Q let me out right here I will walk home from here. I will go call your mother, apologize and tell her I can't make it and that will be that. I don't have to take this." He kept driving and punked out lowering his voice.

"D I'm sorry. I'm just so mad right now." I pointed to the sidewalk outside the car.

"That's O.k. Q, but can you let me out. Right here is fine." He picked my hand up and kissed it.

"D I'm begging you. Please can we just go, please I promise I won't ever blow up again." I yanked my hand from his clasp.

"Ooh I know you won't, well not on me cause I want out." He pulled over to the sidewalk. "D, it is cold and dark so let me take you home O.k.?" I crossed my arms across my chest happy I didn't have to walk home.

"O.k." He exhaled.

"But Diamond please... I don't want to disappoint my mother. Please can you go for me please, and I will never bother you again?" I sucked my teeth and rolled my eyes.

"O.k." The only reason I even remotely agreed is because his mother called me a few hours earlier and asked what I liked to eat, so we were going to Red Lobster to eat seafood. When we pulled up to his house his mother came out. She had it going on to be a single parent. His father was a lawyer and had to give up half his shit to her about 7 years back. She also worked hard at being a nurse so she deserved everything she had. She came out in her fur and I thought, it is not cold enough for that. She was so pretty and she looked all of 25. She gave me a hug as soon as she saw me.

"See Quan this is the type of girl I want for you. She is beautiful and BLACK." (She stressed the word black). I smiled and felt like I needed to curtsy.

"Thank you." He told me his mother didn't like him dating out of his race. She wanted him with a black girl and a black girl only. I couldn't agree with her more. So we got in her Benz and we went to Red Lobster a.k.a Ghetto Lobster on Route 22 in Union. Yo, you always see somebody you know in Ghetto Lobster. We had a nice time and I really liked his mom. She was mad cool and down to earth about everything. Me and her really hit it off. She asked me if I would like to go to the mall with her on Sunday and you know a sista loved to shop.

"Sure. If you're buying me something." She laughed but I was serious (sike I'm fucking with you.) Anyway, I forgot all about Q and he looked down at his watch.

"Ma what time we going on Sunday you know I got practice in the morning." She dissed him real quick.

"No, No Q. We meaning me and Diamond are going not we meaning us 3." I had to laugh at her. I covered my mouth so I wouldn't laugh to loud. I had forgotten about how mad Q had made me earlier. On the way home she was going to just drop me off but he convinced her to drop her self off first and let him take the Benz to take me home. They were just that cool. So we dropped her off and I thanked her for everything and he took me home in complete silence. When we got to my house I went to jump out and he hit the door lock button.

"Wait a minute D. Can we talk?" I looked at my house. "About what?" He reached over and massaged my shoulder.

"I just wanted to say sorry again for the way I acted earlier." I moved over closer to the door so he could get his hand off of me.

"I said its O.k. Q. Enough already." He then moved his hand down to my thigh.

"And I wanted to thank you for still going." I flicked the light on to see the unlock button.

"O.k. Q I'm tired, it is 9:30 and it's getting late and I want to go in the house now." He sighed while I found the button. Click, I unlocked it.

"O.k. D, but does this mean our friendship is over?" I sucked my teeth and placed my hand on the door handle.

"No, I will still speak to you. Hi and bye but what did you say earlier? You said if I did this you would leave me alone. Well I held up to my end of the bargain so..." He reached over me and flicked the light off.

"If that's how you want it D O.k." I pushed the door open.

"Yeah Q I do and I told you I'm tired so are you done?" He turned to face me in his seat.

"Yes D, but before you go can I get a kiss goodbye." I swung both legs out of the car.

"I will see you tomorrow Q, why you blowing it up?" He pulled the back of my coat to avoid me from getting up.

"No D I'm not. I'm really feeling you and I don't want to lose you. Can you please give me another chance?" I sighed.

"I don't know Q let me sleep on it O.k.?" I stood up and he leaned his head out the passenger car door before I closed it.

"D, would you be my girl?" Now I was shocked. I really liked Q, but I still loved Samir and maybe if I didn't see Samir everyday I would have said yeah but I couldn't. I leaned down and stuck my head back in the car.

"Look don't add pressure on me like that Q." He hit the steering wheel with the balls of his hands.

"I'm not trying to D, but you gotta make a decision. It's not fair to me or Samir and you know that. If you don't pick me I will be cool with it but he should feel the same if you don't pick him." I looked down at the ground and my nose dripped.

"Q I still need more time." He pushed the gear into drive.

"O.k. Goodnight." I pushed the door closed and he waited for me to get up the stairs and in the house. Then I heard the car peel off like it was stolen. I knew deep down inside he was right but what could I do? When I got in Sam had left me 4 messages. First he was yelling you better not go out with him and he had enough and I couldn't mess with Q no more. Then he called back saying he was wrong but I really needed to make up my mind and then he called back saying fuck that, you my girl and I got time in and I better make this my last outing with Q cause I was causing mad problems and he was going to handle that nigga and so on and so forth. Then he called back the 4th time saying D as soon as you get in call me. When I finished listening to the messages I hung the phone up to call Samir and it rang. I answered it.

"Didn't I tell you to call me as soon as you got in?!" I remained calm.

"Samir I just got in." He continued to yell.

"So what the fuck you going to do Diamond?!" I studied my cherry red nose in the mirror and my rosy red cheeks.

"With what Samir?" He screamed, "With what?! With what?! With us and with that fag ass nigga Q. It's either him or me." I started to get heated but just brushed my hair.

"Look Samir you can't tell me what to do because first of all you ain't my father and second of all you're not my man. Me and you are just friends and that's all me and Q are. That shit between y'all is between y'all. And if you and him keep acting crazy I won't be friends with neither one of y'all."

"Well don't compare me to that nigga Diamond, and I'm not waiting forever so you need to tell me now who you wanna be with. Me or him? If not I'm out D." I wrapped my hair around and tied my headscarf.

"Well Sam, I'm not going to make a decision now so you gotta do what you feel is real."

He snapped, "Alright then." Click! He hung up on me. I felt the tears well up in my eyes but I held them back. I was tired of crying over his ass and I didn't. I got in the shower, put my P.J.'s on and went to bed.

CHAPTER 17
TOGETHER OR APART?

The next day I didn't speak to Sam in school but me and Q said what up and that was all. Starr was trying to hook me up with one of her out of town guy's friends but I just wasn't feeling it at the time. I just wanted to be alone. Sam and Q had to be partners in basketball practice to show the coach that the beef was over. They still hated each other but tolerated each other for the team's sake. In December I got my permit and started my driving lessons. I was just worried about getting my license. Sam stayed mad at me and started talking to some out of town girl. Q was still chasing a little but I bet he had a chic on the side. Me and his mother Jackie remained cool and still hung out. She was my girl. Q asked me in January to go to his prom and I gratefully accepted. I just wanted to go to show that bitch Yah-Yah up who was graduating as well. The prom was not until the end of May but I was getting designs for my dress early. You know word travels faster then a speeding bullet and when Sam heard I was going to the prom with Q then he finally had something to say. I was coming from Dee's corner store one Saturday and he was coming in from Midtown Miller shooting dice with the boys.

"Yo D! I hate you! And I will never ever take you back if you really go to the prom with that cat." I dug in my Columbia coat pocket for my house keys.

"Sam please! You the one that got a new girl so how you gonna take me back? And who said I want to be back?" He walked across the street towards me.

"No I don't. Me and her are just friends just like you and Q." My bag split and my Bonton potato chips and 16 ounce Pepsi fell on the ground. I picked them up.

"Well Samir I don't care if you hate me. You always

have because if you didn't you would have never cheated on me and we would never have gotten to this point in our lives." His eyes looked red like fire and his eyebrows sunk down so low it looked like they were touching his cheeks.

"You were not even worth 6 years of my life. I wish I never met you!" I threw my keys at him.

"Hold up! I wasn't worth 6 years of your life?! How many times did you catch me cheating? Zero! And how many times did I catch you? O.k. then Samir, put a quarter in your ass cause you played yourself." I snatched up my keys and went to walk up my stairs and he grabbed me.

"D don't turn your back on me when I'm talking to you!" I tried to pull away from him.

"As far as I'm concerned we are finished talking." He yanked me back.

"No we are not!" He squeezed my arm so hard it felt like I had a tourniquet on so with my free arm I hit him.

"Get the hell off me." He squeezed even harder.

"Ouch! D that really really hurt. You so tough. Make me get off you." I tried to pull away and he wouldn't let me go. I was yanking and pulling for him to get off me but he would not let me go. I dropped my Pepsi again and this time it broke. I was really mad then. He pulled me closer to him and started hugging me in a real tight bear hug.

"No D. Stop. Don't fight this." I was trying to push him off but I was getting weak. I did still love Samir and he smelled so good with his Issey Miyake cologne on and his chest was like a rock. I just stopped struggling and let him hug me. I didn't hug him back. I just stood there. We both had on our Columbia ski coats and he was mumbling in my ear.

"What happened to us D? I love you and miss you." I just remained silent and stared into space.

"D I still love you please hug me back if you still love me." I remained unmoved.

"D please come back to me. I love you. Please D. I will never hurt you again." I still remained the same. I was as still as a human statue. He finally let me go and stood back and looked at me. I continued to stare into space. It was like I was looking through him. He had hurt me so bad I couldn't do this. I spoke soft and my voice cracked. I did all I could to keep from crying.

"Samir is it O.k. if I go in the house now? I'm cold and I just want to go in the house." He shook his head yes. I picked up my keys and walked slowly up my stairs. Samir picked up the busted bottle and I could feel the rays from his eyes in my back. I got through my screen door and into my porch. I tried to put my key in the lock and broke down crying at that point. The keys fell and I heard Samir come up behind me. He picked the keys up for me and unlocked the door and pushed it open. I could barely walk I was crying so hard. Samir guided me in and closed the door behind him. He took my hand and led me up to my bedroom. I couldn't reject him any longer. He led me to the chair in my room and sat me down. He peeled back the comforter and exposed my sheets. He grabbed me by the hand again and led me to my bed. He sat me down and removed my shoes; he unzipped my coat and took it off. He laid me back and put my legs up on the bed. He propped my head up on my pillows. As my draws turned from dry to moist, I wanted Sam bad at that moment. He kissed my forehead softly and pulled the comforter up over me. You thought I was going to say we had sex didn't you?

He went into the linen closet in the hallway and got a washcloth, went into the bathroom and soaked it in warm water. He came back and wiped all the tear marks that stained my face. He planted another tender kiss on my forehead.

"D I'm so sorry for all the shit I put you through." More tears rolled down my cheeks. He held both my hands in his and kissed both of them.

"You are the best thing that ever happened to me. Can I just sit in this chair and chill with you for a while?" I was still crying but I shook my head yes. He took off his coat and skully (wool hat) and pulled my desk chair over next to my bed. He held my hand tight and just stared at me and I stared at him. No words were spoken. We were absolutely silent. He broke the silence first.

"D I love you." I couldn't return the words because damn it I was still crying. He wiped my face with the washcloth again.

"D please stop crying." I finally stopped crying and he smiled at me. I mustered up a smile back. He moved the loose hairs from my face.

"D, why you so pretty?" I sighed and turned to look at the wall.

"Boy please." He clasped my chin in his strong hands and ushered my face back towards him.

"No D, I'm serious." I sucked my teeth.

"Samir how am I supposed to know. I guess cause my mom is beautiful." He nodded slowly.

"You right, she is... Diamond I miss you. Can we please stop feuding?" I propped up on my elbows and swung my hair back off my shoulders.

"I am not beefing with you. You beefing with me." He smiled slyly.

"I know D and I'm wrong for that. I treated you bad and you moved on and I deserve it and I know that... D I am so mad at myself. You just don't know. I love you Diamond." I tried to sit all the way up.

"Well Samir..." He pushed me back down.

"Please D let me finish. I'm not asking you to take me back unless you want to but I at least would like to be in your life." I licked my lips.

"O.k. Sam we can work on a friendship." He ran his finger softly up and down my arm sending tingles up and down my spine.

"D I'm not trying to rush you but do you think in the future we might be able to be together again?" I shrugged.

"I don't know Sam." He exhaled.

"D, can I ask you something?" I looked at him.

"Yes Sam, what is it?" He looked down and then at me.

"I know you have friends but um do you have a

man?" I looked away.

"Samir please don't." He grabbed my face to face him.

"You right D, but uh do you?" I answered truthfully even though I wanted to lie.

"No Sam I don't." He started smiling real hard. I squinted up one eye.

"What you smiling at boy?" He squeezed my cheeks like I was a little baby.

"My future wife!" I sat completely up and looked all around my room.

"Where she at Samir? I would like to meet her." He smiled.

"Ooh you got jokes?" He jumped on my bed and started tickling me.

"You want to be funny so laugh!" I was laughing so hard and he was straddled over me and had me pinned down. We ended up locking eyes and then he kissed me. I hadn't kissed Sam in so long it felt like an electrical shock ran through my body. He got up and he backed away from the bed.

"D I'm sorry. Maybe I should go..." I sat up again and fixed my hair.

"No Sam I want you to stay. Please stay."

"You sure Diamond?" I nodded yes and pointed at him and waved my hand as to say come here lover boy. He pointed at himself and I nodded yes and he strolled over and sat on my bed. I laid my head in his lap and he rubbed my hair. I turned and laid on my back so my face was facing his. We just sat like that and stared at each other for a while. I started the convo from this point.

"Sam where do we go from here?" He shook his head back and forth slowly.

"D I don't know." I pushed out my bottom lip.

"Well do you have a girlfriend?" (I knew he did because Starr had told me he did.) He stuttered, "D uh uh um I don't want to lie to you... I do." I scratched my face.

"That's O.k. Samir." I tried to sit up but he held me

down.

"No D, don't run away from this." I sighed.

"I'm not Samir but if you were my man I wouldn't want another girl laying all over you. So I'm giving her the same respect I expect and deserve." He released his grip.

"You're right D." I stood up.

"Samir maybe you should just go." He rubbed the top of his head.

"You right D. My girl... pause (let me tell y'all that made my stomach hurt when I heard him say my girl, anyway)... My girl is so good to me D but I guess I'm not over you and she knows it. She is so jealous of you D." I looked in the mirror.

"She shouldn't be Sam. I would like to meet her." He exclaimed, "For what?!" I put my hands on my hips and turned to face him.

"I just do Samir. I'm saying, I don't want to fight her or anything like that." He raised his eyebrow.

"I know D but um..." I leaned up against my dresser.

"Um what Samir?" He stared at the ripples in my carpet.

"We already not doing too good because of you D, and we on the verge of breaking up so I don't think that is a good idea. She is so sweet though D, she knows I still love you with out me even saying it. I mean she looks at me sometimes and says thinking about Diamond huh? I mean D I do like her, I do but I can't make her happy steady thinking about you." I sat down next to him again and looked him dead in the eyes.

"Sam are y'all having sex?" He looked shocked by my question and he started stuttering again. Finally he filled his cheeks with air and breathed out, "Yes" as he exhaled. My temperature started to rise. I couldn't believe that he was having sex with someone else besides me. I calmed myself down and stood up again.

"Ooh O.k." He stood up as well.

"D please don't be mad. Come on now." I hugged myself.

"I'm not mad Samir... just hurt." He placed his hands on my shoulders.

"Why D? She is my girl." His beeper went off. He sat down to check it. I got an instant attitude.

"Well Sam why don't you go be with your girl." He sighed and sucked his teeth.

"D, I think I'm gonna go cause I don't want to argue." I waved my hands at him.

"Samir ain't nobody arguing. I'm just saying I thought it was me and you, I just never thought you would have sex with someone else." He flopped backwards on my bed and cocked his neck back.

"D, you didn't have sex with no one else?" I threw my hands in the air.

"Hell no! What do I look like?" He looked down at the floor and his beeper beeped again. He just sat in silence while I stood there sulking. I wanted to cry again. So I started with the tears rolling. He jumped up and hugged me.

"Come on Diamond please don't do that." I pulled away.

"Sam please. I need to be alone." He pulled his sagging pants up on his butt.

"No D. Please don't do this." His beeper went off again. I cried and then sniffled.

"Sam please... Your wife must be beeping you if it is beeping like that." He threw his beeper on the bed.

"Damn D that's not fair. We broke up and it was my fault, I admitted that and yes this is my girl beeping me but what am I supposed to say?" I just calmed myself down by breathing in counting to 10 and breathing out. I spoke softly and calmly.

"Yes Sam I know and I understand, I'm O.k. but uh could you just go now?" He kicked his boots off and got completely in my bed.

"No I don't want to. I want to be here with you." I sighed and shrugged my shoulders.

"Well Sam stay then do what you want to do. You

always do anyway." He sat up and scooted to the edge of the bed.

"D hold up." He picked up my phone and started dialing. I sat down next to him.

"Who you calling Samir?" He hit the 7th number. Dag, remember when you could call all over Jersey with just 7 digits?

"Hold up and you will see." All I heard was him and it sounded like this:

"Hello. Pause. Yeah. Pause. At Diamond house! Pause. You heard me Diamond house. Pause. Because. Pause. Look, don't start Tahira. (Tahira was his girlfriend) Pause. I'm saying you know why. Pause. Look Tahira can I just call you later. Pause. I gotta handle this Tee..." At that exact moment I snatched the phone from him. His eyes opened wide and he yelled, "D what the hell are you doing?" He tried to snatch the phone but we wrestled while I started the convo with Miss Tahira.

"Hello?" She sucked her teeth.

"Yeah." I pushed Samir back by his forehead.

"How you doing Tahira this Diamond." She exhaled.

"I know who you are. What do you want?" Samir stopped struggling and looked at me like I was the ghost of Christmas past.

"I want to tell you that me and Samir are just friends nothing more nothing less and you don't have anything to worry about. He told me all about you and I told him I wanted to meet you." She was crying.

"Meet me for what?" I stood up to get room between me and Samir.

"Because I want you to trust Samir. He is a good guy so I just want to meet you so you could see that we are only friends. The only reason he's here is because I was upset earlier and he was making sure I was O.k. Would you like to come over here and we can all hang out or whatever?" He jumped up then and tried to snatch the phone.

"Diamond what are you doing?!" I put my finger

over my mouth to tell him Shh! So she sniffled and blew her nose.

"Sam don't want me around there, he always comes over here."

"Well you can come over here it is O.k. with me, and this is my house so it don't have to be O.k. with Samir." She laughed a little.

"Thanks Diamond. I will come." I smiled.

"O.k. fine."

"I will get my older brother to drop me off." I looked at myself in the mirror and then in the mirror at Samir who was scowling at me.

"Um is he cute?" She laughed.

"Of course."

"O.k. beep Samir when you are on your way around here."

"O.k. bye" We hung up. Sam was staring at me not saying anything and I looked at him and smirked.

"What?!" He shook his head back and forth.

"Why did you do that?" I brushed my hair.

"I just want the girl to see there is nothing going on between us because it isn't. You got someone and I am not interfering in that. Plus, I don't want her to go through the hurt you put me through Sam." He huffed.

"I don't feel comfortable D." I smiled and winked at him.

"Don't worry Samir; I just want to meet her and let her see she has no worries." He snatched his skully off my dresser and pulled it on.

"Ooh yes she does D. If you will have me back I don't want to be with her no more. Can't you see? I want you and only you. I made mistakes in the past but if you be mine again I surely won't make none in the present or future that is for sure." I put my arms around his waist falling for the 'okey doke.'

"You mean that Samir?" He got right up in my face.

"Cross my heart and hope to die." I looked at him and I knew he was serious. I dropped my arms from his waist and he picked up his jacket.

"If she comes here I won't be here." I sighed.

"Sam don't do her like that. Talk to her like a man and tell her the truth." He zipped up his coat.

"I tried." I interlocked my fingers in front of me.

"Well you didn't try hard enough cause you still with her." He picked up his beeper from the bed and clipped it on his Pelle Pelle jeans.

"O.k. today is the day. If I can't be with you I'd rather be alone until I get my shit together." He opened my room door and I followed him down the stairs.

"Well let her come over and we can talk about it." He stopped at the landing on the bottom steps.

"No! Damn who are you Dr. Ruth? Us 3 don't need to talk about shit, me and her need to talk. What does this look like the Get Along Gang?!" I stomped my foot on the step and crossed my arms once again.

"Fine Samir do what you gotta do." He blew it off and reached for the front door knob.

"O.k. D she is history now back to me and you." I looked down cause I felt a little bad, I mean I had just told the girl she had nothing to worry about now I was going to be her biggest competition. What am I saying, there is no competition when it comes to me and Samir.

"Samir handle your relationship first and then we can discuss us. If your break up is official we can talk." He shook his head.

"O.k. I will. Can I come back after she leaves?" We locked eyes.

"Yes Samir." As he went out my parents were coming in from the movies. He stood and talked to them and I said hi and ventured back to my room. I mean what could I do? He didn't want her, he wanted me and who could blame him? I mean I ain't gonna front I wanted him to so too bad for Tahira. He left, I got in my bed and my phone rang.

CHAPTER 18
SHE WHAT?

Well I picked up my ringing phone and it was Danny on the other end. He was screaming at the top of his lungs.

"Diamond you are never gonna believe this!"

"What?" He sighed.

"That bitch never got an abortion." I grabbed my heart like this was my problem.

"She what?!"

"You heard me D. I'm gonna be a damn daddy."

"Well what happened? What happened with the abortion?"

"Well she came by a little while ago saying look Danny we need to talk. I let her in and said what do you want Gina? For the last time its over." She smiled deviously.

"I knew in my heart of hearts you would do me dirty and you did so I did you dirty and I never got the abortion. I faked the whole thing." He went on telling me that all this time she has been hiding it from everybody. She is 4 months and just wearing big clothes trying not to be obvious. He went on to say don't you know this dumb heifer still been taking gym and all that. He said that her mom had walked in her room while she had her shirt off and found out that way, and now her mom wanted to talk to him and Aunt Debra. I thought, ooh boy here we go. Danny was shook because he knew his mother was going to hit the roof. I felt like kicking Gina in her stomach for real this time but I really couldn't be that mad at her because he did do her dirty as hell. Danny wanted me to come over when he told his mother. I didn't want to get involved any further but I had to look out for my brother.

"Danny let me get up and get dressed and I will be

right over." It was Saturday evening and me and Danny were watching TV when Aunt Debra came in. She had a few grocery bags from Pathmark. I jumped up to help her with the bags.

"Ooh my God! To what do I owe this visit from my wonderful daughter who never comes right next door to see her wonderful Godmother?" I smiled.

"Oh Aunt Debra don't play." She put her hands on her hips.

"Well I heard you driving now; I guess I better stay off the roads." I took the things out of the bags.

"I drive better then Danny." He flipped through the channels on the TV.

"Sis you crazy! Ma don't I got the wheel?" She rinsed her hands off and replied sarcastically, "Yeah Danny, whatever you say I guess having the wheel is how you got that dent in your car right?" He laughed.

"No Ma you know that wasn't even my fault." She laughed as well.

"Yeah O.k. boy. What y'all doing?" I had sat down back next to him. I nudged him to go ahead and he flicked off the TV.

"Ma I need to talk to you." She stood over the dining room table and fanned through the mail.

"What boy?" He sighed.

"No ma I'm serious." So she got serious and came over in the living room where we were. She sat in the recliner by the couch we were sitting and he stood up. I knew he wanted to get as far away from his mother's fist as possible. She looked up at him.

"Daniel what's wrong?" That's what she called him when she was serious. He paced back and forth.

"Ma you remember Gina?" She scooted up on the recliner and put her hands on her hips.

"Yes Danny I do. She spent more time here then at her own home." He stuttered, "Well um..." Her eyebrow shot up.

"I know that girl ain't pregnant Daniel?" He looked at

me and I looked away. She jumped up waving her fists in his direction.

"Don't look at Diamond Daniel, look at me! Is she pregnant?" He shook his head yes. She reared back and put her hands on her hips.

"So is she getting an abortion?" He cleared his throat.

"See Ma that's the thing. She was supposed to get an abortion in October." Aunt Debra grabbed Danny by his collar.

"Daniel why didn't you tell me this then?" He raised his hands to almost cover his face incase she was feeling froggy.

"Because she said her aunt was taking her and that was that. I gave her half of the money and was done with it." She wrapped the top of his shirt around her fist and raised her other hand.

"What about all the condoms I gave you? How could you be so fucking stupid? Didn't I tell your hard headed ass... I swear I should..." She smacked him upside his head and pushed him back.

"You know what? Get the fuck out my face Daniel. Give me those car keys, and go some fucking where, get out of my sight quick cause you making me fucking sick." He dug in his pocket for his car keys.

"Fine Ma." He put his car keys on the table and went up to his room. I just sat there and she started to cry. I got up and gave her a well-deserved hug. She pounded her fist into her hand over and over again.

"D I told him over and over again but did he listen nooooo, now he got me 'bout to be a fucking grandmother, well guess what? He in for a rude awakening if he think that girl is raising that baby alone, his ass will be sitting home watching that baby. Fuck that he not gonna be a dead beat dad." I sat down next to her and rubbed her back.

"Calm down Auntie. He made a mistake and y'all gonna work through this." She sniffled and I ran and grabbed her a tissue.

"Yeah you right, and I know one thing you better not come up big bellied." I extended my arm to hand her the tissue.

"Ooh Ma please not me!" I changed the subject off of me.

"Gina's mom wants to talk to you." She wiped her eyes and looked at me.

"That's fine, I just know that bitch better not come over here with no fucking attitude, her daughter the one not smart enough to get an abortion, dumb bitch." I sighed.

"Auntie don't be like that." I then told her the whole abortion story and I after I was done She was fuming. She walked to the bottom of the stairs.

"Daniel get your ass down here!" He came dragging down the top few stairs.

"Yes Ma?" She screamed and waved her finger towards the phone.

"Pick up that mother fucking phone, call that little bitch, and tell her and her cunt for a mother to come over here tomorrow since she wants to talk." (Didn't my Aunt Debra have the nicest mouth in the world?) Anyway, Danny continued down the stairs.

"Ma are you gonna talk like that tomorrow?" She screamed so loud I think the ceiling cracked.

"Look you fucking bastard! You don't tell me how to talk in my fucking house, I can say and do what I want so shut the fuck up, make the call, and get out of my sight!" Danny was not the disrespectful type so he just let his mother talk. He picked up and called Gina and invited her and her mother over for tomorrow and they accepted. He started back up the stairs.

"D come up to my room before you leave." I looked at him and nodded. Aunt Debra clapped her hands 3 times towards him.

"Wait Daniel not so mother fucking fast! Call your punk ass father and tell him. He should be here tomorrow too!" Danny groaned because he had grown to hate his father especially for what he did to his mother. When I was telling him not to do Gina like that I used his father as an example and he was silent when I said that. He got indignant with Aunt Debra.

"Ma I don't want to call him. I hate him!" She screamed on him with some more veins bulging from her neck and forehead. I thought, she is going to burst a blood vessel.

"What I tell you about your fucking mouth Daniel? Did I ask you what you wanted to do?! No I didn't. I told you to do something, and got damn it you better do it. You the one that got yourself into this mess, sticking your little young dick in some pussy raw, so fuck it! Make the call and I don't want to hear no more about it." He picked up and called his father and told him that Gina was pregnant and they were all meeting tomorrow. His father said he would be there. He asked Daniel to speak to Aunt Debra. Why he do that? She grabbed the phone.

"What?! Pause. What?! Pause. Look don't fucking start you half ass sac of monkey shit. Don't be mad at him because he following right in your footsteps. Pause. You know what the fuck I mean David. Look I'm not going through this with you, we not even having this conversation. If you come you come if you don't you don't. Pause. Yeah like I give a fuck about them. Pause. Those are not your only 2 sons you raggedy piece of rat shit, you have 2 others! One in college running wild and one having a damn baby! You might wanna be a father to your sons here sometimes! Pause." She ended with, "You know what David..." Click! She hung up on him. She turned and looked at Danny like a raging bull seeing it's prey. Her chest heaved up and down from her anger.

"Why you still standing here in my fucking view?!" He ran up the stairs.

"Sorry Ma! I'm sorry, but damn you gonna stay mad at me forever?!" She put one hand on her hip and her index finger pointed inward on her chest.

"Did he just get smart with me? I know he didn't just get smart with me." I walked over to her and held her hand.

"Aunt D calm down. Why don't you go next door and talk to my mother." She rolled her eyes, snatched her coat off the chair and walked towards the door.

"Good idea before I commit a murder up in here." She went next door and I went upstairs to talk to Danny. I knocked on his door softly and opened it with out being invited.

"Your mom went to my house." He was sitting on his bed throwing Velcro darts at the dartboard on his wall.

"Good! Damn man she bugging D, I'm saying what the fuck? She got knocked up young too so she ain't no better than me." I picked up a dart and perfected my aim.

"Danny don't you see? She wanted you to be better then her, that's why she's so upset, she wanted you to be older and more mature. Danny don't be mad at her, she just needs to vent, just let her talk to my mom O.k.? I'm getting ready to go home so if you need me call me O.k.?" I tossed the dart. Bulls eyes. I winked at him and he smiled.

"O.k. sis thanks." I blew him a kiss.

"Your welcome. Peace out." I had been over there almost all evening. I threw on my jacket and walked next door to my house. So I see this guy sitting outside Starr and Sam house in a green Lexus coupe. I thought, damn Starr hit the jackpot! That must be one of her friends. Let me walk across here and see who she's dating. When I crossed the street, he rolled down the window of the Lexus.

"Hey shorty how you?" I cocked my head to the side.

"O.k., but who you?"

"I'm picking up my little sis from her boyfriend house." I put my hands on my hips.

"Who her boyfriend?"

"Some cat named Samir." I sucked my teeth and rolled my eyes. I thought, he wont be her boyfriend for much longer. "Ooh." He smiled.

"Do you know him?" I rolled my eyes and turned up my lip.

"Yeah."

"Well is he cool peoples?" I turned my lip up.

"Yeah he ight." He lifted his fitted Yankees cap up.

"Well what's your name?" I twirled a strand of hair around my finger.

"Diamond." He rubbed his chin.

"Well I'm Tahir and I think you're cute." I rolled my eyes.

"No you wrong about that." He looked at me like I was crazy.

"Why?" I swung my hair.

"Kids are cute. I'm beautiful. Why you think my name is Diamond? Cause that is a beautiful jewel and you can only name a beautiful female after a beautiful jewel such as a diamond." He laughed.

"O.k. you got that." He adjusted his hat again.

"You got a man Diamond?" I sighed and batted my eye lashes.

"No." He leaned out the window further.

"What you mean no?" I smiled and licked my lips.

"I'm just single for the minute."

"Why you got your heart broke?" I looked down.

"Something like that." He playfully looked around him.

"Well were that nigga at? I will beat him up and tell him how stupid he is for losing you." I pointed to the Mitchell's house. He furrowed his brow.

"Who?" I laughed.

"Samir." He opened his car door and put one foot out exposing his fresh Timberland boots.

"So you still mess with him?" I looked in his eyes. They were mesmerizing.

"No we're still cool though. I live directly across from here. I know your sister is Tahira right?" He reached for me to come closer.

"Yeah but enough about them, when you gonna let me take you out?" I blushed.

"When you want to?" He pulled my hand to bring me even closer.

"Tonight." I shook my head.

"Naw not tonight. Maybe tomorrow?" He let my hand go and rubbed his together.

"It's a date." We exchanged numbers. As I went to walk away I turned back to face him. I know he would be looking trying to see how big my butt was. It was big so he could look.

"Do me a favor?" He sucked in his bottom lip and bit it.

"Anything for you sexy!" I bought my voice down low.

"Keep this on the low." He nodded his head.

"No doubt." He licked his lips and blew me a kiss. I waved, "bye" and began to walk in the twin's house. Samir and Tahira were walking out. She didn't look happy but he smiled at me.

"Tahira I want you to meet Diamond." She responded very dryly.

"Hi." I smiled and extended my hand towards her.

"Hey Tahira nice to meet you." She didn't say anything and she didn't shake my hand. I dropped it back to my side but kept my smile bright.

"Sorry about earlier I know we were all supposed to hang out but I had an emergency with my brother." She rolled her eyes and put her hand up in my direction.

"Yeah whatever." That's when both my eyes brows shot up with the surprised look. Surprised any bitch wanted to come test the rebel Diamond S.

"Is everything O.k.?" She threw her arms in the air and flung them all over the place.

"No its not! You trying to be all friendly with me and you trying to get back with Samir all smiling in my face, phony self." I stepped back and clutched my imaginary pearls as Wendy Williams from the Wendy William's Experience always does.

"What?!" Sam pushed her arms down.

"Tah, don't blow it all out of proportion, I didn't tell you that at all. I told you that we are just friends like me and you are gonna be, you think it is over Diamond but it is not Tah, I just need some space." She tried to push past him.

"I will give you all the space you need Samir." She went to walk out the screen door on the front porch where we were at. He grabbed her arm and twisted it behind her back.

"Why you acting like that?" I placed my hand on the house doorknob.

"Look Tahira me and Samir is not back together. We are just friends. You don't need to act out towards me cause I'm not the one, I tried to be nice but I don't have to put up with this shit." She moved her neck around like a snake.

"You right you don't." I let the doorknob go and turned around to face her head on.

"What!?" She pushed Samir off her.

"What the hell? Sam why did you get involved with me and you know you want her." He shrugged.

"I don't know." I put the palm of my hand in her face.

"Look I have no time. I'm bouncing. Sam where is my sis at?" He grabbed Tahira who was trying to leave the porch.

"In her room." I turned the doorknob but couldn't let that conversation go unfinished.

"Nice meeting you Tahira and I hope next time we see each other it is under pleasant conditions because I would hate to have to..." She didn't say shit and she better not had. I just rolled my eyes at her and Samir.

"Whatever!" Sam walked her outside and I don't know or care what happened after that. I went upstairs and told Starr all that happened with Danny down to Tahir. She was jealous and ran to look out the window to see if she could get a glance of Mr. Lexus.

"Damn girl I should have strutted my sexy ass outside...Anyway, Sam ain't letting that shit with you and Tahir go down so you might as well pass off." I laughed at her comment.

"Yeah ight. He's mine!" We talked and as I was

leaving Sam caught me coming down the stairs as he was coming up them. He turned me right back around and marched me in his room. He sat on his bed and tossed his sponge ball at the rim behind his door.

"D I'm all confused and shit." I looked him in his eyes.

"Sam I understand. I'm glad we're friends again but I need time to think so I am just gonna go O.k.?" He got up and got the ball.

"O.k. I'm glad cause I need time too." I looked at his bed and noticed it was messy. I turned to him now sitting at his desk.

"Samir did you fuck her today?" He looked at his bed.

"No Diamond, we were wrestling cause she was trying to swing on me." I opened his room door.

"O.k. boo I gotta go." I went to walk out the door and something told me to look back at the bed again. I did and it was an open, empty, Lifestyles condom wrapper at the foot of the bed. I looked at Sam.

"You need to clean this room." He smiled.

"Huh? What are you talking about, my rooms not that dirty." I just stared at the condom wrapper and let his eyes follow my stare. Once he saw the condom wrapper he then looked at me. We locked eyes and I was out the room.

"D wait!" But it was too late. I was down the stairs already. He was chasing me and caught me outside. He grabbed my shoulder and twirled me around to face him.

"O.k. D we had sex. How could I tell you that?" I looked him dead in his face and put my hands on my hips.

"Samir you just did, but its cool." He reached for my hand.

"D please don't be mad at me." I placed both my hands behind my back.

"I'm not, I don't care Samir." As I tried to walk away, he grabbed my wrist.

"Well can I see you tomorrow?" I just looked at him, pulled away, and started walking across the street. He went to softly grab my arm again but I pulled away.

"Samir don't touch me O.k.?" As I crossed the street he cupped his hands around his mouth.

"Diamond..." I kept walking until I got on my steps. I turned to face him in front of his house.

"I'm O.k., its O.k. I will see you tomorrow but right now I gotta go bye." He punched at the air.

"Bye Diamond." I went in the house and I had 2 messages waiting. 1 from Q and 1 from Tahir. I called Tahir back. He picked up on the 1st ring. He answered the phone.

"What up nigga?" Um he sounds so sexy. I had a flash back of his dark brown complexion and pearly white teeth with a little gap between them. That fitted hat was pulled down low. And his body, I could see his muscles through his long john shirt that he wore with out a coat. I cleared my throat.

"Hello may I speak to Tahir please?"

"Yeah dis him who dis?"

"Diamond." He changed his tone to soft and sweet.

"What up sexy?" We talked for 2 hours. We made a date for the next day to go to the movies. He said he would pick me up like 4 in the afternoon.

"That's what's up Tahir. See you then!" We hung up and I went to bed and dreamed about Tahir.

CHAPTER 19
THE MEETING

The next day came and 2 o'clock was the meeting time. Uncle David came to my house like 12. He came early to kick it with my dad. I came downstairs in the den where they were sitting and gave my Uncle Dave a big hug and kiss. He pushed me back and looked me up and down.

"Diamond you better not be having none!" I breathed out.

"Gosh! Why does everyone keep saying that? I'm not!" My dad took my side and came to my defense.

"Not my baby, she is going to wait, right boo?" I smiled."Right daddy." I flopped down on the couch and Uncle David went next door around 1 o'clock to have a man to man with Danny. Danny just let him talk because he couldn't stand him. At 2 o'clock Gina and her mother pulled up and Danny gave me a run down on what happened. He said they all talked about the situation and came to the conclusion that Danny and Gina would raise the baby with little help from their parents. Her mother told her that her running the streets days were over and Aunt Debra told Danny the same thing. And that was basically it in a nutshell. Danny said he was so mad at Gina that he could kill her. I told him to let it go because what's done is done. Starr still took Danny back as her man. I think she did that to make Gina mad. Starr and Danny became inseparable like the old me and Samir. A few hours after the big meeting, me and Tahir went out on our date. Tahir had a pocket full of money when he came and got me. He took me out to eat and to the movies. I was totally clueless about the drug game but I had a feeling I would learn a few things about it from Tahir. When he dropped me off Samir was going in the house. It was nothing I could do or say because he had seen it all. I thanked Tahir, jumped out quick and ran up my stairs quick. He didn't even wait for me to get in the house safe. He just mercked off. When I got to the top step Samir yelled, "Diamond! Come here!" I swung my screen door open.

"What Sam!?" He pointed down the street towards Tahir's car.

"What was that?"

"Sam what?" He started down his stairs towards me.

"Don't Sam what me, wasn't that Tahir, Tahira's brother?" I shrugged.

"Yeah, so?" He stopped dead in his tracks and pointed at himself.

"Ooh so you trying to play me?" I rolled my eyes.

"What are you talking about? We went out. So what's it to you?" He jogged back up his stairs and opened his screen door.

"So? So? D I will talk to you later." He went in his house and slammed his door and I continued into mine. I didn't have time for him. I went in and my dad was shuffling around from looking out the window.

"D where did that guy get that Lexus from?" I shrugged.

"His parents bought it." How the hell am I supposed to know where he got the car from. I went to my room and waited a good hour and called Tahir. He answered the same way.

"What up nigga?" I exclaimed,

"Hey!"

"Who dis?" I sucked my teeth.

"It's Diamond Tahir!" His tone became real dry.

"Ooh can I call you back? I got company." My face dropped.

"Ooh O.k." He hung up. I was disappointed and I knew I had to get him. No guy dissed Diamond off but I guess they do because Tahir didn't call me back that night. As a matter of fact he didn't call me until Tuesday. I was happy as a pig in shit when he called. He was saying he was coming over. I got nervous and started stuttering.

"Wh…Wh..ere?"

"There. Why is it a problem?"

"No it's O.k." I was souped up cause I wanted to spend time with him and be his girl. Why do us good girls like bad guys? DMX sure as hell didn't define it in his hit song, Why do good girls like bad guys, but anyway, he came over and I introduced him to my parents. I could tell by my dad's face that he didn't like him. Tahir was 21 but I told him to lie and say he was 18. He was like no at first but I begged him and he sly smile crept across his face.

"Whatcha gonna do for me if I do that for you?" I shrugged.

"Be your friend what else?" He laughed.

"Yeah ight. I got enough friends." We went into my basement, in the family room, to watch A Nightmare on Elm Street on our big screen TV. He was all over me before the beginning credits rolled on the film. His hands where everywhere. I thought he was a damn octopus. He was kissing me and trying to unbuckle my pants. I had to finally jump up.

"Would you please stop!" He threw his arms up over the back of the couch.

"What's wrong with you? Ooh I forgot that you still a young kid, a baby with Similac on the breath." I was offended by that. I wasn't a baby, but I wasn't a hoe either.

"What? No you're young acting! What you trying to fuck me?" He tugged at my jeans.

"I'm just trying to get to know you better that all." I smacked his hands off me.

"By shoving your tongue down my throat and your hands down my pants?" He pulled in his bottom lip then smiled.

"Would you rather I stick my tongue down your pants?" I blushed instantly.

"What? Ill you nasty." He frowned and stood up.

"No you young and I gotta go." I grabbed his shoulder.

"You leaving?" He snatched his keys off the floor.

"Yep call me when you grow up." He ran up the stairs and left. He walked up out the basement and I heard him say, "Good evening" to my parents and out the front door. I just sat there in the basement; I was mad and sad as hell. I went up to my room and laid on my bed. Sam called me a little while later.

"D why you trying to play me?"

"Damn Sam everything is always about you? Just leave me the fuck alone" Click! I hung up on him. Next thing my doorbell was ringing and my father opened the door and it was Samir. He told him to go right up. He didn't even knock on my closed door. He just barged right in and closed the door behind him.

"Don't you ever hang up no phone on me!... Wait, D what's wrong?" I wiped a tear that escaped my eye.

"Nothing Samir. Nothing at all." He looked me in my face.

"D please. I have known you for too long and I know when something is wrong. What he do?" I rolled over on my side with my back facing Samir.

"Nothing Samir. Is something wrong with your hearing?" He sat next to me on my bed and rubbed my back.

"Look D we're friends before anything else right?" I shook my head yes.

"So what's up?"

"He was just pushing up to hard, I thought he liked me but he just wanted to fuck me I think." Sam stopped rubbing.

You want me to handle that?" I rolled back over to face him.

"No Samir. I'm a big girl now I can handle it." He smiled.

"D, do you wanna go for a walk?" I looked at the clock and it said 9:30.

"To where Sam? It's the end of January, it is freezing cold and it just started snowing again." He placed his hands in the prayer position, cocked his head to the side and batted his eyelashes like a sad puppy dog.

"Please D?" I smiled.

"O.k. Samir. Don't look so pitiful." I bundled up in my Northface coat with the matching hat and gloves, put on my timberlands and we went outside and had a snowball fight. We made snow angels and tried to build a snowman but the snow was too soft. It was like we were little kids again. When we were done he walked me back to my door and said good night. He started back down the stairs. I cleared my throat.

"Excuse me sir where is my good night kiss?" He kept going down the stairs.

"D I don't kiss my female friends." I was still standing there and he turned around.

"Gotcha!" I picked up snow from the top step and threw it at him.

"Whatever Samir!" I jetted into the porch and tried to put my key in the door. He ran up behind me, turned me around, and gave me a long sensuous kiss. My panties got wet and my knees began to shake.

"Sam I gotta go!" He laughed cause he knew what the deal was. He smiled.

"See you tomorrow?" I smiled back.

"You got it."

CHAPTER 20
THIS BITCH DUN BUMPED HER HEAD

O.k. it was March and I was steady taking my driving lessons. The twin's birthday wasn't until October so they had to wait until May to start lessons. I was souped up taking my lessons. Gina was getting big and her baby shower was going to be in May. I spoke to her to keep the peace but Starr didn't and Starr also had Danny on lock down. She was still doing her thing on the side because she didn't completely trust him but that was my sis and I would cover for her. Shit, men did it why couldn't women? Well after 2 months passed Tahir had the nerve to call me like everything was all-good. I wasn't having it. He had tried to play me so I had to return the favor. When he called I told him he had the wrong number and hung up. Me and Sam were still kicking it but just as friends. He told me he was not talking to Tahira anymore. Maybe just once in a while but I bumped into Miss Tahira in the Livingston Mall and she had a different story to tell. It was early April and I was looking for prom accessories to go with my dress. I saw Tahira and I was going to speak but she shot me a look to kill. So I politely approached her on some non rowdy shit.

"Is it a problem?" She glared at me up and down.

"Yeah it is!" I put my finger in the bitch's face.

"Well can you state that problem?" She started getting expressive with her hands and I didn't like it.

"I don't appreciate you still trying to get at my man. He told you he was back with me and you still chasing him. He said he don't want me to come around there cause you crazy and you might try to stab me like you stabbed him. He also told me he has to tell you everyday to move on cause you are pathetic. I'm saying, can't you find your own man? Do you need some help?" I just let her talk and when she was done I busted out laughing. She snapped her fingers at me.

"What's so funny?" I let my laugh and smile fade.

"You!" I screamed on her after that.

"First of all bitch, I don't gotta chase no nigga, just look at me! Niggas chase me including Samir and your brother. Second of all you must have fell and bumped your head if you think Samir is yours, well no let me rephrase that, he might have told you y'all was together but he still trying to get back with me. I told him I don't want him back, I like us being friends." She rolled her eyes and put the palm of her hand in my face.

"Whatever! You're just in denial." I stepped back to get room between me and her.

"Denial?! Bitch you can't deny this black eye I'm about to give you!" I hooked off on her and we started fighting. She was with 2 girls and I was with 1 of my girls, my friend Keisha. Keisha tried to break it up but Tahira's friends thought she was trying to jump in it so one of the girls hit Keisha and Keisha stood back and threw her hands up in the air.

"Oh no this bitch didn't!" She pulled out her mace and maced all 3 of them. We were all choking and coughing and security came and put us in separate offices. Keisha was looking at me like what was that all about? She was totally lost to the whole situation but she is a whatever type chic. Whatever is whatever to her. Yep she is the same one from the skating rink when I fought Kira. I told her a brief run down and she was laughing.

"Diamond yo we crazy." I fought back the tears that the mace was bringing down.

"No bitch you crazy macing up everybody." We started laughing harder. When the security guard came back in the office he asked how old we were and I quickly answered.

"18 Sir." He latched his hand onto his flashlight on his hip.

"You got any ID?" I gave him the puppy dog eyes.

"No Sir. We took the bus here. We don't drive or anything." He sighed.

"Look I'm gonna let you go cause this is more trouble than it is worth. I don't want to see your faces in this mall ever again." We said in unison, "Yes sir," and left quietly. We didn't see those bitches anywhere. We got on the bus and laughed at the whole situation all the way home. I was going to Samir's house as I walked from the bus stop but I said to myself for what D? I knew she was telling the truth about what he said cause he thought it would never get back to me but it did. He just proved my daddy right. Nigga's ain't shit. I was thinking, I don't have time for this anymore.

Samir is finished as a friend and whatever else we could have been. I wasn't going to even let him know I was mad but I was cutting our relationship to strictly hi and bye. Of course I called my best friend to tell her what happened. She didn't feel good. That's the reason she didn't go with me to the mall in the first place. She coughed into the phone.

"D I didn't even know he was still fucking with her. Ever since we got our own separate phone lines I don't know who calls him anymore." I sighed.

"Starr don't worry about it, I'm not. I don't care cause I'm all cried out like Lisa Lisa and the Cult Jam. Anyway let me call Q and see what he doing. I have been treating him bad and that is the kind of boyfriend I need." She laughed.

"I know that's right!" I hung up with her and called Quan and to my surprise he straight dissed me.

"I got company." I was taken back and paused for a second. I then came back to life.

"O.k. Call me later."

"Bet D!" And he hung up. I was heated! 10 minutes later I called back.

"Q, tell her to leave." He started laughing and I huffed. "What's funny I'm serious!"

"Tell what her to leave?" I sucked my teeth.

"Your company." He laughed aloud.

"Well Eric and Dwight is not hers they are hims." I was so embarrassed. I whispered, "I'm so sorry Q, I guess the jealousy bug bit me...I do want to see you if I can."

"Maybe." I screamed, "What?!" He whispered, "D hold up." It was a pause and then he came back. I guess he was leaving the room.

"D you know I really, really like you a lot but you just use me when it is convenient for you. If you're bored or whatever. D let me know what's up?" I sighed.

"Q, you know you're right and I am sorry for that. I want to work on a relationship if it's O.k. with you?" He was quiet.

"Hello? Q you still there?" He sighed.

"D I will be there in half an hour to pick you up O.k.?" I smiled.

"O.k. is my girl at home?" (I was talking about his mother.) He chuckled a bit.

"No she at work but she will be home like 11:30." I jumped up.

"O.k. let me get dressed."

"Bet see you in a minute." I got off the phone and picked out something nice, of course. I picked out tight Armani jeans and a fitted Armani t-shirt. I wanted to look cute for Quan because I wanted to give him some loving that night. I was mad at Sam and I thought at the time I wanted to do something to get back at him. Like half hour later my doorbell rang. My parents had went out for the evening to their second home, Atlantic City, so I raced down the stairs to get the door. I swung it open and it was Samir.

"What up?" He pushed his way in.

"You know what's up!" I sucked my teeth.

"What are you talking about?" He walked up in my face.

"That little stunt you pulled in the mall." I felt my temper flare up and I breathed deep.

"What the fuck are you talking about Samir?!" He yelled, "You punching my gir, I mean Tahira in the face." I laughed.

"Your gir go ahead and finish it your girl. That's what you were gonna say isn't it?! Your girl huh?! Samir you not worth this argument we're 'bout to get into, that's right I hooked your girl and if she ever get smart with me and try to disrespect me again I will hook her ass again."

"Diamond you need to grow the fuck up! That fighting shit ain't cute and it don't solve shit. You think you're so fucking tough, Tahira should have whooped your ass!" I held my stomach as I laughed and bent over.

"Ha! Ha! Ha! That bitch whoop me? That's a joke. If she dream she whoop me she better wake up and apologize and ain't that the pot calling the kettle black, fighting ain't cute huh? Well I can't tell as much as you be fighting! You're the one to fucking talk about growing up and you can't even tell the truth about having a girl! You know what Sam your right I'm sorry (under my breath I said yeah right)...Now bounce!" I tried to close the door and he pushed it back open. I screamed, "Samir look you're bugging, lets not go through this bull shit tonight!" at that moment Q pulled up and I yelled out, "Here I come Q!" I looked at Samir.

"Bye Samir!" He looked at Q and then at me.

"Ooh its like that?" I sucked my teeth hard.

"Like what? Q and me are chilling tonight, what's your problem? You're not going to see your girl tonight? Make sure I didn't lump her shit up too bad? Tell her when she step to me step correct or don't step at all." He yelled,

"Yeah ight!" I chuckled,

"Ooh I see Sam, she more important then me huh? She means more to you then I do Samir?"

"You damn right!" I laughed at him.

"Whatever." I grabbed my jacket from the hook and he was blocking the door for me to leave.

"Move out the way Samir." As I tried to squeeze around him he mushed me. Now it didn't hurt and I didn't fall but still he mushed me and if it was one thing me and Starr didn't tolerate that was a nigga putting his hands on a female! He walked away after he mushed me and I tried to kick him down the stairs. I kicked him in the small of his back and he stumbled down a few stairs. Quan jumped out.

"Yo Samir what the fuck is wrong with you, you don't put your hands on no female." Samir yelled.

"Mind your fucking business nigga this don't concern you."

"Well I'm making it concern me." Samir threw his dukes up.

"Yo you want a piece of me?" Q did the same.

"So what up then?" I ran down the stairs towards them.

"Q lets just go please." Q slammed his car door and walked towards Samir.

"Fuck that Diamond let us get the fair one." I walked up to both of them.

"Q it won't be a fair one cause we will jump him now please let it go." He looked at me and walked back to the driver side of his car.

"You know what Diamond... Ight lets just go." He pointed at Samir.

"This ain't over nigga." Samir threw his hands up.

"So what you gonna do?" Q yelled, "D fuck that!" He came back around the car and swung on Samir. Samir dipped it and hit Q. Q was so tall that Samir's punch landed on Q's arm. I didn't know what to do so I tried to get in the middle of the fight. Quick note to you, don't ever...ever, ever, ever try to break up two niggas fighting because all of the sudden Bam! Q accidentally hit me in my face. My jaw to be exact. It was throbbing instantly. His eyes opened up real wide and he screamed.

"Ooh my God Diamond I am so sorry." I was holding my jaw fighting back the tears. Sam touched my arm.

"D are you O.k.?" I sucked my teeth.

"Yeah I'm fine just leave me alone." Sam's eyes got big.

"Ooh God D your jaw is swelling up quick, you might need to go to the emergency room it could be broken or fractured." I screamed, well tried to scream.

"Don't ewe 'ucking 'orry a-out me 'amir." It hurt to talk and my words came out messed up (I said to him don't you fucking worry about me Samir) Anyway, I was worried that Samir was right. Q pleaded with me.

"D lets go in your house and I will call my mother." I was trying to fight the tears back.

"That's o.k. Q, I want you to leave me alone too." Samir started laughing and I just looked at him. Q ignored Samir.

"Why D? I didn't hit you on purpose." I sighed.

"I know Q but I asked you to just ignore this asshole and you didn't and this would have never happened, but it is all good. Y'all can kill each other now I could care less. I'm going in the house." My jaw hurt to move but I didn't think it was broken. As I was going in Q begged, "Please D let me just call my mother and see what she says." I didn't care anymore; my jaw hurt and I didn't know what to do. Samir followed behind Q.

"I'm coming in too." I couldn't hold back the tears any longer my jaw was on fire. I sat on my couch and Q sat on one side of me and Sam sat on the other. Q had gotten the cordless from the table and called his mother and told her what happened. She told him to put ice on my jaw to keep the swelling down and bring me in. I struggled to get up.

"O.k. let me get some ice." Samir jumped up.

"I will get it for you." He went and got me a bag of ice and wrapped a towel around it. I snatched it from him.

"Samir why are you still here?" He rubbed my leg.

"D I'm worried about you." I moved to move his hand off of me.

"Samir I'm fine." He walked towards the front door.

"Well I will be back when you come from the hospital." He was leaving out and he whispered to Q.

"This ain't over nigga." Q let it go concentrated his

energy on me.

"D I'm sooo sorry will you please forgive me?!" I sighed.

"It's O.k. Q. Lets just get going." We went to the hospital and I was going to live. My jaw was not broken or anything just swollen. The ice numbed it so I didn't feel too much. Q's mother told me to keep ice on it to keep the swelling down. She pulled up a chair in front of me.

"Are you O.k. D?" I started tearing.

"Yes I'm just aggravated with the both of them." She sucked her teeth.

"I told Q a million times that fighting doesn't solve anything. And see what happened?" I felt bad for Q so I defended him.

"Don't be too mad at him, he didn't do it on purpose." When I came from the examining room to the waiting room, Q was sitting there with his eyes red like he had been crying. I touched his shoulder.

"What's wrong Q? I'm O.k., I'm going to live." He gave me a half smile.

"Let me take you home Diamond." All the way home he was quiet. I just looked out the window holding the ice on my jaw. When I got home I saw that my parents had returned. He turned the car off.

"Let me come in and explain what happened." I looked at him like he had two heads.

"Hell no! Are you crazy? I am just going to tell them that I walked into the door at your house. Just forget about it O.k.?" He sighed.

"D I just can't. I am so sorry." I touched his leg.

"I told you its O.k." He looked at me with a tear in his eye.

"No D, it's not. My father use to hit my mother like that and then take her to the emergency room and tell the doctors she fell down the stairs. I remember being a little boy with my blankie (his blanket) in the emergency room at least once a month but since my mom was a nurse we used to go far out to the hospital. I remember saying I will never hit my wife." To make light of the situation I made a joke.

"Look on the bright side, you didn't break your promise to yourself cause I'm not your wife." I smiled; Well what little smile I could get out. He smiled back at me.

"D, you're the best. Do you still want to go to the prom cause if you don't I will understand." I pulled my chin in towards my chest and furrowed my brows.

"What? Of course I do." I tried to smile but my face hurt too much. He looked me dead in my face.

"Diamond will you be my girl, so I can one day make you my wife?" I was speechless but squeezed out, "Ooooh boy of course I will Q." He looked shocked at first but then smiled.

"For real?" I shook my head yes and he leaned over and kissed me on the good cheek. I said, "Bye" and went in the house. I told my parents that bold face lie about walking into a door and that was that. My dad said playfully, "You sure some nigga didn't put his hands on you?" I looked at him dead in his eyes.

"Come on now dad picture that! Did you get a call from the police station saying bring bail cause your daughter murdered somebody? And he fell out laughing, "Yeah you right." Me, him, and my mom laughed in unison and I went upstairs, took 2 Advil's and went to bed.

CHAPTER 21
FOR THE LOVE OF MONEY

My face was swollen for a week. In school I had to keep my cool because people thought I had gotten beat up. I just tried my best to ignore the comments that were being made. When I would be in the hallway with Q and Samir would come, I would hug up on Q extra. I put on the same show for Yah-Yah. By the end of the week, the swelling in my face went down. That following weekend was the beginning of April. Me and Q were at his house watching a movie. He was telling me how he had gotten accepted to Georgetown to play basketball. I got teary eyed. He cupped my chin in his hand.

"What's wrong?" I closed my eyes slightly and sighed.

"You're gonna leave me." He laughed.

"D I'm just going away to college." I sighed again and exaggerated the dropping of my shoulders.

"I know Q. Don't worry about me." He pulled me in for a bear hug.

"D if you don't want me to go I won't." I looked up in his face.

"Q please...I want you to go but when you become big time don't diss me and marry a white chic like those other prick ass ball players do." He released me from his hug and kissed my cheek.

"I won't D. Never that, that's not my style. They're sell outs. Not me. I promise." He leaned over and kissed my lips on that note. We were in his den and I reached for my Fendi pocketbook.

"Q I have something for you." He put his hands out.

"What is it?! Give it to me!" I reached in my bag and got out a condom. I put it in his hand and he looked at me.

"Word D! You ready?" I licked my lips.

"Yeah. I was born ready!" He jumped up and grabbed my hands to pull me up.

"O.k. bet. Lets go up to my room." Once I got in his

room I got nervous but decided the place is here and the time is now. I sat on Q's bed and he sat next to me. He flicked on Mint Condition's Pretty Brown Eyes and it was on. He started to massage my shoulders and I closed my eyes. He pushed my hair to the side and kissed the back of neck. We in turn started kissing. We laid down on his full size bed. I ended up lying on my back while he kissed my neck and pulled my shirt up. He pushed my bra up in a rough fashion and started caressing my nipples with his tongue. I thought, damn what happened to shy little Q. He went down and swirled his tongue around my navel. He then proceeded to unbuckle my jeans. He slid them down and off of me. He then used his teeth to take off my panties. I got ready for him to put on the condom and get busy but instead he got on his knees, took his tongue and began to lick my vagina. I sat straight up.

"What are you doing?!" He looked up from my gushing wet spot.

"What? You don't want me to lick the cat?" I blushed and looked at the wall.

"No it's not that." I had never had it done before. He stood up.

"Well what is it then?" I looked away embarrassed feeling like a kid. He dropped back to his knees.

"Oh! Is this your first time?" I guess the uneasy silence let him know that it was. He rubbed his hands together quickly.

"Well don't worry Diamond. Once I'm done you will wish for your second and third time!" He parted my thighs and began to lick slowly. First the outer vagina walls, then the inner walls, then he stuck his tongue inside me while I thought, ill! That's gross! Then I relaxed and it felt good. I opened my legs wider and pushed his head down to keep it down there cause I didn't ever want him to stop. I thought, no it's not gross Q, do that damn thing! He let his tongue slowly then quickly lick my clitoris and at this time I yelled, "Q stop! I think I'm going to pee." He kept licking.

"No baby! That's not pee." I sat up and tried to push

his head back.

"Please Q. Stop I feel the pee coming." He chuckled and sucked on my clitoris like a tootsie pop.

"That's not pee boo." He kept going faster and harder. By this time I was begging him to stop cause I didn't want to pee in his mouth.

"D, that's not pee but if you think it is then pee in my mouth." I tried to close my thighs but he took his hands and pushed them further open and licked and sucked until I looked like Samir back during our first time. My body twitched and jumped and I hadn't pee'd, I had my first orgasm. Right in Q's mouth and he loved it. He stood up and lied down next to me.

"Congratulations!" I looked away feeling real embarrassed.

"For what?" He licked and kissed on my ear.

"For busting your first nut evidently." I was embarrassed and tried to play it off. I rolled my eyes.

"Whatever." He climbed on top of me and whispered, "Whatever nothing." He tried to kiss me. I turned my head and he got my cheek.

"It's like that D?" I turned my lip up.

"Yeah. You just had your mouth down there." He licked my neck.

"It's yours." I exclaimed, "But I don't want to taste it!" He laughed and tongue kissed my neck. He got me so hot and heated I wanted to yell, "Put it in already" but I didn't. He reached over on his nightstand and got the condom I gave him. Then we finally did it and it was good, damn good. He had a nice size tool to work with. He had this pump pump swirl swirl type of technique he used during sex. That caused me to dig into his back with my acrylic nails and one popped off. He lifted one of my thighs to fit into my spot more perfectly. My mind swam thinking about Q being the first boy to go down on me, wait I'm saying it like I had been with so many other cats but y'all know what I mean. Just think back to your first time your thighs were being used for earmuffs! (smile) I'm catching a flash back.

Wait let me come back to the present. Anyway, when me and Q were done handling our business, he took me home. It was around 9 PM and the stalker appeared. You guessed it Samir! He ran out of nowhere and kicked Q's car. Q jumped out his car and him and Sam started fighting. I didn't know what to do so I ran in the house and got my father. He came out and broke it up. My dad asked, "What's the problem out here?" Samir pointed at Q.

"D (talking to my dad) he's the problem." Q looked at my dad.

"Sorry Mr. Staple for disrespecting your house but he kicked my car when I was getting ready to drive off. I had to defend myself." My dad looked at Samir.

"Sam why you do that?" Samir shrugged.

"'Cause I don't like him." My dad sighed.

"Come on Sam you know better than that... Why are y'all fighting for real, over Diamond?" Sam yelled, "No!" Q replied, "Yes!" Sam got all bent out of shape.

"Like I said no. I ain't got to fight over nothing that's mine!" I cut in.

"Nigga please! Me and Q go together now. You fucked up on more then one occasion." Q looked at me with his eyes wide.

"D watch your mouth." I looked at him with one eyebrow raised.

"Don't tell me to watch my mouth. My dad is cool with it!" My dad butt in.

"O.k., O.k. Enough with all that. If y'all really wanna fight then I will let each of you get a fair shot." I screamed like a crazy person.

"No!... I am so sick of this, I swear if y'all 2 fight again, God as my witness I will never speak to either one of y'all again." I turned to face my new man.

"Q I mean it!" Then I looked at my ex man.

"And Sam you know I mean it, y'all better come to some kind of fucking truce and I mean right now or I will stab both of y'all out here." I started digging in my purse for my handy dandy razor I kept on me at all times. My father waved his hands towards me.

"D calm down. I don't want to be bringing you food packages to Clinton while you in jail." My dad was trying to make light of the situation but once one tear dropped that was it. Funny huh? He is sending me food packages here to Clinton now, but there is nothing funny about jail. Anyway, I blurted out, "No daddy I am so sick of this shit." I turned to Samir.

"You have a girlfriend that you lied about and I should have spit in your face for that but I didn't." I turned to Q.

"And if you want to keep this girl you better get it right and I mean right now, I am not fucking playing no more." Sam sucked his teeth.

"O.k. D calm down. Stop being such a drama queen." I screamed, "Fuck that Samir. I congratulate you on your relationship and you try to shit on mine. What is your problem?" He sighed.

"D ight already! My bad ight? I'm sorry O.k?"

"Yeah Sam you are sorry. A sorry excuse for a boyfriend, that's why you're no longer mine..." He threw his hand up in my face.

"O.k. D you know what? You got it! I will stop; I'm not chasing no chic. I'm Samir and Samir don't chase no chic. Chic's chase me, feel me? Ain't that right Q? Cause Yah-Yah damn sure chased me." I smacked Samir's hand down out of my face.

"Whatever Samir!" I turned my back towards him and faced Q.

"Q?" He looked me up and down.

"That don't be me that be him. See he's starting already, don't nobody want Yah-Yah." I screamed, " C a n we stop pointing the finger?" Q sighed.

"O.k. Diamond whatever, yeah I'll stop." I placed my hands on my hips.

"Shake on it!" They looked at each other and then at me like yeah whatever. I jumped up and down and screamed, "Now!" Nobody budged.

"O.k. Don't. Good bye Samir and goodbye Q!" I began to walk in my house while Sam yelled.

"Damn D why everything gotta always go your way." I walked up on him with my finger in his face.

"What do you mean Samir? Everything has not gone my way or we would at least be friends and you would at least respect me enough to respect my company. You're always starting Samir, damn!" He smacked my hand down out of his face.

"You know what Diamond..." He turned and shook Q's hand.

"Good luck Q." He looked at me.

"There you happy?" I crossed my hands over my chest.

"Very." Samir gave my dad a pound.

"D (my dad), I apologize for all this and I'm gonna be a man about it and walk away." Sam looked at me one last time and then walked across the street and in the house. Q came over and put his arm around me.

"Are you O.k. Diamond?" I tensed up.

"Fine." My dad excused himself.

"I will leave you 2 alone." With that said, he went in the house. Q stood in front of me and put his hands on my shoulders.

"D I don't want to lose you over something stupid O.k." I sucked my teeth and looked up in the sky.

"Yeah I hear you talking but I kinda want to be alone right now." He grabbed my chin and softly kissed my lips.

"O.k." He then kissed me on my forehead and left. I sat on my steps and wanted to talk to Starr but her and Danny went bowling. I figured, I'm gonna sit here until they come home. It was only like 9:30, but it didn't matter. I was going to sit and wait. I saw Sam look out the window and then come outside. I was getting up to go in the house. He crossed the street towards me.

"D wait." I sat back down and waited for him to come across the street. I listened to the bull crap he had to say. He came over and extended his hand towards me.

"Here." He tried to hand me 2 crisp one hundred dollar bills. He had a pocket full of money. I looked at the bills as I took them.

"What's this for?"

"That's to cover your pain and suffering." I handed it back to him.

"I don't want your money Samir. Where you get all that money from anyway?" He sucked his teeth.

"Don't worry about it." I grabbed his face.

"Who you talking to? I asked you a question." He slapped my hand down from his face.

"And I gave you an answer." I sighed.

"Bye Samir, get off my steps." He scrunched up his face in disgust.

"Good D I don't care." I screamed.

"Good!" He screamed louder, "Great!" He started walking back down my stairs. I was getting so tired of this. I stood up.

"Wait Samir... Look we have called a truce in the past and it never works so lets call something else, like how about you act like I don't exist and I will do the same for you. Just act like we never ever knew each other." He slowly clapped his hands together applauding my idea.

"That is the best idea you ever had what ever your name is." I sighed.

"Sam what has gotten into you? You've changed, you're not sweet little Samir I use to go with and love." He stood up straight and made a muscle.

"You're right I'm not little Samir, I'm big Samir and don't you forget it! You're lucky I got so much respect for your father or I would have still been fighting your man. I don't give a fuck." I looked at him and turned my lip up.

"So fuck respecting me and my feelings right?" He looked at me.

"Pretty much D. I lost all respect for you when you were fucking with my man Tahir." I stood up straight and put my hands on my hips.

"First of all, I wasn't fucking with him we were

friends, and second of all that is not your man." He cracked his knuckles.

"That's where you wrong at, that's my nigga." I rolled my eyes.

"Ooh all of the sudden that's your man. When he called his self trying to fuck me you was all ready to fight him, but now that's your man right." He pulled out his knot of money, I guess to impress me.

"Yep he taught me how to get money." I screamed, "You selling drugs now?!" He frowned up his face and covered my mouth with his free hand.

"Would you shut the hell up! Damn Diamond I don't need the whole neighborhood to know unless they want to buy something." He started laughing at his sassy remark. I sat back down on my steps.

"You know what Samir I don't want to hear no more, you disgust me." He put his money in his pockets and shrugged his shoulders.

"Well you will be glad to know your boyfriend ain't so innocent, he sells drugs too. I mean I sell the real deal. Coke and dope. He sells weed but I'm trying to take over his little operation of selling to the white boys at school, so see you're not the only reason we came to blows." I sucked my teeth.

"Samir get your lying ass off my steps." He shrugged again.

"D I'll go, but just remember I got enough money to buy you back if I really wanted to," and he dropped the $200.00 on my steps. I picked up the bills and crumpled them up.

"Hmph! You will never have enough for that mother fucker." As he walked off I threw the money at him. He laughed, picked it up and continued to stroll across the street. He sat on his steps. I couldn't believe him, lying on Q like that. I know he didn't sell drugs but I thought, what about all them beeps he gets and never explains, always saying it is his mother. Maybe he was selling weed. I didn't know and since I didn't get down with that kind of life style

I didn't know how to approach Q on the situation. I looked over at Samir and shook my head. I couldn't believe what he was turning into. I had noticed that Samir had a lot more than before and all new jewelry but I didn't think much of it. I was thinking, man this nigga is off the hook. He just sat back on his steps smiling. I felt like running over there and kicking him dead in his throat. Next thing I know Tahir pulls up and gets out and is talking to Samir. I saw Samir hand Tahir some money and Tahir handed him a bag. Samir ran in the house and Tahir flosses over to my side of the street.

"Hey pretty girl did you grow up yet?" I rolled my eyes.

"I've been grown up." He leaned on my banister.

"So what's up then?" I sucked my teeth.

"What's up with what?" He smiled.

"Us?" I just looked at him and laughed at him trying to talk slick. Sam came back out and yelled,

"Yo Tah, I'm ready." He turned towards Samir and put his finger up.

"Ight Samir hold up." Then he looked back at me.

"Can I call you again?" I looked at the long tips on my nails with the airbrushed colors.

"Nope." He looked shocked.

"Why not?" I stood up and put my hands on my hips, at this age they were no longer my imagination, my hips were real.

"First of all cause you tried to play me, second of all cause I got a man, and third cause Samir hating ass will tell my boyfriend." He touched my hand.

"Samir don't gotta know. We will keep it between us." I shook his hand off.

"Nope you're rude and I don't like that." He smiled.

"My bad about what happened shorty but I had to make sure you wasn't no hoe, I wanted to make you the wife, lace you with nice shit." I turned my lip up in disgust.

"Well I stay laced so I don't need you to lace nothing but your boots up and get up out of here." He laughed covering his mouth.

"Ooh D you gonna do me like that? Come on, give me another chance, let me call you and make it up to you." I breathed out.

"Oh boy! O.k. You can call me... as friends." He smirked.

"Come on D we can start as friends but I want you to be my girl, fuck your man." I sucked my teeth and sat back down.

"Ooh Tahir please don't beat me in the head with da bullshit I don't have a helmet on." He laughed again and shook his head.

"Girl you too much. I don't mind giving away my money if it is to someone sweet like you. I won't be stingy with you if you not stingy with me." He adjusted his neck and tried to look between my closed legs. I rolled my eyes at him, sucked my teeth, and turned my lip up once again in utter disgust.

"Well consider me Scrooge cause I'm stingy with that and if that's all you want then do yourself a favor... don't call." He laughed it off.

"D I'm just playing, I will call you tomorrow." I shrugged my shoulders.

"Whatever Tahir. Where are you and Samir going anyway?" He started walking down the stairs backwards.

"To my house to bottle up." I scrunched up my nose.

"Bottle up what?" He laughed.

"D you so cute, I gotta let you in on the game one day O.k.?" I smiled.

"Yeah ight." He got to the bottom step.

"Look I gotta go I will call you ight?" I winked at him.

"Yeah ight." He walked towards the street and yelled, "Later!" Then he ran and jumped in his Lexus and they pulled off. I started feeling a little excited inside. Tahir was fine as all hell. He was a little darker then I liked them but he would do. He had white teeth, but they weren't the straightest. He had small gaps in them but something about his smile and the way he wore his hat down low drew me to him. I was going to mess with Tahir on the low. He would let me in on the drug game so I could see what was so great about the whole thing. I hoped he didn't tell Samir about our conversation because that would be all I needed. Starr and Danny finally pulled up in front of Starr's house and broke my thought process. I ran across the street and grabbed my best friends arm through the car window.

"I gotta talk to you." She leaned over and kissed him.

"Duty calls Danny. I will call you later." She then came back across the street with me. We sat on my stairs and I told her all that had just went down. Starr had her hands on her hips while she was sitting down.

"Q did what with his mouth to you, cause I'm jealous?" I playfully smacked one of her arms off her hips.

"Come on Starr that is not important, even though it was good as hell, but anyway what is important is that your brother is selling drugs." She rolled her eyes.

"I'm telling on Samir for selling drugs." I put one hand up.

"Starr hold up let me see what I can get out of Samir since he wants to buy me back." She sucked her teeth and let out a disgusted sound.

"O.k. bet, but my brother gets on my nerves, he has changed for the worst." I shook my head in agreement.

"I know that's right. I told him the same thing." She shadow boxed the air.

"Lets jump him like old times." I smiled and joined in with her shadow boxing.

"I'm down!" We laughed thinking back to days of old. I told her what Samir said about Q too and how Tahir wanted to be my friend again. She yelled, "Q too!? What the... Well bump it find out the truth and make him pass off too. And Tahir as well. Play all of they're drug dealing asses." I stretched my arms.

"I don't want no money, you know I am too independent for that. But Samir wants to be throwing it around like he is King Jaffe Joffer from Coming to America, so I will just have to get him for it, and then me and you will just have to split it." She smiled.

"I know that's right! Get that pain in the ass brother of mine. Look sis, I'm tired and getting ready to go to bed, I'm still not feeling too well." I softly touched her arm.

"You O.k.?" She touched her forehead.

"Yeah just coming down with a cold or something." I hugged her.

"O.k. Sis feel better." I went in and called Q and decided against asking him about the drug thing. I figured if he wanted me to know he would tell me. But I decided I would ask for little things like sneakers and hair money. Bump that. If I'm the wife, pass off.

CHAPTER 22

IF I'M CREEPING JUST LET ME CREEP

So the next day Tahir called me, woke me up and asked could he see me. I looked over at the clock.

"I don't know about all that." He sucked his teeth.

"Oh come on girl meet me around the block on that dead end street at 1:00 and don't keep me waiting." I sighed.

"Oh O.k. Tahir."

"We can go far out to eat so you don't have to be nervous your man will find out." I sat up and laughed.

"Whatever! Ain't nobody nervous." I was excited and nervous all in one. Excited to be seeing Tahir, but nervous about going out with another guy besides my man. I hurried and got dressed with a red and white DKNY sweat suit and matching DKNY sneakers and walked around the block. He was the one that was late coming at 1:20. I got in the car with an attitude. I rolled my eyes, sucked my teeth and slammed the door as I got in. He reached over and squeezed my leg.

"Girl please with the fake attitude, you know black folks is on C.P. time so cut it out." I had to give a half smile for that cause we sure as hell was always on C.P. time also known as colored peoples time. Always late. We went to Willowbrook mall which is about a half hour from me, but who did we see all the way out in the boonies? Q's mother. I walked right into her while I was running my mouth to Tahir.

"Hey Diamond" is all I heard and I looked at her shocked. She looked at Tahir. I reached and hugged her.

"Hey Jackie." She smiled.

"What are you doing here?" I lied of course.

"My cousin bought me to the mall to get prom accessories. Tah this is Q's mother." He gave a devious grin.

"Hi how are you? I heard so much about my lil' cousin's boyfriend Q and it is an honor to meet his mother, and what a pretty mother he has." He shook her hand, then kissed it. She smiled at him.

"I'm fine thank you for asking. And thank you for the compliment. Diamond, that's funny you are here cause I called you right before I came here to see if you wanted to go to the mall with me." I smiled while my stomach did flip flops.

"For real? Me and Tah was just spending some quality cousin time together but enough about that, what you doing at this mall?! You know your mall is Short Hills, I'm telling, you cheating on Short Hills!" She laughed and playfully smacked my arm.

"Yeah I know but sometimes you need a change, are you coming over later?" I shook my head.

"Yes probably like 6, by the way where's my boyfriend at anyway?" She sighed.

"Child who knows? I was getting ready to ask you the same thing cause I haven't seen him all day, but anyway I will be there by 6 and I will cook." I grabbed my heart like Fred Sanford from Sanford and Son.

"Elizabeth I'm coming to join ya honey, this is the big one!" I did all that cause Jackie never ever cooks. She was cracking up laughing.

"Oh girl you know you crazy, don't stand me up." I smiled at her.

"I won't. I'll be there." She looked at Tahir.

"Tah is your name right? You can come too if you want." He licked his lips and looked Jackie up and down like he wanted to holla at her (kick it with her).

"Yes it is Tah or Tahir whatever you want to call me and yes I would like to come to dinner at your house." I looked at him as if he had bumped his head and he finished his sentence. "But I have other plans with my girl's family. But maybe next time." She winked at him.

"Yeah maybe." Then she smiled. I thought, damn, Jackie and Tahir would be hooking up if I wasn't standing here. She waved bye.

"See you later daughter-in-law and see you later too cousin of my daughter-in-law." She switched off. I was shitting bricks by then just thinking what would have happened if Q was with her. I know Jackie wouldn't get home good before she told him she seen me and my cousin Tah in the mall. I know it was going to be a problem since he never heard of my cousin Tah. I had to make it look good so I bought him Tommy Hillfiger cologne and matching boxers so he would be happy. As we left Macy's Tahir grabbed my neck and leaned into my ear.

"You owe me D." I stopped in my tracks.

"Why?" He grinned.

"Cause I ain't your cousin. I could have got loud on you but I didn't." I batted my eyelashes.

"You would have betrayed me like that? You know I got a man." He grabbed my hand to pull me along.

"Fuck your man. Just remember you owe me." My mind was swimming, why did I even agree to see him? He smiled while he looked me up and down like I was a meal.

"Let's eat lil' cuz." We went into the restaurant in the mall. He started telling me about his life and how he started in the game and why. He sipped his water.

"D when I was little I was a spoiled brat. For the first time at age 12 I wanted something and couldn't get it and I got pissed. I wanted two leather bomber coats (remember them?) and my mother only bought me one on Christmas. I stormed out of the house and these older cats, Larry Luv and Travy Trav from around the way on Catherine St. asked me what was wrong and I told them what happened and Larry said if I worked for him I could get all the leather bomber coats I wanted and the rest is history. Yo, I gotta get money cause the white man wants to hold you down and clown ass niggas will hate on you. Shit, somebody put me on so that is why I put Samir on. You gotta help others out when you can D." The waitress came and we ordered our food. I sat with my hands under my chin and listened intently to him talk.

"D you gotta get your respect in the streets or cats will try you. Shit, if you gotta pop a nigga to let cats in these streets know you 'bout it. Then you got to. Yo, I got beef from jealous niggas but it ain't a thing cause I keep my gat (gun) for shit like that." I said all loud, "Well what drugs do you sell?" He looked at me like I had bumped my head for real this time.

"You all loud, would you shut the fuck up?! Damn Diamond." I looked down.

"Sorry." He reached across the table and grabbed my hand.

"It's O.k. And for the record I don't sell drugs, you never heard me say that did you?" I looked him in his eyes.

"No, but Samir said, and I assumed..." He cut me off.

"Never assume it makes an ass out of u." At that time the food came and he rubbed his hands together.

"Let's eat!" I guess that meant change the subject cause that's what he did. I was fascinated at the time and still tried to sneak a few more questions in pertaining to the drug game. He sat back straight up.

"I swear to God Diamond you better not be the feds! You ask too many damn questions!" I sipped my soda.

"I'm not no damn feds, be real." He smiled.

"Well you better not be trying to develop a habit!" I screamed,

"What?!" He looked me in my eyes.

"You asking questions like you want to sell or either get high!" I sucked my teeth hard.

"Fuck you pal! I don't have to do no such of thing to get money, I got money and I would never do drugs!" He continued to eat his chicken fingers and pointed one at me.

"Never say never D." I said with an annoyance in my voice,

"Whatever Tahir!" He just smiled at me.

"It don't take shit to get you mad." I picked up my cheeseburger.

"I don't get mad, dogs get mad." He laughed.

"Oh excuse me, you're angry?" I picked up my napkin and wiped my mouth.

"Go to hell Tahir!" He looked at me and made a doof ball face. We both laughed cause he seemed to know how to push my buttons. Let me tell you, if you don't know anything about the drug game, good. That is the best thing for you cause it ain't no joke. There are only 3 ways out the drug game, if you don't decide to get out first: jail, death, or you become an addict. I was feeling Tahir cause he seemed to have shit on lock, and he kind of kept me in my place and that was new to me. I usually ran shit. I thought, the prom is in 2 weeks and then a few weeks after that Q will be going to basketball camp and then to school. I will try to stick things out with Q and keep Tahir on the low. At least until July 5th when Q finally go away to basketball camp for the rest of the summer. I told Tahir about Q and how he was leaving soon for college. He just had to bust my bubble.

"You know he gonna be down there fucking other bitches don't you?" I sucked my teeth at him again and clenched my teeth closed.

"Shut up Tahir. Ain't nobody ask you nothing." He laughed and pointed at me.

"Don't get mad at me cause your man will be fucking other bitches." I started sulking. He laughed again.

"You know, I like you D, you feisty and don't take no shit, but on some other real shit if you ever put your hands on my sister again I will fuck you up." He wasn't smiling and neither was I. I had forgotten about that little episode in the mall. We stared at each other in the eyes.

"Well first of all I ain't no punk about mine, so don't get it twisted and second of all I don't have nothing against your sister, she hates me for Samir's lies." He sighed.

"Yeah I know, I'm just fucking with you, but don't put your hands on my sis no more, for real, you've been warned." I exhaled and replied sarcastically, "Yeah O.k." He waved his glass towards our waitress for a refill.

"That's why I'm not mad at Samir cause I did the

same shit when I was his age. But still Tahira is my sister and I don't want her fighting." I let his ass know in an adult way.

"Well whatever, I don't care, I don't be wanting to fight, girls drive me to it and you're probably still doing it, I mean fucking with mad chic's and lying. You act like you're so old." He got smart.

"If I was you, I wouldn't worry about it cause you got Q remember? And I am old, too old for games. I'm grown and don't have time for kid shit." I smirked.

"Whatever nigga. I think that is real wack of a nigga to lie like that, guys should just keep it real and tell the truth." He finished off his fries.

"You right, we should, but most females can't handle the truth. But I tell the truth at all times no matter what the consequences are, that's why I'm saying I am too old for that now, I don't gotta lie cause with my hoes what I say goes." I rolled my eyes.

"Oh boy please! Speaking of old I will be a year older in a few weeks what you buying me?" He grabbed the brim of his hat and bent it down more over his face.

"Oh Miss Independent wants me to buy her something?" I wiped my mouth and threw my napkin in my plate.

"Wait Tahir don't get it fucked up, I was just asking. I don't need you to buy me shit. If you do its all good and if you don't it don't matter." He waved to the waitress to bring the check.

"Well I don't like my girls cussing a lot, so tone that down and for your b day, how about I surprise you?" I jumped up and headed towards the ladies room.

"You do that, and I cuss when I wanna cuss, thank you." He shook his head and smiled as I walked away. Once I came back he looked me up and down.

"What am I going to do with you?" I looked at my beeper and it was almost 4 and I wanted to get home to change for Q's house.

"Well since we're done eating, we can leave for

starters, so that's one thing you can do with me." The waitress had left the bill on the table. I picked it up to pay my part and he snatched it.

"Don't play me out Diamond." He dropped the bill which was 25 dollars and 2 twenties on the table.

"Lets roll." I thought, big tipper. We were leaving out the door.

"D do you want to come to my place for a while?" I shook my head.

"No cause I don't want to get into it with your sister. Remember I've been warned." He laughed.

"D what are you saying? I got my own crib. And I wouldn't let you and my sis get into it. She got Samir wrapped around her finger anyway, she ain't worried." That's what you think. I sucked my teeth as we exited the mall.

"Well neither am I, but it don't matter anyway cause I don't want Samir at all. But I still gotta say no cause I gotta go to Q's house." He looked at his diamond Rolex watch.

"It is only 4 and the way I drive we will be to my house by 4:30 and chill for like an hour and..." I cut in.

"No thank you, I can't today." He walked ahead of me.

"Fine then." I walked on his heels.

"I know you don't have an attitude?" I didn't want to get on him cause we were to far out for him to be trying to leave me. Once in the car it was silent so I repeated myself.

"I know you don't have an attitude?" He sped out the parking lot.

"Come on now, me? For what?" I crossed my legs.

"Yeah ight Tahir, I will come over tomorrow." He played me out.

"I didn't invite you tomorrow, I invited you today." I screamed, "Ill! I'm coming tomorrow and that is that." He smiled at me. "You know you too much. Maybe you can come over tomorrow if I don't have company." I turned towards him in my seat.

"What?! You better just pick me up in the same

place 4:00 PM when I get out of school and don't be late ight?" We were sitting at a red light and he chuckled.

"Ight Miss Independent." He leaned in for a kiss and I turned my face. He got my cheek.

"Oh O.k. D you got that." I stuck out my tongue at him. "I know." We both laughed. He dropped me off on the dead end block and I walked home quick, changed, and called Q to come get me. When in the car he didn't mention Tahir but when we hit his front door he gave me the third degree asking me about the mall and my cousin I was with.

"Q look do you want to meet my cousin?" He closed his room door.

"Yes. Cause I never heard about him before." I sucked my teeth with much attitude.

"Damn you don't know everybody but you can meet him. As a matter of fact let me get the phone and call him and tell him to come over here right now so we can avoid all this bull shit since it seems you don't trust me." I got up and stomped over to get the phone.

"D, I don't want to meet your cousin, I'm sorry, I trust you." I dialed a few imaginary numbers.

"No! Let me call him and make you look stupid!" He spoke soft and took the phone from me.

"No D. Please don't. I'm sorry." I sat back down and crossed my arms over my chest. I rolled my eyes, but I said a silent prayer cause I know I was a good actress cause I wasn't getting up to call nobody.

CHAPTER 23
THE BABY SHOWER

So anyway the next weekend was Gina's shower and the next Friday was going to be the prom. Me and Starr went to Gina's shower together and since Sam and Danny were best friends you know Samir was there, getting on my nerves. The shower was at the Maplewood Recreation Center around the corner from us. One thing about Jersey is the towns are small. You can have one foot in Maplewood, the other in Union and put your right hand in Vauxhall and left hand in Irvington. It is like a big twister game. Samir was just flossing back and forth trying to kick it to one of Gina's cousins in front of me. He was looking at me while he was talking to this chic, trying to get me mad I guess. I mean it worked a little but you ain't hear that from me. When I walked passed him he touched my butt and I turned around and kicked him in the shin. He rubbed his leg and turned his lip up.

"D why the fuck did you do that?" I put one hand on my hip.

"Keep your fucking hands to yourself Samir." He smiled. I mean he was still cute and sexy as ever. He had gotten a mouth full of gold caps with his name in the front. He grabbed at my hand.

"What up D? Can I take you out tonight?" I sucked my teeth and pulled my hand back.

"Hell no so you can tell Q?" He sucked his teeth.

"D why would I do that? And, you can tell Tahira just as quick." He reached for my hand this time. This time rubbing it real soft.

"Come on D, I just want to go out as friends. That's all." I hunched my shoulders and leaned in closer to Samir.

"To where Samir?" He smiled and licked his lips.

"Uuummm how about The Loop?" (For those of you not from Jersey The Loop is a famous motel that people go to screw a.k.a have sex.) I tried to walk away.

"Bye Samir." He quickly grabbed my arm.

"Sike D, I'm just joking, we can go anywhere as long as I'm with you." I blushed.

"Well you know I'm going to the prom next week and Wildwood for the weekend so maybe we can go out in 2 weeks." He exclaimed out.

"2 weeks? I'm trying to see you tonight." I hesitated.

"Sam... I I I don't know about that." He whispered,

"Come on D, I don't bite, unless you want me too." I playfully hit his leg.

"Samir!" He smiled.

"Just jokes D, just jokes." Krystal seen us talking and she came over to us.

"That's what I like to see." We both smiled at her. Starr looked at me and him and she turned her lip up in disgust. I pulled away from Samir.

"Hold up Sam." I walked over to my best friend.

"What's wrong?" She sighed.

"Oh nothing Diamond." I looked her in the face.

"You sure sis?" She crossed her arms over her chest. "Yeah." I pulled her card quick.

"Starr I know why you disgusted but I love him so much." She sighed again.

"Yeah I know and I hate it. Don't fuck up that good thing you got with Q, for that dead beat piece of shit over there." I touched my best friend's arm.

"Why you hate it so much Starr?" She got all bent out of shape and threw her arms in the air.

"'Cause I hate him. He is not the same and he thinks he is a player and that really pisses me off." I laughed lightly.

"I know Starr, me too but I miss him and I would like to see what's up." She sighed and bulged out her eyes.

"You already know what's up! He got Tahira and he playing her with some other bitches that be calling, is that what you want?" I pleaded for her to understand by staring her in the eyes.

"No Starr, you know if I had to I could and would change him back to my sweet little Samir." She tooted up her lips.

"Hmph! I don't think so, but I'm not hating D, do what you gotta do. But just don't fuck up with Q for that slouch, I'm telling you." I stuck my tongue out at her and scrunched up my nose.

"Be real, Q ain't going no where. That nigga is sprung." She finally smiled at me. Sam yelled,

"Yo Diamond come here." I went back over to where he was and he grabbed both my hands and looked up at me in my eyes.

"So tell me what's up D." My eyes got big.

"I don't know Sam, but right now you playing me to close because all eyes are on me. Look around!" We both looked around and all the chics from school were eye balling me. They probably couldn't wait to tell Quan. I put my hands up in the air as to say, "Well?! Can I help y'all with something?" Chics knew the deal and they knew my temper so they turned around right quick cause they did not want to fight. After the shower me and Sam planned to just chill on my patio. My dad still was Sam's man but he liked Q and he wouldn't be going for me messing with the 2 of them. So Samir would have to stay outside hidden in the back with me. My mom was sitting on the deck eating ice cream when me and Samir came out with our bowls of ice cream too. She cleared her throat.

"Look what the cat drug in? That don't look like Q Diamond?" I sucked my teeth.

"Ill! Oh boy, I know what Q look like Ma. Me and Samir are just friends, is that O.k?" She sucked her teeth right back at me.

"Fine Diamond. I was just playing with you anyway, touchy touchy." Her phone was ringing.

"Let me get that." Her and her ice cream jumped up and she mushed Samir on her way inside.

"Yeah ight Ma!" He laughed at her. She closed the doors and the blinds to give us privacy. Me and Samir sat on my deck and ate our ice cream sundaes. Well, we fed each other ice cream sundaes and shared some French kisses as well. It was like 9:30 at night and I had my cordless outside and it rang. I picked up with a fake sleep voice.

"Hello." It was Tahir.

"Now you know you not sleep so cut the crap." I played it off.

"No Keisha I'm not sleep but I got company can I call you back?" Tahir whispered,

"Oh is Quan there?" I lied.

"Yes he is."

"O.k. cool call me later." I was thinking, I am going to get this off. Sam would never tell Tahir that we were seeing each other because he went with his sister Tahira. Tahir knew that Sam would tell Q if he seen me cheating so he kept our fling on the low and Q, well he would just remain clueless. Hmm. I was the top player, well so I thought. Anyway me and Samir just continued to sit there and enjoyed each other's company when my phone rang again. This time it was Q. I couldn't brush him off, so I answered the phone in the sleepy voice again.

"Wake up! I haven't talked to my baby all day." So I started talking to him and Sam was kissing me softly on my neck. He then started sucking on my neck trying to put a hickey on me. So I jumped and made a little yelp noise and walked to the edge of the patio.

"D, are you O.k.?" I yawned.

"Fine Q just tired is all."

"It sounds like you outside." I fake yawned again.

"No I'm not. I'm in the bed, but my windows are wide open, so I can get some fresh air in here, so maybe you hear the traffic outside." Samir came up behind me and tried to suck on the same spot and said softly,

"Man say bye." I pushed him back and looked at him with my eyes big and my finger over my mouth to tell him to Shh! Q screamed, "Who was that Diamond?!"

"The uh TV Q." He sighed.

"O.k. baby, you know what, you tired, go back to sleep. Goodnight, love you." I was shaking uncontrollably.

"Me too, good night." I hung up the phone. I looked at Sam and sucked my teeth.

"What the hell are you doing?" He grabbed me by my waist.

"Man fuck Q! You still mine no matter what you say!" I sighed and tried to pull away.

"Come on Sam, don't start that shit. You wouldn't like it if I did that to you and you was on the phone with Tahira." Between him pecking on my lips he said,"I wouldn't care. I wear the pants." I looked at him.

"But still..." He put his finger over my mouth.

"My bad D, ight?" He leaned in and kissed me. Yes I got weak and forgave him that quick. In the next fifteen minutes, me and Samir were kissing heavily and he was letting his fingers explore my insides when all of the sudden I heard yelling from the front. It was Starr voice.

"What up Q? I think Diamond in the house sleep." She knew where we were. Q slammed his car door.

"No I don't think so." Sam scattered and jumped over the side of the deck and went up the other side of the house. I heard Q's footsteps coming towards the back of the house down my driveway. I just sat there and ate my melted ice cream. Quan got to the deck and yelled out, "Ah-ha!" I jumped pretending that he scared me.

"What are you doing here?" He said real sassy, "I thought your ass was in the bed?" I had on my PJ short set luckily.

"I was. It was hot so after I hung up with you, I went to pee, came downstairs, got some ice cream and decided to sit out on my deck, and look at the stars, like I always do. You know that is something I like to do." I started guilt tripping him.

"I can't believe that you didn't believe me, and who do you think you are circling my house like you the damn police?" He started stuttering.

"I I I'm so... s... sorry Diamond, I just thought uh

soo.. someone was uh here. I know I heard a voice D, I'm not stupid, and it sounded like Samir. I got a few calls that you and Samir were buddy/buddy at the shower and y'all was planning on seeing each other tonight." I screamed, "What!?" He started up the deck stairs.

"I'm sorry baby that I didn't trust you, but its not you that I don't trust, its him." He walked completely up my stairs to the deck and sat down.

"Forgive me baby?" I yelled, "Hell no! How can I, and you don't trust me? I told you that voice was the TV. I had the volume on like 2 so I don't know how the hell you heard me watching TV. I had Boyz N Da Hood playing in the VCR and who the hell was telling you all that b/s about me and Samir? I guess Samir and Dough Boy from Boyz N Da Hood sound the same huh? I mean damn me and him had a conversation at the shower but that was it. People got us walking down the aisle. You know just as well as everybody else that we still speak. And I assumed you didn't have a problem with that. Mother fuckers are so nosey, I swear." He ignored my question and looked at the table.

"Um Diamond? Whose bowl is that?" I had to think fast cause it was Samir's bowl.

"It is my mother's bowl, she is the one that was out here first so when she saw me in the kitchen she asked me to come outside to join her. She went in the house to answer her phone, so I guess she right in the kitchen running her mouth. Do you want to go in there and ask her, feel free?" (I knew my mother would cover for me at all costs even though she hated to do it and she would lecture me after the fact). He picked up a spoonful of ice cream from my bowl.

"No D, it's alright, can I share some ice cream with you though?" He put it in his mouth. I thought, Ill! Samir just ate off that spoon. I snatched the spoon from his mouth.

"Hell no Q, you can go home though, I am a little pissed with you right now." He stood up.

"You pissed with me? I'm pissed with you, I'm trying

to believe you, so don't make me more mad." I looked at him with disbelief, jumped up and ran to the sliding glass door.

"Ma! Ma! Come here please." She was in the kitchen on the phone with Aunt Debra. She came to the sliding doors and opened the blinds then the door.

"What Diamond? Why you yelling my name like I'm your child?" I pointed at Q.

"Can you please tell Q that we was out here together earlier." She covered the mouthpiece of the phone.

"Hey Q! How are you? Yeah me and Miss Stank Attitude was sitting out there earlier. Anything else?" I snapped my fingers at Q.

"No, thanks." She went back in the doors.

"Well y'all leave me alone now, I'm gossiping." She smiled and closed the door back, but left the blinds open. I walked up into Q's face.

"Thank you very much, and now that I proved my point, good night!" I got the bowls of the table and walked through the sliding glass doors and slid them closed right in Q's face. He was still standing there so I closed the vertical blinds. I was standing in the kitchen holding my heart, thinking, that was to close for comfort. My mother looked at me, rolled her eyes and shook her head slowly back and forth. She began to whisper to Aunt Debra how I almost got caught. I placed the bowls in the sink and left the kitchen to avoid the lecture. I was wondering which hating ass bitch told about me and Samir. I would find out and probably get suspended on Monday. Danny and Starr were sitting on her steps and that was lucky for me. I knew at that instance that I could no longer creep with Samir. The kissing did get me hot and horny but it was not worth it. I went to the front door and peeked through the window to watch Q pull off. Once he was gone I went outside and sat on my stairs. Samir was sitting with Starr and Danny. He came back across the street and sat down.

"That was close huh D?" I looked at him.

"Real close. Sam I can't do this to Q, we can be friends but no physical O.k?" He licked his lips.

"I respect that D." He touched my inner thigh. I pushed his hand away.

"Come on Samir, don't do that." He sucked his teeth. "O.k. D, but damn, you got me all hot and heated and now you talking about no physical." I sighed.

"Don't say it like that Sam? I'm going in the house now O.k?" I got up to walk in the house and he grabbed my arm to pull me back down.

"My bad D, can I see you tomorrow?" I sighed.

"Dag Samir, did you hear what I just said? Maybe Sam, we will see. If you a good little boy." He smiled.

"I'll be your good little boy." I stood up and watched Samir go down the stairs. As Samir got to the bottom off my steps, Q came back around the corner as I was turning the knob to go in the house. He pulled over and jumped out. Samir just kept walking across the street, but I emerged from my porch and came down the stairs to meet him. Q ran up on me.

"Diamond what's this? Tell me what's up?" I said softly, "What's up with what?" He screamed.

"You and him!" Samir just kept going across the street and sat with his sister and Danny. The louder he talked the softer I talked. I placed my hands on my hips.

"I told you nothing right? When I watched you pull off, I came to tell Starr what happened with bitches talking about the shower and he came over here. You know what Q I'm finished. Please just go away, go home or something." I went to walk back up my stairs to go in my house. He ran up my stairs behind me and grabbed my arm.

"No fuck that!" Q's back was to the Mitchell's house but when he grabbed my arm he twirled me around. I looked at Sam stand up to see what was going on. Q turned and followed my glance and yelled.

"Yo, mind your mother fucking business." Sam yelled back.

"What nigga?" I screamed and waved my free arm towards Samir.

"Sam please! Just... don't worry about it." Q grabbed my face.

"D you still fucking him ain't you?" I smacked his hand down.

"What? Hell no! What I look like!" He looked me up and down and twirled me around.

"With those short ass shorts on and that little nothing ass tank top you got on, you don't want me to answer that. And I can't tell you ain't still fucking with him. He standing up like he is ready to defend your honor." I yanked my arm from his grip.

"What the fuck you trying to say Q? These are my pajamas and they can be skimpy if I want them to be. If I want to be at my house naked I can be. Nobody invited you over here. You popped up and I told you that Samir is my friend and that is all, if you and any other nigga is grabbing on me, like they stupid, you think he not going to say something on my behalf?!" He paced back and forth on the next to top step.

"You right, a friend should do that, especially friends that are fucking, let me go over here and get this shit straight right now!" Q went running down my stairs and across the street. I ran after him to try to stop him before this turned ugly but too late, he got over there.

"Yo, Samir you fucking my girl?" Samir smirked at him.

"Your girl? Nigga, that's my girl. Always has been. Always will be." I got over there.

"Samir! Please don't make matters worse. Just ignore him please." Q asked, "So D, it's like that?" I grabbed Q's arm.

"Like what? You know I am his girl, his girl meaning his peoples. Me and Samir are just friends, I just told you that, stop making a scene please." Samir just laughed to piss Q off. Q looked me up and down.

"Yeah his girl meaning just his peoples my ass!" He

turned back to Q.

"I don't see shit funny nigga, if I find out about you and my girl doing anything, you better watch your back." Starr interrupted.

"Be easy Q, it's not that serious. Diamond is your girl. Her and Sam just cool, that's all. Diamond loves you." She turned up her lip at Samir.

"Samir shut the hell up! Diamond is not your girl, like you mean. Stop starting shit, you make me fucking sick. Wait until Tahira call." Samir sucked his teeth.

"Fuck you Starr. Wasn't nobody talking to you or asking you shit. And what you mean wait till Tahira call, yeah that's my wife and?" Q cut in.

"Well nigga since Tahira is your wife, leave mines alone, you've been warned!" He went to walk away but then pointed at my kitty kat.

"This here is mine and I don't want you no where around her or it, if I see you around her or even here that you was, it's on!" Q grabbed my wrist.

"Come on!" He began to lead me back across the street but before we got to the curb Sam got mad.

"Who you threatening nigga? I guess its on then cause I was just with her. Just now before you pulled up. Why don't you look at her neck for evidence, so now what? What you gonna do tough guy?" I looked down as Q looked at my neck. He ran up the stairs and hooked off on Samir who was in the process of coming down the stairs. Sam fell back but they still started fighting on the porch. Danny broke it up. Q looked at me again and then at my neck and sure as my name is Diamond, Samir had put a hickey on my neck. Q shook his head slow.

"Diamond you got it. It's over. Don't fucking call me no more. You be with Samir who will cheat on your dumb ass again. I don't have time for this shit." I pulled at his shirt and almost hit my knees.

"Wait Q, let me explain, it's not what you think!" He turned and faced me.

"Bitch!(the first time he ever called me out my

name) you got a hickey on your neck that I know I didn't put there. Now how you gonna explain that? I think you and I are finished, no matter of fact I know you and I are finished." I put my hands on his shoulders.

"No Q, wait! Samir please, fix this." Samir waved his hand towards Samir.

"Fuck him! I'm not fixing shit Diamond! You shouldn't do shit you can't tell the truth about and the truth is we were just together and I put a hickey on your neck!" I thought of a quick lie. I got up in Samir's face and put my fingers in his face as well.

"The truth is you came over to my house earlier and asked me can we talk and I said yeah and we were in my den and when you didn't get the answers you wanted to hear you grabbed me and put the hickey on my neck. I told you not to play like that but you had to play games, you know what..." I lunged for Samir and Starr jumped in it. Danny pulled Starr off Samir and then me off him. Samir straightened his clothes.

"Y'all bitches is crazy, and that's not all Q, I also..." And Starr was on him again. Danny was breaking them up again but Q didn't stick around. He just started walking towards his car. When I noticed I ran passed him and jumped in the driver seat of his car. He opened the door.

"Move Diamond. I swear to God, you better move. Go be with your man. Do I look dumb to you?" I had to put my academy award winning performance on and start acting. I grabbed the steering wheel tight.

"Move me Q if you want me moved. Cause I'm not moving. You gonna come around here like you Inspector Gadget and not even let me explain. Yes you found out shit I wanted to keep from you, but I did that to keep you from fucking Samir up. Baby you know Samir is an asshole and yeah he put a hickey on my neck and he did it so he could break us up. That's what he told me he wanted to do. How could I call you and say Q, Sam put a hickey on my neck. The first thing that you would have said was why did you let him in, so to keep the peace I didn't say shit. I was aggravated and when you called I was in the process of trying to throw him out. After we hung up he left and then that's when I went outside to tell my mother what happened and ask her opinion but then her phone rang and she left me outside...I'm your girl and you gonna believe that lying ass nigga over me? Is you fucking crazy?! I don't want him cause I got you Q. If I wanted him I would be with him. I can't lie he do be trying to get me to creep with him but I tell him no all the time. Me and him speak to keep the peace. I told you when I watched you pull off and I saw Starr outside, I came out to tell her about the gossiping bitches at the shower and before I could go over there, he came over here (by this time my voice was cracking cause I was about to cry) talking about the same shit, when you gonna let me hit that and I said never and then I told him what was said at the shower, and of course he laughed cause that is what he wants, for us not to be together. I don't fuck with him, I didn't kiss him, and I damn sure wouldn't allow him to put a hickey on me. When I looked earlier it was nothing there. I didn't want to tell you to get you all worked up and beefing over that nobody. He said that shit about us being together to get on your nerves. I'm telling you we were together but not like that. But when you leave its on. I know you don't believe me even though you have no reason not too. But Q baby, I would never cheat on you. I'm not Yah-Yah. But you believe what you want to believe. I will move and let you go." As I started to get out, he said, "Good." I stayed in the car at that point.

"No fuck that Q, I'm not letting you go that easy. You're my man and I expect you to believe me when I say something." He didn't say shit except, "No I'm not your man. You finished yet, I got things to do?" The tears came to my eyes.

"Why are you doing this? Why you believe him over me Q?" He pulled my arm to get me out of the car.

"Cause he don't have no reason to lie Diamond. It all fits. Niggas lie but I know Samir not lying this time. I feel it in my bones." Danny came across the street and added his two cents.

"Yo Q, I'm not getting in your relationship or your business but Samir is lying. I'm saying, D has been telling me for a while that Samir be trying to get with her and I told her just ignore him. When you left Diamond came out to the front. Samir was in the house until he heard Starr yell out to you. I mean he is my nigga but she is my sister and right is right." He gave Danny a pound.

"Ight Danny, thanks." Danny looked at me as the tears kept flowing. Danny left on that note.

"Ight then y'all be safe. D, call me later." He went in his house. The twins were still sitting there arguing over me but I was too upset to hear them. I got out the car slowly.

"Q I love you. I thought me and Samir could be friends but I guess not. You are the one Q. Please don't do this. Don't break up with me. I want to be with you and only you Q." At that time the guilt ran over me. I started hugging Q as he was getting in the car and wouldn't let him go.

"Please hug me back Q." He wouldn't budge. It reminded me of the time with me and Samir and how I wouldn't budge, but I finally gave in to Samir, but Q didn't to me. I wiped my eyes.

"So this is how it ends?" He wouldn't look me in my face.

"Look Diamond give me time to think O.k. cause frankly I can't keep competing with this cat. I'm leaving soon and it will be just you and him. If I can't trust you while I'm 5 minutes away, how can I trust you when I'm 4 hours away?" He got in his car. I yelled at him.

"You can trust me 24 hours away Q!" Before he pulled off he said, "Don't call me D, I'll call you." And that was it. I saw fire in my eyes. I went back over there to the twins.

"Samir why would you say something like that?! I'm not gonna argue with you but just remember payback is a bitch and you know this." I walked back across the street. I wasn't in my room more then ten minute before I was calling Q still apologizing. He kept answering with an attitude.

"O.k. Diamond, I heard you the first 100 times. But I gotta go." He hung up. I kept calling him back until he just took the phone off the hook and it rang busy. I was in my room crying and praying that God wouldn't take Q from me. You never miss your water until your well runs dry and right now I was dehydrated.

CHAPTER 24
THE BLOW, THE PROM, AND PILGRIMS

So the next day, I got up early as hell and I called Q. The phone was still ringing busy so I knew he still had it off the hook and was still sleeping. I also knew on most Sundays him and his friends got up early to play basketball. I decided to try to catch him before he left so I showered and got dressed. I walked that almost hour walk to his house in Curryville (Another section of Union) and rang the bell at like 8:30 AM. Why does it take 5 minutes to drive somewhere and an hour to walk there? His mom answered the door.

"Hey Diamond! To what do I owe this surprise?" We walked in the kitchen and I sat down and started crying right away. She hugged me.

"What is it? What's wrong?" Q came down half way down the stairs.

"Yo Mom who was at the door?"

"Diamond." He sucked his teeth and responded nasty.

"Well what did she want?" She sucked her teeth.

"I don't know Q, why don't you come in here and ask her?" He exclaimed, "That's ight, I'm good! Make sure she leave when you do." He ran back upstairs. She looked at me and handed me a tissue. She smiled.

"Trouble in paradise?" I cried, "Yes." I told her the fabricated story. She shook her head.

"Diamond, I don't know what to tell you. You know that being friends with Samir would cause problems between you and Quan cause they are rivals and both crazy over you." I blew my nose.

"I know Ma, but Samir ain't wrapped to tight, so to

221

keep the peace, I'm nice to him." She got me some more tissue.

"I don't like to get in the middle of your relationship so all I can say is try to go talk to him. If he don't want to talk, then I can't make him. But give him time, he will come around. I have to go back to work now to cover someone's shift. I just ran home to take a shower and I am on my way back to the hospital. Are you going to be O.k.?" I shrugged and wiped my eyes.

"I guess." She patted my shoulder.

"Well be strong, I gotta run so I am not late. Call me at work if you need me." I slowly went up the stairs and went in Quan's room. He was in the shower and I just sat on his bed. He walked back in the room with his towel wrapped around his bottom and looked at me and didn't say anything. I started the convo.

"Hey Q!" He sat down on the other side of his bed silently and put his lotion on. I repeated myself.

"I said hey Q!" He didn't even look up. He just went on putting his socks on. I got up and went around the bed and sat next to him. He didn't even look at me. He just got up and went to his underwear drawer and got out a pair of boxer shorts. He put them on under his towel and then took the towel off. He put his deodorant on and I watched him move around the room like I was a ghost that wasn't there. I begged, "Q please say something." He took a white t-shirt out of his drawer.

"Ight, does your man know you're here?" I started tearing.

"Q, you're my man." He laughed and threw the t-shirt on his bed. I wiped my tears.

"What's so funny?" He laughed harder.

"That joke you just told." I pleaded with him.

"Q please, can we talk." He walked over to his stereo, looked at me and replied, "Nope!" He flicked a rap tape playing I Get Around by Tupac on with the volume on ten. I walked over to turn the radio down and he snatched my hand down. I went to try again and he twisted my arm behind my back.

"Don't ever touch my stuff!" He flung me backwards.

"Q, why are you acting like this?" He mocked me.

"Q, why are you acting like this?" I walked towards his bedroom door.

"Maybe I should leave!" He repeated me.

"Maybe I should leave!" I screamed.

"Q!" He screamed.

"Q!"

"I'm leaving!" And he repeated that as well. I ran down the stairs and opened the door. I slammed it as if I went out but I didn't. I hid by the kitchen entrance and he came running down the stairs and snatched the door open. I said from behind him.

"Looking for me?" He turned around and couldn't help but smirk.

"No I wasn't, I was looking for my mother. Why are you still here?" I smiled and walked towards him.

"You want me to leave?" He didn't smile and put on his serious face.

"Yes!" He opened the front door up wider. I sniffled.

"You serious Q?" He just looked at me and at the door. My smile faded and I began to walk to the front door slowly with my head hung low. I felt this was it. I gave it all I could and now I was walking out on my future. The tears were flowing in a steady stream down my face. As soon as I got to the door he slammed it closed so I couldn't leave. He looked at me and I looked down. He grabbed my chin and made me look at him. I wiped my eyes.

"Q, I wouldn't..." He put his finger over my mouth to Shh! me. He pushed me up against the front door and stared at me. We looked at each other for what seemed like hours but it wasn't more then a minute in reality. Then he kissed me. It was a sensuous kiss that made my draws melt. I felt that it was my womanly duty to drop to my knees and handle my business. He still had on his boxer shorts. I kissed him on his neck and worked my way down his chest until I was face to face with his erect penis that was peeking through the hole on his boxer shorts. I pulled them down and I just started sucking on it like I was an old hoe, not like it was my first time. I guess it felt good cause Q was moaning, "Yeah Diamond, just like that!" He rubbed my hair and pushed the back of my head inward to put his penis deeper in my throat. I thought, I want to throw up but then I thought, no I don't I will do anything to keep my man. When he was ready to blow he pushed my head back and the cum squirted on the outside of my throat instead of on the inside of my throat. My jaws were so sore and I didn't want to swallow. He helped me up and led me up to his bedroom. He flicked on the other side of the tape player and If loving you is all that I can do by Mary J. Blige poured from the speakers. Of course he did me next and we had the best sex we ever had at that moment. I climbed on top of him and rode him backwards. He grabbed my hips and directed me in the way he wanted me to ride him. I held his ankles while I bounced up and down like a pogo stick. He worked me so good I experienced my first tear. Yes, I was young but I loved this man so much that the thought of loosing him bought tears to my eyes. I realized at this point that I really loved Q. That was the silent language of us being back together. All week I was like white on rice on Q. If he moved I was on his heels. I didn't look at Samir or say anything to him. I was being a good little girlfriend, being submissive. Whatever Q said went.

If we were in the caf and he said,"Diamond go get my lunch!" I did it. I didn't question anything he said that week. He could have said, "Diamond push my car cause the battery died," and I would have been out there in my shoe boots and dress pants pushing. So once Friday came, I didn't go to school because underclassmen were not given a half-day like the seniors to get ready for the prom. If you were an under classmen and was going, you either had to take the day off or get ready after 2:39 when that final bell rang. My dress was all ready. This designer Toiya made it. She was owner of Sesa's Fashions. She could sew her ass off. My dress was off the hook. It was just a

Sesa's original. Our colors were black and gold. I had skin showing in many places. Toiya even made my bag and had my shoes covered to match my dress perfectly. Fuck it yo, I was all that and so was Q. We were the best looking ones, if I have to say so myself. My dress got voted best dress and this wasn't even my prom. You know some of the seniors were heated but ooh well.

My hair was done up in an up sweep, compliments of Krystal and she did my make up too. I had gotten my feet, nails, and eyebrows done the day before at Krystal nails. I'm not even gonna front, I was nervous right before the prom because in my town all the kids going to the prom go down to the center of town to Central Six, remember my 6th grade school? and show off their outfits and cars. Starr helped me get dressed saying she was jealous cause she wanted to go. I mean a lot of seniors asked her but do you think Danny was letting that go down? I don't think so.

Quan picked me up at 6. He was driving his mother's black on black 430 Benz that just fit our whole look, which was classy. His mother followed him to my house in his civic. I think she was nervous about him driving her baby. When I came out his tongue almost fell out of his mouth. My father went over and whispered something to Q. When I where on our way Q told me my dad told him to basically keep his hands to himself. My dad thought I was his innocent little girl. Ha! My parents allowed me to go to Wildwood, NJ (the shore) for the weekend because everybody was going. Even the underclassmen. Starr, Danny, Samir, the whole town was going. So we went to the center of town, and it wasn't as bad as I thought it would be. You see everybody from kindergarten up to senior citizens were looking you and your date over. Of course, I played the non-nervous roll but I was really shitting bricks. After that we went to the actual prom. It was fun but not as fun as mines was gonna be with all my peoples I was graduating with. Let me tell y'all I looked much better then Yah-Yah. Her corny stank dick sucking ass (I'm one to talk about dick sucking, hush we have all done it once or twice, some of us love to do it and if you not then your man is probably cheating on you, just jokes.)

Anyway, she wore a cheap red dress that looked like some shit you see hanging in the window downtown Newark and she had on bright red lipstick. She looked a hot mess. Dumb bitch! Sorry I caught a flash back of when I beat her ass down. Anyway she took some 9th grade guy to the prom. She was such a low life. She was trying to sneak peeks at Q all night and when she would look I would grab his face and kiss him and dance with him all close. I was going to say something like, "well bitch", but Q asked me not too. In Wildwood we were all cooling. It is nothing but a big fuck fest after the prom. It was so much trifling shit going on in Wildwood. Everybody was getting drunk and smoking weed. Niggas acting stupid mooning people. You can tell folks that ain't never been nowhere or never been away from their parents. Anyway all in all it was cool but you know Samir was hating on me and Q especially at night when we would close our hotel door:

Well, the next Wednesday after the prom I was sitting at the table eating cereal before school and the downstairs phone rang. My mother picked it up.

"Hello? Well hello Miss, hold on. Diamond Starr is on this phone for you, must be a fashion emergency for her to call my phone." I got up and snatched the phone.

"What's up sis?" She exhaled.

"Diamond I'm pregnant." I spit out the milk and cereal that was in my mouth all over the table and floor and screamed, "What?" My mother yelled,

"Diamond what's wrong? What happened?" I jumped up.

"Nothing. Starr is telling me what happened last night on the Lifetime Movie." My mother screamed, "You spit all that shit out for that? Girl clean this up."

"O.k. One second." I whispered in the phone.

"Starr I will call you right back." I dashed up to my room, all the while my mother yelling, "Diamond get back here!" I was thinking, she gonna have to wait a minute. I picked up my phone in my room and hit speed dial 1 to call to her house. Starr picked up sniffling cause she was crying. I breathed out tired from running up the stairs.

"Now you what?" She repeated herself.

"Diamond I told you I'm pregnant."

"Pregnant?! How did that happen?" She sighed.

"Diamond? How do you think?" I sucked my teeth.

"I know how but I mean how could you let this happen? What is the matter with you girl?" She cried more.

"D please. I didn't think I could get pregnant cause we didn't use a condom just 1 time." I sucked my teeth again.

"Starr please! You sound like one of them dizzy bitches, you know just once is all it takes." She sniffled.

"D please don't yell and be mad at me, not right now." I quickly counted to ten in my head.

"I'm sorry Starr but I am just a little upset right now." She screamed, "Diamond you're upset! How do you think I feel? What am I going to do?"

"What do you mean what are you going to do? You are going to get an abortion." She cried,

"I'm scared to get one D." I got an instant attitude.

"Well have it then Starr, Danny already got Gina for a baby mother what's wrong with having one more?" She sucked her teeth now getting annoyed with my sarcasm.

"Come on D, I'm scared to have a baby too."

"Well look those are your 2 options, keep it or get rid of it, you gotta do what you gotta do. Did you tell Danny yet?" She sighed.

"No I don't want him to get mad." I screamed,

"What?! Get mad?! It took 2 of y'all to do that. Ooohhh, that is why you haven't been feeling good…well you know what you gotta do. We going to Howard next year and you can't take a baby with you. Are you ready to be a mother?" She screamed, "No!"

"Well then call Pilgrims (a popular abortion clinic in Montclair, NJ), and make an appointment so you can handle that." So many girls at school had been to Pilgrims but I never thought either one of us would have to go. She was still crying.

"O.k. I will call." My mother was still down stairs yelling.

"Let me go clean up this mess. I will see you in a little bit." I ran down and cleaned off the table while my mother went off on me.

"You don't listen Diamond and if I am calling you, I don't give a damn what Lifetime played last night you better respond to me understood?" I threw the dishcloth in the sink.

"Yes Ma." I kissed her on the cheek, grabbed my book bag and ran out the door. Me and Starr met up outside to walk to school. She was still teary eyed.

"The appointment is for Saturday." I put my arm around her.

"Well you gotta tell Danny so we can go." She sighed.

"D I don't want him there." I sucked my teeth.

"Oh yes you do so tell him or I will." She bit her bottom lip nervously.

"O.k. I will." When she told Danny he told her he wanted her to keep it. She told me maybe she should and I told her maybe not and we going to Pilgrims. So Saturday came and the 3 of us went. When we got there it was all these people outside picketing saying, "Don't kill your baby we can help you." We pushed our way through and I covered Starr's ears.

"Sis don't listen!" Once inside she had to get blood work and other things done. Come to find out she was almost 3 months pregnant. The procedure was going to be $315.00 and all I could think of is that I was glad we all worked so we could pool our funds together and get it done. She had to wait until next Saturday to have the procedure done. I was mad cause that was the day me and my dad were suppose to go car shopping. I was going to have to think of a lie of why I was leaving so early on a Saturday morning. I had told them for this Saturday we were all going to IHOP (International House of Pancakes) to use coupons from school that were going to expire, but damn I couldn't use that same excuse next week. My dad would say, "I thought they expired last week." During the next week, Danny tried to convince Starr to keep it and every argument he had for why she should I had 2 for why she shouldn't. That Friday night I spent the night at Danny's to not get the third degree cause Aunt Debra left for work early on Saturdays. And Starr's dad went into the city to work every Saturday and you know Krystal did hair so she was up and gone with the birds. So Saturday morning came and we were on our way. Starr was shaking uncontrollably in the car from her nervousness. When we got there the same people were outside picketing. When we got through the first door Starr froze. It was stairs to go up but she couldn't move. I pushed her.

"Come on sis the sooner you go up the sooner it is over." She cried.

"I can't do this." I encouraged her and pushed her in her back.

"Yes you can!" She cried harder.

"No I can't." Danny rubbed her hair.

"Boo if you don't want to you don't have too." I screamed, "Ooh Danny shut the fuck up! You already having one and my friend ain't fucking up her life for you. Come on Starr!" I pulled her by her arm up the stairs and through her sobs she got up them stairs. Danny had his arm around her in the waiting room and I signed her in. When they called her name she went up there and he went with her. They talked to a social worker first that explained that she didn't have to do it but through her cries she said, "Yes I do." So he came back out into the lobby, while she went to have the procedure done. We fell asleep in the packed lobby until we heard, "Starr Mitchell's ride please come downstairs for pick up." When we got down there she could barley stand. The doctor gave me her prescription and told me what she had to do. I told Danny to drop me off and take her to the Garden State Motel (the cheapest one around us) for a little while cause she could not go home like that. My dad was waiting for me to go car shopping. We went to like 10 different places before I saw my car. It was a "1992 5 speed black Mazda MX-3" it had my name all over it and my dad got it for me. My dad said, "I hope you pass your driving test and get your license Monday." I smiled at my new car.

"Don't worry about me I will!"

CHAPTER 25
I GOT IT

Monday, my seventeenth birthday came and I got my license on the first try. I didn't want a party or nothing else except my car and my license and since Saturday I got my car, I knew Monday I had to get my licenses and I did. My dad took me to Motor Vehicle and took all the credit. I don't know why since he paid for me to take driving lessons so he didn't have to bust a blood vessel yelling at me for dumb stuff. My car was a 5-speed stick shift, so I was learning from my dad how to drive a stick, which was a big change from an automatic. I caught on quick because I wanted to drive my car and get rid of my annoying father. He was not a good teacher at all. His patience were too short for me. My mother was mad that I got a stick because that meant she couldn't drive my car. I loved the ring of that, "my car" because she didn't know how to drive a stick. Why do parents have their own cars but always want to drive their kids cars? Drive your own. My mother had a brand new 1993 black on black pathfinder and said, "No way José" when I asked her if I could use her truck to practice. Instead she wanted me to practice on my fathers 1992 maroon big boy Lexus. Which I didn't mind whipping, but my father was a nervous wreck when I practiced the first time and that's why I went through Ace driving school. He said, "Crash those piece of shits they have cause you wont crash up my baby!"

"I thought I was your baby, Daddy!" Guilt tripping him. He replied, "You are pumpkin, that's why daddy is going to buy you your own car for your birthday." I was excited after that and said to myself, I have to pass now. And he kept his promise, he bought my car and I got my license. My mother never came out with me to practice, because she said she was to young to die. Great vote of confidence Mom. Tahir bought me some diamond studs that he gave me on my birthday and I only said, "Thank you" and kissed him on the cheek. He wanted more but I'm not like that. The last few days of my junior year I was whipping my car to school. Me and Starr were chilling. She was still in shock about the abortion but she knew she had made the right choice. When we got home from school on our last day of our junior year, me and Starr found out we got accepted to Howard. That was the best news I had ever heard. For those of you that are slow it is Howard University in Washington, DC. We both came home and our moms were sitting in my kitchen. When we walked in they both had their hands out with the envelopes. One addressed to Starr and one addressed to me. My mother yelled, "Open it!" I took it and looked at it and Starr did the same. I said, "Well they are kind of thick, that means something good I think." Starr's hands were shaking. She looked at me.

"Well you go first, I'm nervous."

"We will go at the same time. Ready? 1,2,3..." We both skimmed the letter and screamed, "We got accepted!" Our mothers were hugging us saying they were so proud then Krystal started tearing.

"Our babies are leaving us!" We just looked at each other like ooh boy. That night both our families went out to celebrate the good news. Me and Samir were cool so the dinner wasn't awkward. And you know Aunt Debra and Danny came so we had a good time. Q was leaving for school in a week and I was getting sad. Georgetown and Howard were not that far from each other but I still had a year of high school to go until I came down there. I hoped our love could stand the test of time. We were having sex everyday to make up for the time he wouldn't be there. When it was time for him to go to basketball camp at school, me and his mother drove him down and stayed in Georgetown for the weekend. I know one thing, it was some cuties at his school. And that was only the athletes that were there. I tried to keep my eyes forward as we helped him with his things to the dorm. The dorms they were staying in were the non-athletic freshman dorms. They had a roommate and were used only for the summer basketball camp. His dorm assignment was at another location that was decked out. Each athlete had their own room and private bathroom. He would be coming home in about a month or so to get the rest of his things and his car. He swore he was going to remain faithful to me but I just couldn't see that happening. He said this at breakfast in front of his mother and she said, "Q don't make promises you can't or won't keep, you know how I am about the truth!" He cut up his pancakes.

"I know Ma, I'm serious." I just remained quiet. On our ride home me and Jackie talked about the future. I told her I hope me and Q could last. She reached over and patted my leg.

"Me too Diamond, put he is young and a male, and I hate to say that because he is my son but some guys ain't shit, excuse my language." I laughed.

"You sound like Daniel Staple cause that is his favorite line." We just laughed and left it at that. All I could do is hope and pray but just incase he went flat I had a few spare tires in Jersey. When I got back from Georgetown, me and Tahir was kicking it more but we still kept it where Samir didn't know. It was easier now that I had a car because I could go see him and nobody knew were I was at. He only lived like 15 minutes away in Linden. It would be times Samir would call Tahir and I would be there. It was funny how I was getting this off. So I thought I was. Tahir was pressuring me to have sex but I said no and I meant no. I told him Q was still my boyfriend and I wasn't cheating on him like that, point blank. One day I called Tahir and he was acting funny, saying, "Well why am I going to keep letting you come here and you fronting on the draws."

"Is that all you want Tahir? A piece of ass?" He exhaled.

"No but damn I've been putting in mad time and doing mad shit for you, how else you gonna show your appreciation?" I sucked my teeth.

"Well I always say thank you, and I don't ask you for anything, you do it on your own." He chuckled.

"Yeah you right, it don't matter cause I got some pussy on the way. So I'll get at you."

"Whatever Tahir..." He hung up. I was steaming and then my phone rang back and I leaped for it thinking it was Tahir but it was Q.

"Hey baby!"

"Hey sweetie!" I know I was a phony bitch, tell me something I don't know. He told me about camp and I just listened. Q was calling me everyday, I guess making sure I wasn't doing nothing on him but, me and Sam were still seeing each other on the side. I'm sorry I couldn't resist. I forgave him for what he did but I didn't forget. Samir was even hitting me off a little with sneakers and money for me to get my hair braided or nails filled in. And all with out me having sex with him. Tahir on the other hand had more dough and he was giving me more stuff cause he could take me out to where ever and buy me Coach bags. We would be in the mall getting stuff from Express and Limited. I was playing both of them. Well so to speak.

The first weekend in August Q was suppose to come home but said he couldn't because of some b/s excuse about camp being extended a week. I just knew it was another chic but I didn't say shit. I knew that the freshman girls were down there already. I wasn't stupid. He told me a while back the freshmen had to come 2 weeks early for all types of classes and orientation. Hey, I was doing me so I figured he might as well do him. But then the following weekend, actually Friday evening, he popped up at my house unannounced and with no warning whatsoever. I was at Tahir's house. My mothers number came up 911 and I called her back from Tahir's phone making sure to block Tahir's number from her Caller ID. That was the good old days when you could block a number and then Bell Atlantic had to go and get all fancy having the feature that people can't block their numbers from Caller ID's anymore. Damn them. But anyway, she said, "Hello!"

"Hey Mom! What's up? You beeped me 911?"

"Hold on Diamond!" Q got on the phone.

"Hey D, where you at?" I stuttered.

"Uh uh huh?" I was scared as hell. He repeated himself.

"I'm at your house, where you at?" I played it cool.

"Ooh I am at Keisha's, I will be there in a minute." I hung up. I started putting my sneakers on.

"Tahir I gotta go, Q is home." He sucked his teeth.

"Bye! Run to your little boyfriend, but you made me rent Beat Street and Krush Grooving for nothing?! I didn't want to see this bullshit you did, but now you leaving?" I picked up my keys from the end table.

"Tahir what do you want me to do?" I went in my pocket and threw a 10-dollar bill at him.

"For your troubles!" I smiled and winked at him. He turned his mouth up to the side and   put the ten in his pocket. I laughed and left. Q was sitting in the den watching ESPN when I came in. I made it home in record time. I was so happy to see him and jumped on his lap, hugged him and kissed him on the cheek. He tickled me.

"Did you miss me?" I laughed.

"And you know it!" He returned my kiss on the cheek.

"D why don't you come down to the school for the weekend to help me move in?" I didn't want to go because me and Tahir was supposed to go paintballing on Saturday and Sunday me and Samir was suppose to go to the city to Time Square to get our picture drawn, but you know being a girlfriend in a long distance relationship called for sacrifices so I thought fast.

"O.k. Q let me ask my mother." I was going to say she said, "no" but guess what? He held my hand.

"I already asked her and she said yes!" I smiled and clenched my teeth.

"Great!" In my mind I said, "Shit!" But I called Grey Hound and ordered a 1-way ticket to get back from

Georgetown. A few hours later, me and Q were on our way to Georgetown. He lived in a coed dorm so it didn't matter who came in and out on the first days. They didn't I.D. people. It was nice taking a road trip with him, but helping him move all his stuff into his dorm was not the move. We got there like midnight and he wanted to move most of the stuff in then. I pouted.

"Oh no Q, I will not break a nail. I will carry the light stuff!" I had on tight guess jeans and a little guess t-shirt and you know guys was outside hanging around looking and he was getting mad at me. He slammed the trunk closed.

"Diamond un tuck your shirt." I put one hand on my hip. "If I un tuck it, it still wont cover my butt Q, it's a damn baby doll tee, I'm yours O.k., I'm not thinking about these other cats. Here we go with the trust issue." He sighed.

"No you right, I'm sorry. I just don't want them looking." I laughed.

"Newsflash Q, you go with a dime, no bump that a fifty cent piece! They will look on my worst day!" He laughed and handed me a light bag.

"Ooh boy! I must have the most conceited girl in New Jersey!" I smacked my cheeks.

"Maybe in the world Q!" We both laughed. Then a few of his boys from the team came over and introduced themselves to me and said they would help him move in if I bought some friends back that look like me. Q commented, "Well she don't have that many friends, and none look like her, I got the best!" I got an attitude.

"You crazy boy, but my sister and my other girls is on my level!" He agreed about Starr.

"Yeah Starr is, I won't front on that but some are not, lets leave it at that!" I put my hands on my hips.

"Are you saying some of my girls are ugly?" He adjusted the bag on his shoulder.

"I didn't say it, you did!" We all laughed and the one cute boy Dre said, "Well leave the monsters at home but bring Starr and the other cuties with you next time." I smiled.

"I will try." They started taking the TV, VCR, and other stuff up the stairs. Once we got all the things upstairs, we came down to run and get something to eat. I knew it was a lot of hoochie mama chics on that campus. I was not feeling that. When we came back from McDonalds one yelled out, "Hey Quan!" You would have swore my name was Quan the way I turned around. And it was damn near 3 in the morning so why was all these people outside chilling. She rolled her eyes towards me.

"Hello! But I wasn't talking to you, I was talking to Quan." She said this in a smart tone. I threw my hands in the air.

"What up!" Not asking her how she was doing what up, but what up calling my mans name like y'all together or something. He pulled me along.

"Hey Rashida, this is my wifey Diamond!" She flicked her hand towards me.

"Nice to meet you! BUT ANYWAY, what's up for next week Quan? You going to freshman orientation?" He didn't stop to talk but replied, "Yeah the team gotta go." She yelled at his back, "Well I will see you there! You better believe that." He was in the door.

"Ight." She was trying to play me out and I couldn't let that go down. Then she yelled, "Nice to meet you Cubic Zirconia!" I turned around in the door.

"Ugshida, its Diamond, the rarest and most precious stone to mankind!" She stood up off the wall she was leaning on with her friends.

"It's Rashida!" I began to walk towards her.

"I know what it is bitch. I called you Ug-shida. Cause you're not cute!" She started walking up on me.

"What bitch, I'll fuck you up!" I started taking off my jewelry.

"Q, hold my earrings!" He grabbed me up with the food in his right hand and my collar in his left.

"Hell no! Rashida get out of here with that dumb shit, I'm not messing with you, don't disrespect my girl like that. Go head with all that nonsense." She stopped in her tracks.

"What Q, she started it." He waved his food filled hand at her.

"Whatever. Come on Diamond!" He let my collar go and snatched my arm. I turned around and stuck my tongue out at her. She was steaming and when we got in the room I got the third degree. He slammed the food down on his desk.

"You can't keep acting like that Diamond! That fighting, you gotta cut it out, you getting to old for that!"

"Yes Q." I pushed him down on the bed and mounted over him and you know what happened next. When I went home Sunday I was so sad because being away from Q made me realize how much I missed him. He had gotten so much bigger in a month like he was on steroids. I mean his back and abs were all cut up like crunches was his middle name. My baby had it going on and I knew the vultures on the campus knew it too. That is why as soon as I stepped foot into my house that Sunday evening I called Grey Hound and made reservations for the following weekend to go right back down to Georgetown.

CHAPTER 26
GREYHOUND CHIC

So that next Friday I took the Grey Hound to see Q again. I caught a cab to his school because my bus came in early. He was waiting for me outside. It was so many more niggas there because now all the students were there. I wish I would have bought Starr. The moment I saw Q I realized how much I missed him from one week. I gave him a big hug when I got out the cab and some other corny country bama looking bitches was staring. So when I noticed them looking to hard I tongued him down right there in front of them.

"Whoa Diamond can we take this inside you got me all hard and shit." I smiled and stuck my tongue out at him.

"Yes we can. Can you get my bag?" And he nodded, "Yes My Lady." And he did just that. We went in the dorm where everybody had their single rooms. It was Friday afternoon and I was leaving again on Sunday. So we couldn't get in the room good before we were going at it. Damn we had just had sex less then a week ago but still I missed Q a lot. I felt bad about creeping behind his back, not bad enough to leave Samir and Tahir alone but sorta bad. I knew deep down in side that this long distance shit wouldn't work for long and he would be fucking one of these bitches that I thought was a country bama bitch by the end of this school year. Anyway, we had a good weekend except for the run in with the girl Rashida again. She tried to start some thing in the caf where all the athletes and their girls, well the ones with girls, were sitting eating brunch on Sunday, by saying to the old cafeteria aid,

"She don't go here so she not supposed to be in here." But you know the athletes run the school and his boy Dre, with his cute self, stood up.

"Baldie locks mind your business, it's always the

239

ugly bitches trying to start shit. You shouldn't go here cause you to ugly." What she didn't know is that Q paid for me to eat in the caf. It was 10 dollars for non-students. So the cafeteria aid said,"Thank you Miss Informant but she can be in here, she paid to eat and she can." I rolled my eyes and my neck.

"Thank you! Bitch!" Q placed his hand on my shoulder to stop me from getting up.

"Ooh boy here we go!" She slammed her tray down on the table opposite ours.

"Well you the bitch and your man is playing you!" She sat down at the table next to the basketball team. Why she do that? Before I could respond or say anything, 4 of the guys from the basketball team dumped their trays of food on her and she looked stupid. The whole caf was in an uproar laughing at her and I couldn't say nothing. I joined in the laughter while the brutes a.k.a basketball players smacked hands. She ran out the caf looking like a damn fool. After brunch it was time for me to go catch my 3:00 bus back to Jersey. Q took me to the bus station and went in with me to see me off. While we sat side by side and waited on the bus he took my hand in is.

"D please don't cheat on me. I'm doing this college thing for us, me and you." I sucked my teeth.

"Come on Q. I won't! You should know that by now." I looked the other way. He grabbed my face to look him in his eyes.

"D I'm serious promise me!" I blinked my eyes closed and held them that way for a second. I opened them and exhaled.

"What did that chic mean by your playing me?" He let his face go and brushed over his waves with his hand.

"Be real, she didn't mean anything by it, she is jealous cause she want to talk to me and I don't care if she was a dime, I'm not cheating on you. Nothing is worth that. Now promise me, you won't cheat!"

"O.k. I won't." All the while my fingers where crossed behind my back. I crossed my feet.

"You promise me that if you meet someone else that you are remotely interested in you will tell me." He sucked his teeth and put his head back on the seat.

"I wont meet someone else." I sighed and pulled his head up to face mines.

"Please Q, just promise me if you do then you will do that for me." He crossed his heart.

"I promise." They announced my bus and we kissed like we would never see each other again. After I teared a little and got on the bus I wanted to hurry and get home cause I couldn't wait to see Tahir. I called him when I got in at like 8:00 PM and told him I was on my way. For the last part of the summer me and Tahir were attached at the hip, still on the low. I was really starting to feel him. We did some heavy making out but no physical sex as of yet but I was getting weak. We did a lot of dry humping but sometimes I wanted to give in and let him in but I didn't. The weekend before my 12th grade year was to start I decided I was going to have sex with Tahir for him being so patient with me and it was all planned. I told my mother I was staying with my friend Akira who lived on the other side of town and Akira knew if my mother was to call that she would say I was in the bathroom and I would call her right back. Then she was to call me at Tahir's house so I could call her back. It was all set for Friday night.

CHAPTER 27
SPENDING THE NIGHT OUT

So Friday night I went to Tahir's house. He had cooked for me and rented movies from Blockbuster. We ate dinner, which was t-bone steaks, baked potatoes, and string beans with red kool-aid to drink, and then we popped Scarface in the VCR. We started kissing and getting into it and his beeper went off. He looked at it.

"Diamond hold up this money." He made a call and all I heard him say was, "How much? O.k. I got you. Give me 10 minutes." He jumped up off the couch.

"Diamond I will be back in 15 minutes." I pouted. He looked around for his keys and I was holding them on my pinky finger.

"Thanks D. Don't be like that. Fix your face. Business before pleasure." He leaned over.

"Don't be mad at me O.k.?" He gave me a soft kiss on the cheek. He patted my private area.

"Keep that nice and wet for me, I will be right back to put in some business on that." I scrunched up my face.

"Ill Tahir!" He laughed.

"Sike D. 15 minutes I promise." I laid back on the couch.

"O.k. Hurry." When he left I decided to be a snoop in those 15 minutes. I went through his dresser drawers and found girls phone numbers, pictures, and I even found a pair of red thongs. I thought, he not getting nothing when he come back. So I finished watching the tape and 15 minutes had turned into an hour. I fell asleep and that hour had turned into 2 hours. I was beeping him off the hook and he wasn't calling back. I was mad as hell thinking, he must be with another chic. I started getting my shit together to leave and I looked at the clock. Shit I was suppose to be at Akira's house and it is damn near 1 in the morning and I can't go home at that time of the morning. I fell asleep again and when I woke up it was 4 AM. I called my house to check my messages and when I picked up I noticed the ringer was off. The caller ID said 20 new calls. He thought he was so slick. I just knew he was with another bitch. I called my machine and Tahira had left me a message.

"Diamond this is Tahira, it is very important that you call me. My brother is locked up. He said you were at his house and I kept calling his house and you not picking up. Whatever time you get this call, call me." I was scared to call cause first of all I was scared for Tahir and second of all I knew Tahira would tell Samir I was at Tahir's house. I dialed the number and she picked up on the first ring.

"Tahira what happened?" She sniffled.

"He had went to his customer's house and when he came out the cops pulled up behind his car and put their lights on and asked if they could search it and he said O.k. because he knew he was clean but when they popped the trunk, he had drugs and a gun in the car with him." She was crying telling me to hold on cause Samir was clicking in on the other end. I cut her off.

"Wait Tahira before you click back over please don't tell Samir I'm here."

"Why not?" I begged, "Please don't, it is none of his business who I see." "O.k. I won't." She clicked over and in a few seconds she clicked back. Next thing I know my pager was going off and it was Samir beeping me 911. I knew that bitch had told. I asked, "Well what did Tahir say for me to do?" She blew her nose.

"He wants you to get his money and drugs out of there in case the police come to his house." She told me where everything was and I got the drugs, money, a gun and put it in my over night bag and left. It was near 5 AM and Samir kept beeping me. I still couldn't go home so I was riding around with my head spinning and all this illegal shit in my trunk. My pager was still going off so I finally pulled over and called Samir back from a pay phone. The blasting began because he was calling me everything but a child of God. I just let him put me on blast and I didn't say anything. I just put another quarter in the phone and listened. He was asking me how could I? He said I was a slut for fucking Tahir. That is when I spoke up.

"I am not fucking him. Ask him, we have just been hanging out and having fun."

"Well I bet Q would be very interested in knowing this D." I came back at him.

"Well I bet Tahira would be even more interested in that hickey I put on your chest the other day Samir so don't play with me." He tried to change up.

"Well if you wasn't happy with Q why you didn't come to me."

"What are you talking about? I am happy with Q and I'm happy with your friendship and Tahir's." He sighed.

"D, me and Tahir are boys, what the fuck is wrong with you?" I sucked my teeth.

"Well I'm friends with y'all too."

"You know what D I'm not mad at you. You got that, but remember what goes around comes around." I sighed.

"Samir look lets go out to breakfast and talk about this. IHOP opens in a minute." He sucked his teeth.

"Hell no." I begged,

"Pppplllleeeeeeaaaaaaaaaasssssssssssseeee Samir!"

"O.k. D, damn, don't beg." I smiled.

"Get dressed and meet me on the Ave." (The Ave was on the corner of our house.)

"O.k. Diamond." I picked him up. Once he got in I questioned the stuff in the trunk.

"What am I suppose to do with this stuff in my trunk?" He rubbed his temples.

"We will put it at my house. I gotta move that for Tahir." I whispered like the Feds were in my car.

"Samir I don't like you selling drugs." He sucked his teeth.

"Diamond don't start. It is to early in the morning for all that bullshit and you like those new Nikes you got on that

I bought you." I just agreed to keep the peace.

"Fine Samir." He bought the topic of the hour back up.

"Now back to you and Tahir." I looked straight ahead.

"Well me and him are just friends." He leaned up and looked me in my face.

"You sure about that?" I glanced over at him.

"Look first of all me and you on the low anyway and you got a girl that you love and..." He cut me off.

"No I don't love her, I just like her. I don't tell her I love her." I shrugged my shoulders.

"Well whatever Samir, me and Tahir is just cool, we have mad fun cause I don't let him get over and I'm not a gold digga like them other bitches. So he fuck them and get them some Reebok classics and he not fucking me and I get nice Air Max's." I laughed but he didn't.

"Sam it was a joke, me and him are like best friends, I can tell him anything and I do." Sam adjusted his seat to go back far as if he was sitting in the back seat.

"Well let him keep buying your sneakers I will keep my dough in my pocket. And why you didn't tell Q about your new found friendship." I sucked my teeth.

"For the same reason you don't tell Tahira about me and you and it is not like you could call her and tell her we together right now, she wouldn't understand and neither would Q and right now you acting like you don't understand." He shot me a look.

"Come on I understand but that's not the point. Me and you are more then friends. We still do couple like activities." I stopped at a red light and looked at him.

"Well what is the point Samir? I don't kiss Tahir. He is like my big brother, I know about the other chics and all that. We are just cool. That's all. You can't question my life, I'm damn near grown and can do what I want when I want." He looked at me and then out the window.

"Oh O.k. Diamond it's like that?" The light turned green and I pulled in IHOP in Elizabeth.

"Come on Sam. Please can we not get into it? Lets talk rationally." He jumped out the car and left me to go inside.

"O.k. Diamond." I walked behind him.

"What are we going to do about Tahir?" A tear formed in my eye, I was thinking about how serious this could be. We got in and got seated immediately. Samir got serious again.

"Diamond this shit is not going to look good for Tahir. He had 200 clips (that's 10 viles of coke rubber banded together to make 1 clip) in the trunk and a loaded gun with the serial number scratched off and I think he shot somebody with that gun, so I don't know what is going to happen. He told Tahira he think his boy set him up cause he didn't know those drugs or that gun was in the trunk. He said he could have swore it was in his house." I sighed.

"Damn if he would have just stayed with me." Samir raised his eyebrow.

"Ooh yeah D?" I sucked my teeth.

"Ooh no Samir not like that. He cooked me dinner and we was watching movies and just chilling." Samir scratched his head.

"And you were spending the night Diamond? Do I look stupid to you?" I sighed.

"Please don't start this up again Samir, you don't trust me Samir?" He sipped his orange juice the waitress brought.

"No I don't." My draw dropped open and my eyes extended wide open.

"You know what Sam, I don't believe you. After all the shit you put me through..." He placed his hand in the air to shut me up.

"Oh boy here we go again." I slammed my fork on the table.

"You got damn right here we go again." The waitress came over and asked us to please keep our voices down and refrain from the profanity. I dropped my eyes low and whispered.

"Look Samir I'm not fucking him, you don't believe me. Don't. I don't care. Case closed." We sat in silence and I wouldn't look at him. After like 20 minutes and our food came, he reached across the table and rubbed my hand.

"Diamond I believe you." I shrugged my shoulders as to say so who cares what you believe. I thought, damn I'm good. I poured syrup onto my French toast and taylor ham.

"O.k. So what are we going to do?" He mixed his grits around and added his scrambled eggs to them. He was disgusting right?

"We gotta wait D, cause his mother not going to do shit for him. He also said his Uncle Poppi that lives in New York will help. I know Tah got money." I looked around before speaking. I dropped my voice below a whisper.

"Yeah I got like 3,000 from his closet." Sam laughed.

"Ooh trust me, he got way more then that chump change." I cut the edges off my French toast off and ate the middle like a kid.

"Do you really think he getting out?" He sighed.

"Man I don't know, that's my nigga though and I gotta help him out. I got money saved for my car, but I will put it up for my nigga if I have too." We finished eating and arguing and talking and right back to arguing. And when we left IHOP it was like 8 AM. When we got in Samir leaned over and tried to kiss me and I wouldn't kiss him back. He got mad.

"What's wrong with you?" I turned my head.

"Nothing Samir, its just, well, me talking to Tahira this morning..." He cut me off.

"D, please don't start that stupid shit." I sucked my teeth.

"Damn Sam, why don't you never like to talk about it? You do have a girlfriend Samir and I do have a boyfriend." He waved his hand.

"O.k. D. just drive." I pushed the stick into reverse.

"Samir please don't be mad. You know I still love

you, I would break up with Q for you in a heartbeat. How about that? I will leave Q and you leave Tahira alone." I don't know what was making me say that. He looked at me.

"Say word D!" I winked at him.

"Word." He sat up straight.

"D, don't play around." I sighed.

"I'm not we obviously can't stop messing around and it is getting harder everyday to not give into you." He leaned back in the seat.

"You right D. Tahira is out of here. Diamond you not backing out of this. So when is you calling Q to handle that?" I got nervous.

"Soon." Samir blacked.

"No fuck that D! Soon is not good enough." I put my hands up.

"Wait a minute Samir I feel rushed." He put his hands behind his head.

"I will give you 2 weeks." I shook my head up and down slowly.

"O.k." The next weekend before school started I was going to see Q again. I didn't know what I was getting myself into but I had said it now. I yawned and stretched.

"I just want to go home and sleep." When we got to the corner of the Ave and our block I made him get out and walk just incase our parents were up. I was going to tell my parents I had diarrhea if they asked why I was home so early. They weren't up so I snuck up to my room and got in the bed and got ghost until 1. My dad came in my room.

"D what time did you get in?" From under the covers I said, "Like 8 cause I had the shits and didn't want to tear Akira bathroom up." He was laughing at me. I added in, "I guess it was those brownies and ice cream." He eased out of my room.

"That will do it every time." I felt bad about lying in my dad's face but oh well. The bell rang and my dad went and got it. It was Samir and my dad let him in and he came right up. I was in the bed with the covers over my head. He snatched them back.

"Come on D, we got to go." I stretched.

"Where?" He leaned in and whispered, "To see about Tahir's bail." I sat up straight and stretched again.

"O.k., O.k." He flopped down next to me.

"We gotta go to NY to get instructions on how to handle this from his uncle." I covered my mouth as I yawned.

"I'm not driving to NY Tahir." He mushed me.

"My name is Samir." I hit his arm.

"I'm sorry Samir but I'm still not driving to NY." He sucked his teeth obviously annoyed with me.

"Come on girl don't be such a scardey cat." I sighed.

"Why can't you just call his uncle Sam?" He laughed.

"His uncle is big time and he don't talk over nobody's phone line." I rubbed my eyes.

"O.k. let me get up." He peeped under the covers. All I had on was my t-shirt and my panties. He licked his lips.

"Damn I miss that." I yanked the covers back up over me.

"Bye Samir. Wait downstairs." He rubbed his hands together.

"I prefer to wait here." I yelled, "Downstairs!" He got up and went to the door.

"O.k., O.k." I got up, took a shower and got dressed real quick. When I got downstairs Samir was in the kitchen eating a bowl of cereal. I grabbed a mini orange juice out the fridge.

"Come on Samir." My mother was rolling dough out for a pie.

"Where y'all going Diamond?" Of course I had to I lie.

"To the mall Ma." My mother wiped her hands on her apron.

"Diamond since you got that car you ain't been going to work in the shop. You don't think you have to work no more?" I sucked my teeth.

"I was going but my stomach was hurting this morning and Starr can handle it, could you come on Samir." Sam washed out his bowl in the sink then placed it in the drain.

"Bye Ma." She smiled and waved.

"Bye you 2." He stopped in the kitchen entrance.

"Ma you cooking today?" She sucked her teeth playfully.

"No! Not for you." He walked over and kissed her on the cheek.

"Come on Ma." She rolled her eyes.

"O.k. I will. You can eat when you two get back from the mall. Have fun." We went to NY, met his uncle, got some money, and a number of a lady to call to actually bring the bail to the bail bondsman. You had to have a job with pay stubs to show proof of income. He gave us every instruction and made us write it down so we wouldn't fuck up nothing. His uncle was smart and knew his stuff. Samir had met him a number of times from hanging with Tahir. We were in his Uncle's living room. He took a pull on his Kool cigarette and blew the smoke in Samir's direction.

"Who is the bitch...'oh excuse me sweetheart' (he said that towards me)... that was at his house when he got locked up?" I slightly raised my hand.

"You looking at her." He dubbed out his cigarette in his ashtray.

"Oh I didn't mean it like that, please excuse me but I told Tahir about mixing business with pleasure." I just looked at him. He smiled.

"I'm sorry miss forgive me." I rolled my eyes.

"Whatever." He looked at Samir.

"Ooh Samir she is a feisty little one huh?" Samir smiled.

"Yeah Poppi (that was his street name) she rough and tough and all that stuff, so she think." I rolled my eyes.

"Yeah ight Samir." He then took out some e-z wider weed paper and started rolling a joint.

"So are you Tahir's girl?" I watched him carefully as

he rolled the marijuana.

"No, not at all. We just friends." He looked me up and down real sexual.

"What kind of friends?" I screamed, "Ill! Not that kind of friends you fucking pervert."

Samir screamed, "Diamond!"

I yelled, "What?!" Poppi smiled.

"I like her she don't take no shit." He put the weed on the glass table and came and put his arm around me and I flung it off. Samir jumped up to get us out of there.

"No Poppi this is..." He stopped. I know he was about to say this my girl or my friend or whatever but Poppi was Tahira's uncle too. So anyway he said, "This is my neighbor." Poppi picked up his joint and licked it.

"So you put Tahir on her?" He pulled me up by my arms.

"Yeah Poppi but look enough about that we gotta go and get back to Jersey." He placed the joint in his mouth and allowed it to hang as he finished his sentence.

"You right go handle that. Miss don't worry we gonna get Tahir out for you." He smiled and lit his joint. He then threw the lighter on the table.

"If my nephew anything like his uncle he will be running home to that... Samir you want to hit this?" I didn't smile. I was getting ready to say you old goat but Samir covered my mouth with his hand and pulled me to come on.

"Naw Poppi, I'm good. You so crazy. Will see you later." On our way out of his building in Queens Bridge I looked at Samir.

"Why he ask you did you want to hit that joint? You smoke weed now?"

"No nosey I don't. He was just being cordial. Lets just go." When I got home I could hear some collect calls that had been made to my machine and I knew who they where from. I sat and waited for him to call back while Samir was downstairs stuffing his face with my mother's lasagna and garlic bread and apple pie for dessert. He called a few seconds later and I accepted the call with the quickness. All I remember saying was, "I accept... Hello?"

"Hey Diamond. Damn Diamond I fucked up." I told him about how me and Sam went to see his uncle and all that we had to do. He chuckled.

"You and Sam huh?" I talked into the receiver and covered it with my hand just incase there were any nosey parents listening from the hallway.

"Yeah your sis told him I was at your house and I hope he don't tell Q." He assured me he wouldn't.

"He won't. I will talk to him." I let Tahir in on what I told Samir.

"I told him that me and you were like best friends." He laughed.

"Cool I will follow through with that lie." We both laughed. I laid back on my bed.

"Well thanks." He whispered to me in a seductive voice.

"Yeah you welcome and you know you owe me..." I cut him off.

"I know Tah... I know." He came back to his regular voice.

"I should be bailed out by early next week." I sat up on my bed.

"I cleaned up and locked your doors." I heard a bunch of noise in the background.

"In a minute nigga!" I was confused.

"Hello? Tahir?"

"Yeah my bad D. Niggas in here always wanting to try you. The nigga trying to rush me off the phone. He better just fucking wait his turn like everybody else in this bitch. But anyway thanks for cleaning up. I gotta tell you I'm feeling you a lot. I hope all this works out for the best so we could be together." I smirked.

"Yeah I hope." He got all serious on a nigga.

"D I'm serious!" I exhaled and flopped backwards on my bed.

"O.k. Samir." He sucked his teeth.

"My name is Tahir." I sighed nervously.

"My bad. I'm just tired is all." He sucked his teeth again.

"O.k. Get some rest then, cause I don't go for being called no other nigga name, I will call you tomorrow."

"O.k. Bye."

"Peace out." And he slammed the phone down in my ear. Sam came up to my room.

"Who you was talking too?"

"WhaT?" (you know with that sharp T on the end.) He sat down on my bed next to me.

"I don't stutter D. Don't play with me, who was that?"

"Why Samir? Don't start acting all possessive and shit." He stood up.

"D what you talking about? Whatever man I'm out." I sat up and threw a pillow at his back.

"See ya! Wouldn't want to be ya!" He left out and came right back in and closed the door. He pushed me back on my bed and started kissing me all hard. Between kisses I squeezed out.

"Sam where are my parents?" He kissed me on my neck.

"They went to the movies." He kept kissing me and trying to unbutton my shorts. I was saying, "No" but my body was saying, "Yes." We were tussling and I knew I couldn't give in. I was moaning.

"Stop Samir." He was whispering.

"Diamond do you want me to stop?" I was shaking my head back and forth.

"I don't know." He pulled my shirt up and was kissing my smooth stomach. He was making circles around my navel with his tongue. My body felt like it was going to melt until my phone rang. I reached for the phone and Samir reached for my hand.

"D don't get it." I struggled to get from under him.

"I have to." He stopped and I picked up the phone. It was Q. Of course it was. I looked at Samir.

"Hey Q!" Sam was mouthing, "Tell him D, tell him" and I was shaking my head no. He wanted me to tell him over the phone that it was over but I wasn't ready. So Samir just sat there, damn near in my lap in my convo. Q was telling me about his classes because school starts early when you're in college. He asked, "Enough about me D. What have you been doing?"

"Missing you." Sam looked at me with one eyebrow up. I tried to get up to go in another room but he pulled me back by the top of my shorts to sit me back down. I sat there and listened to Q tell me he missed me and he couldn't wait to see me next weekend and he had a surprise for me and blah blah blah. Well all I heard was blah blah blah cause I wasn't listening, I was to busy being scared Samir was going to scream on me. He finally said he was going to a party later on so he was about to go so he could get ready. He blew me a big kiss through the phone.

"I miss you Diamond." A tear formed in my eye.

"Me too."

"I love you Diamond."

"Me too."

"O.k. baby, bye-bye."

"Bye." He butt in.

"Wait D… You sure you not seeing anyone else?" I crossed my fingers like I was a little kid. "Positive. How about you?"

"Of course not you the only one for me, the only one I got eyes for." I smiled.

"Awe that's sweet. Don't be up on no chic at that party you heard!" He laughed.

"Never that! Bye wifey."

"Bye boo." I looked at Samir and he looked at me.

"What he say?" I looked away.

"Nothing Samir." My mind was swimming Quan Samir Quan Samir. It was the same shit different year. Samir started kissing my neck and I jumped up. I need to control this situation and right now me and Samir having sex wasn't the answer.

"Stop Samir not now, not like this. Lets do the break

ups first." He smiled.

"Fine Diamond." I walked to my room door and opened it.

"Samir can I be alone please?" He stood up and walked towards the door.

"O.k. D whatever you want I'm out." He leaned over and tried to kiss me. I turned my head.

"D what's that all about? Are you sure you want to do this?" I looked down at my hands.

"Sam I don't know." He picked my chin up.

"Well let me let you know something. This ain't your world and I ain't a squirrel trying to get a nut you heard? So you better decide quick!" He left it at that and walked out of my room.

CHAPTER 28
PERMISSION SLIP

O.k. so next week came and I went to see Q. I wanted to drive down but my parents said no because I was still a new driver and that was to far to drive by myself. So there I was back on Grey Hound again. My surprise was a Bismarck chain with a double plated nameplate with both our names. It said Quan and Diamond. I was so excited about it and I couldn't wait to wear it. Also he had gotten a picture we took in Wildwood on the board walk blown up to a poster size and had it up on the wall. I waited until I was leaving Monday to try to break up with him. You notice I said tried. This is how it went down.

"Q I think we should take a break." He screamed, "What?!" I sighed.

"Q calm down. I'm saying you down here and I'm up there and it is all these girls..."He grabbed me around the waist.

"Fuck them I want you." I gently pulled away.

"O.k. Q that is all good but you can keep tabs on me in Jersey from all your peeps but..."He got up in my face.

"But what? I don't keep tabs on you Diamond, I trust you and I thought you trusted me." I sighed.

"Q I do trust you..." I walked over to his bedroom window, "Come here Q... You see her and her and her over there? It is them I don't trust. You can't tell me that when you go to them parties that girls don't be checking for you." He pulled me away from the window.

"D I can't lie, they do..." I butt in.

"See..." He cut me off, "See what?!" I looked down at the floor.

"Q when I start back to school what is going to happen?" He hugged me.

"We gonna maintain." I tried to pull away.

"Q I don't want to get hurt no more... look at me...

256

you big on the truth, tell me there is not one girl on this campus that you are checking for?" He let me go from his hug.

"D, what the fuck? I'm not blind, of course there are pretty girls here, but I got a pretty girl already. D look, if you don't want to be with me no more don't beat me in the head with the bullshit." I hugged him this time.

"Q of course I want to be with you but I can't sleep at night sometimes thinking about what you doing." He kissed my forehead.

"Well let me save you any more sleepless nights. I'm not doing anything Diamond, I swear... how about this. You come here 1 weekend a month and I will come their one weekend a month. And when B ball officially start I wont be able to come there but you can come here 2 weekends a month and I will pay for it." I looked in his eyes while we were standing with are arms around each other.

"Pay for it how Q? You selling weed down here on campus like at home?" He laughed.

"If you must know, yes. Niggas got habits, expensive weed habits at that and I'm there pusher man." I sucked my teeth.

"Well whatever. Don't get kicked out of school for being stupid." He then grabbed my chin.

"Wait how you know I was selling weed at home?" I smiled and winked at him.

"The streets is watching, but like I said be careful don't get kicked out trying to be the damn pusher man." He laughed again and kissed my lips.

"Never that." I was trying everything under the sun to put this break up on him but he was willing to do so much. I gave him a small squeeze while still hugging him.

"Q we will see how it works out." He pulled away from me and screamed, "What Diamond? What more do you want from me?" I sighed.

"Well Q I am giving you permission to see other people." He yelled louder.

"What?! I don't need your permission for anything

and you don't have mines to see nobody else but me and if you my girl, you my girl and that's it, now if you want something different Diamond, then maybe we are not meant to be!" I didn't say anything. It was almost 3 hours before my bus but I was going to go to the bus station now and sit and wait. I picked up the phone and dialed the number for a cab and in the middle of me saying, "Please pick me up at..." he hung the phone up. He grabbed my shoulders and shook me.

"What's the matter with you?!" I didn't answer. He screamed, "Diamond are you seeing someone else?!" I screamed back.

"No!" He got in my face.

"Are you sure?" I moved back.

"I said no right? Then I'm sure." He paced back and forth.

"You know a few cats told me you were fucking with Samir again but I said no not my Diamond and I didn't question you cause I trust you. Now you acting up so I can't help but believe it." I got an instant attitude.

"Well believe what you want, I'm not." I got my bag and tried to leave. He stood in front of the door.

"Where you think you going?" I adjusted my bag on my shoulder.

"I think I'm going home Q." He pushed the bag off of my shoulder.

"No you not, not yet. We not finished talking." He pushed me back. A tear fell down my face.

"Q I don't want a long distant relationship no more." He rubbed his chin.

"So Diamond are you fucking him again? Is the dick that good to you it got you bugging like this." I pushed him hard and he fell up against the door.

"What mother fucker! Are you fucking him? What kind of question is that? And may I ask you what him are you referring too?" He sucked his teeth.

"Oh you know who Diamond, it all fits. You come down here, we have a good weekend, and all this b/s comes from no where, it must be someone else and I think it is Samir."

"Well you know what Q? You thought like lit, you thought you had to pee but you had to shit!" That was some old saying my mother says to me. Q looked at me all confused.

"What?!" I rubbed my temples.

"I don't know." We locked eyes and started laughing. He grabbed me and hugged me tight.

"D, I don't want to lose you." I whispered.

"Q I don't want to lose you either. I'm scared Q, I am really scared." He kissed my cheek.

"D I am here to protect you not hurt you. I am not your enemy, I'm on your team. I don't want to hurt you, no let me rephrase that I wont hurt you, I promise... I don't think you cheating... Are you?" I looked him in his eyes.

"No." He pinched my nose.

"O.k. then case closed." My eyes teared.

"Q I just miss you, I miss seeing you everyday." He ran his fingers through my hair.

"D, I miss you too but we can make this work can't we?" I shrugged.

"I guess." He grabbed my face in his hands.

"No D, don't guess. Know that we can." I smiled.

"O.k." In my mind I was thinking, I'm not gonna break up with Q, I'm going to tell Samir he gotta take my friendship and be happy with that. Next me and Q made wild passionate blow your back out love and I can remember how sweated out my wrap (a hairstyle I use to wear in high school) was. Um it is taking me back. After we finished and freshened up, he took me to the bus station and we waited for my bus to come. As I was getting on Q said, "Diamond, I love you. Don't do nothing, please. Trust me. I'm not messing with no one else but you. I put my life on it. Show me the same respect ight?" I wiped my tears away.

"Yes Q. I will." I sat in my seat and waved as the bus pulled off.

CHAPTER 29
JCH (JUST CAME HOME)

So when I got home from Grey Hound with my mother Samir was at my house chilling with my father waiting for me. He followed me to my room.

"So we going back to school a couple?" I sighed.

"Yes Sam we are." He smiled.

"That's good." I mumbled.

"Yeah a couple of friends." He screamed.

"What!? You trying to play me!?" I looked up at him.

"No Sam I couldn't do it, I tried." He caught glimpse of my chain.

"Oh I see. Nice chain." I sighed.

"Sam please don't start..." He flicked the chain.

"So you tried huh? I guess you tried to get that hickey on your neck too." I pleaded with Samir.

"Sam please, can't we just be friends like we were?" He gave me a pound.

"Yeah D, sure, whatever!" He went to walk out of my room and he stopped.

"Oh yeah your boy is home. He came home today."

"For real?! Where he at?" He sucked his teeth.

"Didn't I just say home?" I smiled and placed my arms around his waist.

"Sam let's not beef, you know I love you but right now is not the time for us. You will always be my first love and have a piece of my heart, but for now friends is all I can offer. Now, let's go see him." He turned his lip up and pushed my arms down off his waist.

"O.k. But only cause I want to take him his stuff." I smiled.

"Oh so you using me for a ride? That's O.k., just go get the stuff and let me take a shower real quick and get dressed." He looked me up and down.

"Why you gotta shower and get dressed? You didn't wash after you fucked Q?" I rolled my eyes.

"Oh boy Samir! I didn't fuck Q! I was on a nasty bus sitting next to a stinky old man and I feel dirty. So I want to take a shower, is that alright with you my lord?" He sucked his teeth.

"Whatever! Just hurry up. I got other things to do!" I put my hands on my hips.

"Like what? Fucking Tahira?" He pulled his lip in and rubbed his hands together.

"If you must know, yes that is what I gotta do. I gotta tear my girls ass up and as a matter of fact you can just drop me off over there when we leave Tahir's house." I shrugged my shoulders.

"No problem Samir." He stepped out the room.

"Hurry up, I will be at my house." I sat on my bed and took my clothes off. Damn it, Samir is always trying to hurt my feelings and it always works. After my quick shower I called Tahir.

"Me and Samir are coming to see you."

"Come alone cause you owe me." I had just got my period. I guess Quan bought it down and even if I didn't I had just had sex with Q. I was not that trifling. I laughed.

"So you want to meet Aunt Flow from Red Bank?" He laughed hard.

"Ill! You got your period." I laughed, "Yep."

"O.k. You off the hook this time but you still owe me."

"No you owe me for doing what I did."

"Yeah you right about that. Thank you so much for that, now hurry up I miss my best friend." He laughed.

"Whatever Tah, we are on our way." I grabbed my keys and got in Nelly (that was my cars name). I honked the horn and Samir came out, threw the bag in the back, got in the car and turned my radio up. He looked out the window. I touched his knee.

"Are you mad at me?" He flung my hand off.

"For what Diamond? I don't feel like having a 2-hour

conversation about the shit. You didn't break up with him, so that's fine. Now drop it before shit get ugly. Drive please." I didn't say anything cause I didn't want to argue. I just drove to Tahir's house. When me and Sam went to Tahir's apartment he talked about that he was looking at maybe 1-3 flat meaning he needed to do 1-3 years but he could be released from jail as early as 6- 18 months. He said his lawyer might get him off cause he didn't have a record and he might just get probation. When Sam looked away, Tahir would blow me kisses. He tried real hard to play that best friend role in front of Samir. He was smacking my thigh.

"How was your trip? And how is Q? Nice chain, when is the wedding?" I clenched my teeth.

"He's fine but we not getting married now." He was going the extra mile.

"Good to see you 2 still together." I smiled, "Yep." He gave me the thumbs up.

"That is so good." I flipped the script on him.

"How about you Tahir? We gotta get you a girlfriend." He laughed.

"No not me, I'm a player, I don't want no girl." And them 2 was laughing and slapping hands and inside I was heated cause when Tahir was behind bars he wanted me to be his girl. Tahir then pointed at his bedroom door and nodded towards Samir.

"Diamond excuse us for a minute. We gotta go talk business." They went in the room with the bag with the drugs, gun, and money in it. I guess that's what was in it. I didn't ask Samir what he had done with the drugs or any of it. The less I knew the better. They were in the room for about a half hour while I watched TV and then came out. Samir hit my leg.

"Diamond you ready?" I threw the remote on the couch and stood up and stretched.

"I guess." He smiled at Tahir.

"We need to go so Tahir can get him some ass. He has been locked up and needs to get some." I turned my lip up.

"O.k. but why you gotta be so graphic?" He playfully punched me in my air.

"Cause you like one of the guys right?" Tahir cut in.

"Yeah D, this is how the guys talk and since we all cool, this is how it goes down. You don't think when Q kick it with his boys he don't say I'm getting some ass or whatever?" I smirked.

"I don't think so since he is not getting any. I am abstaining from sex." They both looked at me as to say bullshit. I looked at both of them in their faces.

"Don't look at me like that, I'm serious." Tahir clapped.

"Well word Diamond, more power to you. I'm not and that is why y'all gotta go right now cause this chic should be here any minute now." I sucked my teeth.

"Fine. We gone." Him and Tahir shook hands and mumbled some drug stuff behind me. When we were leaving out some stank bitch was getting out a cab. She had the biggest nastiest butt I have ever seen and she had on some nasty sweat pants and it looked like she had no draws on. Tahir was in the door and Samir gave him a pound.

"Ight Tah." The girl waved towards Samir.

"Hey Samir!" I just looked at her with utter disgust. Samir winked at her.

"Hey Tani, don't hurt nothing tonight." She smiled.

"I'll try not too." When she reached the top steps she hugged Tahir. He hugged her back gripping her big nasty ass and tongue kissing her. I mercked off with an attitude. I mean damn he didn't have to do all that in front of me. I sighed.

"Which way to Tahira house?" He sat back.

"I changed my mind 'cause I don't need you knowing where she lives at." I sighed again.

"I could care less Samir, if you want to go I will take you." He flipped the radio station.

"No just take me home and I will catch a cab to her

house." I didn't want no problems. I just kept driving.

"Whatever you want." I was to pissed about the Tahir situation to get into it with Samir. I mean the nerve of him telling that girl Tani to come over there while I was still there. When we pulled up to my house he got out and didn't say anything to me and I didn't say anything to him. We left it like that. School was starting Wednesday and I was just ready for my 12th grade year to come and go. It was our 12th grade year and nothing had changed. People made a big deal out of 12th grade but it was just another school year as far as I was concerned. Me and Starr were still best friends and running shit as always. Over the next few months, there were some loopholes in Tahir's case and he didn't have to do any time at all because the cops didn't have any reason to pull him over so he got off. Samir kept up cheating on Tahira, but not with me because after I didn't break up with Q me and him didn't speak too tough. I know I did get sick of seeing him with all these chics in school. I am glad I had decided to cut our creeping off completely, or I would have been suspended everyday. We spoke a little but not too much. Mitch got this big promotion at work and got a 25,000 bonus. He bought Starr and Samir cars. Starr got a purple MX-3 like mines and Samir got a black bubble back civic trying to be like Q. Well he would never admit it but Q had a civic first so as far as I am concerned he was trying to be like Q. They got their cars about 2 weeks before their driving lesson and Samir had put rims and a system in the civic. It was looking good but guess what? On the day they went to get their license, Starr got hers but Sam didn't. It was so funny. He was trying to be so cool and drive with 1 hand and they failed his black ass. So he had to wait for about 6 weeks and his mother and father didn't let him drive with out that license either. The next time he went to get it, he acted right and got it.

Me and Tahir finally had sex near December, it was not worth cheating on Q for. Did you ever hear that song about a 2-minute man. Well they were talking about him.

He wanted me to suck his, you know, and I didn't even do that for him. His name wasn't Q. He was making all these growling noises like he was some type of wounded animal while we had sex and I wasn't feeling it at all. He kept saying when he was done, cause I never got started.

"Yeah I can look in your eyes and tell you hooked." I couldn't say shit for fear of laughing at him. It was the worst I had ever experienced. The only reason I took it there is because his grandmother died and he was sad and I went to comfort him. One thing led to another and you know the rest. No sex was like sex with Q so you know we maintained. We kept up with our visits and I kept up with not having sex with Tahir no more. Any and every excuse I could use I did. I couldn't do it. I felt like a tramp and couldn't deal with that feeling so I told Tahir I had a yeast infection and couldn't have sex for 6 weeks, then I told him I had my period, I also told him I had a urinary tract infection. I made up all types of infections. I know he was thinking ill something wrong with this chic, but not really cause he was always still trying to get some of my good stuff.

CHAPTER 30
HIGH SCHOOL IS OVER

O.k. I know you like enough about high school. I will sum the 12th grade up. Me and Q stayed together. Tahira finally got fed up with Samir cheating so she broke up with him and he didn't give a shit cause once you get a taste for cheating you like it and act like you can't stop.

Q's basketball team was in the finals and they were playing out West and he couldn't go to the prom with me last minute so Sam suggested, "We can go D." Of course Q was steaming. He had bumped his head when he said this:

"Why can't you go by yourself Diamond?" My response to him:

"Did you go by yourself La Quan?" We got into about the situation but he finally gave into my wants. He did warn me that if Samir were to so much as touch a hair on my head then it would be on. And if I felt the need to touch him then it would be over. I told him we were just going to the prom and that was all. Me, Sam, Starr and Danny all went in a limo and had made fun. I wore black and silver and Starr wore black and gold. Toiya made my dress again and Starr's too. We went down the school, which was the center of town. Remember I told you about that when me and Q went, if you forgot you gotta turn back to Chapter 24. It was titled "The Prom and Pilgrims," but enough about that. It was drizzling the day of the prom so we got out real quick, showed off our dresses with our extra big umbrellas and got right back in the limo. At the prom me and Samir won prom king and queen. I was shocked cause we were not a couple but people were so use to us being together since the 6th grade they voted for us. After the prom we all went to the Loop (remember about the Loop) but Sam wasn't getting none. He was mad but hey, he got over it. We just sat up in the room and kept knocking on the couple's room doors that were having sex and then we would run. Hey, we were hating, but oh well. When we went home that night, we packed for Wildwood. It was still the same couples from the prom that paired up in Wildwood, but this time when the doors closed to the motel room on Saturday night, me and Samir took it there. I didn't realize how much I missed Samir until that night. I was scared as hell that it would get back to Q but Samir swore to me no matter what he would never breathe a word of what happened to anyone. So, by him making that vow, Sunday night in Wildwood we had sex one more time for the road before we came home. We said to each other, "What ever happened in Wildwood stays in Wildwood."

So once Starr got her car she was dipping and dabbing on the side but Danny was her main man. She thought he was still creeping with Gina but she didn't have solid proof so she kept her sidepieces. We loved his baby. She was so cute. Little DaGina Cheri. That ghetto shit. When you take your name and your man's name and creating a name…some ghetto bullshit. Gina kept going to school and graduated and was set to start county college in the Fall. She didn't go to the prom because she didn't have a date. Danny didn't want to leave his daughter so he was going to Montclair State University in New Jersey to play ball. He was staying in state on campus about a half hour from where we lived. Samir was going to Hampton in Virginia to play b ball. You know me and Starr was going to Howard to play niggas ooh and get an education while we were at it. Tahir was still a sidepiece. I was still trying not to have sex with him as much as possible but sometimes it had to happen and I was disappointed every time. At graduation we tossed those hats up and kissed out child hood goodbye. That afternoon I had a graduation/18th birthday part blow out in my yard. Jackie came and Q surprised me and came up for my graduation and my 18th birthday, which was a week prior. He was going to be home for about 2 weeks until basketball camp started in July. I was so happy to see him that I sat up under him the whole time of my party. Samir kept his word and didn't even look me and Q's way. That was a good thing. While sitting in the back Q linked his arm through mine.

"I see Samir must be over you huh? He not even looking over here or nothing." I squeezed his arm.

"I told you we were just friends. Don't start please Q." He winked at me and smiled, "I'm not." We just ate, drank, and were merry. Everything was so nice. It was all the cool graduates and their parents. You know my Godfather came and bought his wife and kids. Aunt Debra stopped caring because she had met her somebody too. He was an older guy, but he was nice. He gave me a hundred dollars for my graduation so I liked him. Danny was O.k. with him as long as he treated his mother good he was cool. Also, the fact that he gave Danny $250.00 for graduation didn't hurt. My dad went all out for me. He came over and kissed me on my forehead.

"Your only daughter only graduates once and only turns 18 once." I got 18 one hundred dollar bills from my dad. All together from family and friends I came off with about three grand. That was going to be a nice fund to go shopping with for Howard University. There were so many parents there and you know that meant plenty of liquor. When the party was over, I walked Q and his mother to their car. He was going to hang out with his friends to let me and my friends be together. We rode around with our cars all decked out with the shoe polish words smeared all over the car saying, coming through the door in 94! We honked our horns all through the town to let people know we had made it out. Once we finished riding around me and Starr dropped off the girls that were in our cars and came on home. We met up with Samir and Danny who were coming home from doing the same. We were all standing in front of my house and Samir rubbed his growling stomach.

"D, is there any food left?" I laughed thinking about

all the food that was left over.

"Now Samir you know Ann cooked enough for a third world country!" We all laughed and went into my house straight to the kitchen. We got left over fried chicken out the fridge and all the cold salads out. We took our food and went out on the deck. I don't know whose bright idea it was but the 4 musketeers snuck and got drunk on the left over liquor. All me and Starr had was some Boones Farm mixed with Mad Dog. Now you know back in that day they called Mad Dog liquid crack. Danny and Samir were drinking Mad Dog straight and chug a lugging Budweiser's. It was close to midnight and we were getting twisted like Gumby on my deck. We decided to play Truth or Dare after we got 'nice' (cute way of saying drunk) and Samir started the game off with me.

"Truth or dare Diamond?" I burped and then covered my mouth.

"Truth." He looked in my eyes.

"Is it true that you still love me?" I looked down and my face instantly flushed and turned beet red,"Yes." He smiled and I covered my face. Starr's drunk ass waved her finger at her brother.

"Ooh boy Samir, you had to ask her that, you know that already, she has always loved you and she told me if you pushed up hard enough you could have her back." I screamed, "Starr!" She covered her drunken mouth.

"Oops! I'm sorry sis...wait...I'm going to be sick!" And with that, she threw up all over the deck. I jumped up trying to avoid it splashing on me.

"Damn Starr with your big mouth, if you would have kept it closed nothing would have came out!"

I know you are saying what the hell is Starr talking about? Well, at graduation when the superintendent was giving his same old boring speech, I told Starr that I really loved her brother and if he was persistent he could have me back, but I didn't tell her so she could tell him. He was just looking so good to me in that cap and gown and all the old feelings came over me. 5 years old to 18 years old flashed in front of my face. Now you know when people are drunk they are goofy as hell. Samir and Danny wee laughing at Starr and between burps and more throwing up she said,

"Shut up y'all, it is not funny!" I was busy stumbling trying to get the hose to get the throw up off my mother's newly stained deck. I got the hose from the side of the house and turned the water on to clean off the deck. I ended up spraying all of them and calling a water fight. We were outside screaming and laughing loud and my mother came to the sliding door with her robe and her rollers in her head. I was pointing the hose at them as they ran passed me trying to get down the steps and my mother opened the door and yelled, "Diamond!" I stumbled then tumbled around.

"Huh?" As I turned, I didn't put the water hose down and soaked my mother up. She was drenched from head to toe and her rollers were soaked and hanging. She screamed, "Are you crazy girl?!" I dropped the hose and my eyes got big.

"My bad Ma! Turn the water off one of y'all!" Samir ran over and turned it off but of course them being drunk they couldn't stop laughing that I soaked my mother. Doing something like that would get a drunk person sober real quick. I had got most of the throw up off the deck but some was still there and my mother came out on the deck with her hands on her hips and looked at us.

"Who threw up on my deck Diamond?" I tried to keep myself together by standing still.

"Starr did." She looked at how goofy we all looked and picked up one of the cups from the table and smelled it.

"Who was drinking?" We all pointed at somebody different. My mother began to storm into the house.

"All of y'all in the kitchen right now!" They were all snickering coming into the house dripping wet. I was the only one that wasn't wet but I was stumbling with the others. We tried to keep our composure in front of my mother but we just couldn't. She looked at all of us with utter disgust.

"So y'all think y'all are grown and you like to drink huh? Have a seat!" We all sat down and she went and opened the liquor cabinet. She pulled out a bottle of Hennessy and 4 shot glasses. She placed a glass in front of each of us.

"Since you like to drink, you will finish this bottle of Hennessy with out throwing up or y'all all will be grounded for the entire summer." I raised my hand.

"Ma we don't..." She snapped.

"Shut up Diamond! Y'all want to be grown right? Show me your grown. Keep these shots down! Bottoms up!" I thought, my mother has watched to many episodes of the Cosby show, remember the one when Vanessa got drunk? She poured the first round. Starr took a sip and put the glass down. The rest of us threw back our shots and we were looking at each other with our chests burning. My mother kept pouring.

"No-no Starr, you gotta get it down. Now hurry up and finish that first shot so you can get this second shot." We all had to throw back second shots. I rubbed my forehead and thought, I'm not going to make it! Samir and Danny were throwing back their shots while I slow rolled with my third one. Starr was still staring at her first one and my mouth was filling up with saliva and I knew if I placed that shot to my lips that would be all she wrote. My mother slammed her hand down on the table.

"Hurry up Diamond and Starr! Bottoms up!" With that, Starr earled (threw up) all over herself. I put the third shot to my mouth and my lips started quivering. I vomited all over the table and myself. My mother shouted, "That's two grounded for the summer. Now guys lets see what you made of cause you're men right?" They both shook their heads yes. She kept pouring and they kept drinking. They got to the bottom of the bottle and Samir was next. He threw up all over himself. Danny got to finish off the bottle. My mother patted him on the back.

"Congratulations Danny, now finish off this corner and you will be the only one free this summer." Danny rubbed his hands together.

"No problem. I can do that." He turned the bottle up. He held the liquid in his cheeks and finally swallowed. He jumped up and down and posed like he was the iron man. But after a minute he covered his mouth.

"Uh oh!" And uh oh was right because like they say what goes up must come down, well with him what went down must come up and it did. My mother shook her head and turned up her lip. She barked out orders like she was a drill sergeant.

"Look at all of you! Starr go in the basement and get the mop and some hot soapy water and mop up this mess off my damn floor and don't just mop the throw up, mop the whole floor!" She pointed towards the deck next.

"Diamond finish cleaning off that deck! Get some hot soapy water and the scrub brush from under the sink and get that shit off my deck!" She wasn't done there.

"Samir help your sister bring the water up stairs and mop up this floor and Samir clean off the table with disinfectant spray and scrub it until it shines!" I went outside and felt like throwing up again but I forced myself to keep it down. I finished rinsing off the deck and scrubbing it and came back inside. I walked across the part of the floor that was dry and my mother looked me up and down.

"Take your ass in that den and join Samir. Wait for the other two to finish!" Once Starr and Danny were done they came into the den. My mom paced back and forth in front of us.

"So what did we learn tonight boys and girls?" I slurred, "If we drink, don't get caught?" She snapped her neck towards me.

"You think that's cute Diamond? Go to your room and don't come out until I say so!" I was struggling to stand up and wanted to say "But Ma..." but I rejected that urge and went upstairs. I don't know what happened after that cause I laid across my bed and the room was spinning. I got up and stumbled to the bathroom and threw up all over the toilet seat. I started to cry silently to myself because I knew I had to clean it up. I just wiped off the toilet seat to make it look presentable, sprayed Lysol and went and laid back across my bed and fell asleep fully clothed and all.

I knew in the morning what happened because Drill Sergeant Ann made all of us get up at 6 AM and clean the yard from the graduation party. We did it without a complaint. Once that was done the rest of the troops could go home but I had to clean the bathroom since I didn't do it properly the night before. When all was said and done it was about 8 AM and my mom gave me 2 Tylenols and let me get back in the bed. I stayed there for the rest of the day. I turned my ringer off and my beeper off. She told my father and their parents what happened and that she had taken care of the punishment and to leave us alone. I felt like I had suffered enough. This must have been how Vanessa Huxtable felt on The Cosby Show that time she got drunk but her parents gave her tea not real liquor. When I got up that afternoon and stumbled to the kitchen, my mom made me hot tea and soup. She sat the empty bowl for the soup in front of me and poured my tea.

"How you feeling Diamond?" I took a sip of my tea.

"Better Ma, thank you!" She stirred the soup.

"I hope so Diamond. I'm not mad at you for drinking last night. But I hope you learned your lesson." I laid my head on the kitchen table.

"Yes Ma...I did!" She came over with the pot and poured soup in my bowl.

"O.k. cause if I can't trust you at home how can I trust you at Howard?" I sat up at the table.

"Mom you can trust me!" She handed me a spoon for my soup.

"I hope so cause anymore slip ups from you this summer then you will not be going to Howard understood?" I slurped my soup.

"Yes Mommy." She sighed.

"Well you were punished enough and so was the

other 3 musketeers so you're free this summer. Let's just put this behind us." I smiled.

"O.k." My dad walked in and thought it was funny. I personally didn't. Q had been calling all day and my mom said he came by and she told him I had ate something that didn't agree with me. He called me early the next day while I was lying in the bed watching Richard Bey (remember him, use to come on Channel 9 back in the day).

"Hey boo. You O.k.?" I yawned.

"Yes, better Q." He sighed.

"That's good D, cause I want to be attached at the hip for the next 2 weeks while I'm home." I sat up.

"No problem! I want that too!" And that is what it was. We would be together all day long and it was the same routine. We either went out to breakfast, lunch or dinner and always ended up at either his house or mine to hit the sheets depending on whose parents were home.

Since I was leaving for school in about a month, my mother decided to open up a small soul food restaurant down town Newark called Auntie Ann's. She was there all day with my dad getting the shop set up to be open so me and Q had free rang to my house most of the time. My mom said she was going to need something to do since her baby was leaving. It was set to open the day after Labor Day. I would be long gone to Howard by then.

By the time Q left back for school Tahir had built his self back up of course and he got a bigger place. Actually, he bought a condo in Elizabeth away from where he did his dirt in Peers Manor Projects and a new truck, a blue Ford Expedition to be exact. Tahir had built his self back up of course and he got a bigger place. He was my honey for the rest of the summer after Q left on the down low of course. He tried to be thuggish but behind closed doors he was a sweet pie. The day before me, Samir, and Starr were set to leave for school, I went to see him and he vowed he would be there to see me on the regular. I didn't pay that any attention, I just let him talk. We had just finished having half way decent sex and he walked me to the door.

"D, as soon as you get there call me with the number so I can plan my first visit." I rolled my eyes in my head and he grabbed my hand.

"D, I'm serious. Call me and I will come." We kissed and hugged in the door way and I got misty eyed. He smiled that million-dollar smile.

"Ooh shoot, so now you gonna cry over a nigga?" I wiped my eyes and then rolled them.

"No I'm not, it's just my allergies." He tickled me.

"Yeah ight! But for real Diamond, I'm going to miss you and that's from my heart." I couldn't respond to that or I would have cried him a river. I left and blew him a kiss as I pulled off.

Anyway, we got up at 6 AM and my parents and Starr's parents rented a van because we were all driving down together. The plan was to stop at Howard to unload me and Starr, who were roommates and then all of us go down and drop Samir off at Hampton in Virginia. Then our parents would come back through D.C. to drop me and Starr back off at Howard. We got to Howard at about 12 noon that first day. I remember getting our key from check in and my dad, the geek, was video taping our every move with his brand new camcorder. I was signing my name on the paper accepting my key and the camera was right in my face.

"Daddy! Please! I can't take that camera no more can you give it a rest?" He kept taping.

"No baby girl. It's not everyday your little girl goes off to college." I stuck my tongue out and crossed my eyes at the camera and Starr pulled down her eyes and pushed up her nose. We made grunting noises like we were apes in the jungle. My mom walked over and hit the stop button.

"O.k. honey that's enough for now the girls are tired of starring in your home videos." My dad put the cap on the camera and hung it around his neck.

"I bet you didn't get tired of starring in them last night." Me and Starr looked at each other with our eyes big. I covered my mouth to keep from tossing my cookies and my mother smacked my dad's arm and laughed.

"Oh Dan you so crazy!" He walked away like he was the man and I screamed, "New subject! Lets go see our room." So we walked towards the elevators and they were broke. Damn, this was the projects. This was going to be my home for the next four years. This event was going to mark the first steps of my adult life. I looked around Frazier Hall and smiled but damn it was hot. Our room was 316. As we carted our stuff up and down the stairs to the third floor I threw my arm around Samir.

"You're mighty quiet. You O.k.?" He kind of pushed my arm off of him.

"Yeah Diamond, I'm fine." I stood back and watched him walk away from me and decided to leave him alone. When we were done bringing things up and setting up we grabbed a quick lunch and got on the road to Hampton. Once we reached the school Starr began to get teary eyed. I hugged my best friend.

"Sis, I am going to miss my brother." I squeezed her tight.

"I know you are. I am too but we will be coming down here harassing him all the time." I then leaned in and whispered in her ear.

"Look around at all the cuties." She wiped her eyes and looked around. A smile crept across her once crying face. She shook her head in agreement with me. She smiled at me knowing her best friend, meaning me was a nut and that's why she loved me. It took Samir about an hour to get moved in. Of course moving one person in takes much less time and is much easier then two. Samir was reading the freshman rules on the board and freshman's had an 11 PM curfew during the week and 1 AM on the weekends. He slammed his hand on the board.

"What? 11 and 1? What is this?" Me and Starr pointed and laughed because Howard didn't have a curfew. Our parents didn't like that but ooh well, it was too late now. We couldn't wait to get back to Howard so our official being grown could begin. We left Hampton about 7 and I jumped in the van so I didn't have to say bye to Samir. My mother hugged him first and cried. Then his mother hugged him and she joined in the symphony of cries. Then my dad hugged him. He taped Samir's whole moving in adventure as well. My dad was sad but didn't cry. He patted him on his back.

"My only son going to college!" Either I was seeing things or Samir had a small tear in his eye.

"Aw Big D go 'head! I will be home all the time." Next Mitch grabbed his son and hugged him tight.

"I'm proud of you Samir. Stay focused. Keep your mind in them books and off all these pretty little girls down here." He gave his Dad a pound.

"Now Dad you know I gotta keep one eye on the girls." All the men laughed. Then Starr hugged him and boo hoo cried. I sat in the van shaking my leg and flipping through a magazine. I waved at him quickly through the window and dropped my head back down. I tried my best to fight back the tears I felt knocking on the back of my eyelids saying 'let me out!' He waved back at me. Everybody got in the one van because we left the other one parked in D.C. As Samir waved from the curb and his dad put the van in drive. I sat up.

"Dad wait a minute please." Mitch turned and looked at me and put the van in park. I slid the door open, got out and slid it back closed for a little privacy. I looked down at my feet and Samir walked up on me. I spoke in a voice barely above a whisper.

"Well Samir, I don't know what to say." He shrugged.

"Me either Diamond. I was drunk that night but I never said that I still love you too." I raised my head to look in his eyes.

"You didn't have to say it, I know it in my heart...Well let me get going. Don't hurt nothing down here!" He grinned.

"I'm not but you don't crush 'em to bad in D.C." I looked down trying to hide my tears.

"I wont Samir." I extended my hand to shake good-bye. He smacked my hand down, grabbed my chin and pulled me in for a bear hug. The tears ran down my face as I hugged him back. I whispered in his ear,

"I'll miss you Samir." He blew in my ear.

"I'm going to miss you too D. Let me, let you go."

"O.k. Samir." Neither one of us let go. We both pulled back slowly and gave a quick peck on the lips. I walked and got in the van. He waved good-bye as we pulled off. Nobody said anything to me about what we said to each other. Starr was sitting next to me and she put her arm around me.

"D it will be O.k. but guess what? We go to Howard!" I couldn't help but smile. We got back to school close to 10 PM and our parents were staying at the Howard Inn around the corner. They were going to leave in the morning. They dropped us off and as we got out my mom waved at me and Starr.

"O.k. you two, we will pick you up for breakfast at 10 AM, be up and ready." I shook my head up and down and slid the van door closed. We walked towards the building but after they turned the corner we walked right back out. There were people outside hanging all over. You know guys flock to me and my sis like magnets so some began to come over. We talked to cats from where we were from. The tri-state area (NJ, NY and CT) ooh and we included Philly in that equation. But it was definitely some cuties from Boston, Baltimore, D.C. and Chi-Town. Cuties were from all over and we didn't discriminate too much. We stayed out until about 1 AM and decided to go in. Walking up the stairs Starr looked like she was on cloud nine. She ran up the stairs and looked at me.

"Yo Sis, this is only the freshman. Can you imagine next week when the upperclassman get here?" She smiled and put her hand up. I slapped her high five and returned her smile.

"Yep Starr, I can't wait!" We continued talking and went into our hot room. The fan was blowing but that was not helping and no air conditioners were allowed. Ooh well, we rolled with the punches. I picked up the phone and called Q and Tahir to give them my room number. Starr picked up and called Danny to give it to him. Once we had on our P.J.'s our phone rang and it was Samir giving us his new number. He had switched rooms because someone wasn't coming to the dorm that was scheduled to come so this way he would have his own room. When his roommate came he said he was a cornball and had to get away from him some kind of way and this worked out perfect. The next morning we did breakfast with the folks, told them the Samir situation and then gave them the boot. We were free at last!

O.k. so our first days at Howard I will never forget. As the upperclassmen filled in it was so many people down there. Everybody would hang out on Georgia Ave at the McDonald's. All the DC cuties use to be their especially scooping out the fresh meat from Howard. You know Starr played her game on campus with the college cats but me I wasn't in to it cause Q was right at Georgetown. College was hard. I am not going to front like it wasn't. Especially the first year. We partied, went to class, partied some more and barely slept. We were both in school for Business Marketing and had to wear business suits to our business class once a week. We took all the same classes at the same times. It was mad fun and I wouldn't trade in those memories for nothing in the world. Tahir kept his word and was coming down to the school almost every other weekend to see me. He had some peeps that lived in D.C. so he said that is why he came so much but we all knew it was to see me. I was still going to see Q every other weekend and Starr had a friend at Georgetown she was going too see. As a matter of fact, it was Dre. You remember Q's teammate? They didn't have sex but did heavy making out. She stayed with him to not have to be in the room with me and Q boning.

One weekend Starr missed Danny so we took the bus home to NJ instead of to Georgetown. She liked Dre a lot but she loved Danny. She was going to surprise him but when we got there we got the surprise. It was Friday afternoon and she rang the bell. Gina answered the door. It was me and Starr so I said, "Hey Gina," and pushed my way in. Gina was always their dropping the baby off. When we got in Danny was standing in the living room with his boxers on. He was shocked and yelled out, "Starr?!" Starr crossed her arms over her chest and put all her weight onto her right leg.

"What is this Danny?" Let me tell y'all, he couldn't even lie and say she bought the baby over cause the baby wasn't even there. Starr had a tear in her eye and he looked down.

"Starr I'm sorry I never meant to..." She cut him off.

"Meant to what Danny?" He looked up at the ceiling.

"Hurt you." She pointed her finger from him to her and then from her to him.

"So what's this?" Gina butt in then when she shouldn't have.

"What does it look like STARR? This is us trying to work on getting our family together." Starr looked at her and put her hand in her face.

"BITCH I didn't ask you. I have been about 2 minutes off your ass for a minute now so don't test me Gina cause you don't want it." Gina walked up to Danny and put her arms around his waist while he kept his eyes glued to the floor.

"What? Huh get over it cause we back together so why don't you move on." Starr looked at me and shrugged her shoulders.

"D I'm sorry but 2 minutes is up!" She punched Gina dead in her mouth. Gina held her bleeding mouth screaming, "Danny!" Starr pushed up her sleeves to get ready to administer another blow.

"Bitch don't call Danny! Now you get over it and get over that knot I just put on your lip." I grabbed Starr.

"Come on Starr you don't need this shit." Danny got in front of me.

"Sis holds up." Danny looked at Starr.

"Starr wait." She cried and screamed.

"Fuck you Danny, you could have told me the truth but nooooo you call me every day saying you miss me and love me and it is all nonsense." He said with an attitude,

"Well why you sneaking up on me anyway? You didn't tell me you was coming home?" Her eyes got big as ping-pong balls.

"What! I called myself surprising you but surprise! I got the shock." He sighed and shook his head.

"Starr I just... I don't know." She smirked,

"You know what. It is all good Danny." She put her hand out to shake his. He looked at her hand like she had the plague.

"Starr you not mad?" She shook her head back and forth and kept her arm extended towards him. I knew that shit was a set up. His dumb ass believed it, smiled and put his hand out to shake her hand. Then she kneed him right in his nut sac. Ooh well. We left and both went to our homes. I went to see Q's mother. She was so happy to see me she took me shopping. We stayed for the weekend and Tahir took us back Sunday. I told him he might as well move down to D.C. since I see him more then I saw Starr and she was my roommate. The next weekend Samir came up from Virginia to see us. It was only October but his body got broader since I had seen him in August. I had a thing for big muscle bound backs. His back was banging. I'm sorry y'all please don't think I'm a slut but with him looking that good I had sex with him. Starr was pissed but she got over it. She was more mad we put her out the room to do it. I hadn't seen Q in a few weeks. I was still going for our every other weekend visits even when Starr didn't go, but sometimes he would cancel last minute. Now that I was down there you would think he would want to see me more but he didn't and me being at Howard he never wanted to come see me. I was getting fed up so I said to him one day, "Look why can't you come to my school sometimes?" He stuttered, "Uh with uh basketball it would be to uh much and uh since Howard and Georgetown play um each other it is a conflict of um uh interest." I wasn't feeling that b/s but I just let him talk. Starr was on the rebound from Danny and started kicking it with some cat from campus along with still talking to Dre. The guy from Howard was nice and he was from NY. He was cool as hell. I think his name was Smitty. He wanted me to talk to one of his boys but I wasn't playing campus cats close cause Tahir was coming to see me too much. I found out in November why Q didn't want to come to Howard to see me. Drama, straight drama.

CHAPTER 31
NEGRO IS YOU CRAZY?

Me and Starr were in the caf getting ready to have dinner one Thursday evening. I was standing in line and overheard these girls at this table talking. The one girl was telling her friend that she was going to skip her evening class on Friday to go see her man at Georgetown. The friend then leaned in and asked, "Girl is he cute?" The girl rolled her eyes and took a sip of her juice.

"Come on now what you think? I don't mess with ugly guys. He is tall and handsome and he is one of the star players on their basketball team." That is when my ears opened. The girl fingered her short bob style hair cut. She smacked her lips together as she finished her sentence.

"Yeah girl, he from Jersey and I'm trying to get him to come home to Chicago with me for Thanksgiving. He said he can't cause it is just him and his mom and since she is a nurse and too busy to come down and see him, he wants to go home and spend time with her." I had my tray in my hands and my arms began to get weak. My palms filled with sweat and I swallowed hard as I eavesdropped on the rest of their conversation. The friend smiled.

"That is nice of him. He sounds sweet." The girl did a little dance in her seat smiling and waving her fork around.

"Girl he is sweet. That's my boo, Quan. Everybody calls him Q but I call him Quansey." I couldn't believe what I was hearing. My arms gave out and *Bam*! I dropped my tray all over the floor. I felt like I was starring in Ferris Bueller's Day Off the way the whole caf turned to look at me. Everyone was wondering who the klutz was. I bent down trying to keep my face covered and began to pick up the utensils that fell. Tears spilled over my eyelids like a cup that was overflowing. One of the staff members came over to help me with the mess and I handed him the tray.

"I'm, I'm so...sorry I I I gotta go!" I ran from the caf like my name was Flo Jo. Starr was standing in line waiting for her cheeseburger and she yelled behind me.

"Diamond hold up. Where you going?" She was on my heels and grabbed my shoulder to spin me around.

"Sis what's wrong? What's the matter? What happened?" I was hyperventilating trying to tell her the story. We sat down outside the caf on the edge of the wall.

"Sis what should I do?" Now hold on, I know y'all like what comes around goes around but bump that. He could have cheated with a chic from another school, why he pick Howard? Starr handed me a tissue from her Coach bag.

"D, don't you worry we are going to handle it." We walked back to our dorm and talked about our plan. I knew the chic was going the next day to see Quan. Me and Starr didn't have school on Friday's. We hooked our schedules up for no evening classes and no Friday classes. We decided we would make a late night trip to Georgetown the next day.

The next day came and I was getting cold feet about the whole thing. I thought, it might be another Q on the team but my mind mentally smacked me Pow! Wake up Diamond, you know better! Now mind you, I had talked to Q Tuesday and Wednesday. He was telling me how much he missed me. When I pulled myself together after the incident I talked to him that night. Once again he was saying how much he missed me and loved me. I held the phone with much attitude.

"Diamond I can't wait until the following weekend to see you." I cleared my throat.

"Well Q since you miss me and I miss you so much, I'm not doing anything this weekend so I will come tomorrow to see you instead." He dropped the phone and then picked it up.

"My bad D. Butter fingers. Anyway Boo I would love to see you this weekend but I am going to my man's house in Virginia this weekend. His mother is cooking and you know how I love to eat." I sighed.

"Dag Q, I wish I could come."

"Baby I wish you could too but this is a fella's weekend. You understand don't you?" A tear formed in my eye because he was lying to my face, well to the phone. I cleared the lump that was setting up shop in my throat.

"Yes Q. I do." He then added insult to injury.

"Next weekend can't come quick enough. Is them Howard cats chasing you boo?" I choked back my tears.

"Yeah as always but you know I love you and I'm not thinking about them. I am only thinking about you. I would never cheat on you boo. Never. Is them Georgetown hoochies still trying to get at you?" He laughed.

"Yeah but you know it but you the only apple in my eye girl." I grasped tight to a sarcastic tone.

"Oh really?" He softened his tone.

"Yes really boo. Why you say it like that?" I sighed.

"No reason...Look Q I really want you to start coming over here so I can show my man off around campus." He cleared his throat.

"O.k. I will try but you know the coach be bugging about us going to rival schools." The tears streamed down my face looking like waterfalls.

"Yeah...I know Q." Starr was sitting across from me shaking her head as to say that's a damn shame. She picked up her line in our room and listened in muting the phone. I had to hang up at that minute because I was ready to go off.

"O.k. Q let me go study, you have a safe trip and call me the minute you return." He blew me a kiss through the phone.

"You know I will, we are leaving tomorrow around 4 or 5 so I will call you before we leave."

"Ight then bye."

"Wait D, you forgetting something?" I dabbed at my eyes.

"What?!"

"I love you D." I whispered, "Me too Q, me too." I

hung up the phone and the tears came down like a monsoon. Starr got up and came across our spacious double room to my bed and hugged me.

"Don't cry sis. We gonna bust his ass tomorrow." The next day like clockwork Q called me at 5 and said he was going to Virginia and around 4:30 I seen miss thing walking across campus to a cab. Me and Starr went and took the bus to Georgetown that night. We got there like 11:30 and since it was Friday night, it was people all over the place.

When we got to Q's dorm I paid a guy twenty dollars to sign us in so we can get into the building. Once me and Starr got to his floor I knocked on the door and then we pressed our backs up against the wall next to his door so when he opened the door he wouldn't see us. Q snatched the door open.

"What up?" When nobody was standing there he stuck his head out of the door. He looked from left to right and on his right was me. I popped up off the wall.

"Surprise Q! Are you surprised?" In a shaky stuttering voice he replied "He.He.Hey D! Wh wh wh what 'cho doin' here?" I heard a female voice echo from his room.

"Q who is that?" I answered for him. I pushed Q out of the way and ventured into his room.

"His girl. Who you?" Starr followed close behind me with Q coming in third. The chic looked me up and down and laughed.

"That's funny because I'm his girl." She was sitting on his bed with her blouse half unbuttoned and her jeans open. Q was in his Tommy Hilfiger lounge pants without a shirt on. It was the same shit Starr dealt with, just a different nigga. Q reached and touched my shoulder.

"Um Diamond what are you doing here?" I shrugged his hand off my shoulder, crossed my arms over my chest, and looked him up and down.

"I should be asking you that exact same question cause you told me you was going to Virginia with your boys remember?" He stuttered once again.

"Um well um um it um got um cancelled." I furrowed my forehead.

"Interesting Q. How can something get cancelled that was never planned?" The girl then stood up and pointed towards me.

"I know you. You go to Howard." She began to button her shirt.

"Yeah, you the girl that dropped her tray yesterday in the caf." I unfolded my arms.

"Yeah that's me. I over heard you talking about going to see my man at Georgetown and I guess it shocked me and I dropped my tray." I took a glimpse around Q's small single dorm room and he had taken my pictures down and replaced them with hers. She walked over and stood in front of Q facing me.

"Well Q, it seems she is mistaken so let her know please so she can go." I screamed, "What you stupid bitch?! If anybody is getting let known something it is you and if anybody going anywhere it is you, not me! Don't get it twisted! I got mad time in." She put her pointer finger up.

"First of all I got your bitch and second of all, ain't you the one with the boyfriend with that black truck from Jersey that be at the campus all the time." Starr came to my rescue. She stepped in front of me and got in the girls face.

"First off bitch, the truck is blue not black and don't look so hard next time cause he be coming to see me. Stop riding my man and his truck dick." She laughed sarcastically.

"No I am not riding your man or his trucks dick. I was getting ready to ride my man until you bitches came. Now can you bitches disperse so I can do just that or would you like to watch and get a lesson so you can keep your man next time?" I was staring at Q and he was staring at the floor. Starr pushed her sweater's sleeves up.

O.k. I'm gonna give you that first bitch for free but the next time you call me or my sister, Diamond a bitch it will cost you that whole top row of teeth." She laughed like this was a big game.

"Yeah Whatever!" I sighed to stop this petty argument.

"Starr don't even waste your breathe, lets just go, I seen all I need to see." Q grabbed me.

"D wait!" I did 2 moves in one. I pulled away and swung on him in the process. He dipped it and grabbed my arms to restrain me.

"Diamond calm down." I yanked away from him bumping into Starr.

"Calm down?! Calm down?! We been together almost 3 years and you always giving me this shit about us and how you wouldn't cheat because of your father and and..." My voice became faint and I began to cry. Starr put her arm around my shoulder.

"Sis don't cry. Fuck him." Q's eyes grew large.

"Ooh Starr it's like that?" She sucked her teeth.

"You damn right, you made it like that. You cheating on my sister Q, what the fuck? What's up with that?" He rubbed his forehead.

"I didn't mean for this to happen." Starr pulled his card.

"Mean for what to happen? The cheating or getting caught? Whatever it is, it happened and what you plan on doing to make this shit right?" An inner voice said, "Open his closest." When I did, the back of closest housed our big poster size pictured neatly rolled up and a box with my pictures in it. I pulled the stuff out. I waved a few pictures of us at her.

"See. Look. Pictures of me and Quan." She briefly glanced at the items I was holding.

"See what? I see that they are in the back of the closest where they should be because you're his ex?" I unrolled the poster and ripped it in half. Q snatched the 2 halves from me.

"Diamond no. Why did you do that?" The girl placed her hands on her hips.

"Q why do you care? Look this is getting old, what

are you going to do?" I walked towards the door.

"I will decide for him. I'm out. Come on Starr." He blocked the door and covered his nuts. I had told him about the Starr/Danny incident. He softly touched my arm.

"D can I explain?" I quickly closed my eyes and shook my head back and forth. He intertwined his fingers in the begging motion.

"Please Diamond. Please?!" I didn't say or do anything because I didn't have the energy. He didn't know what to do so he introduced us. Dumb.

"Kendra this is Diamond. Diamond this is Kendra." She flopped back down on the bed and rolled her eyes.

"Charmed I'm sure." I muttered.

"Whatever." He began to ramble on about her.

"Um D, I met Kendra at a party last year, as a matter of fact I met her that night we was talking last summer and I was going to that party? Do you remember?" I shrugged my shoulders.

"Vaguely, but whatever that makes it acceptable then." I was being sarcastic y'all. He interjected.

"Hold on D. Let me finish. We started talking as friends first and then it turned into more." I scratched my head.

"Ooh is this the same night that you told me you loved me, and asked me 'are you seeing someone else' and I told you no and then I asked you the same question and you said you only had eyes for me? Is that the fucking night in question Q?" He looked down and softly squeezed out, "Yes." I screamed, "So I need to know cause I just don't get it. How could those same eyes less then an hour later change?" He sighed and leaned up against his dresser.

"I didn't know we would take it here. I thought I could keep it just as a friendship but... either way she has been coming to see me on the weekends you don't come." I softly uttered, "So you change the pictures on the wall every week?" He looked down and shrugged.

"Pretty much." I clenched my teeth together and

balled up my fists.

"So are you having sex with both of us Q." Kendra jumped up at that time.

"Damn Q that's fucked up but I forgive you. Ooh well a man will be a man and we know men ain't shit, but whatever. So Q who do you want? Well it is obvious it is me." She looked at him and me and Starr looked at her. Q hung his head low.

"I don't know who I want to be with." My neck jerked towards his direction. I went off the deep end at that moment.

"You don't know? You don't know? What the fuck you mean you don't know? Earth to Q! We have been together for 3 years and you don't know who you want. You know what, you know who you want and you know it's not me because I told you Q, don't hurt me. Didn't I?" He slowly shook his head up and down. I snatched his face up by his chin for him to look at me in my eyes.

"No nigga you gonna look at me. I asked you over and over again did you want to see other people and you said no. I even told you that it was O.k. to see other people but you said noooooooooooo! And that was the weekend after you met her Q! I will never forgive you for this Q! Do you hear me? Never! I am going back to Howard now and I will make sure I call your mother and let her in on this." He pleaded with me.

"D please don't call my mother. This is between me and you." I shrugged my shoulders.

"So. I want her to know what a piece of shit you are and why I'm not having Thanksgiving with y'all." He looked at me with sad eyes and sighed.

"Diamond..." I looked at him with ice daggers in mines and screamed, "Quan!" I grabbed Starr's arm.

"Come on Starr lets blow this joint. This scene is getting old." Kendra waved her hand towards me and Starr and winked.

"Thanks for stopping by. Good night and have a safe trip back to Howard." I stopped in the door and semi turned and decided against fighting her. I was getting to old for this bull. We left his floor, went and reclaimed our ID from the front desk and called a cab outside of the dorm. The cab station said it was a shortage of cabs but one would come soon. While we were standing out side on this unseasonably warm night for November, Quan came running out. He ran up to me and I looked him up and down.

"My didn't we get dressed quick." He had thrown on some gray Nautica sweat pants and a white t-shirt along with his Tims. He softly touched my hand.

"D please don't leave like this. Lets talk about it." I pulled my hand away and turned my back on him.

"Bye Q, beat it!" He grabbed my arm.

"Diamond we need to talk." I pulled away again.

"Go talk to Kendra. She must be the real reason you couldn't make it to Howard to see me." He looked down.

"Damn you Q! Stop trying to act like the victim. You disgust me! You ain't no better then Samir. You talked about him like a dog saying he ain't shit for hurting me but you know what? He is much better then you will ever be cause at least that shit he pulled... we was in high school with those juvenile games, now we are in college and you still playing? I thought college made you smarter. I know one thing you need to get a refund cause it has not helped you in the least." He folded his hands behind his head.

"D I deserve that and much more but I made a mistake can you please forgive me?" I sucked my teeth.

"You can't be serious! Fuck you Q and the heifer you rode in on or should I say was about to let ride you. I wouldn't forgive you if the world was coming to an end. I wouldn't piss on you if you were on fire and there was no water. If we were the last 2 people on earth and it was up to us to have kids, the world would die out as we know it. Do you get it? It is over, finito, finished, hasta livista!" Our cab was pulling up. Perfect timing.

"This is our cab. Q make love to your girl Q." He

pulled on me again.

"Diamond, if I put her out right now will you come back?" Starr opened the cab door. I pulled away from him.

"No deals Q." Then I spit in his face. He grabbed my arm and used his t-shirt and free hand to wipe his face.

"Wait D please." He pushed Starr out of the way so she couldn't get in. He leaned in the back of the cab.

"Go 'head man. They staying." She tried to push him out the way and yelled at the driver.

"No he is lying. We are going." Q closed the door and Starr would open. I jumped on his back and kicked the door closed. The cab driver got annoyed and pulled off. I jumped off his back.

"Asshole! Why did you do that?" He grabbed me up.

"Cause we need to talk D. Starr please, can I just talk to her?" She rolled her eyes and shrugged her shoulders.

"She is grown so ask her." I looked down while he grabbed my chin.

"D, please can we talk." I looked at Starr and winked at her. Then I looked at Q.

"Yes we can." He grabbed my wrist.

"Let's go in the lobby and talk." I pulled back.

"I want to talk in your room." He scratched the back of his neck.

"Um my room?" I crossed my arms over my chest.

"Yes, your room. What happened, I thought you would put her out of I stayed?" He sighed.

"O.k. let me just go get her out." He began to jog and we followed him.

"Wait up Q. we coming too." Starr pulled my wrist and whispered in my ear.

"So sis, you going to forgive him?" I turned my lip up.

"Of course not! I'm just making him put that bitch out. Show her that Jersey girls are the best in the world. Can't no Chi-Town bitch take no nigga from me and think I will let it ride. Make that can't no bitch from nowhere take a nigga from me and I let it ride. Once he put her out we will leave too." Starr laughed.

"Good idea!" He was way in front of us and by the time we got in he was already up the stairs. We tried to sneak past but the guard caught us. We couldn't get in because we had to be signed back in. I picked up the phone in the lobby and dialed Q's 4-digit extension. He didn't answer. I called again and then again. Me and Starr ended up sitting on the couch in the lobby. In the next few minutes they came down and he was damn near dragging her. She approached me and Starr while Q went to get her I.D. She jumped in front of me and put her index finger so close to my face I thought I was seeing cross-eyed.

"You no good bitch! You said you were leaving!" I smacked her hand down and jumped up and got in her face almost nose to nose.

"I said I was but now I'm staying and you are leaving so good-bye bitch." She moved back a tad bit giving herself space between the 2 of us.

"Fuck you! I love Q and you and nobody else is going to take him from me!" I inched back up closer to her face.

"Bitch he was already mine so I ain't gotta take shit I already got, so get your bama ass out of here before you catch a bad one." Well we had a live one here. She smacked the shit out of me and I was in a state of shock. Q yanked her back and saved her from an ass whoopin'.

"Kendra what is wrong with you? That is my girl." Starr jumped up and approached her from the side. She punched her in the face and kicked her in the stomach. She threw her hands down to hold her stomach.

"No! My baby?" Me and Q replied in unison.

"Baby?!" She rubbed her stomach.

"Yeah, y'all heard me, BABY!" I felt light headed like I was going to faint. I grabbed my head and massaged my temples.

"Sis go call us a cab." Starr ran over to the payphones in the lobby and they had a hundred different cab numbers stuck all over the phones. When we used the payphone outside it only had one number but now we had a variety of cab companies to call. I began to walk away and Q grabbed me. By this time we had an audience.

"No D, don't leave she is lying!" I squinted my eyes almost closed.

"Are you fucking this bitch raw Q?" She moved her hips like a snake and pointed at her private area.

"Yes he is. He be busting all up in this!" He mumbled,

"Only a few times." I screamed over to Starr.

"Sis call all of the cabs cause I gotta get the hell out of here!" The security guard finally got up off his fat twinkie eating butt.

"If you don't live in this here dorm, you gotta go!" I sucked my teeth.

"Oh we going you better believe that but this bitch don't go here either so she gotta go too." The security guard began to push us towards the door.

"O.k. then out with all of y'all!" I wanted this bitch to come outside in the night, so I could get in her ass. We left the door with Q on my heels. He grabbed my elbow.

"O.k. I put her out. I thought we were going to talk?" I turned and faced him.

"Are you fucking crazy? I don't want you to talk to me again, let alone touch me. You fucking that nasty bitch raw and she might be pregnant?" He grabbed me again.

"D, she is lying!" She was in front of us at the curb and our cab pulled up. She tried to get in it and Starr ran up on her and yanked her back.

"Bitch this is our cab!" She tried to get back in the cab again.

"So!" She was a live one. Starr sighed.

"I had enough!" She punched her dead in her mouth and they started fighting. I ran up to where they were and we jumped that bitch. I didn't even care if she was pregnant. She had too much mouth. That cab pulled off fast as hell but another type of cab pulled up. Was the white cab also known as the police. We were stomping that bitch like back in the day with Shakira. I know if she was pregnant, she wasn't anymore. The cops jumped out and broke the fight up. Q ran in the building. I couldn't believe he was leaving us. The cop yelled.

"Everybody freeze!" Your all going to jail." I pleaded,

"No officer please you don't understand." The cop had a smart mouth.

"No Miss. I understand. I understand your going to jail." He told all of us to put our hands behind our back. Me and Starr did but Kendra had a lot of mouth and a bloody lip to match it. She moved her neck around and pointed her finger at the cop.

"I'm not putting my mother fucking hands no were! Fuck that! These bitches just jumped me and you want to lock me up. I don't think so!" She went on and on and me and Starr just looked at each other and shook our heads as to say this bitch better shut up. Me and Starr were cuffed, while Kendra kept arguing with the cop. She finally was cuffed and Q and his coach came running out. The coach happened to know one of the cops. He knew the one that Kendra was cussing out. The coach went over to him and whispered, "Josh this is just an innocent little brawl. Please let them go. You know how girls are over my basketball players." Josh laughed.

"Yeah you know I know. We have to break up about 10 of these fights a week... No problem for these 2 (pointing at me and Starr). Those 2 are quiet and can go, but this one (pointing at Kendra) she is disrespectful and rude and she is going." Me and Starr smiled at each other as we were uncuffed and Kendra commenced to screaming.

"No it is not fair. They jumped me you saw them!" The other cop spoke up.

"Don't tell us what we saw. We didn't see shit!" She cried.

"Q you saw. You saw, please help me!" He lied.

"No I didn't. I saw you smack Diamond in the lobby along with everybody else." She cried as they placed her in the car.

"I can't believe you Q. I thought you loved me." He shook his head back and forth.

"I have never ever told you that I loved you. I said I liked you but not now because I just found out you was so violent." The second cop looked at me.

"Miss would you like to press charges?"

"No... but she does go to Howard with me and I am scared (yeah right! Me scared, I was fronting for the cops)." The cop looked worried.

"Well Miss, you should get a restraining order." I looked nervous to keep up the scared act.

"I will." Me and Starr saw another cab, grabbed it and got the hell out of dodge while Kendra sat in the back of the police car. Q was still standing there shocked. I stayed strong until the cab was out of his view then I started to cry. Starr put her arm around me.

"Don't cry sis you got Tahir, and Samir." We laughed.

"You crazy girl." She tapped the back of the cab driver' seat.

"I know and I learned from the best. Excuse me, can you turn this up this is my song." The cab driver did and Candy Rain by Soul 4 Real poured out the speakers. We sang along and it made me feel a little better. We got back to school and didn't look back. Except just to watch our backs.

CHAPTER 32
A TIME TO GIVE THANKS

You know that old saying you always go back to what you know well when I got in I called Samir. It was like 4 in the morning. He was my old reliable. Some girl answered in a sleepy voice, so I hung up. I didn't want to mess up his new thing because mine went sour. After that night, we didn't see Kendra for a couple of days but when we finally did see her she was taking her stuff out of the dorm. Apparently she had a full scholarship from a non-violent organization in Chicago and when they found out she was arrested and charged, they yanked her money. Her family didn't have the money to keep her in Howard so she had to go home. Oh well, that was her problem not mine. Good reddens because that campus was not going to be big enough for the 3 of us. Me, her and Starr. And let me tell you, the chic was never pregnant. One of her friends was a friend with one of my friends on campus and you know how that goes. I knew all of her business in a matter of hours and I am sure she knew some of mine. The only difference is I didn't get to Howard and need a best friend mines with me so I only told Starr my deepest darkest secrets. I didn't keep a lot of girls around me because that always meant trouble. You know sometimes girls have too much hate in their blood and I didn't need the extra-added drama with gossiping bitches. I had enough drama of my own. Also, I was a professional college girl. I didn't want to go up top on anyone at school. (That meant, punch someone in the face.)

Anyway, Kendra was a homebody virgin from Chicago who couldn't do anything or go anywhere at home and got to school and lost her damn mind. She went buck wild smoking weed and drinking and also having sex WITH MY MAN. Quan messed her head up and ran game on her. She told her friend that Quan was the one she saved herself for and she wanted to have his baby. And, you are going to laugh at this one; Quan told her he was a virgin too. I know, I laughed too when I first heard it. What the hell is up with that lie? What dumb broad would believe that? I mean Q was a fine, 6'2 basketball player from Jersey and he was supposed to be a virgin. I don't think so! I mean it could happen, not often, but it could happen but in Quan's case it wasn't happening. I guess a guy will say anything to get into those panty draws! So we went home for Thanksgiving soon there after and Q's mother called me when I got home on Wednesday and asked me to come see her. I had called her and told her everything that went on. She was madder with Q then I was. The reason she was so mad is because she said she had told him so many times not to play with people's feelings. I hadn't told her the whole story, like the fighting that went on or the raw doggin' (having unprotected sex.) I just told her that he had cheated and he got caught. While on the phone with Jackie I said, "I'm sorry Ma, I just can't come over there because I don't want to see your son." She chuckled, "Oh D he is not even here. Please come. He will be gone for a while. He went to see his boys." I looked up at my ceiling.

"Oh alright. Just for a minute." I put on a high neck sweater and some fitted jeans, pulled my hair back in a ponytail and left. When I got there I pulled into the driveway. As soon as she opened the door she hugged me saying she missed me and how good I looked. Tears formed in my eyes because I was still upset about our break up. She grabbed me by the hand and led me in the kitchen.

"D don't cry cause you gonna make me cry and I am ugly when I cry." So I smiled and wiped my tears. We sat at the kitchen table and she was telling me about work and her new friend she was dating. I told her about school and Starr. As we laughed in unison at something I heard the front door creep open. My heart sank as I tried to catch my breath. I knew it was Q and I didn't want to see him. He sauntered in the kitchen with a humungous smile plastered across his cute face. His mother turned up her lip at him.

"What are you doing home so soon?" He rinsed his hands off in the sink.

"Eric, Rashon, Dwight or Tariq wasn't at home." He dried his hands off and came close to me.

"Hello Diamond." He smiled but I didn't. I stood up.

"Hi." I grabbed my brown butter leather jacket off the back of my chair.

"Well I guess I should be going." Jackie stood up as well.

"No Diamond don't leave." She then sucked her teeth.

"Bye Quan, she came to see me not you. Go somewhere." I put my jacket on.

"I'm sorry I have to. I should have never come over here in the first place." Quan stood in front of me and put his hand on my shoulder.

"Diamond I want to talk to you...please?" I kept my eyes glued to the floor.

"No Q, please just leave me alone." Jackie intervened, "Q would you please leave her alone, don't you think you did enough damage? Go call that hussie, what's her name Kenya?" I corrected Jackie.

"KENDRA!" Then I stared at Q. Q sulked while pouring himself some O.J.

"Aw, come on Ma. Don't play me out. I am not stunning Kendra. I love Diamond." Jackie placed her hands on her hips.

"Oh you love Diamond do you Q? What did I tell you about that word love? You don't love her or you wouldn't have cheated on her! Q get out of my sight because the sight of you is making me sick standing in here looking like your cheating ass father! Diamond, will you please stay for me." I flopped back down in the kitchen chair near tears.

"O.k. Ma, I mean Jackie." She rolled her eyes in Q's direction.

"You can still call me Ma even though he messed up and you won't be my daughter in law it is O.k." Q touched my shoulder again.

"Diamond I am sorry for what happened, would you please forgive me?" He pulled the empty chair next to me, plopped down in it and scooted over close to me. He took my hand in his.

"Pretty please Diamond?" A tear fell from my eye and his mother rolled her eyes up in her head.

"Q what did I tell you? Get out of her face. Leave her alone and go somewhere." He jumped up from the chair.

"Dag, ight Ma. Diamond, please don't leave with out us talking. I will be in my room." He backed out of the kitchen looking at me the whole time.

"Yeah...O.kayyyy Q." (I was being sarcastic.) He stopped in the kitchen door way.

"D come on now, I'm for real." I fought back the other tears in my eyes. I mean my tears were like soldiers. One never came alone.

"O.k. Q. I will." His mother sat back down and waved her hand towards her son.

"O.k. bye Quan, I won't tell you again." He left out the kitchen and ran up the stairs. His mother placed her hand over mines on the glass table.

"Diamond you don't owe him anything, you don't have to talk to him if you don't want to." I wiped one quick tear that escaped my eye.

"Yes Ma I do have to talk to him. I want to get this over and done with or he will keep bothering me." I stood up and she did as well and gave me a hug.

"O.k. Diamond whatever you want. Trust me baby, I have been here and the hurt will get less and less until it stops. Then you will meet somebody new or you will be back with him. Whatever you want to do make sure it is what you want to do and not what he wants you to do." I hugged her back tighter.

"Thanks Ma." I went up the stairs and knocked on his room door. From the other side I heard, "Come in." I opened the door and stood there. He was lying on his bed and sat up. He patted the spot next to him on his bed.

"Come here D and have a seat please." I rolled my eyes and folded my arms across my breasts.

"I'm fine right here Q, what did you want to talk about?" He stood up and walked towards me.

"D I am so sorry." I crossed my arms over my chest.

"We already established you are a sorry bastard, that's old now is that all you wanted?" He stood in front of me casting a shadow over me with his 6'2 frame over my 5'6 frame.

"I don't know what possessed me to cheat on you Diamond. I don't know what came over me." I began to back up away from him almost into the hallway.

"O.k. then I don't know either, so I'll see you later." As I turned to walk forward he grabbed my wrist and swung me back towards him and pulled me in his room.

"Diamond wait." I looked up into his eyes and the ice began to melt away from my heart a bit.

"Yes Q?" He pulled me closer to him.

"D don't be so nice to me. It makes me feel worse." I shrugged.

"Well I'm sorry Q. I don't feel like being mean and evil." He dropped my wrist.

"What are you sorry for Diamond? I'm the one that did you wrong. Don't be sorry D, do something. Curse me out or something please." I slowly shook my head back and forth.

"Nope Q. I won't do all that. This is old. I'm over it. Me spitting in your face was bad enough and I apologize for that." He sat down on his bed.

"No that's O.k. D, I did deserve it..." He looked up at me and began to speak again.

"D, I... uh...cut Kendra loose that night cause you mean more to me than she ever will. D you are my whole world and I am lost with out you." I used my neck muscles and swung my ponytail back off my shoulder.

"Oh so does she still call you?" He tried to act real annoyed and kicked his foot out.

"Yeah man she still calls me. All the way from Chicago too. She said we could work it out. Please, I don't want her. She says she forgives me for everything and I never even apologized to her. I told her to move on but she said she just can't, I'm the one for her...whatever man, I told her you're the one for me." I laughed sarcastically.

"I'm the one for you? Please Q, that's a joke! Well maybe you should reconsider being with her since you had UNPROTECTED sex with her and we were oh so in love and we never had sex with out a condom so that when we graduate we can do this thing the right way. Get married and then have kids. Isn't that what you said La Quan? But no, you didn't just cheat on me, no that wasn't enough you had to take it a step further and raw dog the bitch...real nice Q, real nice. What if she got something?" He looked down at the floor and then up at me.

"I know D, but she was a virgin. It is no feeling in the world like being with a virgin. It felt so good with out a condom and I couldn't help it, I can't lie but I am sorry!" I dropped my arms to my sides.

"Well, you better stay with her then since it 'felt so good' to you and you know that is not right taking that girls virginity and then treating her like this. You know better then to play with someone's heart like that. It's just not right. What would possess you to do something like that?" He sucked his teeth.

"I know it's wrong but what's done is done and I don't care about her. D, I want to be with you." I grabbed my ponytail and smoothed it down.

"Well Q that's not gonna happen cause I don't want to be with you and if you can treat her like that then I'm sure you wouldn't have a problem doing the same to me. Besides, I want to be alone. I have never been alone and I kinda like it. So you better call her and get her back or move onto your next victim." He jumped up.

"Come on now D I told you I don't want her or nobody else. I want you and I will be alone too until we can work this out." I laughed.

"Oh yeah? Don't hold your breath! Look I gotta go, anything else Q?" He stretched then yawned not covering his mouth.

"Yeah D there is one more thing. Can we at least be friends?" I clenched my teeth closed because I was getting aggravated.

"We are friends Q." He cocked his head to the side and looked at me with the puppy dog eyes. You know those are my weakness.

"You call not speaking friends? If so I don't and if we are friends then can I still call you?" I twiddled my thumbs.

"Don't you call anyway?" He smiled.

"Yeah...I do but you don't accept my calls. You always say loud enough for me to hear 'Starr tell him I'm not here' or when I catch her on a bad day she picks up and hangs up. And let's not talk about if you answer. You always pick up and when you hear me say hello you say 'wrong number' and hang up." I couldn't help but laugh a little. He laughed with me then reached out and rubbed my hands. I guess he thought because we were both laughing that it was all-good because he had the nerve to say, "D, I love you can we just start again?" I pulled my hands back from his.

"You can't be serious and if you are hell no! We can be cordial but that's all Q. I cant be but so bothered with you, you hurt me and you knew how I felt about being hurt again, but I'm strong and I will bounce back so don't you worry about me." I tried to turn and leave and he reached over my shoulder and pushed the door closed. He looked down at me while I looked down at the floor. He grabbed my chin to look at him.

"Can I have a hug D?" I will admit I was getting weak. I closed my eyes and slowly shook my head back and forth. He leaned closer into to me with our bodies slightly touching. He whispered into the core of my ear.

"Please D?" My body briefly shuttered as his breathy words tickled my eardrum. I opened my eyes and looked at my so-called Prince Charming. I didn't move an inch. Again he leaned in close to my ear.

"Pretty please D?" This time before he pulled back he let the tip of his tongue slightly trace the outside of my ear. My knees damn near gave out that time. He pulled back and looked at me. Then he pulled in his bottom lip. That was it! He was looking scrump-deali-ocious! I knew I better hurry and get out of there before we were doing the horizontal polka. I tried to turn to leave and he gently but with force pushed me up against the door and put his face in mines with our lips barely touching.

"Where you going D I got your car blocked in so you can't leave until I'm ready for you to leave and right now I'm not ready." I stuttered, "Q, I, I, I, I gotta ggggoo please." He kissed me with one single real soft and sweet kiss on the lips then took the tip of his tongue and licked my lips real quick and enticing. This time my knees did buckle and my panties felt like I peed on myself. He smiled as he held me up by my elbows.

"Are you O.k. D?"

"Um hum." He took my hands in his and pushed them above my head up against the door. He leaned in as if our bodies were one and whispered in my ear again.

"Diamond no matter what you believe I love you and I swear that on my life. I made a mistake D, you do remember what a mistake is right? Just like you did when you tried to creep back with Samir that time and I caught you. I forgave you right? So please forgive me, I wouldn't lie about my love for you D." I turned my head so I didn't have to look at him. Tears began to come like always and I couldn't believe he was bringing up the past. I pulled my cheeks in and chewed on the insides of them both. He gently pushed my head back towards him.

"You gotta believe me Diamond, you just have too." I was all choked up.

"I, I, I do Q but I, I, I gotta go. Please let me go." He looked at me one last time and smiled at me.

"Not with out a smile Diamond." I mustered up all my strength to produce a smile. He then kissed me again this time with tongue. I didn't fight him. I kissed him back just as passionately if not more. I reached up and cradled his neck and hugged him. He smelled so good. He had on Polo Sport cologne and deodorant. We released from the kiss but continued to hug. Tears streamed down my face because I knew I had to leave him alone. I was the first to pull back.

"Q can you please unblock my car now?" He used his thumbs to wipe my running tears.

"Anything for my little Diamond." He kissed me on my forehead.

"Yo D, I love the shit out of you and I want you back. I don't care what I gotta do to get you back I will do it. I'm telling you, I'm going to get you back. D, can you do me a big favor?" I smiled at him. I know, dumb right?

"What is that Q?" He grabbed his keys out of his sweat pant's pocket.

"Whatever you do, please don't go back to Samir." All that lovey dovey shit we had just been through, right out the window. I got an instant attitude.

"Can you just let me out please Q?!" He shook his head back and forth.

"Nope not until you promise me that." I pushed him back away from me.

"I don't owe you jack but just incase you must know Samir has someone new. He is not thinking about me. Now please let me go." He sat down and slid his boots on.

"I'm going to let you go D but he got somebody cause I had you but I know him and he will be back real soon." I put my hands on my hips and rolled my neck.

"For your information, no he won't. He has a girlfriend that he is feeling at school so don't worry about me and Samir. He said he wants to marry her, but don't worry about me and you either cause it's not happening." He stood up and winked at me.

"Whatever you say D, I'm going to get you back, fuck what you heard. I'm not even having this conversation because I don't want to debate about it. Samir can marry her because I am marrying you. You can bank on that. I will let you out now beautiful." I just rolled my eyes and didn't say anything else. I opened the door and ran down the stairs. I ran into the kitchen.

"Bye Ma. I gotta go." I left out like a bolt of lightning. She said to my back.

"O.k. D but I hope to see you before you leave." I said from the front door, "As long as your son is not here." She came to the door to watch me leave.

"Diamond let's do brunch on Sunday before you leave."

"O.k. it's a date." I was in the driveway getting in my car. She yelled out to me, "Girl you like the daughter I never had. I can't lose you know." I waved at her.

"O.k. Ma. I will see you Sunday." Q came out the door she was standing in and kissed her on her cheek. She playfully wiped it off. He got in his car and she went in the house. He sat in his car for a while until I flung my door open and looked back at him. He blew me a kiss, smiled and backed his car out to let me leave.

Thanksgiving was all-good. My family, Starr's family, and Danny's family all ate together at my house. Q's mother had to work so I made her a plate full of desserts and bought them to the hospital. She cooked a small dinner but nothing like Ann's spread and she didn't make any desserts. She had store bought cake. That is a no no when you are around Ann. Anyway, I knew Q loved my mom's cooking so I made him a plate and a plate full of desserts as well and headed to his house. It was after 5 and I know him and his mom ate at about 1 because she had to be to work at 3. I rang his bell and he yanked the door open and smiled. I extended the bag of food in his direction.

"Here!" He took the bag.

"What's this?" I shifted the weight from one foot to the other.

"It's a plate and some dessert. I know your mom didn't make any." He smiled and opened the door wider.

"Thanks D, do you want to come in?" I looked down

at the steps.

"No thanks just being nice on Thanksgiving." He lifted my chin to look at him.

"Let me rephrase that, I would like it if you came in D." I squeezed past him in the door.

"Just for a minute Q." He closed the door and followed me into the family room. He was watching football and I sat down on the couch. He went into the kitchen and warmed up the peach cobbler I packed for him. He came back in the family room with vanilla ice cream piled on top of it. He sat down and ate a spoonful.

"Damn D, I miss your mother's peach cobbler." I smiled broadly and sat up straight.

"Well I made it this year!" He put the spoon down in the bowl and looked over at me.

"My baby made this?" I stood up to leave.

"Q...come on now..." He pulled me back down next to him with his free hand.

"I'm sorry, you know what I mean, but it is good and it tastes better than your mothers. Let me call her and tell her." My eyes got wide like teacup saucers.

"No, no don't do that. Nobody knows I came here. I just did." He flicked the TV off.

"D, tell me the truth. Did you miss me?" I shook my head yes. He flicked the TV back on.

"Well we will leave it at that." He started to eat his dessert again.

"Damn I'm rude D. Do you want some of this?" I shook my head no and just stared at Q. He put a tad bit on the spoon and put it to my lips.

"Please have a little for me." I ate it off his spoon and then he licked the spoon behind me. He put the bowl down and leaned over and kissed me. I didn't stop him. I leaned back and we kissed some more. While he was getting on top of me and unbuttoning my coat that I never removed my beeper vibrated between us. I pushed him up and off me to check my beeper. It was my mother beeping me and I think that was a sign. I sat up straight.

"I'm sorry Q, I gotta go." He reached over and touched my hand as I buttoned my black pea coat.

"Will you call me later?" A single tear dropped from my eye.

"I don't know Q, I don't know." I stood up and he did as well. He wrapped his arms around my waist.

"Well will you come back later?" I shook my head no. He gave my waist a little squeeze.

"Please D, please come back we can make this work." I put my hands over my ears, closed my eyes, and rocked back and forth slowly. He grabbed my arms down.

"I'm sorry, we don't have to talk about us, we can talk about sports, the weather, school anything D, please just come back later." I walked towards the door.

"I will see Q." I ran from the house like it was on fire. I was saved by the bell because if my mother didn't beep me when she did, me and Q would have had sex. When I walked through the doors of my own home my mother sent me back out to the store. That is why she paged me. She wanted me to pick up more Martinelli's apple cider from Pathmark.

When I got back in Tahir had called and left a message. When I called him back he invited me out to the movies. I went out with him to keep me away from Q. We had such a nice time that once I returned home I didn't even think of calling Q. He called me though and left me a message saying he understood how I felt because that is how he felt when he thought I was cheating on him. He ended by saying he will give me my space and when I was ready I could call him. On Sunday Q's mother called me like 9 in the morning.

"Good Morning Miss Diamond, I.H.O.P. at 11?" I stretched.

"O.k. I will meet you there. The one in Elizabeth right?" She laughed.

"Come on now, you know that is the only one I eat at. You know I have my own private waitress Aneesah up in there." Little did we know Q was listening on the other phone and walked into I.H.O.P. after me and his mother were seated. He tapped on the table.

"Can I join y'all?" She looked at me and I shrugged my shoulders. He scooted me into the booth and stared at me as I drank my tea.

"What Q, What are you staring at?" He smiled.

"My future wife." I had de ja vous cause I remembered when Samir said that same line to me in the past. I didn't answer him. I just let it slide. Me and his mother talked a bit while he gawked at me. We ate our breakfast and said our goodbyes. I gave Jackie a hug and then he opened his arms. I gave him a hug too and he whispered in my ear, "D I love you. I will call you." I pulled back and didn't say so much as a word to Q. I got in my car and pulled off. I was confused and just needed to remove myself from the situation. I went home and got ready to go back to Howard.

CHAPTER 33
I GOT A NEW MAN WELL OLD BUT NEW

Me and Starr went back to school and for the rest of the school year we were just cooling. You know Starr cut Dre off because he was Q's boy and she didn't want to go up there alone so she told him they could be friends. He said whatever, it didn't matter. She said that was better for her.

When we came home for the summer we did us, meaning whatever we wanted to do we did without worrying about what a man would say because we were young, single and free. Starr didn't even look Danny's way when she came home. I know it hurt to see him and Gina outside playing with DaGina but she was strong. She would put on some short shorts and a halter top, jump in her Barney colored MX-3 and keep it moving past them. On a few occasions I caught Danny looking at Starr because Gina had gained over 30 extra pounds from little DaGina and hadn't lost it at the time. He tried to explain to me all the time about what happened and why and that he was sorry. He also asked me if him and Starr could be friends but I shut him down letting him know I didn't want to hear that shit and I told him just like that. The same way my sister told Quan forget about it, I told Danny the same thing. Me and Danny's friendship wasn't the same since he tried to play my sister out. He was and always would be my God brother but I wasn't feeling him.

During the summer me and Starr worked in my mother's restaurant as waitresses. We had had enough of the beauty salon and plus all the cuties use to come in my mom's downtown spot. We left with more phone numbers at night then tips. Her business was doing well and she loved it. She did all the cooking herself. Don't let nobody even step foot in her kitchen and try to stir something or she would act the fool. I would have flashbacks to when I was a kid. Tahir was still on my team egging me on to be his girl since Q had messed up. I decided to take him up on his offer. I was now Tahir's girl. It happened like this, he came to get something to eat and I let him have it on the house. At the time he was leaving out the door Quan was coming in the door. Quan or Tahir had never seen each other face to face so they didn't know each other. As Quan came in the door I was standing in he said, "Hey Diamond, how you been?" Tahir stopped in his tracks and looked at Q. I rolled my eyes.

"I'm just fine Q." I sucked my teeth.

"What are you doing here anyway Q?" He smiled.

"Getting some of Momma Ann's cooking and trying to see you." Tahir let a slow smile creep across his face then stepped up close to me and Q.

"Baby what time do you want me to pick you up tonight?" At first I was lost because we weren't supposed to be going out but I caught on quick.

"Like 9 is good boo." Tahir then extended his hand towards Q.

"How you doing fam? I'm Tahir, Diamond's boyfriend." Q looked at his hand.

"So." Tahir began to laugh at Q.

"Damn fam, it's not that serious, I was just introducing myself so you can see what a real man looks like and don't be trying to see my girl for nothing except if you want to place an order." Q made a face and walked towards his car.

"Yeah ight! Whatever!" I smiled at Tahir.

"Your girl huh?" He put his hands on my waist.

"That's right! My girl!" I shrugged.

"If you say so." He gave my waist a little pinch.

"I did!" I playfully rolled my eyes.

"So!" He pulled me in close.

"So you mine got it?" I put my hand to my head as if I was in the army saluting an officer.

"Yes sir!" We walked arm and arm to his truck. I kissed him good-bye and floated back inside. I walked right up to Starr and told her what happened. She laughed out loud.

"Good for Q's dumb ass!" Nobody ever knew about when I went over to Q's on Thanksgiving, but once I got back to school and the reality of it all hit me again and again, I couldn't take it with Q anymore. I floated around on cloud 9 for the rest of my evening shift. I kept saying, Tahir's girl over and over in my head. As I drove home that night my mind focused in on Samir, I don't know why but it did. Samir had his new girl and he was all in love. She lived in South Jersey and he was going to see her all the time. That night me and Sam were both coming home at the same time. We sat on my stairs and had a long talk like old times. We laughed, then got mad at old stuff all over again and then we laughed again. He told me about his girl and said it was something about his girl that made him think she was the one. I wanted to cry because I was suppose to be the one not her. I told him I was happy for him even though I was lying. He said he didn't ever have the urge to cheat on her and he began to apologize to me for the past. I told him to just forget it, we were both young and dumb. He then stood up to go home and threw in, "Well D I hope you find true love because you deserve it." I smiled.

"Samir I hope so too and I got something to tell you." He looked at me with his eyes opened wide waiting to take in what I had to tell him. I was taking too long.

"What is it D, tell me!" I looked down, exhaled and then looked up again.

"Don't get mad O.k." He sat back down.

" I wont D, now what's up?" I cheesed (smiled big.)

"Well Tahir asked me to be his girl today and I said yes." At first he was quiet and then he breathed out.

"You know what D…that's cool but just be careful." I was confused at what I needed to be careful about.

"What does that mean Samir?" He looked up at the sky.

"Well you know how Tahir is. Just don't put your heart all into it he is not the most faithful person in the world." I jumped up.

"Ain't that the pot calling the kettle black, don't be a hater Samir." He sighed.

"What are you taking about Diamond?" I rolled my eyes.

"I'm talking about you trying to hate on him." He stood up next to me.

"I'm not trying to be a hater Diamond, I am trying to be a friend to you and stop you from getting hurt. Do you think he is the faithful type?" I came back at him and hit him hard.

"Does your girl think you are?" He looked me in my eyes.

"I am cause I don't cheat on her ever!" I chuckled.

"Well you can't prove it by me Samir." Our voices began to elevate. He walked down the stairs.

"Diamond you know what...I gotta go." I snapped, "Bye!" He turned to face me from the bottom step.

"But before I go don't say I didn't try to warn you." I waved my hand in his direction.

"Good bye Samir." He started walking away and then turned back towards me.

"Hold up, you know what D, we not kids anymore. I care about you and I love you and I don't want you to get hurt. I know Q hurt you and I'm sorry about that but I'm just saying, Tahir is deep in the streets and girls throw themselves at him. That's my man and all that and I wouldn't kick dirt on him or kick his back in unless I cared more about the other person and in this case I do, I care more about you Diamond. Just be careful O.k.?" I crossed my arms over my chest.

"Whatever Samir, you do the same." He just shook his head and headed for home. Deep down I knew Samir was right about Tahir but I was feeling Tahir and all his power he had in the streets. With Tahir I didn't want for nothing, meaning like if I needed my hair done or wanted a new Coach bag or belt. The only thing I wanted for with him was time. He didn't put in enough time with me and that upset me. He always said, "Diamond, my money won't make its self!" and I would just accept that. When I was with Samir and Quan I could see them everyday all day if need be but with Tahir everything was about his money and nothing ever came before his money. That was something he made clear to me from the beginning. I mean I knew these things but I thought with us being a couple it would be different. Boy, was I wrong.

CHAPTER 34
4TH OF JULY

It was the weekend before the 4th of July and Q's mom invited me over to a cook out for the 4th. We were on the phone rambling on like old school girls when I asked, "Can I bring my boyfriend?"

"Sure you can and tell your mom, dad, your Aunt Debra, your cousins and the Mitchell's. Just tell everybody!"

"O.k. Ma will do let me know if you need some help." She laughed.

"Girl please I am having it all catered. I hired a set up and clean up crew. We are not going to do anything but enjoy ourselves." I laughed at her.

"O.k. then see you next weekend." So the next weekend came and everybody but Samir decided to go. Q and Sam still weren't feeling each other so Samir decided to go to South Jersey to see his girlfriend. I called Tahir to remind him that he needed to stop by.

"D it is the first of the month and money is flowing, you know how I am about my money." I rolled my eyes at the phone and exhaled.

"I know Tahir but please just come by, even if it is just to say hi, please?" He sucked his teeth.

"Yo I will just come, eat and bounce." Just like a typical nigga. I got dressed and went to the cook out with out him. He beeped me two hours before he came and said he was on his way. I told him the address and it didn't take 2 whole hours to get to Q's house from wherever he was but I didn't say anything when he came. I was like a little puppy dog around him and was happy as a pig in shit to see him come in the backyard. He sauntered in the back with his swagger on and I smiled like I hit the jackpot. My father turned his lip up in disgust because he did not like the likes of Tahir but ooh well, you can't please everybody. Tahir threw up his hand to the crowd of people, "Hello everyone." Some of the young nurses and nurses' assistants from the hospital were eyeing my man up and down. I quickly jumped up and grabbed his arm and lead him in the direction I was sitting in. He sat down, extended his legs and crossed his feet.

"Yo D, make me a plate please?" I jumped up like I was Ms. Celie and he was Mister from The Color Purple. My father leaned up and peered over at Tahir.

"Tahir are your hands broke?" My mother nudged my father while I stopped dead in my tracks and whipped my neck around. Tahir pulled his legs in and leaned up to look at my dad.

"No Mr. Staple, I ..." I butt in, "Excuse me Mr. Staple he didn't ask you to make the plate, he asked me and I don't mind making my man a plate. As a matter of fact I want to make it! I would be honored to make it!" I knew that pissed my dad off but he pissed me off. Tahir already didn't want to come and I had to practically beg him to come. I didn't need my dad getting smart and running Tahir off. My father tried to stand up.

"Look Diamond, I don't know who..." My mother yanked him down in his seat.

"Danny, please!" My father took a swig of his Budweiser and shut up. I'm glad he didn't embarrass me any further. While at the food table, Q walked up next to me. I was piling a little of everything on his plate. The spread she had was unreal every cold salad you can name, baked beans, crabs and shrimp, all kinds of meats. She had gone all out. Anyway Q nudged me in my back.

"Yo Diamond I don't appreciate you inviting that nigga to my house. I think that is real disrespectful." He was across the cook out talking to every female that wasn't nailed down but I was disrespectful. I rolled my eyes and picked up a plastic fork and napkin.

"I'm glad you don't get paid to think." With that said

I walked away with my man's plate. Tahir saw me coming and sat up and rubbed his hands together. I handed him the plate. Before my butt could touch the seat Tahir had another request.

"Yo D, can you get me a Heineken?" I walked over to the cooler and bent down and got one out of the icy cold water. I came back over and handed it to him. He put his plate down and grabbed his opener from his keys. As he tipped up the bottle to his lips the Russell St. Clan all looked at him. He slowly took the bottle down from his lips and flashed them that million-dollar smile.

"I'm legal, do you want to see my I.D.?" My mom and the rest of the females laughed but my father didn't. As Tahir chugged down his beer and knocked off his whole plate he requested another beer. I gladly got up and got it for him once again. After about 3 or 4 beers he stood up and stretched.

"D I gotta go. Can you walk me to my truck." I jumped up and smiled.

"Of course I can." He had only stayed for about an hour but I was pleased with that. I linked my arm through his and he waved goodbye to everyone in the yard. Jackie passed us taking a pot in the house and waved at us. She was still doing a bunch of running around and didn't even have time to come over and meet my new man. As we approached his truck, I gave him a kiss goodbye. I tucked my red, white, and blue tank top into my white shorts and noticed one of my white K Swiss sneakers were untied. I bent down and tied it while Tahir started his truck. I stood up and he rolled down his window.

"Tah can we please go see the fireworks tonight?" He playfully punched me in my arm.

"Didn't you see them last night in my bedroom?" I crossed my arms over my chest.

"Whatever!" I started blushing acting like a little kid. I don't know if it was because he was my man now or what but the sex had gotten better, much better. I think he was more into trying to please me instead of just pleasing himself or maybe one of his exes told him to get a book because his loving was trash. Whatever the reason, it was now satisfying me. He looked down at the clock and then back at me.

"I guess we can Diamond, I don't know but I gotta get going." I sucked my teeth.

"What? Don't make me put you in a headlock!" He put his hands up playfully covering his face.

"Oh, Oh, please don't hurt me. Please don't hurt me tough girl, the fireworks it is." I laughed at his silly behavior. He shifted the truck into drive. He stuck his puckered up lips out the window. I gave him a peck.

"Ight D, I will see you later."

"O.k. Bye!" He pulled off. I watched his car until it turned the corner. I walked in the back on cloud 9 when Jackie let the air out of my cloud. She grabbed me by the arm.

"Sooo Diamond that is the mysterious Tahir huh?" I looked up in the sky all goggly eyed.

"Yes! Isn't he all that?" She let my arm go and looked me up and down.

"He most certainly is Diamond and you know it looks a lot like your cousin Tahir from the mall a few years back." My face dropped. I completely forgot about that incident in the mall at prom time a few years back. I stuttered, "Ma let me..." She closed her eyes, cocked her head to the side and put her hand up.

"Diamond you are grown and there is no need to explain to me, but it looks like my son is not the only dishonest one that was in your relationship." I tried to touch her hand.

"No..." She pulled her hand back.

"Diamond its O.k. save it! I don't even want to know..." And on that note she walked away. We kept the conversation lo key so nobody knew what was up but I was hurt. How could I be so stupid as to invite Tahir? My stomach tied up in knots and I felt the urge to go number 2. I stood there with my eyes closed holding my stomach. Q walked up and tapped me on the shoulder.

"You know, I was thinking...Nigga in a truck, every other weekend from Jersey to see you. That was him. He was coming to see you not Starr. You were cheating on me the whole time." I sucked my teeth.

"What?! Duh Q, is he the only nigga in Jersey with a truck. No and he just got that truck so get your facts straight. That was Starr's friend that was coming to Howard to see her." Q grabbed my arm.

"Yeah right and when I see that nigga again I will ask him." I smacked his hand off of me.

"You do just that. I will give you his house, cell, and beeper number." He looked me dead in my eyes.

"No I don't need all that. We will bump heads soon enough." I threw both of my hands in the air.

"Well bump them then Q, I don't care. You cheated, got caught, it's over case closed! I got somebody new now so leave it alone already!" He got heated and started throwing verbal jabs below the belt.

"Yeah ight Diamond. I should have said it was over when you were cheating with Samir but I didn't. You came over and sucked my..." I put the palm of my hand in his face.

"Whatever Q. I wasn't cheating with Samir and stop trying to put your mess ups on me. Yeah I came over and sucked it because I loved you and as much as you kept your face between my thighs I thought you were going to set up residence down there. I am surprised your mail doesn't come addressed to 'Diamond's Punaneeeeeee.'" He smacked my hand out of his face.

"Whatever Diamond you will want to be back with me." I furrowed my brow and snapped my neck back.

"Are you drunk Q? It is over do I have to spell it out? Leave me alone already!" He laughed.

"I'm not bothering you and I'm happy it's over. That's why I cheated on your dumb ass. Fuck you!" I took both hands and covered my kitty kat.

"No No boo. You wish you could fuck me but you

will never get that chance again." I turned and walked away.

"Bitch!" I stopped in my tracks, shocked because he had never called me out of my name. I just looked at him and stuck up my middle finger and kept it moving. I decided I needed to leave this stage, exit left. I waved for Starr to come over to me and told her I was leaving.

"Not with out me you're not." I dipped out of the backyard with out saying anything to anyone. Starr came out behind me. When I got home I beeped Tahir. He didn't call right back so I kept beeping him until he did. He called back and said tell Starr to be ready too because his boy Quadir was coming. I called Starr and told her what Tahir said.

"Hell no D, I'm not going Quadir is ugly as hell!" I laughed.

"Yeah sis but he got money." She sucked her teeth.

"Well he better have a lot of it!" I laughed at her remark.

"He does sis, he does." Quadir would always ride up to Vauxhall with Tahir and check for Starr, but she wasn't checking for him. He would beg me to hook him up with Starr but it wasn't going down. I just told him she was seeing someone. I had to convince Starr in some form of fashion to go with us because I knew Tahir would act funny if it was just me him and his boy. They would be talking and I would be looking stupid. When Tahir pulled up to pick us up Quadir jumped out of the passenger seat. He opened the back door for Starr as she approached the truck. He looked her up and down and licked his lips.

"Hey beautiful!" She cut her eyes at me and clenched her teeth.

"Hey..." I jumped in the passenger seat so I didn't have to look at Starr. You don't think Tahir got out to open the door for me do you? Quadir was ugly but he dressed his ugly ass off and it didn't hurt that he had a drop top BMW. Starr was conversing with Quadir in the back. When I tried to talk to Tahir he turned the music up. He was so rude sometimes. We went to see the fireworks at Bear Temple Park in Union. Afterwards we went to Dairy Queen on Stuyvesant Ave in Irvington to get ice cream. Tahir then dropped us off saying the block had mad money out there and he needed to check up on his runners (the cats that sold his drugs for him) to make sure they were doing what they were supposed to be doing and he would talk to me later. Qua asked Starr if he could call her later and she smiled and gave him her number. He was such a nice guy that it made up for the ugliness. Me and Starr then sat on my stairs looking up at the stars, talking about old times. She told me even though Quadir was ugly she was going to give him a chance because he was so nice. At that moment, Samir pulled up on two wheels. He jumped out of his car and his shirt was ripped. His lip was bleeding and he had a lump on the side of his head. Me and Starr jumped up and ran over to him. I screamed, "Samir what happened to you." He walked behind his car.

"Shh girl! Nothing, where is Tahir at? I reached out to touch his face.

"I am not telling you until you tell me what happened." He got annoyed and sucked his teeth.

"None of your business D, this is serious, I need to know where Tahir is. This is not a game." I saw the seriousness written all over his face.

"He just left like a half hour ago and he said he was headed back to the block." He ran past us in the house and Starr ran behind him still asking him what happened. I stayed outside and went and sat on my steps. Starr came over and sat back with me.

"He won't talk to me and he just beeped Tahir and he is on his way back over here." Less then 20 minutes later I saw his blue Expedition turning onto my block, damn near on 2 wheels. It was 2 twin niggas I didn't know in the truck. He stopped in front of Samir's house. Samir was coming out and I was walking towards his truck.

"Tahir what's up?" He looked me up and down.

"Not now Diamond, me and my peoples gotta go

handle something." Sam came out and jumped in the back of the truck. He didn't look at me. I tried to open the back door but Tahir hit the door lock.

"Tahir I want to go." He screamed on me in front of everybody.

"Hell no Diamond! This is nothing that concerns you now go your ass in the house and I will call you later." He pulled off damn near running my toes over. I smacked my forehead, fuck that, he gotta drop Samir back off so I will sit here until they come back, he does he think he was talking too? I went in the house and got my cordless and Starr ran across the street and got her cordless and Samir's cordless. She came back over to my house.

"Something is up D. Samir's girlfriend just called here on his phone and asked did he get home yet and I told her no and she said well please, please tell him to call me when he gets in. I told her O.k. but she didn't sound right. She sounded like she was crying or something." I snatched his cordless from her hands.

"Well let's call that bitch back cause Tah just came and got Sam and you know that means they are up to no good." Starr snatched the phone back from me.

"Fuck that D I'm calling her back!" She pushed *69.

"Hello can I speak to Blair? (That was his girlfriend's name.) How you doing Blair, this is Samir's sister Starr, you just called here and I need to know what happened?" I stuck my head next to Starr's ear to ear and we put the phone between our ears so we could both hear. The girl was saying that her ex boyfriend was at her house and she tried to get him to leave cause she didn't ask him over and when Sam came him and the ex got into it and then him and his boys tried to jump Samir and then Samir finally got in his car and pulled off and she wanted to make sure he was alright. Starr jumped up and snatched the phone up with her.

"What the fuck bitch, are you trying to play my brother out because I will fuck you up!" I stood up and stuck my head back to Starr's to hear Blair's response.

"No Starr, never that. I would never try to play your brother out. I love Samir and I never meant for this to happen." Starr paced back and forth again cutting off my ties to hear the conversation.

"Yeah I will tell him you called and y'all stories better coincide or that's your ass!" Starr clicked the phone off. I got nervous at that moment.

"Oh no Starr, I hope they didn't go down there." Starr looked at me like I was retarded.

"Where else could they have gone Diamond?" My eyes got big.

"What, where does she live at? I don't want Tahir getting locked up over some dumb shit." Starr rolled her eyes at me, "What about Samir Diamond?" I nervously fidgeted my fingers.

"Yeah him too. I ain't got nothing but time on my hands and we are sitting out here waiting for them to return. She picked up Samir's phone again.

"I can do you one better then that. Hold up." She pushed redial to get Blair back on the line.

"Yo, what's your address?" I heard the echo from Blair's voice.

"WHY?!" Starr sucked her teeth.

"Look, I'm not going to ask you again, bitch what is your address?" Blair hung up on her. Starr's eyes got wide and she looked crazy as she flailed her arms around.

"No this bitch didn't just hang up on me! Hold up sis..." She ran across the street to her house. She came back out in less then 2 minutes and it was a card that Blair had mailed to Samir in June. Bingo, it had her address in the corner. She lived on Coral Way in Neptune, NJ. I snatched the envelope and turned up my lip.

"Who the hell lives in Neptune? I thought it was a planet?" Starr took the envelope back, folded it and put it in her pocket.

"Obviously this bitch does. I know Neptune is off the Garden State Parkway. Let's roll!"

CHAPTER 35
THE SMACK DOWN!

We jumped in her car and got on the parkway. It took close to an hour to get down to Neptune. We got off exit 102 South and pulled into the first gas station and asked for directions to Coral Way. We found her house and she was sitting on her steps looking nervous. I tapped Starr on her side.

"Starr pull up in front of her house and let me handle her." We had only seen a picture of her but we knew it was her at first sight. She was light skinned with cheek length hair and she was thick with a big butt. I jumped out before Starr came to a complete stop.

"Blair?" I said her name like we were old buddies. She stood up.

"Yeah who dat?" Starr then jumped out of the driver's seat.

"Bitch don't you ever hang up no phone on me. I'm Starr!" I threw in, "And I'm Diamond." Blair began to walk up her stairs backwards. Starr walked up to her gate.

"Bitch where are you going?" She had a petrified look on her face.

"What do y'all want?" Starr unlatched her gate.

"The truth! Where is your punk ass ex at now and his punk ass boys?" She squirmed around in her spot,"I don't know." Starr opened Blair's gate.

"Well bitch if my brother tells me something else, I know where you live and I will be back. I stretched my neck around Starr's.

"Correction, we will be back!" She nervously turned the doorknob to her front door.

"If y'all don't leave I am calling the police." I waved my hand in Blair's direction.

"Just like a punk bitch, fuck her let's go sis." Starr tried to go up her stairs with me pulling her back.

"Bitch you think I'm scared of some police? O.k. I see your work! You don't have none! But you will see mine! Just wait bitch! I will see you!" I pulled Starr harder because she was getting over amped, "Let's go Starr. It ain't worth it."

Blair ran in the house and we went to the car. She was peeping through her curtains from the front room of her house. As Starr pulled off I saw her come back out on her steps to watch us pull off. Starr looked in her rearview mirror.

"Oh shit D! Is that Tahir behind us?" I looked back and saw his plates "GY204T" coming down the street. I got scared.

"Hell yeah! Let's go before he has a fit. Merck! Merck! Merck!" She mercked (pulled off fast) down the street and we got back on the parkway and got home in like 40 minutes. We jumped out of the car looking guilty like we just robbed a bank and sat on the steps. We were sitting there laughing at how much of a punk Blair was and how we just got away. I was praying Tahir didn't see us because I would have to hear that. Once we sat there for about a half hour, Tahir came pulling up. He had dropped off the other 2 boys so it was just him and Samir. Sam was smiling from ear to ear and as he got out the truck he gave Tahir a pound.

"Thanks you my nigga!" Tahir smiled.

"You know that!" Tahir yelled over in my direction.

"Diamond come over here now!" I rolled my eyes.

"No." He slightly elevated his voice.

"Diamond don't play with me. Get yo' ass over here now!" So I got up and walked slowly towards his truck like my shoes had cement bottoms. He frowned his face and threw the driving column in park.

"Diamond do I look like I'm fucking playing? Hee

325

hee haa haa, hell no, now get your ass over here now!" I didn't appreciate him trying to scream on me in front of the twins, so I kindly turned back around before I reached his truck and went and sat back down on my stairs with Starr. He jumped out the truck and came over to me. He spoke nice and calm to Starr.

"Hey Starr, can you excuse us please." She stood up and yawned.

"Yeah I'm tired anyway, I will see you tomorrow sis." I watched her walk down the stairs.

"O.k. sis good night. See you tomorrow." Tahir sat next to me and watched Starr and Samir go in and close the door. Then he grabbed up skin on my forearm and pinched the hell out of me.

"Yo, when I tell you to do something you better fucking do it." I sucked in air and made that sucking noise with my teeth because he was hurting me. I pushed his hand off, "What?!" He pushed his Atlanta Braves fitted hat upward so I could see his eyes.

"You heard me Diamond. Don't make me put my 9 and a half in your ass." I laughed.

"Yeah whatever nigga! You don't look like Daniel Staple to me. As a matter of fact he is in the house sleep, so I know you not my damn father!" He put his hand on the back of my neck and squeezed it like he was squeezing a lemon for lemonade. I scrunched my neck and dropped my head backwards to stop the pain.

"Yo D, I didn't ask you all that did I? I don't have to be your daddy to tell you what to do. And if I say I'm your daddy, then I am and right now I'm your daddy." The look in his eyes was like he hated me, and it was at that time that I knew he was dead serious and this was not a game. He let go of my neck and slapped me upside my head.

"Diamond don't make me..." His beeper went off. He stood up.

"Look I gotta go." I sucked my teeth at him.

"Who is beeping you at damn near 2 in the morning?!" He stood in front of me and pointed his finger in my face.

"Do I ask you who be beeping you? No! So don't start trying to play the possessive role. You my girl and all that but don't take shit far, you feel me?" He used his finger to mush me on the side of my head. I jumped up.

"What?!" He threw his hands up as if to invite me to try him.

"Do you have a problem with your hearing?" I sat back down and waved my hand in his direction.

"Bye Tahir. Get the fuck out of here before we be out here fighting." He pulled his hat down over his eyes.

"Oh so you think I'm playing with you? You think I'm some joke ass nigga?" He then yoked me up by my tank top collar.

"Come on we need to take a little ride." I was nervous as hell and trembling a bit. I took both hands and tried to push his one off of me.

"No I don't want to take a ride." He squeezed the yoke he had on me tighter.

"You don't have a choice!" He basically dragged me to his truck, opened his passenger side door and tossed me in like a rag doll. I tried to get out but he hit the car remote door lock and locked me in. He hit it in time for him to jump in the truck and pull off. He reached over and squeezed my thigh.

"We need to talk in private Diamond." He pulled down the street and around the corner to our meeting place on Oswald Place when we used to creep. He shut his truck and lights off. He reached over towards me. Pow! He smacked the shit out of me.

"That's for your mouth." Whap! He smacked me again.

"That's for your hard head." Smack! He smacked me one last time.

"And that's just because." I held my face and my chest heaved up and down. I was mad and wanted to attack. Tears welled up in my eyes and I lunged across the seat at him like I was Tina and he was Ike in What's Love

Got To Do With It. He knocked me back and started choking me.

"Diamond this ain't no fucking game and I'm not fucking playing with your ass! Do you hear me." He began to close his fingers around my neck tighter and shake me harder. I choked for air and squeezed out, "Yes. I hear you, I hear you. Get off me!" He squeezed even harder.

"I am not sure you understand, do you understand?" I placed my hands over his to try to remove them. Tears ran down and leaked into my ears. I screamed out, "YES!" He let go and backhanded me.

"What did I just finish telling you about your mouth? Oh you will learn right here and right now to answer me the right way! It is yes Tahir. Say it, say yes Tahir." I rubbed my neck because my throat was dry and sore. I answered nicely scared for my life.

"Yes Tahir." His beeper went off again. He hit the lights and started the truck again.

"Now sit up and fix your face before I really give you something to cry for." My mouth fell open. I felt like a child again when my mother would spank me and then tell me that same bull shit ass line. I would think well if that was nothing to cry for then what was. My face was stinging and I pulled the visor down and looked in the mirror. I had a big red handprint across my left cheek. He looked over at me checking my face out.

"I'm sorry D but don't make me crazy and I won't act it. Do as you're told and you will be fine. I don't like no hardheaded bitch. When I tell you to do something, do it. It's just that simple." I couldn't believe what I was hearing. I spoke in a calm voice barely over a whisper.

"Tahir can you take me home please?" He put the truck in drive and began to drive.

"I am D. Are you O.k.?" I clenched my teeth closed, "Fine!" He slammed on the breaks and I flew forward.

"Do you have an attitude Diamond?" I reverted back to my whispering voice.

"No I'm just tired is all." He started driving again.

"Oh O.k. be dressed by 11 tomorrow morning cause I'm coming to get you." I didn't answer. By this time we were back in front of my house. I tried to jump out but he hit the door lock button again quickly and locked me in. He had dark black tints on his windows so I knew if anyone were up on the block they wouldn't see him abusing me. Tahir hemmed me up again.

"Diamond you are gonna have to learn the hard way I see." I cried out.

"No Samir, please let me go!" He smacked me three times in a row. Whap! Whap! Whap!

"Bitch are you fucking him? My name is Tahir Diamond you better get it right or I will kill you." I whimpered like a wounded dog.

"Sorry Tahir. I'm so sorry. It will never ever happen again!" He shook me like a snow globe.

"You better be sorry and it better not ever happen again! You dumb bitch." In the next breath he returned to his normal self.

"O.k. baby just be ready in the morning." I looked at him with one eyebrow raised.

"Why? To get beat on again? No thank you!" He reached over and rubbed my face and my hair that had grown down past my bra strap.

"No D not to get beat on but you just got to listen and stop being so disobedient." I couldn't believe my ears. What was I a fucking dog? I replied sarcastically.

"Yes Master." He rubbed his chin and looked straight ahead.

"Master? Hmm...I like the sound of that." He smiled and reached over and grabbed my hand.

"Look D I gotta go. Give Master Tah a kiss." I didn't want to, but damn I liked my life and I kissed him to get out alive. He unlocked the doors. I got out. I went in the house, washed my face and got in the bed. Then I cried, what else? It was close to 3 AM and Starr called.

"You O.k. sis? I just saw Tahir pull off." I sniffled.

"Yeah I guess." She adjusted the phone.

"Are you crying D? What happened?" I cleared my throat.

"Naw I'm not crying. We just had an argument that's all." I was not about to tell my best friend that I got all smacked up and punked out. I changed the subject quick.

"Did Samir and them see us down in Neptune?" She exhaled.

"No and I am glad they didn't. I asked him what happened and he told me not to worry about it because it was handled and to mind my business. That piece of shit. I went down there cause that bitch played him and he is getting all snotty. Fuck him, next time I won't care."

"I know that's right sis. Look, I'm tired and I'm getting ready to go to sleep."

"Me too cause…(her phone beeped) who the hell is this calling, D hold on!" She clicked over and clicked right back.

"Sis, no I am not going to bed. That is Quadir on the other end." I smiled happy for her.

"Ill! Tell him don't be calling at no damn 3 AM. You know the rules. Anything after midnight 'It's a Booty Call!'" She laughed.

"Shut up sis, you know it is not even going down like that. It is O.k. cause I kinda like him with his ugly self, bye!"

"Bye girl!" I rolled over and went to sleep. The next day at like 11:15 my phone rang and it was Tahir.

"Are you ready Diamond?" I smothered my face in my pillow.

"Tahir please not today. I just want to sleep." His temper flared.

"Diamond what did I just tell you less than 24 hours ago about being hard headed?" I pleaded with him, "Tahir please I just need some rest." He shuffled the phone.

"Be ready by 12 Diamond." I moaned.

"But it is 11:20 now Tahir."

"Well I suggest you hurry…" And he hung the phone up in my ear. I was scared of a repeat of last night so I did what he said. I got dressed in a mini black DKNY jean skirt and a gray and black t-shirt that read, "DKNY" and tied it in a knot in the back. I slide on my black and gray DKNY sneaks, grabbed my small black coach bag, slung it around my body and waited outside. Tahir pulled up. I walked to the truck and lifted the handle. Once I opened the door there was a dozen red roses in the passenger seat with a card attached that read, "I'm sorry." I picked them up and sat down. I looked out the window and not at Tahir. He reached over and touched my thigh. I jumped. He rubbed my leg.

"Diamond I am not going to hit you. I'm sorry baby. I was drinking and I know I can't drink cause I can't hold my liquor. I get all violent and shit." He looked so sincere and he had a wife beater on with his muscles rippling like he was the rapper, Fifty Cent. I looked him in his eyes. He leaned over and kissed me on my cheek.

"Diamond I am so sorry, I never meant to hurt you cause you know I am not like that." I put the flowers to my nose and smelled them. I smiled and then thought back to last night.

"I know you're sorry Tahir but last night you scared me." He ran his fingers through my hair.

"D please forgive me, I need you D, for real. Please baby give me one more chance. I will never put my hands on you again." He flashed me that million-dollar smile and my cold heart towards him turned warm. I returned his smile.

"It's O.k. Tahir but don't ever do it again O.k.?" He licked his lips eyeing my revealing thighs.

"O.k. don't let me drink again." I reached over and held his hand.

"Deal. Can I have a kiss?" He leaned in and gave me a quick kiss before driving off.

"Guess what? Quadir and Starr are going too. They are going to meet us down there." I still didn't know where we were going.

"For real? Down where?" He looked over at me like I was crazy.

"Seaside Heights. Where else?" I fell back laughing because he loved to go down there just to jet ski. I turned up the air conditioner and reclined my seat. I was happy for Starr. I hope Quadir didn't treat her like Tahir had begun to treat me. We all ended up meeting up at the McDonald's on the parkway in Union. Quadir and Tahir followed each other down to Seaside. That morning they both got a new toy. Cell phones. You remember the ones that came out and where big and gaudy. They were calling each other all the way down to Seaside. I snatched the phone from Tahir on like the seventh call.

"Quadir let me speak to my sister." Starr got on the phone.

"Hey sis you alright." She said loud enough for Quadir to hear, "Yeah I guess I am alright. I don't have nobody to talk to since Quadir is on the phone with his boyfriend Tahir instead of talking to me." Quadir cut in from the background.

"I'm sorry baby. I won't talk to Tahir no more until we get there." She laughed.

"O.k., you heard that Diamond? Tell your man to stop calling, we're bonding." I laughed.

"Oh O.k., Tahir Quadir told Starr to tell me to tell you, don't call him no more cause him and Starr are bonding." Tahir playfully snatched the phone.

"Ill Starr bye. Me and my boo will bond then. Good bye!" He hung up and we laughed. He reached over and pulled me in to lie on his chest. His underarms even smelled good. They smelled like Degree. Once we parked and got on the boardwalk Quadir looked a tad bit better in the daylight. Don't get me wrong, he was still ugly but I'm telling y'all he took pride in what he wore and the whole personal hygiene thing. Him and Tahir looked like the bopsy twins with the same type of Enyce sweat suits on. Quadir did have a nice body. He had done 3 years in prison so that explained that big back. He had the type of muscle bond back you only get in prison. He was still on parole too. If he violated his parole he would have to go back to prison for 2 more years and finish out his sentence. We were all bugging out on the boardwalk talking and he came out of nowhere with, "I'm going to see my P.O. (parole officer) even on my days off. As a matter of fact, what time is it. I might make a surprise visit to her today." We all laughed. We were on the boardwalk chilling. We went and jet skied, got on rides and played plenty of games. We took the old black and white gangsta pictures together. Tahir and Quadir dressed like the gangsta's while me and Starr dressed like the old time females with the big umbrellas and frilly dresses. We ate cotton candy, candied apples, and funnel cakes. We were the perfect couples that day even though Starr and Quadir weren't. You couldn't tell by looking at them that they weren't. It seemed all-good but I still didn't want to test Tahir so whatever he said, I did. I was trying to avoid a nice black eye or a front or side tooth missing like I see chics with. Tacky just tacky. Anyway that was July and all the rest of July and August was peaceful. Well sort of. I mean I got popped a few more times but I dealt with it. I finally broke down and told Starr about Tahir hitting me and she just looked at me and shook her head.

"D why you putting up with that bullshit? The old Diamond wouldn't."

"Look Starr this is my life and my relationship so if you can't listen as a friend with out giving your unwanted and uncalled for comments then I just won't tell you anything." She just kept quiet and left me alone.

Her and Quadir became friends quick, fast, and in a hurry. He was an all around nice guy. The only thing was he had 4 kids with, 4 baby's mammas and a lot of baby mamma drama. One time Starr was at his apartment and one bitch bust out her driver side window. All 4 of his baby's mammas were crazy as hell so he didn't know which one did it. It didn't matter because Quadir paid for it. One of them keyed her car, Quadir paid for it. The one that keyed the car called there after she did it and her and Starr got into. Starr just let her know you can keep messing with my car but your baby's daddy will keep getting it fixed so you just taking food out of your child's mouth not me nor mine. Quadir must have had the bomb in his pants because those chics were off the hook. I don't know why the ugliest guys always run around making a whole bunch of babies. You know you ugly so why you want to do that to your kids.

Anyway, the first week in August Quadir missed an appointment with his P.O. because he got locked up in N.Y. for driving with out a license. He shot an alias and the cops told him that he had a warrant. The whole crew of guys that Quadir and Tahir ran with were not the brightest individuals that walked the face of this earth. They all used the same alias name which was 'Hassan Turner' when they got into anything with the police and I guess the last person that used the name didn't go back to court or pay the fine so Quadir got locked up. When he was released and went to his P.O. the next week, Po Po (the cops) were waiting for him and he got locked up. He was going to have to finish out his 2 years. Starr was so upset when Tahir told us. She had really started digging him. She lay on my shoulder and cried a bit.

"Damn D, I don't have no luck with niggas." I kept reassuring her, "You can write him and we can come up from school on weekends to see him." She sighed.

"You're right but I'm still depressed." I hugged her.

"It will be O.k., at least he is locked up and not dead." She wiped her eyes.

"You got that right D. I don't know what I would do if that happened." I looked down.

"Me either sis, if something happened to Tahir I would lose it. I love that boy too much. Too bad he don't feel the same about me." Starr put her arm around me.

"He loves you D." I shrugged.

"Oh yeah? He has never said it. I always get on him about not saying it and he be like come on girl why I gotta say it you know it already." She sighed.

"Typical nigga with dat typical nigga shit." I laughed at her.

"Well I am glad I didn't give Quadir none or I would

really be missing him. Even though we didn't, we came close and he was hung like a horse. When we were dry humping I felt that thing rise and boy oh boy, I might not have been able to walk after he finished with me." I playfully smacked her arm.

"Girl you so stupid!" See we had a rule and the rule is this: you shouldn't be able to count on more then one hand the number of guys you sleep with before you get married. That means you need to ration it out. Don't sleep with everybody. If they don't wife you then don't give them none. If you're good enough to lay down with then you should be good enough to be the girlfriend and then be the wife. If they start getting it on the regular before they even ask you to be their girl why would they ask you to be their girl? Why buy the cow when you can get the milk for free. Remember when Aunt Debra taught me that at 6 years old? I listened.

CHAPTER 36
IT'S SO HARD...

The last week in August Tahir was taking me and Starr back to Howard for our second year of college. We were going early Saturday so we could get some partying in down there before classes started on Wednesday. We were going to be in the newest dorm which was the Annex. It was a nice dorm and it was co-ed. We couldn't wait to get down there. Tahir called me like 2 AM to tell me that he would be there by 10. I told him O.k., clicked my ringer off and tried to go back to sleep. I lay on my side and thought about our relationship and how it was so different from Samir and Q. I was thinking, after Tahir drops us off at school I am going to tell him we need space cause I don't trust him and I know he be cheating. I mean, we didn't spend that much time together and sometimes he would say he was coming and wouldn't show up for hours or until the next day. Then I would beep him and call his cell phone and wouldn't be able to get him. The phone would ring but he wouldn't answer it. Then he never told me he loved me and I didn't have time for that. Let me go to sleep and sleep on it. I got up about 9 and noticed I hadn't put my phone back in the charger. My battery was dead. So I flicked my ringer on, slammed it in the charger and got dressed. Then I pulled all my stuff I had downstairs. All our big things like TV's and winter clothes were in storage down in D.C. So all I had were clothes. 10 AM came and no Tahir. 10:15, no Tahir. 10:30, no Tahir. 10:45, no Tahir. At 11, me and Starr were in the kitchen waiting. I listened out for my phone to ring in my room but I knew the battery wasn't charged fully so I reached for my mother's cordless and started beeping him off the hook and calling his cell phone. He knew if I didn't answer my phone to call my mother's line. The cell phone went right to voice mail and the beeper couldn't get any more beeps. Starr sat at the kitchen table flipping through an Essence magazine watching me frantically dialing him over and over again. Starr tossed the magazine across the table.

"This is not the first time he didn't come when he said he was. He probably laid up with some girl over sleeping." I sighed.

"Starr come on now. Why you gonna say something like that? Don't say that Starr." My stomach began to churn thinking of the possibility of him snuggling with another chic. She snatched the phone from my fingers.

"Well I am calling Greyhound and getting us bus tickets cause ain't nobody got time to be playing with Tahir's ass all day." Inside I was pissed at him but I didn't want to be agreeing with Starr letting her think I didn't have faith in my man so I tried to beep and call him a bunch of other times. Starr ordered 2 bus tickets for the 4 o'clock bus to D.C. and we were going to get on it since Tahir was acting shitty. If he showed up before we left I still wasn't going with him. I had made up in my mind that it was going to have to be Splitsville for me and him. While I waited for Tahir to call back I laid across my bed and listened to my What's the 411 CD by Mary J. Blige. I got up at 2 to look around for last minute things I might have forgotten and we were set to go to Penn Station at 2:30. My parents were going to drop us off. Neither one of our parents could take us back because they were all going to dinner and a show in NY. Before we left out of the house my dad started in, while we stood in the kitchen.

"I told you about that Tahir, but you didn't want to listen to me. I told you he was a piece of shit nigga. He knows you girls gotta get back to school and now he goes and pulls this disappearing act." I whined.

"O.k. Dad! Don't rub it in! God-lee! I know..." My mother intervened because she saw I was getting upset.

"Dan please. Diamond you and Starr don't have to

lug all that stuff on the bus. You and Starr pack an overnight bag and pack the rest of it in the Navigator. We will bring it down to you tomorrow O.k.? Or when Tahir shows up he can bring it down to you O.k.?" I gave my mother a hug and cried on her shoulder.

"Thanks Mommy." She whispered in my ear,

"Your welcome baby. Don't worry about Tahir. He will either get his shit together or get lost right?" She grabbed my shoulders and pushed me back. She grabbed a tissue and dabbed at my eyes. She smiled at me. I smiled back.

"Yes Ma." I hugged her tight because I was so hurt that Tahir could do me like this. I knew he wasn't locked up because his sister would have called Samir and she didn't. Samir asked me did I want him to call her but I said no because I didn't want to deal with the hurt of him with another woman. I can just see him laying on his back with some bitch sleep on his chest. They probably was at a motel on 1 &9. Just thinking about it angered me. I grabbed the kitchen phone and called Starr and told her to pack her stuff in the Navigator. Once we were both done we headed down to Newark's Penn Station. We got in, got our tickets, and bags checked. We sat down in silence because in line Starr was browbeating Tahir.

"Diamond you need to cut that zero, he is a good for nothing nigga!" I sucked my teeth.

"Starr look don't pass judgment on my man. He is mine and you don't have to worry about him." I then rolled my eyes in her direction.

"Hmm, look where Quadir is at, I guess he's a better man huh?" She reared back and put her finger in my face.

"Let me tell you one thing Diamond...you know what, fine, don't say nothing to me and I wont say anything to you." I exclaimed, "Fine!" People turned in the line to see what was going on. We both stood apart and didn't say 2 words to each other. Before our bus came at about 3:50 I saw my mom, dad, and Samir come running in the bus station. I smiled at them. I walked towards them with Starr slowly trailing behind me.

"Hey Ma did you miss me that soon, you just dropped me off." But nobody was smiling. Samir had tears in his eyes. I grabbed his shoulders.

"Samir what's wrong?" My dad put his arm around me.

"Diamond baby...we need to go home." I backed up from my dad.

"For what? What happened? What's wrong?" My mother sighed and then stuttered, "Diamond...baby...Tahir was killed last night." The room began to spin and I put my hands out to brace myself.

"Tah who? No, no he wasn't. I just talked to him this morning at like 2, you got it mixed up." I sat down. She sat down next to me.

"Diamond it was him, he got shot in the head 6 times about 5:30 this morning." I was shaking my head back and forth.

"No Ma, not my Tahir. That is another Tahir that got shot not mine. Right Daddy? Tell Mommy she's wrong and I'm right." He sighed and sat on the other side of me.

"Diamond I'm afraid not." It started to finally settle in. Tahir was gone and was never coming back. I commenced to screaming, "NO! NO! NO! NO! NO! NO! NO! NO! HE'S NOT DEAD! NOOOOO HE IS NOT GONE! SOMEBODY WAKE ME UP! PLEEEAAASSSEEE WAKE ME UP! I AM HAVING A NIGHTMARE!" I jumped up and ran at Samir, "Samir shake me and wake me up!" I turned to Starr, "Sis please don't just stand there. Shake me! Wake me up from this bad dream!" Samir grabbed me and hugged me tight.

"Diamond I wish I could wake you up but its true Diamond. It's true." I pushed Samir off of me. I dropped to my knees in front of my dad and clasped my hands together.

"Daddy Daddy! Take it back Daddy. You can do anything Daddy, don't make him dead Daddy make him alive!" He hugged me.

"Baby I can't, I wish I could but I can't." I was crying uncontrollably and through broken sobs I said, "Bring him back pleeeaassseee! I need him here. Samir I need him here!" Samir tried to help me stand up.

"I do too D, I do too." After Samir helped me up, I fell back to the floor and started pulling my hair. I tried to pull it out at the roots to make sure this was really real. I rocked back in forth on the floor balled up in the fetal position. Starr dropped to her knees and wrapped her arms around me.

"Come on D. Please don't do that, get up sis, you gotta get up." I was weak and couldn't move.

"I can't Starr. I want Tahir to come get me up." I pushed her back and yelled, "Did you hear that Tahir, come get me up. Please come get me up. Don't leave me here Tahir...Starr go beep him, I know he will call back this time I can just feel it." The bus station was announcing the 4 PM bus to D.C. had arrived. My dad wrapped his strong arms around me and lifted me up.

"Come on Diamond. Let's get y'all bags and go home." I let my whole body go limp so my dad had to drag me.

"No Daddy no! Tell me it's not true. Tell me sike or something!" But nobody said sike. This was real and I was a mess. Samir grabbed one arm and my dad had the other. They helped me to the Navigator. To this day I still don't remember how I walked to the truck. They must have picked me up or something. All I remember is sitting between Starr and Samir yelling, screaming and crying. I could see in the rearview mirror my dad had tears in his eyes. My mom reached over and touched his hand.

"Ann this is the first time I can't make things right for my daughter. My mom squeezed his hand.

"Don't beat yourself up Dan, it is not your fault." I grabbed the tops of the 2 front seats and pulled my body up so my face was between my mother and father's.

"Daddy please ride past his house, I know he is there." My dad looked over at me and sighed.

"Diamond baby he is gone. We are going to deal with this the best way we know how." I let my head drop down in the space between the seats.

"Nooo Daddy. Please ride by his house, he is there waiting for me. He must still be sleeping." So to make me content and make me shut up my dad rode past Tahir's house. He lived in a second floor condo in Elizabeth. Samir gave him directions. There was yellow tape all over. My eyes got big and I yelled, "Dad stop the car. Samir let me out." Samir got out but held my hand as I went to see. I saw blood that had began to turn brown and have flies around it and I fainted on the spot. My dad jumped out. He picked my head up and tapped my cheeks.

"Diamond, Diamond wake up!" My eyes popped open and when I tried to open my mouth I began to throw up. My dad sat me up so I wouldn't choke on it. He helped me stand up and got a bottle of water he had in the car.

"Here Diamond drink some of this. Baby come on you gotta stop this. You're making yourself sick. I jumped up and down and screamed at the top of my lungs.

"Tahir! Tahir! I'm outside so come out here Tahir, please come out here. I'm ready to go Tahir. Tahir do you hear me?" The little old lady that lived under him came outside. I ran up to the porch.

"Hey Mrs. Boone, Tahir is upstairs right. Please tell me I'm right and everybody else is wrong." Mrs. Boone looked down at the bloody concrete.

"I'm sooo sorry dear..." I flailed my arms around like I was having a conniption.

"Nooooooooooooo!" My mother come over and grabbed me. She pulled me to the truck.

"Come on Diamond let's go home." I pulled back to pull away from her.

"No Ma, No Ma please I can't. I don't want to." They got me in the car some how and the harder I cried the harder Starr cried because she hated to see me like this. Once we were riding I completely had lost my mind. I tapped my dad's shoulder.

"Daddy hurry, Tahir is at our house and I don't want him to leave, he was just running late, you'll see." Starr pulled me over to lie on her shoulder.

"Come on Diamond...it's gonna be O.k." I lifted off her shoulder.

"What is going to be O.k. Starr? He is not dead I know he didn't leave me here Starr, I know he wouldn't do that to me." When we pulled into my driveway, no Tahir. I collapsed on the curb and cried.

"Why Tahir? Why? Why you leave me baby? I loved you Tahir. Come back to me please Tahir. I will do anything, just come back to me." My mother lifted me by my elbows.

"Come on Diamond, let's go in the house." I dragged myself up the front steps and then up the stairs to my room crying with every step. Samir and Starr were on my heels. I picked the phone up and I heard the pause in the dial tone indicating I had messages. I dialed in my code and I yelled, "I know this message is from him. He is not dead." I listened to the recording.

"First new message, 5:12 AM." Then it went to the message.

"Yo D! This your man, Tah. I'm tired as hell from hitting this block picking up my money. I'm drunk and I'm horny. I'm pulling up to my house now but I thought you might have woke up so a brother could come through your block and see you but I guess you knocked out slobbing (then he started laughing) Well boo, I will see you in a few hours, Yo D, I love... What nigga? Who the fuck is you? Do you know who I ..." the voice then said, "Fuck you and who you are nigga!" And shots rang out. I heard the cell phone drop and I guess what was Tahir's body falling. I heard another guy in the background say, "Get that watch he got on nigga and his pockets oh, oh and that cell phone he was on." The first voice picked up the phone.

"Hello, Hello? Well whoever this is, Tahir is dead!" The car screeched off and then the phone went dead. I screamed, "Oh my God Tahir!" The recording then came back on.

"To replay this message press 1, to save press 2, to erase press 3." Samir bust through my doors like he was superman.

"What's wrong D? What happened?" I sat there frozen with the phone in my hand. Samir took the phone and listened. The recording repeated the instructions again and he pressed 1. After he listened to the message he pressed 2 and sat down next to me.

"Oh my God D, he called before he died." I didn't move. I didn't even blink. Samir yelled for my mother and father to come to my room. They came running in. He let them hear the message. After my mom heard it she covered her mouth and tears welled up in her eyes.

"Diamond? Diamond?" I couldn't respond. All I could do was sit perfectly still. The longer I sat like that, it wasn't real. My mom sat down next to me and started hugging me and pulling me like Oprah did in The Women of Brewster Place. I began to cry again feeling this pain in my chest. It was real and my heart ached. I took the phone from Samir and listened to the message over and over again. Samir finally took the phone from me and saved the message. I dropped my head in my hands and cried. Oh my God, that is the first and last time he said he loved me or tried to say it and he couldn't even get it all out because some punk took his life. I sat up and punched my fist in my hand.

"Tahir is dead!" Samir hugged me.

"D yes he is gone and we will get through this." I jumped and screamed, "No! It is all my fault! If I didn't turn my ringer off he would be alive right now." Samir grabbed me and looked in my eyes.

"No it is not your fault D! Niggas was plotting on him for a long time. They wanted him and they got him. This is nothing new to Tahir. He knew he was wanted for years now. They would have got him no matter what time it was, when the streets want you the streets get you." I pushed him off me and turned my back to him.

"Well I didn't get to say goodbye." He hugged me again.

"Diamond baby please don't do this to yourself. Tahira called me like 3 and I called your parents and that's when we came. D, it is going to be O.k." My dad went to call the Elizabeth Police and tell them about the message to see if they wanted to hear it. They came and I stayed in my room. They called Bell Atlantic and got the message extracted from my voicemail box and kept it for evidence towards his case. My dad requested a copy for me and they said they would get it to me. Everyone was downstairs with the police and I was in my room looking in the mirror. I looked around the border of my mirror at the pictures we took in one of those booths where you get 4 poses. That was the day we were in Seaside Heights. The first pose we smiled, the second one we stuck our tongues out, the third one we made a silly face and the last one we kissed. I turned from the pictures. The memories hurt too bad. All I know is for the next few days I didn't move out of my bed. I didn't eat, sleep, or use the bathroom except to pee. So you know that meant I didn't wash or brush my teeth. Come on y'all, I was hurt. I just lied in my bed crying and miserable. The wake was set for Tuesday and the funeral was going to be Wednesday. Me and Starr were supposed to be at school and we were supposed to go to Virginia Beach for the Greek Fest for Labor Day weekend which was that weekend. I knew I wouldn't feel like going anymore. Before the wake Starr came over and helped me get dressed.

"D, I know your upset but I think we should still go to Virginia Beach. It would be good for you." I looked at her and my eyes said, "Not!" When the wake time came I was a total wreck. We pulled up to Cotton's funeral home in Newark and I couldn't get passed the front door. It was me, my mom and dad, Samir and Starr. My mom put her arm around me.

"It is O.k. if you don't want to go in." I stood up straight.

"No no I do, I do." It was so crowded in there it was ridiculous. Girls were all over crying and guys as well. Some guys were falling out, while their boys tried to be strong for them. Outside it was guys on motorcycles doing wheelies in dedication to Tahir. They had t-shirts made up which Samir bought one for all of us. At a later date I had my own special t-shirt made up with our picture we took in Seaside Heights saying R.I.P. Tahir! I love you! Well my parents couldn't take all the commotion and went and sat in the car. Me, Starr, and Samir proceeded into the wake. It was so many people crying I couldn't think straight. I had taken another picture me and Tahir had taken to put in the casket along with a letter I wrote him that morning. The letter was short and brief.

Dear Tahir,

I love you and I miss you. I know your money was important to you but was I Tahir? I mean anything you have ever done to me I forgive you. I am not holding any grudges because life is too short. I love you Tahir, I know you had to go for a while but we will meet again. I am and always will be your wife and you will always be my life. Again I love you Tahir.

Love,
Diamond

Once I reached the casket he didn't look like himself. Cotton's try to fix his head the best they could but it looked bad. I stood there and cried and leaned on his arm. I placed the picture and the letter in the casket and I kissed his ice-cold cheek. As I stood up from kissing him tears welled up full force. I touched his hand.

"Why Tahir? Why? Why you leave me? Get up Tahir, get up!" Starr pulled me.

"Come on Diamond, its O.k. lets just go." I buried my head in Starr's shoulder.

"Why he leave me Starr, why?" She hugged me tight to keep me from falling out. As we were walking away from the casket and towards Tahir's mother to pay our respects, I heard a girl say from behind me, "Oh no this bitch didn't..." I turned around to see her pick up my picture and my letter and tear it up into little pieces. I dropped to my knees.

"Noooooooo! Why did you do that?" I got up and walked up in the girls face.

"Tahir was my fiancé and no bitch will be putting anything in..." I put my hand in her face. The old Diamond was coming back.

"Whatever with all that, why you rip my stuff?" She smacked my hand down and stepped up a step closer into my face.

"Cause I felt like it!" I moved closer in her face.

"Oh yeah you stupid bitch!" I reared back and punched her dead in her temple right in front of the casket. She lost her balance a little and came back at me. Some of Tahir's boys including Samir came and broke it up. Tahir's mother jumped up and yelled.

"Now y'all just stop it! Cut out all this foolishness! My son is lying here dead and y'all is acting straight crazy. He was with all of y'all! All y'all in here that think you were the only one, you weren't..." She grabbed her chest and fanned her face with her handkerchief. She started pointing at different chics.

"I met you and you and you and he was with all y'all!" She waved her handkerchief in the girl I hit direction.

"Now Dawn you was wrong for ripping that picture. That's Diamond and he was seeing her just as much as he was seeing you. Now I'm not saying it is right but it is the truth. Now could y'all at least show my dead son and me and my family some type of respect and take that garbage outside?" I looked down.

"I am sorry Ms. Edwards." The girl Dawn looked down as well.

"Yeah Ma (she emphasized Ma) me too." I had only met his mother 2 times. She was at his house cleaning when I came over. He was spoiled like that and she came to clean his place and wash his clothes. I began to walk away from the casket but as I did I yelled, "Tahir I love you!

Rest in peace baby!" I ran back over and kissed him on his dead cold forehead. I looked at Dawn and we exchanged nasty looks and that was it. On my way down the side aisle I saw Tahira coming out of the bathroom. She looked so pitiful and sad. I went over and gave her a hug.

"Tahira, I am so sorry. If you need anything call me." She hugged me back and tried to smile.

"Thanks Diamond." She looked at Samir and he reached for her and pulled her into his bear hug. She started crying hard then. He rubbed her neck length hair.

"Baby it is going to be alright, Samir is here for you." He waved at me and Starr.

"You guys can go ahead, I'm going to stay here with Tahira. One of the boys will bring me home." Through her sobs she squeezed out, "Thanks Samir." He kissed her on her forehead.

"Don't worry about it boo." I was too sad to be pissed but when I thought about it later I was. I am such a jealous person. I hadn't been with Samir in years and my man was lying in his casket and I was mad he was calling her baby and boo. Anyway the next day at the funeral wasn't any better. When I read the program it had the girl Dawn listed as his fiancé. I was upset but I was too weak to get mad over that. He had a son with her and he never told me. The baby was only a few months old. Do you know his son, Tahir Jr. was born on my born day. June 12th. It said in the program, Tahir just was blessed with a son on June 12th. I got real sick then. When they closed the casket to start the services I felt like I was having a heart attack I was crying so hard. Hollywood Cemetery in Union would be Tahir's final resting place. When the preacher said, "Ashes to ashes, dust to dust..." I wanted to jump in the hole and be covered with dirt right along with him. In the car on the way out it was me, my mom, dad, Starr and Samir and I started up again.

"Why? Why? Why?...Daddy I can't breathe. It hurts Daddy, it hurts..." He reached over the seat and touched my leg.

"D you gotta calm down. Breathe D, breathe!" I was hyperventilating and my heart felt like a knife was slowly cutting through it. My dad didn't want to take any chances and pushed the Navigator until he reached the doors of Overlook Hospital.

CHAPTER 37
I HAD A DREAM

Once in the emergency room they gave me oxygen and fed me with an I.V. I hadn't eaten or drank anything since Tahir died and I found out I was dehydrated. The doctor wanted to keep me over night. Starr stayed with me and I dozed in and out of sleep. Every time I woke up I was crying. I had the worst headache and I felt dizzy. I buzzed the nurse. She came in and checked my temperature. She rubbed my hand.

"Sweetie you've got to stop crying O.k.?" I sniffled.

"I can't." She softly patted my hand.

"You're going to make yourself sick." I shrugged my shoulders.

"I don't care cause I want to die, I want to die." Starr woke up in her chair and got up and hugged me.

"D don't say that! Do you want to die and leave me here? We're supposed to grow old together?" I cried.

"I know Starr but I can't take it. It hurts." She rubbed my hair.

"I know sis, but we are going to get through this." At 11 PM Q's mother some how found out I was admitted and came to check up on me. When I saw her come in the door I started crying again. She kissed my cheek.

"Hey Starr...Diamond baby you gotta stop crying. I know it is hard but you have to try. Just think about all the good times you and Tahir had." (Q must have told her Tahir got killed because I hadn't spoken to her since the cookout. I thought she hated me. I don't know who told Q about Tahir but he left a message saying he was sorry) She added, "You really liked him and he liked you." I tried to sit up.

"Jackie I did and I wasn't cheating on Q with Tahir. I swear to God me and Tahir were just friends at that time,

I swear it, but I said he was my cousin because it was easier then saying my friend because..." She put her hand up.

"It's O.k. Diamond, I believe you. I am not upset with you at all. You're young, pretty and sweet. Just like me. Of course guys love you and love to be around you. I love to be around you too. You're still my daughter no matter if you call me or not. You might still be my daughter-in-law who knows. I hope so cause you know I don't like this new chic he is seeing." She smiled and I forced myself to smile back. I reached up to hug her.

"I miss you so much Jackie and I love you!" She put her hands on her hips.

"Well if you love me stop crying and think about all the good times you guys shared even before you were a couple. He is in a better place now D." she leaned down and kissed my forehead.

"Get some rest now Diamond so you can go home tomorrow and we go shopping." I smiled at her.
"There is that pretty smile I love to see. Get some rest now sweetie. Bye Starr." I waved, "Bye Ma." I looked over at Starr.

"Bye Jackie. Diamond are you O.k.?" I turned over to get some rest.

"I will be sis. Thanks for staying with me and I'm sorry for yelling at you about Tahir at Penn Station." She adjusted her cover over her legs.

"No problem sis. I love you. Goodnight." I flicked the TV off.

"I love you too. Goodnight." I instantly feel asleep. I dreamed that I was at a party and Tahir walked in. I ran up to him and grabbed him and hugged him.

"Tahir I knew you wouldn't leave me!" He hugged me back and then pulled me back to look in my eyes.

"D I'm fine. I am O.k., are you O.k.?" I laughed at grabbed his hands.

"I'm fine Tahir especially now that you're here." He took my face in his hands.

"D you will be fine even if I am not here O.k.? I grabbed his arm and led him to the dance floor.

"O.k., whatever Tahir. Let's dance." At that very instance a fight broke out. Tahir grabbed my hand.

"D we gotta get out of here!" I grabbed him close to me.

"No we can't! I can't lose you again!" He pushed me off of him and towards the door. It was commotion and pandemonium all around us.

"D I gotta go this way and you need to go that way. We gotta separate and get out of here. I will be fine and so will you. I will see you soon. I love you." He ran in the opposite direction and I stood in the middle of the floor screaming, "No Tahir! Come back!" I tried to follow him but lost him in the crowd of people. I ran outside up and down the streets screaming his name at the top of my lungs, pulling on people asking had they seen him. Nobody would stop to help me. Everybody was running to safety. My eyes popped open and I sat up. I had a single tear fall from my eye and I wiped it. I lay looking at the ceiling analyzing my dream. In the morning I told Jackie about the dream.

"Diamond that is Tahir trying to tell you he is O.k. and you will be O.k. too." I felt a weight had been lifted off of my chest. A few hours later I was released, me and Jackie got our friendship back on track and I stopped crying. Me and Starr were leaving the next day, which was Friday to go to the Greek Fest after all. We took the bus down to D.C. and rode with some of our NY girlfriends from school. Once in Virginia Beach I watched the money making cats pull their nice cars up and down Atlantic Ave. like it was a car show. I was sad thinking about how that should have been Tahir out there with them.

Me and Starr started school back that Tuesday. We only missed our Wednesday and Thursday classes the week before. I remained solo for the rest of the year. I couldn't talk to any guys for fear they might get killed too. Q was still calling me but he never really left Kendra alone. I found out from my same mutual friend that he was still talking to her and she was planning to go to his school to see him. All the way from Chicago that is. Q did have the bomb in his pants so I didn't blame her. His new girl's name was Stephanie and she was in New Jersey getting played out while he was doing him. Jackie said she didn't like Stephanie because she seemed like a little fast ass. I didn't really care about Q, Stephanie or Kendra because I was still mourning. When he called I just let him talk. I didn't have the energy or the want to tell him I knew everything.

One weekend close to the end of the school year Samir came to see us. Blair had transferred to another school so she wasn't at Hampton anymore. Me and Samir were sitting watching TV in my room and Starr was at the Library. Samir flicked the TV off.

"D, how are you?" I smiled.

"Good. School is hard and you?" He looked down.

"I'm fine but D I have something I want to tell you." I scooted up to the end of my bed.

"What's up Samir?" He rubbed his forehead.

"Well the night of the 4th of July..." I cut him off.

"Yeah what about it?" He rubbed his hands together.

"I went to see that bitch in South Jersey (talking about his ex Blair, come on y'all pay attention) and her ex was there. They had just got finished fucking and I slapped her ass and homeboy white ass tried to fight me. I beat his ass like he stole something. He left while me and her continued to argue and as I was leaving he came back with his boys and those fags tried to jump me." I looked at him with my eyes wide open.

"Yeah, well I know the rest of the story from there..." He grabbed my hand.

"No D I want to tell you what happened that night when me, Tah, and the twins Roc and Kerm went back down there." I sat up straight wanting to hear anything about Tahir.

"Well what happened?" He took a deep breath.

"Well see it went like this..."

CHAPTER 38
THESE ARE MY CONFESSIONS

"Well when we left Vauxhall Tahir went and scoped up 3 other cats. Shareef, Moe, and Monster. So us 7 went down to Neptune to handle our business. Old boy was walking by himself looking happy until the New Jersey Hot Boys jumped out on him. We beat him up so bad he was damn near unconscious. Tahir put a gun in his mouth while Monster put a shotty (shot gun) to his guts. The twins held him up by his arms while Moe and Shareef stood look out. Tahir spoke to him in his ear and asked him, 'Do you see the people that did this to you?' Old boy had a tear run down his face. He shook his head back and forth. Tahir then took the gun out of his mouth, cocked it back and put it back in his mouth. He then asked him, 'Are you sure?' Old boy was petrified and said, 'Yeah' with the gun still in his mouth. Tahir jiggled the gun around in his mouth and said, 'So you positively absolutely don't see anything right?' The dude shook his head up and down slow this time with more tears running down his face. You know Tahir didn't give a fuck. He then took the gun out of his mouth and pointed in my direction. He said to the boy, 'You see my man over there? He is better then that skank ass hood rat ho bitch so you keep her, but if you ever try my man again, I will kill you, that's my word. I will take my nine and blow your mind. I mean literally. I will take this gun and blow your brains out all over this mother fucker.' By this time old boy was crying and wet his pants. It was sight D. Tahir then wiped his pistol on the boys shoulder getting his slob off the nose of his gun and took the butt of it and beat him in the head until he was unconscious." I was shaking my head back and forth not believing what I was hearing. Samir took my hand in his and finished his story.

"D, by the time we left him, we rode to Blair, that bitches house and Tahir parked his truck down the street from her house. She was standing on her stairs and he told us all to stay in the car he would handle it. He walked down the street and entered her gate like he knew her for years. I don't know exactly what he said to her but he said he basically told her that her ex was fucked up and if she so much as breathed a word to anyone that Samir and him had beef he would kill her. He pointed to his truck and told her it is a truck full of niggas up there and if you identify me or Samir one of those niggas in the truck will be back and they will kill you and your whole family. As he got up to leave he lifted his shirt and showed her his gun and put his finger over his lips and told her, 'not one word.' As he was leaving her stairs he said to her, 'this is not a game and I am not playing. If the cops so much as question Samir say bye bye ho. I know where you live and if I don't get you I will get your family, and don't bother reporting this to the cops because I got half of them on payroll.'" I put my hand up to stop the story.

"What did he mean he had cops on payroll in Neptune he was doing stuff down there too?" Samir looked down.

"Diamond Tahir was not a drug dealer, he was a drug supplier. He sold weight. He sold it to niggas all over. Newark, Elizabeth, Vauxhall, Neptune, Asbury. He was large. That means he sold big bundles to drug dealers for them to package and sell on the streets. You didn't see half of what Tahir had. He had another house in West Orange that he shared with Dawn and his son." I snatched my hand from Samir.

"Oh and about his son being born on my birthday. Why didn't you tell me?" He looked down and exhaled.

"D I just couldn't. That was for Tahir to tell you but can I finish my story please?" I rolled my eyes and he went on.

"Well I know the whole thing went under

354

investigation but there were no witnesses and no just cause so it was dismissed." I looked at Samir imagining him ready to kill somebody or even be witness to it.

"D, you know I miss Tahir. That was my nigga." I wiped a tear from my eye.

"Yeah mine too." I smiled remembering the Neptune/Blair incident.

"Do you know that me and Starr went down there that night too. We saw y'all when you were pulling up on the block and we pulled off fast." He laughed.

"What were y'all doing down there?" I fell over laughing thinking about the incident.

"Threatening Blair!" He laughed harder getting a visual.

"You and Starr?" I shook my head up and down.

"Yep me and Starr. You know I still loved you then and I was mad jealous of that bitch. You were saying she was the one and you were going to marry her. I was the one nigga!" He looked at me.

"For real D? I thought you hated me." I stretched.

"Hated you? Yeah right. I had to put up that front." He smiled at me and I smiled back.

"Samir I'm sorry for blacking on you when you were trying to protect my feelings from Tahir. I knew deep down that you were right but he had me hypnotized." Samir smiled.

"Yeah he was like that." I looked down at my hands.

"So you knew Dawn huh?" He looked down and sighed.

"D don't do this, don't torture yourself. I told you he was a ladies man but that bitch was not his fiancé." A tear fell from my eye.

"Well that shit hurt." He reached over and took my hand and kissed it.

"D Tah loved you too, no matter what he did, you were his girl too." I repeated the last part of his sentence.

"His girl too?" He looked away.

"D...it was a few of y'all." I dropped my hands in my

lap.

"Samir why didn't you tell me?" He raised one eyebrow.

"I tried." I screamed, "Well you didn't try hard enough! How could you allow me to get played?" He took my hands in his.

"I didn't. When I tried to tell you a little bit you went off on me!" I lowered my voice and my eyes.

"You're right, I did, but you should have smacked me and said snap out of it...I can't believe they never found his killer or killers. I want justice to be done!" Samir made tiny circles with his thumbs on the top of my hands.

"Yo D in time the shit will surface and then it will all hit the fan, just have faith." I cried, "Samir I will never find another Tahir. Even though he was a piece of shit, when we were together I felt like it was all about me." He smiled to take away my tears.

"Well it was, I'm telling you he was feeling you a lot. He would tell me all the time, 'Yo I'm going to marry Diamond' and I would say, 'Over my dead body!'" I sat up and looked at Samir.

"Why would you tell him that Samir?" He locked eyes with me.

"Cause that's what I meant. Y'all would have got married over my dead body...you not the only one that still had feelings." I lightly smacked him on his arm.

"WHAT?!" I was shocked because I thought Samir was so big on Blair.

"You heard me D, but anyway he was truly big on you but he just was a ladies man...back to what you were saying about finding another Tahir. No you won't find another Tahir but maybe you will find someone better for you." I played with my hair.

"I don't think so Samir." I looked down and Samir lifted my chin.

"I think so D and maybe, look at me D, maybe you will and maybe you have." I was real confused.

"Huh?" He looked me in my eyes.

"I'm talking about me Diamond." I shook my head back and forth.

"What? No Samir, I'm not ready."

"Ready for what?" I looked at him.

"A relationship Samir." He sighed.

"Diamond I'm not asking you for all that, I'm just telling you that I'm here for you O.k.?" I smiled.

"O.k." He put his arms out.

"Can I have a hug Diamond? I really miss your bear hugs D." I hugged him. I hugged him so tight all the old memories from our relationship came rushing back and tears ran down my face. He hugged me even tighter then I hugged him. He whispered in my ear, "D you feel so good right now. Yo I miss you so much." I whispered back.

"Samir can you let me go please?" He pulled back and looked me in my eyes.

"D what's wrong?" I looked down.

"I can't Samir. I just can't. I can't talk to or deal with anybody anymore. Make that ever Samir. I can't go through what I went through no more Samir, damn I'm still mourning now." He kissed me on my forehead.

"Diamond its O.k. but boo you can't live your life like that. I know Tah is gone but life goes on and you know that." I cried, "I know." He kissed my nose.

"Ight then I'm gonna go in the other room. I just heard Starr come in." I lay on my bed.

"O.k." I know he wanted me to stop him but I just couldn't. I was done with relationships for real. I did think about what he said and he depressed me all over again. The year dragged by for me. I didn't socialize much and lost 25 pounds. I was 145 from the beginning but now I was down to 120. I looked sick and people probably thought I had the package. Oh you know what the package is, if not use your imagination. It's like Nas the rapper said about Cameron the rapper. Nas said Cameron got a House In Virginia, oh now you get it.

That summer I came home and got my first tattoo. It said, 'Tahir Edwards R.I.P. with a tombstone on my left arm. Starr got a star and a crescent on her arm. No she wasn't Muslim now but we always used that symbol because her first name was Starr and my middle name was Crescent. At the end of the summer I went and got the same one. We both had them tatted on our right ankles. My parents were pissed off inside that I got Tahir's name tatted on me, but they knew I was still upset and didn't say anything.

Me and Starr had talked our parents into letting us get an off campus apartment and bringing our cars down with us for our 3rd year. We knew it was going to be on and popping. I couldn't wait to get back to school the next semester and have my own place. Samir didn't want to go to Hampton anymore so he transferred to Howard with us. He couldn't have an off campus apartment his first year there, college rules.

During the early part of the summer, me and Samir started out being friends again. While Starr was out with Smitty, the one she was kicking it with from Howard who was from New York, me and Samir would sit home and play Monopoly or watch movies. We would go to Friday's or Ruby Tuesday's or do outside activities as buddies. We took it slow because he knew I was healing. As we got closer I told Samir I couldn't be hurt again. I told him I would take his life if he did. He laughed at me. He was pushing the issue for us to be a couple again. We were sitting in my basement watching Harlem Nights.

"D what more do I have to do to make you my girl again. I spend all my free time with you and I want you to commit to me." I laughed at the scene in the movie when Della Reese and Eddie Murphy were fighting.

"Samir there are mad girls on Howard's campus and we can just remain friends until after school starts in case you see something you like." He stopped the movie.

"Look Diamond I got enough friends. I know what I want and it's you. It's always been you. We've been through so much and I love you Diamond." I stuttered, "I...I...I...love you to Samir." He put his arm around me.

"Do you really D?" I looked down.

"Yes Samir but..." He cut me off.

"But what?" I looked away.

"But I'm petrified and terrified to get hurt again Samir or lose another person that I love and care about." He pulled my hands in his.

"Diamond I know that and I am not asking you for anything more then you are willing to give me. Deal?" I exhaled.

"Deal!" He smiled at me and started the movie back. Me and Starr found a cute 2 bedroom upstairs and downstairs apartment less then 5 minutes driving and maybe 15 minutes walking. It was close to one of the off campus dorms, which was Slowe Hall. That happened to be the dorm that Samir was placed in. He was going to play basketball for Howard and Starr she was going to continue to play her game as always, cause she had caught Smitty out there with a new freshman the weekend after we got back.

She was really starting to open her self up to him but after that stunt she went back to missing Quadir who she continued to write through it all. She wasn't able to go see him much because it was only 4 visiting days a week and his baby's mothers had those days on lock and she didn't want no problems for him. If they knew she was coming they might not bring his kids to see him and his kids were his world. Me, I had given up on gaming all together.

After we got back to school we knew everybody and everything about D.C. and were getting tired of college parties and wanted to move up to the big league partying. Samir loved it at Howard. He said it was more lively than Hampton and he had more freedom. Me and Samir kept kicking it and then slowly but surely we became inseparable like the old days. Yes it was sickening. I was taking it day by day but I wasn't sure what was going to happen.

Starr ended up still kicking it with Smitty because the freshman girl, her name was Brandy, she thought she was cute and tried to play Starr out. Starr wanted to show her who was cuter and won Smitty over. After she won him back she didn't want him. She said she wanted someone fresh and new. Someone not from Howard.

CHAPTER 39
D.C. IS LIVE!

One night me and Starr got all dolled up and went to this club called D.C. Live. This was not college night so girls had to be 21 to get in and guys 23. Since we were only 20, we got fake I.D.'s made said that were 23 and when we got in, we were drinking like we were 41. That was the night Starr met him. Her one and only true love, so she thought.

He was standing at the bar. He had his elbows leaning on the bar as he watched the crowd. He bopped his head up and down slowly enjoying the music and the atmosphere. He had a low hair cut with his hair waves spinning. He had on a diamond stud, well I don't know if it could be classified as stud as big as it was. He looked like he had a baby fist up on that ear. He was about 6'2, nice build with connecting side burns and he was a nice chocolate brown complexion. Homeboy was standing there looking like Hershey's milk chocolate should have been stamped on his forehead. He smiled and his teeth looked like hand picked pearls from the ocean. He was a pretty boy to the fullest. He was a young Morris Chestnut in training, but not how Morris looked in Boys N The Hood, but how he was looking in The Best Man. Remember when he walked into that restaurant. Yes Lord! He had on a long gold chain with a Jesus piece and a matching bracelet. His diamond pinky ring was humungous. They must have used the mate to his earring to make his ring. It was the end of November or the beginning of December and he had on some black dress pants and a black button up top. He had it hanging open with a white wife beater on underneath. I ain't even gonna front. He was looking good. All eyes were on him like Tupac. He was at the bar with his own bottle of champagne chilling. Me and Starr were tapping each other on the low telling each other to look at him. He knew he was the shit cause he was laid back and just looked around like 'yeah whatever.' Starr whispered to me.

"Damn D, see a nigga like that could make me 100 percent faithful." I giggled.

"Yeah you're right! He got it going on, but he knows it." She elbowed me.

"Yo, we gonna floss passed him and see if he try to push up on either one of us." I sucked my teeth.

"A cat like that ain't pushing up on nobody. He knows chics gonna push up on him." She smiled slyly.

"Well let's walk to the ladies room and see about that." Starr had on a black leather mini skirt and tall matching black leather boots. She had on a short sleeve pink cashmere sweater that showed a bit of her flat stomach. I had on beige suede pants with a brown and beige silk button up top. We adjusted our clothes and as we walked passed this mystery man he reached out and grabbed Starr's arm. She stopped and turned her nose up.

"Can I help you?!" He flashed her a smile with out releasing her arm.

"I know you seen me checking you out all night." She pulled her arm from his grasp and adjusted her gold bangle bracelet.

"No I didn't. I'm so used to all the nigga's checking me out all the time you're just another face in the crowd." I looked at her with my eyes wide. I wanted to laugh because I couldn't believe she was playing him out like that. He laughed at her comment. His cologne was smelling good and I was a bit jealous cause he was looking like Mr. Right. He stopped laughing and started grinning real hard.

"Oh that's cute and I gotta agree with you, I see nigga's looking at you and your friend here and that's why I'm trying to snatch you up first and get your friend for my man." Starr rolled her eyes and flung her hair off her shoulders.

"Who said we wanted to be snatched." He rubbed his hands together and licked his lips.

"Ooh y'all do. I can tell. What's your name pretty girl?" She batted her eyelashes and looked down like she was oh so shy.

"Starr." He grabbed her hand and held it.

"Star? Like superstar?"

"Exactly like Superstar but you spell it with 2 R's so spell it right when you're writing it down." He laughed again.

"Oh that's cute, just like you and your momma named you right cause in that skirt you're looking like a star to me." He looked her up and down like she was a gigantic Popsicle that he wanted to lick.

"Well thank you." He reached for her other hand and now he had both of them.

"You got a man Starr?" She pulled her hands away.

"No." He rubbed her cheek.

"Why a pretty girl like you don't have a man?" She sucked her teeth.

"Cause there are no good men left." He touched his chest and leaned back a bit.

"Don't say that Starr, you're breaking my heart. Just say you haven't found a good man yet." She shrugged and rolled her eyes upward.

"O.k. what you said?" He put his hand on her shoulder.

"Well what if you were looking dead at him? Would you know it?" She looked him up and down.

"I might." He pulled his hand back and rubbed his hands together.

"Well, what's a good man to you Starr?" She placed her right index finger to her temple with her left hand holding her right elbow steady. She looked up at the ceiling and pondered his question.

"One that don't cheat or BEAT on you." She looked over at me and I looked down because I didn't want to argue with Starr in front of this Negro. She was describing Tahir in her response and I wasn't feeling her. Old boy threw his hands in the air.

"That's it? Well I can handle that." She put her hand

up.

"Wait a minute that's not it but those are the 2 main things. I mean I haven't found a man that doesn't cheat yet so I couldn't tell you anything else." He grabbed her hand to put it down.

"So you telling me a good guy could be fat, black, blind, crippled, and crazy but as long as he don't cheat on you or beat on you then it's cool?" She laughed.

"No you know what I mean." He pulled her in closer to him because the club was getting crowded.

"No I don't Starr that's why I want you to tell me." She sucked her teeth.

"Well that might take a while." He licked his lips.

"Well look if I give you my numbers will you call me?" She shrugged again.

"I don't know, I guess but I don't even know your name." He smacked his forehead.

"Oh my bad Starr. I was so blinded by your beauty I forgot to introduce myself. My name is Kareem but everybody calls me Reem." He extended his hand and she shook it.

"O.k. then 'Reem' maybe I will call." He looked her up and down.

"Sweetheart, you can't do no better then a maybe?" She looked over at me, winked and then back at him.

"O.k. I will call you, do you want my number?" He shook his head back and forth.

"No I want to see if you serious or working with the bull shit. I'm not about games so let's see whose playing one." He wrote down his numbers and handed them to her. She took the paper and tucked it in her black coach bag.

"Ight then 'Reem' I'll call you." He grabbed her wrist as she tried to walk away.

"When?" She kindly yanked her wrist away.

"Soon?" He grabbed it back and pulled her in close enough to kiss her.

"How soon?" She smiled and licked her lips at him.

"How soon do you want me too 'Reem'?" He

massaged her shoulders.

"Tomorrow. Please?" I nudged her and extended my eyes open to let her know enough with the difficult role already. He pointed in my direction.

"Starr who is your pretty friend." She smiled at me.

"This is my sister Diamond." I extended my hand.

"Hi nice to meet you." He shook it.

"Same here. I gotta friend for you if you're interested. He is right over there." I looked and saw a nice red bone cutie wave in my direction and raise his champagne glass in my direction. Kareem tapped me out of daze as I gawked at his friend.

"That is my man and we only date dime pieces." I frowned up my face.

"Really, only dime pieces? Well me and my sister are not the ones for y'all." He furrowed his brow at me.

"Well why not?" I put my hands on my hips.

"Because we are 50 cent pieces!" Starr jumped up louder screaming, "Nuh un. We dollar pieces!" We high fived up high and then down low. He laughed at us.

"Ight! Ight! You got that, y'all is." We were all laughing and Kareem ordered 2 glasses from the bar. He handed us the glasses and poured Moet for each of us. It was empty after he poured us some. He tapped the bar towards the bartender.

"Yo, can I get another bottle please." He waved for his boy to come over.

"That's my boy Zak. Diamond when he gets down here you better do your thing."

"Hold up! My sister is not interested because she goes with my brother." Kareem's eyes got big and then he scrunched up his eyebrows.

"Whoa shorty! T.M.I. (to much information), your sister goes with your brother? What that be about?" Starr playfully hit his arm.

"No silly this is my best friend/sister. We're not related by blood but she is still my sister for life and she goes with my twin brother." He smiled and grabbed his chest.

"Oh I was a little nervous." He smiled again flashing those pearly whites and damn he had a dimple. He was all that. His other bottle of Moet came. He popped it open and freshened up me and Starr's glass. Starr stretched her neck to look around the club. They were playing Go Go Music and she wanted to dance. Sardines, Hey and Pork N Beans! Kareem snapped his fingers in Starr's direction.

"Well I see you ready to go dance so I will let you go and finish getting your mac on but I will hear from you tomorrow right Starr?" She did a little footwork because they had changed the song and the speakers blared out Get in the Water! As she shook her tail feather she shrugged her shoulders.

"Yeah 'Reem' I don't see why not." He grabbed her arm.

"I will be waiting for your call so don't play me. I don't like to be played." She blew him a kiss.

"Neither do I boo, neither do I." His friend approached at that time. It was so crowded he had a hard time getting through.

"Ladies." Kareem smiled.

"Zak this is my future wife Starr and her sister Diamond." He smiled.

"Nice to meet y'all. Diamond do you got a man?" Kareem answered for me.

"Yeah she do but it don't matter push up anyway." I just shook my head at Kareem.

"That's rude." Zak laughed.

"Naw Shawdy (shorty you know they were a bit country) he playing, I ain't even gonna do it like that, but are you allowed to have friends?" I smiled.

"I guess that would be O.k." He picked up his glass and helped himself to some Moet.

"Where y'all from." In unison we replied, "Jersey." Biz Markie was the Dee Jay and he had turned the Go Go off and put on rap music. Starr was pissed. She just leaned up against the bar next to Kareem. Zak leaned in close to my ear.

"Well is that where your man is at Diamond? In Jersey?" I shook my head.

"No he is down here in D.C. too." He snapped his fingers.

"Dag, that is too bad. I still want to get to know you if that is O.k." I looked at Starr and she shook her head up and down frantically.

"Yeah I guess." So he gave me his number and I gave him mine and that was that and we walked away. I noticed bitches looking like, 'who they think they are?' 'The New Jersey Hot Girls that's who.'

Anyway, the next day she debated about calling him but I pressured her to. When she called him he was telling her he was 25 and owned a barbershop with Zak, he drove a navy blue big body Benz and he owned a condo in Silver Springs, Maryland. He had given Starr his house, cell, beeper, and shop number. He told her he did all that to show her he didn't have a girl and he was serious about her.

While on the phone she asked him, "Well you wanted to know why I didn't have a man. Why don't you have a girl?" He told her, "Cause I haven't found the right one yet. I want some one for me not for what I got or who I am." She asked him, "Well who the hell are you?" He chuckled, "I'm Kareem. Maybe that don't mean nothing to you, but my name rings bells in this hood!" She replied, "That's nice." She was being sarcastic.

"So Starr when can I see you again."

"When you want too?"

"Today! Can I take you to dinner." She accepted. Then Zak called less than an hour later and asked if I wanted to double. I said, 'O.k.' and had to find a slick lie to tell Samir to get him to not come over. I called him and told him I had to study for finals with a study group. He was trusting and said, "O.k. I'm going to basketball practice and then come back to my dorm and study too."

"O.k. boo I love you. See you tomorrow."

"I love you too. Have fun studying. Bye." I hung up and started getting dressed. One good thing about our apartment was my bedroom had a master bathroom while Starr had her own bathroom. We flipped a coin and I won the master bathroom bedroom.

We all went out that night and had a nice time. They picked a restaurant in Virginia since we were so close to Virginia. We sat in a big plush booth at a candle lit table. Zak talked to me, and Kareem talked to Starr. Zak was a cutie. He reminded me of Q with his polite mannerisms. He was so polite and sweet. He was telling me he had a baby on the way and my mind was screaming, ain't nothing happening cause I don't do baby mammas. He was saying how the girl poked holes in the condoms for 3 months and he didn't know it. I shook my head back and forth thinking how trifling can a bitch get. He continued, "D, I thought I had a case and was ready to sue Lifestyles Condom Company. Me and Nia (the baby's mamma) were just friends with benefits. I made it all the way to 27 with out having kids because I'm careful and never wanted a baby's mother. I wanted a wife and then a baby."

I cut in, "You sound like me. I want to be married and then have kids." He smiled at me with the candlelight silhouetting off his face.

"You never know, it might be like that with us." I put my hand up to stop his thought process.

"No offense but I always wanted my husband to have his first child with me so we can share in the experience together for the first time." He reached for my hand.

"Well I respect that but trust me, I'm not sharing in anything with her. I don't go to her doctor's appointments, I don't call her, and I don't care. I normally wouldn't act like that but since she sabotaged the condom she turned me off. When she first told me she was pregnant I said how cause I always check the condoms to make sure it didn't break. She said you never know it could be a small hole you didn't see. So, I wasn't happy but I am a man and I told her I would support her with whatever she wanted to do. I was praying she said abortion but she is 31 and she is ready for a child." He stopped and took a sip of water. I smiled at him and raised my eyebrows high.

"Wow she is 31 and your 27?" He choked a little laughing while drinking his water. He picked up his napkin and wiped his mouth.

"D why you say it like that and why you make that face? You crazy girl, yeah she a little older then me but its cool. Age ain't nothing but a number right?" I shrugged.

"I guess, I just can't see dating a younger guy. That is not me." He pulled in his bottom lip.

"Well I am glad I am not younger than you am I?" I sat back in the booth and pointed at myself.

"Do I look older then 27? True woman never reveals her age but I am legal and I'm not over 27." He smiled.

"As long as your legal but can I finish my story?" I extended my hand towards him.

"Proceed."

"So I am being a good man right, and calling her everyday. I am bringing her food and stuff to her house and her job. Mind you, I don't even like the chic like that. Then about 2 weeks ago I popped over there to bring her some fresh fruit and tell her I was getting her, her own apartment and her sister stopped me at the front door. She whispers to me, 'Zak you are a good guy and I have to tell you something, my sister was poking holes in the condoms for the last 3 months y'all were having sex.' I went ballistic. I repeated over and over in my head I am going to kill that so and so." I cut him off, "You said so and so?" He put both hands up.

"No but I try not to curse and especially not in front of the ladies, that's rude." I smiled becoming more and more impressed with my date.

"Oh O.k., continue."

"So I sat at her house where she lives with her mother and 2 sisters and their 5 kids between them and I'm sitting and waiting. Kids are jumping all over the place and

I am heated. So she comes in the house and says hey honey, like we a couple. I stood up and asked her if I could talk to her outside.

So we went outside and I said look you dumb so and so, I'm giving up all rights to your child, I don't want it, I don't want to be bothered. I am going to court and let them know that you poked holes in the condoms. She asked me who told me that and I told her don't worry about it. She stormed in the house and started arguing with her youngest sister who she had shared that information with. Her sister hooked off on her and they were scrapping (fighting.) Allah forgive me but I wanted her sister to beat that baby out of her." I cut him off again, "Are you Muslim?" He smiled.

"Yes I am." I smiled back at him.

"Oh O.k., go ahead." He finishes the story by saying, "So then I feel bad and I go break the fight up. They are all over the floor and punching kicking and biting. She was 3 months then. I think she is going on her 4th or 5th now but I cut her off so I don't know. I got all my numbers changed so she contact me." I sucked my teeth.

"Dag she played you." He sighed.

"Tell me about it." Kareem and Starr were in their own world and conversation but Kareem butt in our conversation on that note.

"I told you from the door don't fuck with that old hood rat but you didn't listen. I told you...you should have beat that baby out of her. Stank bitch!" Starr's face took on a look of surprise. He smiled at Starr.

"Naw baby it's not like that. Don't think I put my hands on females cause I don't, but she did my man dirt-ty feel me and I didn't appreciate it." Zak began to get annoyed talking about that.

"Whatever let's not talk about that chic no more, let's change the subject." Zak and Kareem were partners with the barbershop and were in the process of expanding and getting a salon as well. Zak drove a white Range Rover and he drove us that night. I knew they did more than cut hair but big timers don't go around bragging and boosting about selling drugs. Our night was nice and peaceful. I liked talking to Zak.

After that night Starr and Kareem went out almost every night after that until we went home the week of Christmas. I saw Zak when I could because Samir was my right leg most of the time. Starr told me that she was really feeling Kareem. I was happy for her. She had stopped writing Quadir all together and he was to come home soon. I liked Zak but I couldn't put Samir out for him and he understood. He was cool with us just being friends. Me and Samir had started having sex again. I missed having sex with Samir cause he did it nice and slow and it was what real lovemaking was all about. The day before we left for Christmas break to go home she finally invited Kareem and Zak over to our place. I told Samir to go hang out with his buddies and me and Starr were going to hang out with our girls. She cooked spaghetti for him cause it was the only thing she could cook. She made it good but the buck stopped there on her cooking skills. I made lasagna and fresh garlic bread. We sat down and ate our Italian feast together.

After we ate Zak excused himself to the bathroom and Kareem tapped me. He whispered, "Yo, are you feeling my man or what cause he is feeling you?" I smiled.

"Yeah I am but I am still with Samir and thank you Kareem but Zak is O.k. with our friendship right Zak?" He was coming back to the table and sat down.

"Yeah I'm just O.k. with it. When he messes up you're mine you heard Shawdy?" I smiled.

"Yeah I heard." We smiled at each other. I usually didn't like light skinned guys but this one was growing on me quick fast.

After we cleared the table me and Zak washed the dishes and Kareem and Starr went in her room. Me and Zak sat in the living room and watched TV and talked more about his baby mamma situation.

"Yo D, she be coming to my shop everyday so I had to go get a restraining order against her." I chuckled.

"Dag that is something a girl would do. You really ran and got a restraining order? Let me find out you scared of her." I winked at him and he laughed.

"Diamond I know that is a bitch, excuse me, move but I had to or I would have to chip this girl up and that is not my style. Do you know she keyed my truck today?" I screamed, "You lying! You want me to beat her up?" He smiled and playfully tapped me in my chin.

"No killer don't get her. You're too much of a lady for that. I'm 'bout to get my cousins from the projects to tear her ass, excuse me D, up and she don't want that." I laughed at him always excusing himself after he cursed.

"You don't have to say excuse me every time you curse. I'm O.k. with it, trust me." He rubbed my knee.

"I know but that's me." After me and Zak were done talking I looked at the clock and noticed it was getting late. So I walked him to the door and he kissed me on my cheek.

"Call me when you get home to Jersey. I will drive up to Jersey to see you if you want. I got cousins in Newark. You know where that is." I laughed because Newark was 10 minutes from me.

"Of course I do I live about 10 minutes from there." He walked down the stairs.

"Well then hit me up." I waved at him.

"No doubt. I will." Kareem ended up staying the night. They didn't have sex y'all they just sat up talking all night cause I could hear them. The next morning Starr walked him to the door and gave him a kiss as if she would never see him again.

"Yo Starr be good up there in Jersey. Call me so we can hook up." She waved at him going down the stairs like I did Zak a few hours before.

"I will. I will be home in a few hours I will call you then. I will miss you." He got to his car and hit the door unlock.

"Me too baby." He blew her a kiss and she pretended to catch it. She closed the door after he pulled off and laid up against it. She exhaled and looked in the sky like she was a lovesick puppy. I broke her concentration.

"Can you come on I'm ready to go back to Jersey."
She got herself together so we could go home.

CHAPTER 40
HOME FOR THE HOLIDAYS

We went home for Christmas and Starr wanted to cut our time short in Jersey to get back to D.C. to see Kareem. Christmas Eve I went by to see Q's mother and bought her, her favorite perfume set, White Diamond, for Christmas. When I rang the bell Q opened the door, "Hey Diamond." I pushed passed him.

"Hey Q. Your mom here?" He closed the door behind him.

"Yeah she's in the kitchen with my girl." I stopped in my tracks but exhaled and continued into the kitchen.

"Hello everybody!" Q's mother jumped up from her seat.

"Diamond! Hey babe, how are you?" I gave her a hug.

"I'm fine. I have a gift for you." I handed her the bag, while Q's girl Stephanie looked me up and down. Q's mother took her bag and looked inside.

"Oh Diamond my favorite. Thank you baby." She hugged me again.

"You're welcome. Hold on let me go get yours." She left the room and it was me, Q and Stephanie.

"Diamond this is Stephanie. Stephanie this is Diamond." She looked at me and responded very dryly, "Hi." I turned my lip up and waved. Him and her were rolling out dough for Christmas cookies. Jackie came back in the kitchen and handed me an envelope.

"Here D open it." I ripped it open like a kid and it was a gift certificate to Macy's for $250.00. I squealed and then hugged her.

"Thank you Ma. I love it, I will spend it on the 26th." She smiled.

"I am glad you like it. Do you want to stay for dinner?" I looked at the couple.

"I'll pass because I have things to do but I will see you before I leave." I began to walk out the kitchen. Jackie pulled my arm.

"Wait Diamond let me walk you to the door." I gave a half wave.

"Bye. Merry Christmas." They said in unison, "Same to you Diamond." They laughed at their comment being the same. I felt nauseous at them rolling out cookie dough together. Jackie walked me out to my car.

"Isn't it just disgusting Diamond? I can't stand that girl. She is always here like she doesn't have a home." I playfully hit her on the arm.

"Be nice Ma. That is your future daughter-in-law." I got in my car and she held the door open.

"Humph! Over my dead body." She kissed me on the cheek.

"Merry Christmas baby. See you soon. Love you." I waved at her while I started my car.

"Love you too. Merry Christmas." I pulled off and played Biggie Small's One More Chance. I cared a little bit about Q and Stephanie but didn't want Jackie to think I was pressed. I'm funny like that because I didn't want him but I didn't want him with anybody else either. I felt that way about all my men. Once mine always mine. Jackie never told Q the truth about Tahir and I loved her for that. Zak called me on Christmas day.

"Hey Shawdy what did you get me for Christmas." I laughed.

"Nothing you Muslim...sike, it's a surprise." I was thinking, when he sees me I will yell surprise because I didn't get him anything.

"Well I got you something. I hope you like it. We are coming up that way this weekend, do you think I can see you?"

"Of course. I will see you then." I hung up and thought, oh shoot! I gotta get him something. So that Friday a booster came in my mother's restaurant and had 2 Coogi sweaters. I bought one for Zak and Starr bought one for Kareem. They were $400.00 sweaters and we paid $100.00 for them. For all they knew we were struggling college students even though we were not. For Christmas Samir bought me a new VCR because he broke mine and he loved when I wore timberland boots and DKNY sweat suits so he bought me some brand new Constructs (nickname for Timberlands) with 2 DKNY suits. One gray and one blue. I bought him his favorite basketball jersey, which was the New York Knicks at the time and 2 outfits, one Phat Farm and the other Enyce.

　　That weekend Kareem and Zak came up. Saturday, Me and Starr told our parents and Samir that we were going to Philly to see our friends, Kito and Tyra that went to Howard with us. We met them on Irvine Turner Boulevard in Newark because that is where they were staying. They came up Friday night to go clubbing in New Jersey with their cousins, Andrew and Tyree. They ended up going to Broker's in East Orange. When we got there they were not ready so we went in. Andrew and Tyree's girlfriends Toya and Teka were there. They were looking at us funny because they wanted Kareem and Zak to meet some of their friends but wasn't nothing happening. They came in the living room where we were sitting and both extended boxes towards us. Kareem bought Starr a fur coat that she liked in the fur store at the mall. Zak got me a tennis bracelet that I loved but couldn't wear because Samir was at my house on Christmas and he knew that wasn't one of my gifts. Once we left out we gave them their sweaters and they were happy. We ended up going to Philly to South St. because Jersey wasn't safe for a girl like me who had a man. I was starting to like Zak and I knew it couldn't be good for business. I smacked my forehead and thought, once we get back to D.C. I am going to have to cut our friendship to a minimum before I get caught up.

　　When we got back for the spring semester Starr and Kareem were kicking it hard. She was missing classes for him and staying at his condo. It had been a little over a month and they were having sex already. I told her, "Make sure he is strapping up (wearing a condom.)" She shook her head, "Of course you know I don't get down like that." I personally thought they were getting too serious too quick but who was I to judge. My best friend was happy and that made me happy. Samir met Kareem and wasn't feeling him. He said, "He is O.k. but I think he is a little too nice." I waved my hand at him.

"Yeah he is nice but maybe that is how D.C. cats are, not all mean like you Jersey cats." I said that because I knew Zak was a nice guy and it was genuine. He respected me and Samir's relationship and the fact that I couldn't see him much.

That May at the end of that semester Starr and Kareem were a full-fledged couple and after knowing him for about 6 months she was pregnant. Yeah you heard me, she was pregnant.

Zak's baby mother, Nia had a boy. When she went into labor he called me after Nia's mother called him.

"Diamond guess what?"

"What?"

"Nia is in labor. Her mom just called me. I don't know why and I don't know how they got this number. I don't know why she called me because I am not going to the hospital." I cleared my throat.

"Zak I know you are going to get mad but that baby didn't ask to come here and it deserves a father, especially one like you."

"I hear you talking Diamond but I'm not having no parts in that."

"So if the baby gets older and brings you on the Ricki Lake Show or Maury or even Jerry Springer for that matter, what will you say?" He laughed.

"I would tell him your mother was a trifling so and so that poked holes in the condom and I wanted to kill her and because of her I missed out on being with Diamond, the one that I should have been with and the one that should have been your mother." I started to blush.

"Aw Zak you are so crazy. Shut up boy and go see your baby being born. If you don't want to do it for you then do it for me." He sucked his teeth.

"Don't even try it Diamond." I begged him.

"Pretty please Zak?" He sighed.

"O.k. I will go for you but you owe me."

"O.k. O.k. I owe you go ahead and call me when you get back." Well once she delivered he called me from the Hospital like I was the wife. He was excited and screamed, "Diamond it's a boy!" I smiled.

"Congratulations! What's his name?" He cleared his throat.

"Zechariah Johnson Jr." I laughed.

"Oh O.k. I see, a junior huh?" He chuckled.

"Don't start Diamond! But he looks just like me. I can't wait for you to see him. I'm still not forgiving her ever and I mean that but you were right. I am glad I was able to see my son being born. He didn't ask to be here and this is going to be my lil' june june." I smiled into the phone.

"Yeah I can't wait to see him either. Once I get home I will come back down and see you and the baby."

"That's what's up. Have a safe trip home." I blew a kiss into the phone.

"Thanks. Talk to you soon." Me and Zak were like best friends now and I finally told Samir about him a few days before we left for home. Not how I met him, are you crazy? But that he was in one of my classes and we got cool. Samir wasn't feeling it but when I lied I said, "Him and his fiancé had a baby the other day..." Once I said that Samir was a little more relaxed. It was funny because once I got home I told Zak what I told Samir. He laughed.

"My what? She would never be my fiancé D, don't make me go up top on you." I laughed with him. I always laughed when people used the phrase go up top.

Now back to Starr, I was pissed with her since AIDS was a fucking epidemic and not to mention other diseases but she was ecstatic and she was keeping it. She had it all mapped out, take off from school for a year, have the baby and Kareem would watch the baby so she could finish school. She waited until she got home to tell her parents face to face and they hit the roof. They told her she was coming home and she blacked out.

"No I'm not. I love Kareem and I am staying with him and there is nothing you can do about it." From there they had a big blow out and she ended with basically telling her parents to kiss her grits like Flo used to say on the TV show Mel's Diner. Sam was disappointed in his sister, but hey, she was smelling herself and she was ripe! Her parents ended up telling her.

"Well if that is your man let him support you and that baby because your funds are cut off!"

"Good. I don't care I don't need you or your money, my man has plenty of it and I am going to live with him!" With that she packed that night and left. I tried to talk to her but she was persistent and wanted to go so as a best friend I supported her decisions. That was still my best friend even if her parents and brother were mad. I went down during the summer to see her and would stay with Zak. No no no we didn't have sex. We kissed a few times and got a little heated but for the most part we really just became best friends. He confessed he had never been friends with a female but he liked being my friend. It was cool. We would hang out and do things together. I just stayed with him because I didn't want to stay with Kareem and Starr and our D.C. apartment was being renovated during the summer to update the house. Zak's son was a cutie pop. He looked like Zak spit him out but with a tad bit more color. One day the baby was over and I was holding him. I looked at Zak and then at little Zak.

"You couldn't deny him if you tried." Zak laughed knowing I was telling the truth. Little Zak was breaking my pockets because I was buying him everything cute I saw.

When August finally came I started my 4th and final year alone. Samir was still there and he took Starr's place in the apartment. Her parents cut off everything living expenses and college tuition. With me and Samir living together I really wasn't able to see Zak but we hooked up and hung out once in a blue. I even ended up introducing Zak to Samir so it wouldn't seem like I was hiding anything. So of course once Samir met him it was not all good because he thought Zak was an ugly geek nigga. When Zak pulled up in that white Range Rover Samir frowned.

"D I don't know about this friendship you have found." I sucked my teeth.

"Samir we have been friends almost a year now. Don't act ugly you know we have classes together. That is why I wanted you to meet him...you don't trust me? His fiancé trusts him and she knows we're cool. She is secure in their relationship, are you not secure in ours? We are not kids anymore Samir."

"You're right Diamond. I'm cool." Zak got out and played his position. He shook Samir's hand and even asked did I have a book yet for class to make it look good. He stayed a minute while I pretended to write down the assignment and handed it to him. On the note I wrote I put, 'thanks a million, you're the best!'

Starr was happy as a pig in shit. She told me everything was great and Kareem told me she was the best thing that ever happened to him until...

CHAPTER 41
THE BABY'S BORN

About a month before the baby came I gave Starr a surprise baby shower at our, well me and Samir's apartment and her parents refused to come. I mean everybody else did like my parents, Aunt Debra, Jackie and even loud ass Aunt Michelle who was even louder then ever. All our old girls from home and college girls came. Starr had hurt her parents too bad and they didn't raise her like that so they didn't come. Krystal and Mitch were mad at the others for coming but nobody wanted to take sides. They all knew Starr was wrong for her actions but the baby was going to come anyway no matter who liked it. Krystal called me and told me she was mailing the stuff she bought for the baby to my house. I said it was fine because I understood how Krystal felt. I had told Starr she was wrong but I didn't want to upset her during her pregnancy. Before me and Krystal hung up from our call she said, "Diamond mark my words, it will not work out and she will be crying to get back here."

"Probably Ma, but you know we're young and think we know it all. I already told Starr about herself and the situation but she says I don't know what I'm talking about so I leave her alone."

"Well you're a good friend Diamond. I'm glad her and Samir have you down there. I don't know what would have happened to either of them with out you!" I laughed.

"Thanks Ma! You know I love my sister and my boyfriend even though they both drive me crazy!" She laughed.

"I love my kids too, but Starr needs tough love and

she will just have to learn the hard way."

"You're right." We talked a bit more and hung up. The shower was a surprise and it was nice. Starr was crying when she saw her parents didn't come. I pulled her aside.

"Don't trip! Starr you have been acting up and they are tired of your mess. Have you even apologized? The answer to that is no so cut out all the dramatics and just enjoy your shower." She rolled her eyes at me. I didn't care. Kareem's mom, Chickie and sister, Sheya came. Then when we were almost finished opening gifts some of his ghetto hood bugga female cousins came all weeded up. I was disgusted with them. Kareem came real late and was acting standoffish. I pulled Starr aside again.

"Starr what is Kareem's problem?" She started tearing up again.

"My weight is turning him off." My eyes got big.

"Well what does he think a pregnant person does lose weight? I'm going to say something to him." She pulled me back by my shirt.

"Sis please don't say anything to him. Just leave it alone." It was my turn to roll my eyes at her and walk away. Kareem's mother was a sweet woman. She was a Deaconess at her church and she loved Starr. She helped me clean up in the kitchen and talked to me.

"I love Starr and I wish they were married before they had a baby but I am working on my son. I want them to start coming to church but Kareem says no." I knew that Kareem loved his mother but he didn't pay her any attention. Kareem came in the kitchen and kissed his mother on the cheek because he was leaving. He had borrowed Zak's Range Rover to pack up all the gifts to get them home. His mother tugged on his arm.

"Son, when are you going to do right by Starr and marry her?" He yanked away from his mother and gave her a look that read, 'please, I am not marrying her!' and he left out of the kitchen. I shook my head at him and she did as well.

Anyway, on March 23rd 1997 Starr had my beautiful Goddaughter. Kareemah Diamond Blackwell named after her father and me and with his last name. After Kareemah was born, that is when the trouble began. Starr hadn't hardly gained that much weight, maybe 15 pounds tops but she would call me crying saying he called her 'Lard butt' and 'Fat ass.' She asked me to keep whatever she shared with me a secret from Samir and I had to respect that. She told me Kareem would stay out all night and not bother to call. She would call him and the phone would ring but he wouldn't answer and when she would keep calling back he would turn his phone off. He didn't half ass be bothered with Kareemah even though it was his bright idea to have a baby. Other girls had started calling the house for him and she said she would tell them, "Look this is his girl, don't call her anymore!" and he girls would laugh and say things like, "Kareem got many girls boo" or "Look I ain't trying to be the wife, he just eat pussy good have you seen him?" She told me she would invite bitches over to fight but they wouldn't come. I told her she can't be inviting chics over to fight with Kareemah there. She ended with saying the bitches that were calling were just jealous. I said, "Well Starr if they are lying how did they get the number?"

"Look Diamond I don't need your shit on top of this. I just need a friend or better yet a supportive sister right now."

"I'm not trying to give you shit, I'm trying to open your eyes to his game."

"Damn Diamond! I never thought you would be jealous." I yelled, "Of what?!"

"I gotta go Diamond!" Then she hung up on me. Me and Starr had begun to drift apart, way apart, because we couldn't see eye to eye on Kareem. She couldn't go out because you don't think for one minute that he was going to baby sit do you? And he would tell Starr his family would not baby sit for her to go out and be in the club. He told her she was a mother now and she was going to act like it. He didn't change diapers because he said that was a woman's job. I was telling Zak all that was going on and how I couldn't take his boy. He said he would talk to him, which he did, but it didn't work. He told Zak to mind his business and stop listening to the shit I tell him because Starr be over exaggerating and adding shit in when it is not like that at all.

One night I went out with some girls from school and Kareem was up in the club all hugged up on some chic. I approached him like I was his girl.

"What the fuck is this?" He looked me up and down.

"Diamond what's up?" I waved my hand up and down.

"I was just about to ask you the same question Kareem! What up with this?" I pointed at the girl and he smacked my hand down."

"Look girl, mind your business." I screamed out.

"What?! This is my business. Are you trying to play my sister out?" He pointed towards the other side of the club.

"Go 'head now Diamond with all that bullshit! Don't make me tell you again!" I frowned up my face and put my hands on my hips.

"Excuse me? You must have bumped your head nigga!" I turned to the girl.

"Excuse me miss, you don't know me and I don't know you but this is my sister's man and they live together and she home now with his daughter they just had not to long ago." She began to walk away from him.

"Oh excuse me then...I don't do girlfriends." He pulled her arm back.

"Wait up Monique baby. This bitch is lying! Don't believe her!" She stopped in her tracks while I questioned him.

"Bitch? Who the fuck you calling a bitch?" He put his finger in my face.

"You! Now get the fuck out of here and stop riding my dick, I know you want me but I told you before chill! You not my type!" I thought, this good for nothing trying to play me. So I screamed on him.

"What?! You rat bastard! Want you? In your fucking dreams. My sister barely wants your shriveled up dick ass!" The girl laughed a little. I tapped her on the shoulder.

"Look believe what you want to but I don't got no reason to lie!" I turned to walk away and she did too. He started walking behind me yelling, "Diamond get your ass over here now!" I kept walking thinking, this nigga must have fell and bumped his head for real. He grabbed my shoulder and spun me around to face him.

"You stupid ho bitch! Nobody gets in my business and that includes you and your dumb ass sister!" Pow! He pimped smacked me. I was in a state of shock for a minute but quickly popped out of it. I thought fast, grabbed a drink out of somebody's hand and threw it in his face. The bouncers were on us. They separated us and put us out. Kareem was yelling, "Yeah bitch watch your back! I don't play with bitches in my business. I'm gonna fuck you up." I yelled back, "Make my fucking day you fucking punk, putting your hands on a girl. You is a bitch ass nigga and I'm gonna have to pull that skirt up!" The bouncers told us to both shut up as they threw us out. Luckily I drove my own car or I would have been assed out. I don't know where the girls I came with were because I had excused myself when I see the slime ball with the girl across the club. It was so crowded that I couldn't even see where they might have been.

Once outside Kareem yelled, "You stay the fuck away from my daughter you bitch!" I screamed, "Fuck you! That's my Godchild and my sister's daughter! You don't half ass take care of her so fuck off!"

"You just wait bitch, I'm gonna fix you. I'm the king in my castle and what I say goes. Your sister is sprung and will not go over what I say goes. Your sister is sprung and will not go over what I say or she knows what will happen!" I jumped around.

"Well I'm waiting for you to fix me and I'm shaking in my boots! Nobody tries to play my sister and you wait until

I tell her. It's over for you buddy. If anybody is sprung it's your punk ass! My sister would never turn her back on me over no sorry ass nigga!"

"Watch and see ho!"

"I'm watching you piece of shit!" He got in his car parked in front and screeched off. I did the same. When I got in the car I used my cell phone to call the one girl Alnisa who I was with. I told her I got put out. My other friend Miriam didn't have a cell phone and Karen didn't answer hers so I told Alnisa to relay the message and for them to call me tomorrow. As soon as I got in my front door my phone was ringing. It was Starr. Thank God Samir had went out with his boys. I began to speak first.

"Starr let me tell you what happened..." She cut me off.

"I already heard and you owe Kareem an apology." I screamed, "A what?! What was you smoking tonight Starr, that good shit?" Kareem had beaten me home and told Starr some bullshit ass story and she believed it. She repeated it to me.

"Diamond, Kareem said he was in the club talking to his cousin and you busted over there and started disrespecting him..." I then cut her off.

"No it wasn't like that at all. That girl wasn't his cousin, he was trying to talk to her! Then he smacked me!"

"Well I can't believe my Kareem would do something like that." For the second time that evening I was in a state of shock.

"So you saying you believe him over me?" She sighed.

"I don't know who to believe." I sucked my teeth.

"What? BYE STARR!" I hung up on her. Zak called me a few minutes later.

"D are you O.k.?" I exhaled.

"I'm fine, don't worry about me. It is my sister I am worried about."

"No D I am worried. You are my peoples and Kareem owes you an apology. He is drunk as hell though

Diamond. Can you please forgive him for me." I yelled, "What? Naw! Fuck him!" He sighed.

"For me D? Remember you owe me from when I went to the hospital with that... You know what!" I smiled.

"Ight, Ight! I'm not going to forgive him but I will not talk about the situation no more. It is dead and buried. He told Starr this bull story about him talking to his cousin. What did he tell you?"

"Some story about you walking up on him. He didn't say who he was talking to but I know it wasn't his cousin and he said that you threw a drink in his face and then he smacked you." I corrected the story for Zak.

"No he smacked me, then I threw a drink in his face. Whatever I don't even care. It is over and done with. I'm not stressing and I'm not beat."

"That's my girl, I will call you tomorrow O.k.?" I smiled.

"Yeah, yeah. You're lucky you're my friend." I scratched my head. It is going to be hard to stay friends with Zak when Kareem is such an asshole.

Once Samir came in I was in the bed and had simmered down from the situation. I told him very little of what happened but not about him smacking me because I didn't want Samir approaching Kareem. I knew Kareem was deep in the streets of D.C. and Samir was just a college guy. This wasn't Jersey where he could get his street niggas to help him handle the situation. The next day Starr called back.

"I think we have both cooled down now and I wanted to know if you could apologize to Kareem to keep the peace? He told me that you are forbidden from coming here or being near his daughter but if you apologize I am sure he will change his mind." I furrowed my brows.

"Starr are you fucking crazy? Fuck him and his house, but that is your daughter just as much as it is his and you gonna repeat that bull shit he told you about me not seeing Kareemah?" She began to stutter.

"Well I will sneak..." I cut her off.

"Sneak hell! If you gotta do all that Starr then just forget it. You know I love Kareemah more than life itself but you acting up. Did you forget who was in the delivery room with you when he was nowhere to be found? And who bought diapers there when she only had one left and he was nowhere to be found..." The list went on but she cut me off mid sentence.

"O.k. Diamond I have thanked you for all that over and over again. Are you gonna hold that over my head forever?"

"No but you're turning into a wimp letting him run you."

"I am not! I'm just trying to keep the peace up in here." I sucked my teeth.

"Well I ain't apologizing for shit. He smacked me Starr and he was playing you. I can't believe you're still there but do what you gotta do." She screamed, "I will D!" We hung up on each other. I couldn't help but tell Samir what had just happened because he heard me in the bedroom arguing with her from downstairs. He called her and they got into it as well. He was still mad at her for playing Johnny jackass and having a baby in the first place. After he hung up with her, he was more pissed off than me and I rubbed his shoulders.

"Sam don't worry about it. She will come around...I hope." I stopped massaging his shoulders and sat and thought back to all the things me and Starr had been through and began to cry. I mean this nigga was fucking our whole friendship up. I thought back to things with Kareem that just didn't add up. Now, he owned a barbershop, which he expanded into a beauty shop but Starr couldn't come there to get her hair done. I thought, he probably fucking the beauticians. And how he was always so busy all the time. He would give her a little cash and then not see her for days saying he had business to take care of. He didn't pack a bag but would come home with different clothes on. When his beeper would go off or cell phone would ring he would straight up get up and go in the other room and close the door to use the phone. When she would tell me this stuff I would say, "Starr that doesn't seem right. You sure he is not seeing another woman?" She would suck her teeth every time.

"Oh boy Diamond. Everybody don't cheat like Tahir and Q." I got fed up with her saying that because she didn't have the most faithful ex boyfriends herself.

"Look you always talking shit about my exes when you didn't have the most trustworthy exes yourself but you know what? I won't say shit to you about your relationship and don't tell me shit else about yours!"

"I won't!" She hung up on me once again. I was getting sick of her with that shit. If there is one thing I can't stand that's for someone to hang up on me. It is rude and it makes you want to fight. We didn't speak for 2 weeks until she called me crying. Check this shit out...

CHAPTER 42
YOU FIND THAT HARD TO BELIEVE

Starr found out that Kareemah had a sister 1 month younger than she was and she was through with him. She called me crying asking me if her and Kareemah could stay with me and Sam for a while. She was still my best friend so I opened up my home and my heart. Once she got to my place we sat down on the couch to talk. She started the conversation.

"Diamond I am sooo sorry for all the shit I've been doing and putting you through. You are my best friend. Always have been and always will be. Why didn't you tell me not to fuck with him no more a long time ago?!" I screamed, What?! I did! I guess the dick must have blinded you!" We both started laughing. She adjusted Kareemah in her lap.

"Damn! For real girl, you ain't never lied!" I fell back laughing on the couch.

"And you know this! It had you bugging!" She slapped my thigh.

"Sis, I ain't gonna front, it is good! And the tongue ain't too bad either!" We started laughing and Kareemah did too. I tickled her stomach.

"What you laughing at girl?" She was so cute with Starr's complexion and a head full of curly hair. She looked like Starr spit her out. Starr sat up straight and crossed her heart.

"Sis, I am done with him. Cross my heart, hope to die, stick a needle in my eye!" I laughed at our childhood phrase we use to recite when we were dead serious. I threw my hands on the air.

"Hallelujah! Thank you Jesus! It's about time." She whined, "Deeeeeeeeeee!" I rolled my eyes and crossed my arms over my chest.

"Don't Deeeeeee me. I'm sorry Starr but he smacked me for protecting you and you took his side over mine. Me, your sister and best friend. That hurt bad Starr, I won't front like it didn't." She sighed and wiped away a tear that had formed. She looked down at the floor and sighed,

"I know D and deep down inside I knew you were telling the truth. I am so sorry sis for betraying you. I know better then to put a nigga first and I vow I will never do it again...I tried to leave him D, I swear I did but I just couldn't. He pays for everything and I was scared to leave because I didn't know what I was going to do." She looked up and we locked eyes. I examined her face with my eyes. I quickly grabbed her chin towards the light once I noticed her cheek was red and swollen.

"Starr what happened to your face?" She pulled away from me and looked down at Kareemah.

"Oh uh nothing. I just uh walked into a door, that's all." I jumped up from the couch.

"Oh yeah, I remember about 5 years ago when I told that same lie now what really happened?" She put Kareemah down on the couch next to her. She exhaled.

"Well, me and Kareem were arguing about the girl that said she had a baby by him and he punched me in my face." She sniffled.

"See the girl called the house and said, 'yo, can I speak to Kareem?' So I huffed with an attitude and screamed, 'who dis?' The girl on the phone said, 'look sweetie don't get no attitude alright, Kareema needs some things and Kareem has been M.I.A. (missing in action) and I just had to call him at your house because I didn't make her by myself. His daughter...' I cut her off confused saying, 'his what? His daughter Kareemah is sitting right here.' The girl laughed and said, 'no boo, not your daughter Kareemah, MY daughter Kareema. Your precious Kareem has a daughter with me as well.' Sis, I instantly got sick to my stomach thinking of him and this girl and their daughter. I was silent on holding the phone and Kareem walked in.

He kissed me on the forehead and asked, 'who you on the phone with?' I told him, 'I don't know Kareem wait a minute. Excuse me, what is your name?' The girl said, 'It's Walida.' I turned to Kareem and said, 'I am on the phone with Walida your other daughter's mother.' He snatched the phone from me and I watched him. He took the cordless and went into kitchen. I put Kareemah in her swing and turned it on and followed him in the kitchen. When he noticed me he had the nerve to cover the mouthpiece and scream on me saying, 'excuse me! I'm on the phone!' I shook my head at him and ran upstairs and started packing. A few minutes later he came up the stairs after me and almost bust down the bedroom door and grabbed me by my collar and asked me what did I think I was doing. I pulled away from him and told him I was leaving because I didn't need his shit. I screamed, 'enough is enough already Kareem. I give you everything I have and it's not enough and now you got another daughter named Kareema? I'm gone.' He tried to pull on me and explain saying it was a mistake and I should forgive him and that baby's name was spelled different. D, he was telling me all this crazy shit. Once I didn't stop packing he blacked out on me and told me I wasn't going nowhere and punched me in the face. I fell to the floor and he began to kick me until I said I was staying." She lifted her shirt to reveal the bruises that occupied her side and stomach. I looked in terror at the discoloration of her skin.

"Oh my God Starr. How did you get out?" She shrugged and fixed her shirt.

"That was a week ago..." I grabbed her shoulders and shook her.

"You stayed with him another week after he did that to you?!" She flung my arms off of her and screamed, "Yes Diamond damn! Get off my back! I didn't know you were the only one aloud to be dumb over a nigga that can't keep his hands to his self." I flopped down and sighed.

"That is fucked up Starr. I was young and didn't know any better. What's your excuse?" She exclaimed,

"There is no excuse! Look D, I'm sorry, I'm really sorry but I can't believe the situation I got myself into." I hugged her.

"Well don't worry. You don't need him. We will handle this situation." She looked out into space.

"I wonder if my parents are still mad at me?" I touched her hand.

"Call them." She shook her head back and forth slowly.

"No...I, I, I can't." I picked up the phone and handed it to her.

"Yes you can and you will!" She looked at the phone for a while and then slowly dialed her parent's number. She puts the phone to her ear.

"Hello...Mom?" From there she started crying.

"Mommy I am so sorry...I, I , I don't know what got into me." She looked over at me.

"No, no Ma. He didn't hit me." I tried to talk but she covered my mouth and looked at me with her eyes big. She sniffled.

"O.k. Mommy. Maybe I will come up this weekend." She wiped her eyes.

"I love you too Ma!" She hung up and fell over in her lap crying. I rubbed her back.

"You O.k. sis. What did she say?" She threw her head back as she sat up straight.

"She told me don't worry about anything just come home and we will deal with it." I smiled at her.

"That's good." She grabbed my hands in hers.

"Diamond please don't tell Samir about him hitting me. I forgot to put my cover up make up on. Don't worry I will fix it up now." She snatched up her pocketbook and ran in the bathroom and then came out with the make up caked on her face. She extended her arms and pointed to herself.

"Ta-da! Good as new!" Then keys began to jingle in the door. Samir was home. He walked in, looked at her, at her bags by the door and then at me. He snapped his fingers and pointed towards the stairs.

"Diamond. Bedroom. Now!" Starr smiled and stood

up walking towards her brother.

"Hey Samir." He looked around her at me.

"Diamond. Now!" I ran up the stairs with him following me.

"Diamond tell me, what is her and all her stuff doing here? Did he put her out?" I put my arms around Samir's neck.

"No Samir. She found out he had another baby on her and she left him." He threw my arms off his neck and paced around.

"So. Is that our problem? After she has given us her ass to kiss we are supposed to feel sympathy?" I sat down on the bed and gave him my best puppy dog eyes.

"Sammmiiiirrr! That is your sister and your niece down there. Not to mention my best friend. I am not going to put them out on the streets!" He put his finger in my face.

"Look, Kareemah can stay forever but as far as Starr is concerned. She gotta go!" I pushed his finger out of my face.

"Samir come on now. Just let her apologize please so we can move on." He sucked his teeth.

"Not even. I'm not beat for Starr or her apology." I jumped up and ran out of the room.

"You are an impossible pain in the ass! A number one PITA! (pain in the ass)." I stormed down the stairs, sat next to Starr and took Kareemah from her. She looked at me concerned.

"What is his problem?" I kissed Kareemah.

"You and your life Starr. You and your life." She stood up and put her hands on her hips.

"What?!" She took off up the stairs while I played with Kareemah. They argued at the top of their lungs for almost half an hour before they peaced it up. That weekend me, Sam, Starr and Kareemah went home to New Jersey.

Starr had completely shut her parents out so they never saw Kareemah except in pictures ooh, and the home videos Dan the director AKA my father shot when she was born. He thinks he is Spike Lee or Robert Townsend with that camcorder. Her parents tried numerous times to see Kareemah but Starr wouldn't return their calls or let them in when they came down to see me and Samir. I think Kareem made her stay away from her parents. She was addicted to him like he was a cult.

So once we got home and Starr entered the house her mother started crying and hugging her. I was holding Kareemah and Krystal extended her arms.

"Diamond is that my grandbaby?" She started crying some more as she took Kareemah in her arms. She kissed Kareemah on the forehead.

"She is absolutely beautiful."

"Thank you!" Rang out from my lips and Starr's. They looked at me and we all laughed. Krystal kept giving Kareemah kisses and Kareemah kept laughing. She was such a happy baby. Mitch was sitting in his den reading his paper and didn't budge. Her mom leaned over and whispered to Starr, "Your father is just hurt Starr. You need to go talk to him." She slowly walked in the den looking around like she hadn't been there in years. She stood in front of him and lowered her eyes.

"Hi Daddy." He kept reading his paper.

"Hello Starr. She looked up at the back of the paper. She peeked over the top of the paper at her father.

"Daddy are you upset with me?" He slammed the paper down in his lap and sat up from his Lazy Boy recliner.

"What do you think Starr? You answer your own question!" She fidgeted around in her spot.

"Daddy please..." He stood up and cut her off.

"No Starr, please hell! What do you think this is? We raise you and give you everything and you meet some piece of shit nigga and give me and your mother your ass to kiss? You think we are supposed to just have open arms when he does you wrong and your heart is broken? Well it doesn't work that way Starr!" She kept her head hung low as the tears continued to follow each other in a straight line down her face.

"No daddy, I'm sorry. It wasn't my fault." He sat

back down in his recliner and reached for his pipe.

"You damn right you're sorry Starr. And you standing here saying it's not your fault. Well whose fault is it Starr?" She wiped her tears but kept her face down.

"It's loves fault daddy. I can't help who I love. Love is blind and so I didn't see this coming but you know what Daddy? If you don't want me here, me and my daughter will just go." He cleared his throat to keep his own tears from flowing.

"Now that's just like Starr. Run out when shit gets tough on you. You know what Starr, just do what you want, isn't that what you have been doing anyway? What you want to do?" She fell to her knees in front of her father. She screamed, "Daddy what do you want from me? Blood? I'm saying I'm sorry and I didn't mean for any of this to happen and if I could take it back I would. I swear I would Daddy but Kareemah is here now. She's here and she didn't ask to be. I love my daughter no matter what..." I walked in the den and up to Mitch.

"Mitch would you like to see your granddaughter?" Krystal passed her to me and I handed her to him. He looked up at me with tears in his eyes. He looked at her and pinched her cheek.

"She is beautiful Starr." Starr was collapsed on the floor on her knees in a ball. She sat up and looked at her father and her daughter. He kissed Kareemah and she laughed. Starr touched her dad's knee.

"Look daddy she loves you and I love you too." She pulled herself up and hugged her father with Kareemah in the middle. He tickled Kareemah.

"Hey grandbaby! Grandpa loves you too!" He looked at Starr.

"And I love you too Starr." Kareemah was smiling and laughing like always. She was such a happy baby. After some serious one on one talking with her parents she decided to stay in Jersey for a while.

She really didn't want to, but at the time she had no other option.

CHAPTER 43
STALKER MODE

It was June and school was out. Samir had started speaking to Starr again like they used to. Up until she went home to Jersey he would tell me he couldn't believe they shared a womb. Me and Samir were in D.C. because he had to work. He worked for a top law firm in D.C. as a paid intern. When we got back from our Jersey trip Kareem had left over 20 messages filling up my voicemail box. He was looking for Starr and Kareemah. Her and her car were back in Jersey and I wasn't going to tell this asshole this. Samir put the phone on speaker as we listened to his messages get more and more crazy.

He was saying he was sorry and he was the reason she cut her family off but he wanted to make it right in the beginning but by the 7th message he said, "Diamond you better get my family back here and Samir if you're listening your girl is a hoe. She is fucking my man Zak." He was lying because me and Zak were just friends. Not so much as a kiss on the cheek happened since we really started being best friends. Samir slowly turned his neck to look at me as I stared at the speaker on the phone not believing what I heard.

"D what is he talking about? How does he know Zak?" I cleared my throat, nervous as hell.

"Well, that is his friend too. Zak is from D.C. they know each other but he is lying you know I am not fucking that boy. You met him and you know it ain't nothing. We speak and that's all and you know that. He just looked at me with the corners of his mouth turned upwards. My eyes automatically bulged out of my head like someone was choking the life out of me.

"What is that look Samir? You believe him over

me?" He turned away from me.

"Did I say that Diamond? Don't put words in my mouth ight?" I sucked my teeth.

"I didn't say you said it but it is not what you said it is how you're looking and you're looking like you don't believe me!" He jumped up and tried to walk away from me.

"Oh boy D, now you're a body language reader? Let me know!" I jumped up and pulled him back towards me.

"No Samir I'm not but let me call Zak right now if you want me to because I don't have nothing to hide!" He got up in my face.

"Why go through all that Diamond if it ain't nothing!" our doorbell rang. Saved by the bell. I stormed away from him and looked out the peephole. It was our neighbor, Ms. Bailey. She watched our apartment while we were gone.

"Hey Diamond, that boy, Starr's boyfriend? He has been riding past here every 20 minutes looking at the house since y'all left." Samir came up behind me.

"Sam did you hear Ms. Bailey. Kareem has been stalking us, riding by here every 20 minutes." He looked at me and then at Ms. Bailey.

"Thanks Ms. Bailey." She waved bye and left. Samir grabbed his car keys.

"D I will be back I am going to the store so go ahead and call Zak now and get your stories straight." I tried to grab him but he pulled loose from my grasp.

"Samir!" He continued out the door with me hot on his heels. He ran to his car while I screamed from the entrance.

"Look. I don't need your shit Samir, if you don't believe me then lets just break up. I don't care no more. I thought we were grown but I guess not, let's take it back to high school. Fuck it, it's over!" He unlocked his car door.

"Fine Diamond, I ain't trying to keep no bitch that don't want to be kept." I began to walk down the stairs to that comment.

"Keep a bitch? Nigga you must have bumped your head! If you ever..." He jumped in his car and made his tires screech as he pulled off leaving a cloud of smoke for me to argue with. I stomped up the stairs thinking, I'm going back to Jersey for the summer. I don't need this shit! I ran in the house and locked the door placing the chain on there as well so he couldn't get in. I ran up the stairs and began packing my things. 10 minutes into my packing someone laid on the doorbell. I didn't stop because I knew it was Samir. He kept ringing and ringing until I slowly sauntered down the stairs and snatched the door open without removing the chain. Well, it wasn't Samir but Kareem. Our eyes met and locked.

"Diamond can you open the door please." I sucked my teeth and closed it in his face. From behind the door I screamed, "Get your lying ass off my steps. You left that message about me and Zak trying to be funny. Fuck you!" He knocked on the door as if I wasn't standing right there.

"Diamond can you open the door please?" I yelled, "What about no don't you understand? You left that shit on the machine and now me and Samir is beefing. I wouldn't open the door if you were on fire and I had the only water to put your black ass out, you fucking bastard!" I was close to the door and he kicked it with all his might. It almost gave way and bumped me in the nose. I rubbed my nose while he stood outside and screamed.

"Bitch, where is my family?" My temperature began to rise with every breath I took.

"I got your bitch you punk mother fucker! The family that you are looking for, MY family is not here. I don't know where they are." He punched the door but this time I was standing away from it. Damn Samir for leaving me here alone!

"Don't fucking play with me Diamond. Are they in New Jersey?" I yelled, "Why would they be there? You made her cut her fucking parents off, you made her cut me and her brother off, so fuck you Kareem get off my steps before I call the cops!" He kicked the door one last time.

"Bitch, I'm gonna get you! You better get my family back down here quick." I sucked my teeth.

"Whatever!" Next thing I heard was Smash! That Negro bust out the left window on my MX-3. I snatched the chain off the door and swung it open with all the force in my body. He jumped in his car and I ran down the stairs and yelled behind him, "You fucking punk! You will pay for that!" Ms. Bailey came out and asked was I O.k. I said yes and went in called the police. They came and I made a report. When the cop was leaving he handed me his card.

"Miss unfortunately the only way to get him to pay for your window is to take him to small claims court. If you have a 500 deductible it doesn't make sense to report it to your insurance company because the window might be 250." I walked the officers to the door.

"Thank you officer." As the cops were pulling off Samir was pulling up. I let the door close in his face and went in the kitchen. The cop had helped me put plastic over the window. Samir slammed into the house.

"D what happened to your window?" I opened the cabinet to get the Advil bottle.

"Kareem happened!" Samir punched his fist in his hand.

"Yo I'm sick of him. I will be back." I tried to jump on his back to stop him from leaving but he threw me back off of him. I hit my back on the wall and he continued out the door.

"Sorry D but I have to handle this." I sat up rubbing the pain that engulfed my back. I stood up and wobbled to the kitchen. I had taken out 1 Advil for my headache but I opened up the bottle and took out 2 more. I needed 3 for the pain I was in. Headache, backache, and heartache.

CHAPTER 44
WHERE IS ROSCOE?

I slowly walked up the stairs to finish packing my things. I dragged my Tommy Hilfiger duffle bag down the stairs packed to the top. I ran back up the stairs and got my big, green army duffle bag and dragged that down the stairs as well. I sat on the couch waiting for Samir's safe return before I left his sorry ass. Samir came back in a half hour later screaming at the top of his lungs.

"That mother fucker pulled a gun on me! I can't believe this shit. He had the audacity to pull a gun, ON ME! No, I ain't letting that shit ride." Samir had a gun in our apartment, upstairs in his bottom nightstand draw. I had already moved it just incase anything like this ever happened. He ran up the stairs and I followed him, "Samir are you alright?" He kept walking around talking to himself saying, "A gun. On me?" and ignored my question. He went right to his drawer to look for his gun.

"Diamond where is Roscoe (that was our 380's name)?" I sucked my teeth and looked down.

"How am I supposed to know. It was in your drawer." He pulled the whole draw out and turned it upside down.

"D I'm not in the mood for your shit! I want my gun and I want it now, so where is it?" I sat down on the bed and looked at him.

"You sure you not in the mood for my shit because you gonna have to get in the mood because I am not giving you no gun to go kill that nigga so you can go to jail for the rest of your life. It is not worth it Samir, just let it go!" He got in my face and grabbed me by my collar.

"Diamond, I have never put my hands on you but I will beat your mother fucking ass in here, right here and right now if you don't give me my mother fucking gun! I am not playing with you, now where is my shit at Diamond?" I was not moved by Samir's threats so I jumped up and balled up my fists.

"Ball first Samir! Lets get it on!" He pushed passed me knocking me on the bed. He pulled open my drawers.

"Diamond you think everything is a game but I got something for you. I will tear this apartment up piece by piece until I find my gun." He dumped everything out of my top drawer, then the middle and finally the bottom drawer. He scratched his head and looked around.

"Let me look in the kitchen." He took off the down the stairs like a bolt of lightning. I followed him with my sore back. He began to throw every pot and pan out of the cabinets. I screamed at him.

"Sam stop it!" He kept taking everything out of the cabinets and the pantries. He paced back and forth and thought about possible hiding places. He ran back upstairs into the bedroom. He opened our closet. I jumped in front of him. He pushed me aside and started ripping clothes from the hangers like he was Mommy Dearest. I dramatically fell. I pulled myself up to my knees and yelled, "O.k. Samir you win. I will give it to you." I walked into our master bathroom and opened the cabinet and dug behind the Clorox bleach. I produced the gun and handed it to him. I then began to lecture him.

"You know what Sam once you leave it is..." He looked at the gun and then at me. He waved his hand at what I was saying.

"Yo D save drama ight? Where are the bullets?" I screamed, "I don't know!" He looked me up and down.

"Oh you don't know?" He flung the linen closet open and pulled out all the neatly folded towels and flung them all over the floor. I cried.

"O.k., O.k. let me get them. Please stop." He kept his stone face and watched me. I went under the bed in one of my many Via Spiga shoeboxes and pulled out a box of bullets. I slammed them into his hand.

"Here! And you might as well know I am leaving

your black ass. When you go I am getting the hell out of here and going home." Samir loaded his gun, "D I will deal with you later." He traipsed down the stairs with me following.

"I won't be here when you get back!" He put the safety on the gun and tucked it into his jeans.

"Look Diamond you better be sitting your ass right here when I come back or I swear to God I will fuck you up. Now if you think I am playing with you, just try me." He picked up his car keys and then looked at mine. I tried to beat him to the table but he pushed me backwards and took my car keys. He had the spare set on his keys so I was stuck. I had to sit there and wait. I was shaking uncontrollably and needed to talk to Starr. I dialed her number and told her what happened thus far. She screamed at me.

"D I gotta go. I gotta call Kareem." I begged her not to call but she did anyway. She hung up in my face. I was sitting on the couch crying with my left leg shaking like I had Tourette's Syndrome. When I would push down on my left leg my right leg would start in shaking. About an hour passed and Samir came in the door. He sat down next to me and put his gun on the glass coffee table. He looked at me.

"D, I couldn't find him. I am so sorry." I jumped up and extended my hand in his face.

"Sorry? Huh! Can I have my car keys please, I'm leaving. I'm going home for the summer." He got down on his knees and buried his face in my stomach.

"Come on D, let's work this out. I'm sorry." I pushed him off of me and stepped over him flinging my Hilfiger bag on my shoulder.

"There is nothing to work out Samir. You pushed me a bunch of times. You called me a bitch, told me you ain't trying to keep no bitch that don't want to be kept, threatened to beat me up if I left...I don't need this shit Samir. He crawled up and flopped down on the couch pulling me down into his lap. He took my face in his hands.

"I'm saying sorry D! Sorry for all that wrongdoing. I love you D and I love my sister. What did this nigga have over my sister that caused her to let him tear our family apart and tear y'all apart? She better not never mess with him again and I mean that." He looked like he wanted to cry. I didn't want to tell him that I called her and she was concerned about Kareem. I pulled him into my bosom and gave him a tight hug.

"It's O.k. baby. It will be alright." He let out a quiet sob.

"No it won't! That nigga pulled a gun on me." I reached behind him and rubbed his neck.

"Samir baby, we are getting ready to graduate and you will be a lawyer soon enough. We don't need to be bothered with street stuff anymore. It is not worth it to mess up your chances for him." He looked at me and I kissed him on his forehead.

"D, I know that but right now I don't care about none of that. I am not a punk and I won't be disrespected like I am." I massaged the top of his head.

"Samir that is still Kareemah's father. She didn't ask to be here so don't do anything that you will regret and make her hate you later on in life." He sighed.

"I guess you're right D." Shit, I was always right. I mushed him.

"You know I am right...and I am still leaving your ass!" I tried to get up but he pulled me down and pushed me on to the couch and got on top of me. He held my wrists over my head and sucked on my neck.

"Samir get off of me right now!" He licked from my neck to my ear lobe.

"No! You not leaving me! I'm sorry dammit! I love you D, I can't be with out you!" He softly blew in my ear getting me hot and bothered. We began to kiss and I snapped out of it.

"No way Jose, no kitty kat for you! You are on punishment!" He stuck his tongue down my throat, "Man stop playing." I pointed to my face.

"Do I look like I'm playing? Look at my eyebrows! You can tell I'm serious! Now get off me!" He looked into my eyes.

"O.k. I will get up if you promise to stay?" I looked away and then looked back at him.

"I will stay if you promise to clean this mess up!" He kissed me and got up.

"O.k. deal...but uh D?" I sat up and looked at him.

"What Samir?" He put his arm around me.

"You gonna help me right?" I flung his arm off of me.

"Hell no! Now get started." He smiled and jumped up. He went in the kitchen and started picking up pots and pans. I stood in the doorway and watched him.

"Drill Sergeant I can do this with out an audience." I sucked my teeth and walked into the living room.

"O.k. smart ass!" I went up to the bedroom and started cleaning up the mess in there. I was standing in the closet door hanging up clothes. He crept up behind me. I turned around and we were face to face. He put his arms around my waist.

"D, what would I do with out you?" I looked him up and down.

"I don't know, what?" He smiled at me and me at him. I couldn't help but give him some. We played butt naked boodie tag in the closet, but afterwards he was back on punishment. I didn't give him no loving for a good 2 to 3 weeks. He had to learn his lesson for treating me bad.

CHAPTER 45
GUESS WHO'S BI-ZACK?

Well the next week came and Starr was back in D.C. with Kareem. He had kicked some slick shit in her ear and she came running right back to him. Now mind you, this is after he busted out my car window and pulled a gun on Samir. Krystal and Mitch were at their wits end with Starr and so were me and Samir.

She called me like everything was all-good that she was back with him and I had to rip her a new asshole. I think back to that day and still want to cry at the things that we said to each other. The phone conversation went something like this. The phone rang and I answered on the first ring, "Hello."

"Hey D! Guess what?!"

"What?!" (I said it with much attitude because I hadn't spoken to her since she hung the phone up on me the week before.)

"I'm back in D.C." I looked over at my caller ID and sure as my name is Diamond, I saw Blackwell, Kareem on the screen and I lost it.

"Starr?!"

"Yes?" I called her name again.

"Starr?!" She began to laugh.

"Yes D, it's me." I cleared my throat.

"Well the reason I keep calling your name is because I'm trying to figure out who the hell I am talking to because I know this is not the Starr I grew up with as a best friend and a sister." She stopped laughing, "What do you mean?"

"I mean that my sis and best friend Starr wouldn't ever let a nigga disrespect her or me or Sam for that matter. She wouldn't ever let a nigga dictate her life. She wouldn't ever let a nigga get her pregnant and dictate her whole shit and fuck up her life by making her drop out of school. My best friend would have never been that fucking stupid to let some sorry ass nigga come between her and her family and beat her ass and she still goes back to him. She would have never gone back to him after he has a baby on her. She would never go back with him knowing he bust out her best friend's window and pulled a gun on her brother. This can't be the Starr Angel Mitchell that I know. My best and friend and sister, it just can't be..." She was quiet and I started to feel bad about the things I was saying. She was sniffling and then crying.

"Diamond I can't believe you of all people would talk to me like that. I'm just trying to do what is right for my child. I am sorry..." I cut her off.

"Oh Starr please! Having Kareemah in a violent household is the best thing for her?! I don't think so! Has he knocked you upside your head yet for leaving him or is he waiting for a special occasion?"

"No D, you got it wrong. He does not hit me like that."

"Bullshit bitch!" She screamed on me.

"O.k. Miss Know-it-all, maybe once in a while but that is when I deserve it. He does a lot for me and Kareemah and I sometimes don't act appreciative enough, but I thought you were a friend and would be more supportive and less judgmental. I have never said anything about your relationships!" I sucked my teeth.

"First of all, he is supposed to do for Kareemah. You didn't make her alone, did you ask to get pregnant? NO! He got you pregnant. He trapped your dumb ass into thinking you need him and you don't. What happened to being an independent woman and not needing a man for shit? He has you brain washed to think that you need him. And bottom line, I am not being judgmental I am being real!"

"No Diamond that is not it at all! I am not brain washed. I am here because I want to be here, I love being here. You think you know every fucking thing and you don't! I never thought my own best friend would be jealous of me!" I screamed at the top of my lungs.

"Bitch, I think on your trip back to D.C. you lost your mother fucking mind and need to go look for it because what would I be jealous of you for? Oh let's see, I want a nigga knocking me upside my head if I so much as breathe wrong and I would love to be dependent on a nigga for everything and not be able to do anything on my own. And oh, oh..." She cut me off.

"Fuck you Diamond, you dumb bitch!" She hung up on me and I hit *69 on my phone.

She picked up on the first ring with Kareemah screaming in the background. I heard her say, "Just shut up Kareemah...What Diamond?"

"No Fuck you Starr and you're the dumb bitch not me, you dumb bitch!" I hung up on her. There was this burning in the pit of my stomach and I needed to see Starr. I had to go over there and see what was going on with my Godchild. I got in my car and drove over there. Kareem's car wasn't there so I rang the bell. Starr opened the door and looked me up and down.

"What do you want?" I looked behind her to see if I saw Kareemah.

"My Godchild!" Starr blocked the door.

"You are not her Godmother anymore!" I pushed passed her.

"Whatever Starr!" I walked into the all white living room and Kareemah was sitting in her swing sucking on her pacifier. I picked her up and gave her a kiss and a hug. Starr ran over to me.

"Give me my child!" She tried to yank her from me. I handed Kareemah to her.

"Here take her Starr...but God as my witness if you ever tell her to shut up again I will personally fuck you up!" She put Kareemah down in her swing.

"Oh yeah, well try me! This is my fucking house and my fucking child and I'm raising her so you can just get the hell out! I don't remember inviting you over here!" I placed my right hand in the air and closed my eyes. I was praying

408

for God to give me the strength to knock some sense into Starr.

"You know Starr, you tripping. No matter what you say or do this is my Godchild and I will see her and do for her for the rest of my life!" Starr sat down on the couch and looked at me with tears in her eyes.

"D, let's just stop all this foolishness right here. This is your Goddaughter and if anything ever happened to me I want her with you and Samir. I had it put in writing. D, I am sorry our friendship has come to this, how can I make it right?" I sat next to her.

"Starr you know how!" She looked at me.

"No D I don't." I tooted my lips up.

"Well think about it real hard Starr!" She sighed and looked away.

"D, I'm not leaving him if that is what you are suggesting. He said he is going to marry me and leave all them other chics alone. He said he made a mistake! Diamond nobody is perfect. When Tahir was tapping your chin you stayed with him." I exhaled.

"Yeah Starr but I got out of that relationship." She got up and got Kareemah who had started whining.

"Yeah I guess you did since somebody blew his brains out!" If she wasn't my best friend at that time and she wasn't holding my baby I probably would have fucked her up off G.P. (general principle.) I walked towards the door.

"You know what Starr, keep fucking with him and he will probably blow your brains out!" She followed behind me.

"Whatever D!" I turned and looked at her.

"You know what Starr, I hope he does because you deserve it!" She laid Kareemah down in her playpen with her bottle.

"If I deserved it, so did Tahir! I'm glad he's dead." And why did she say that? I'm glad my Goddaughter was safe and sound in her playpen because I charged Starr and she fell back on the floor and I pinned her down. I wanted to beat the crap out of her but I didn't. I wanted to fight her because I thought I could beat some sense into her. She tried to push me off of her.

"Get out of my house!" I slowly got up and pulled her up too. I took her shoulders in my hands and began to shake her.

"Hell no! Not until you pack your shit and come with me. Starr you are making me so mad right now I could kill you. What is so great about this nigga that you are willing to trade in your family and friends for him? I don't understand Starr. I need to understand!" She grabbed my arms and shook me back.

"I don't know D! I just don't know..." By this time we were both boo hoo crying. She sat down on the couch and I joined her.

"D in due time I will leave him but not right now." I looked around for my keys. They had flung across the room. I picked them up.

"Look I gotta go!" Kareemah had started crying from us yelling and I went and picked her up and kissed her goodbye. I handed her to Starr. As I was leaving, Kareem was coming in. He flew passed me almost knocking me over.

"Starr! What the fuck is she doing in my house? I told you I don't want her here or around my daughter didn't I?" I stood in the door listening for Starr's response.

"Yes Kareem I know but she just barged in passed me. I told her no but she wouldn't leave. I'm sorry baby."

"Next time you better call the police. I don't want her here and I mean it!"

"Yes Kareem. Whatever you say." I couldn't believe what I was hearing. I didn't say no more. I just closed the door and then I flung it back open and stared at the 3 of them. I knew I was done with her.

"Starr that's it! We are through! Do you hear me? Through!" Kareem walked up on me.

"Good bitch! She don't need you!" I backed up out of the door.

"She will need me before I need her!" The tears

were running, I was hyperventilating like I had asthma and needed a pump. I was outside fighting the air like I was Tre in Boys N the Hood. I got in my car. I had never been so hurt in all the days of my short life. I got home and climbed the stairs barely getting in the door. I collapsed by the front door crying hysterically. Samir ran over and helped me up.

"D What happened to you?" I told him the whole story while we sat on the couch and he stroked my hair. He listened while shaking his head slowly back and forth. He hugged me tight and whispered in my ear.

"D, she will come around, don't cry baby girl. Don't cry." I couldn't stop crying. Every time I tried more tears came like my face had the negative side of a magnet and the tears were the positive side and they were attracted to each other.

"Samir why baby? Why did she treat me like that?" He reached over my head to the end table to pick up the phone.

"I don't know D but I am going to find out." I snatched the phone from his hands.

"Please I just want to move on!" He kissed my forehead.

"O.k. D, whatever you want." I closed my eyes and imagined better days between me and Starr. Samir rubbed my hair until I fell asleep in his lap.

CHAPTER 46
COURT DATE

A month went by and I didn't speak to Starr or see Kareemah. Samir had spoken to her or better yet, argued with her because he said she had completely lost it, meaning her damn mind. He cut her off because of the stunt she pulled with me at the house. During the argument he said, "Starr don't call us and we won't call you!" She screamed, "Good! I don't need y'all! I only need Kareem. He is my family now!" Samir hung up on her. Since me and Starr wasn't speaking I didn't mind taking Kareem to small claims court for the damages to my window he had busted. I had to go alone because Samir was at work.

Once in court he pleaded guilty and was ordered to pay for it. As we left the courtroom he winked at me, walked passed me and whispered, "Diamond, you can't get Starr to leave me alone, the dick is just that good." Then he had the nerve to say, "When you want to try it just let me know. I got enough to pass around." I screamed, "You sorry piece of shit!" I tried to charge him but he backed up laughing at my rage. The bailiff grabbed me.

"Miss that is inappropriate behavior in a courtroom." I adjusted my Couch bag on my shoulder.

"Sorry but..." He put his hand up in my face.

"Up...No excuses. Don't let it happen again." I looked him up and down.

"Fuck you!" My mouth got me in trouble again. The court fined me for disorderly conduct and I had to pay $250.00. Kareem had to pay $300.00 so I only ended up with $50.00. It was better then nothing. My window had been fixed the day after he busted it, but I took him to court behind the principle of the situation.

After I was done standing in that long line to pay my

fine, I walked out into the parking lot to my car. Kareem was outside leaning on my car waiting for me. I approached with caution.

"Kareem please go 'head. I'm not getting locked up behind you. Get away from my car." He smiled and looked me up and down.

"Damn Diamond! Why it got to be like that? I want to call a truce." He was licking his lips like I was something good to eat. I mean I am but...O.k. back to the story. He put his hand out for me to shake it. I was a little scared I have to admit because it was just me and him in that abandoned parking lot. I looked at his hand.

"O.k. truce but I'm not shaking your hand." It was getting dark because it was the evening time and I didn't feel safe with him. Especially since I didn't have my stun gun in my possession. Yes I had a stun gun and it was under my seat for any crazies that were out there. Too many nuts, not enough cops. I fumbled with my car keys noticing my mace.

"Kareem can you please just move?" He crossed his arms over his broad chest.

"If I move what you gonna do for me?" I exhaled.

"I won't knee you in the nuts for starters." He grabbed his family jewels and sexually rubbed them.

"Ooooh you soooooo cold D! I need these babies for something...you know I like your spunk D. I should have pushed up on you that night I met you and Starr." I felt like spitting on him.

"Whatever, can I please get in my car?" He licked his lips.

"Diamond you know you want me cause I know I want you. I would turn your ass out just like your friend. It can be our little secret. It can be OUR little secret." I sucked my teeth and turned up my lip.

"You would never ever get the chance! Now move!" I walked up on him and tried to push him aside. He blew in my ear.

"Well the offer is always open. Don't forget." He

smacked me on the butt as he walked passed to his Benz.

I stood there frozen not believing what had just happened. I couldn't wait to get home and call Starr and tell her about his no good ass. Maybe this would be the straw that broke the camels back.

CHAPTER 47
DINNER AT THE BLACKWELLS

Well once I got home I ran upstairs to my bedroom to call Starr and caught a glimpse of myself in the mirror. I walked over to the mirror and stared at myself. I then began to talk out loud to myself.

"Diamond, what's the point? She won't believe you anyway so you might as well just forget it. Move on with your life. Get over the fact that your best friend has chosen her man over you." As the last words tumbled from my tongue, the tears tumbled from my eyes. I grasped my chest and sat on the bed. I fell back and looked at the ceiling. As the teardrops flooded my eardrums the phone rang. I cleared my throat and answered.

"Hello."

"Diamond."

"Yes?"

"Diamond, I can't take us not talking anymore. I miss you. I miss us. Kareem told me that you guys called a truce and..." I cut her mid sentence.

"He what?!"

"He said you guys came to an agreement to be friends so I was thinking...Well maybe we could too?" I sat in silence and she took that as a cue to speak again.

"Diamond if I cook will you and Samir please come over? I miss y'all so much and D, Kareemah misses y'all too. She is getting so big and she has 2 little teeth coming through. Can you believe soon she will be five months old? D, please can you come? If not for me D please do it for your Godchild. Even if you never forgive me, don't do her like that. She didn't ask to be here. Don't you miss her D?"

Tears were marking my face like a tattoo. They seemed to be permanent. I couldn't say one word or she would have known I was crying. She screamed into the phone.

"Diamond?! Please don't do this. I am so sorry for all that mean stuff I said to you. I love you and you have always been there for me, no matter what and I know that...you are my best friend in the whole world not to mention my sister! D, please say something...anything!" I finally choked out, "Starr I will call you back," and hung up the phone. I sat there thinking and concentrating on Kareem and how he really wasn't shit and what would happen if I took him up on his offer and then let Starr find out. Hell no! I didn't want him so don't get it twisted but I figured I would rather her hate us both to get her to leave his ass alone. But who was I kidding. She wasn't leaving him alone for anything and I didn't want to do anything that would risk my relationship with Samir. I sat in the same spot until he came from work. It was about 7:30 when he came through the bedroom door. I got up and hugged and kissed him. He pulled his tie a loose and looked me up and down suspiciously.

"Diamond what's up? I know it's something, so what is it?" I smiled and ran my finger up his arm.

"Why would you say that? Can't I just love you and want to hug and kiss you?" He sat down on the bed and removed his black Kenneth Cole Loafers.

"No you can't so spill it, whatever it is." I sat down next to him and rubbed his shoulders.

"O.k., O.k. your sister called. She wants us to come over..." He put his hand over my mouth to stop my sentence.

"Oh hell no! That nigga disrespected us and now she wants us to break bread and be cool with him? Fuck that. We're not going." I placed my hand on his thigh.

"Samir baby please calm down. Don't you miss Kareemah?" I knew he had a soft spot for her. He looked off into space.

"Yeah I miss my baby." I touched his face to turn it towards mine.

"Well then can we go over there and see her?" He looked me in my eyes and pushed my hand down from his face.

"What did I say Diamond?" I sucked my teeth.

"Samir please just do this for me? I miss Kareemah and Starr for that matter..." He jumped up from the bed and flung his tie at me.

"Well D I do too but..." I jumped up and got in his face.

"But what? Look we going and that's that!" I walked over to get the phone. He came up behind me and snatched it from my hand.

"Diamond you kill me, always thinking you running shit." I snatched the phone back from him.

"No I haven't killed you yet, but I am going to kill you if you don't go." He snatched the phone back and extended his arm way up in the air so I couldn't reach it. He smiled.

"Damn, why are you my girl?" I began to tickle him and made him drop the phone. We raced to pick it up and I won.

"I'm your girl because you love me." He playfully licked my cheek.

"Yeah I do." I wiped it off and wiped my hand on his shirt. I ran for him to chase me. I only made it to the bedroom entrance. He grabbed me and roughly pulled my hair back to kiss my throat. He licked the bulge of my Adam's apple while I stood there enjoying every minute of it. I dropped the cordless on the floor and wrapped my arms around his neck. We began to passionately kiss. Ring! The phone. I picked it up from the floor.

"Hello!"

"Diamond are you guys coming?" I looked at Samir who had one eyebrow up looking at me.

"Damn Starr I'm trying to get me a quickie but besides that, yes Starr, we will come." She playfully sucked

417

her teeth.

"Ill! Y'all are boning this early in the evening?" I sucked me teeth back at her.

"Yeah, what's it to you?" She laughed.

"Nothing! Kareemah does need a playmate. I'm joking but can y'all make it today? Please come today." I rolled my eyes.

"O.k. Starr is Kareem there?"

"No but he said to hit him on his cell if y'all were going to come." I sighed.

"Well it is almost 8. Let Mr. G.Q. get out of his suit, showered and changed and we will be there. I would say by 9." I hung up and looked at him. We took it to the shower to finish what we started. Samir wanted to fight Kareem bad as hell but he was going to try to be civil for the sake of me, his sister, and Kareemah.

Once we got to the house we stood on the stoop. I rang the bell. Samir leaned over and whispered in my ear,

"D you're lucky I love you so much, if he start one thing we are going to..." The door flung open.

"Hey y'all!" She reached and hugged both of us. As we entered the house Samir finished his sentence in a whisper.

"...fight tonight Diamond and I mean that." I just looked at him and then at his sister. She looked thin. She lost all her baby weight and even more. She use to be a size 8 before Kareemah but now she looked like a 2/4. I guess a nigga stressing you can do that anytime. I scrunched my face up.

"Damn Starr, you lost mad weight." She twirled around to show off her new anorexic shape.

"Girl I had to if I wanted to keep my man." She turned to walk towards the kitchen. I looked at Samir and he rolled his eyes. I followed her towards the kitchen.

"Starr where is my baby at?" Starr pointed into the far end of the living room. Kareemah was sitting in her swing playing with her hands. Samir ran and snatched her up first.

"Hey baby girl! Uncle Samir missed you." He kissed her and she laughed and felt his face like she was grown. I put my hands under Kareemah's arms.

"Give me my baby Samir." I kissed her.

"Hey my little pumpkin butt!" She smiled and I kissed her like a million times. I can remember her smelling so good like a baby girl should. Sam pulled on my arm.

"Come on D, give her back to me." At that time the front door swung open and Kareem came in.

"Hello everybody!" He approached us like everything was all-good. Me and Sam said in unison, "Hi." We both had our teeth clenched together. He walked passed us to Starr.

"Hey baby." They kissed on the lips. He then put his arm around her and looked at us and smiled.

"Hey Kareemah baby, I see you got company." He was smiling extra hard in my direction. Kareemah laughed then got whiny for her daddy. He waved at her playfully.

"Oh girl, I don't want you. Stay with your Uncle Samir." He smiled like it was all peace. I wanted to tell Samir lets jump him but I decided against it. You know me and Samir thought we were Bonnie and Clyde. I took Kareemah from Samir and Starr handed me her bottle. She fell asleep in my arms and I took her upstairs to lay her in her crib. I looked around her room. Everything was pink. A tear came to my eye as the memories of me and Starr's first sleep over at my house flooded my mind. I watched Kareemah sleep peacefully. I went downstairs where everybody was already seated in the dining room for dinner. Starr made spaghetti, what else. It was still the only thing she knew how to make. Starr put the noodles on the table and Kareem reached for them.

"Damn Starr spaghetti again?" He laughed and looked at me.

"D I know you can cook. You need to come by more often and help her out." She laughed it off.

"Kareem you know I'm trying." He smiled as he spooned sauce onto his noodles.

"I know babe but you should take lessons from Diamond for real." He looked at me and I looked at my plate to stop from spitting in his face. After the whole table was served, we all were silent. You know that uneasy silence. Kareem broke the silence first.

"Yo I got something to say. Samir my bad for all that happened dog. I hope we can get past all that for your sister and niece's sake." He stood up and extended his hand towards Samir. I know my man and by the look written all over his face he wasn't feeling it at all but he shook his hand anyway. He came over next to me.

"And Diamond I want to apologize again and pay for your fine in court." I cut in, "That's O.k. Kareem." Samir put his fork down.

"D, what happened in court?" I took a sip of water to think of a lie.

"Nothing much. This guy stepped on my foot and didn't say excuse me so we got into an argument and because I wouldn't shut up I got fined." Samir stared at me.

"Diamond...why didn't you tell me?" I shrugged.

"Because it was no big deal. Now please just leave it alone." I looked down at my plate. Kareem was still standing next to me.

"Diamond can we shake?" He extended his hand and smiled. It took all I had to shake his hand, but let me tell you, I don't know if y'all are up on this but while we were shaking hands, he bent his index finger inward towards the palm of my hand and gently rubbed the palm of my hand. To some of you that may sound like nothing but where I'm from that basically means I want to have sex with you. I snatched my hand back but the twins didn't pick up on it. I hated Kareem for real at that point. He threw his hands in the air.

"Well now that, that is all squared away, mi casa su casa!" For you non speaking Spanish folks that means my house is your house. Kareem looked at Samir and then back at me.

"I know you 2 love Kareemah and she loves you

too, so feel free to see her anytime." He then began to walk towards Starr. He touched her shoulder.

"Starr?" She put her fork down and looked up at him like he was Mother Teresa.

"Yes Kareem?" I noticed every single time he called her name she said, 'Yes Kareem.' It made me want to spew or throw the hell up for you de classe people. I know one thing, she never said yes to her parents, but anyway he dropped down on one knee. I thought, Oh God no! Please don't get engaged! He took her hand in his.

"Starr baby. I love you. You know that. Even though sometimes you are disobedient I still love you..." Now wait stop the tape! This nigga really had the nerve to say disobedient like she was a damn dog and he was her master. Who does that remind you of? If you said Tahir, you score 10 points. Just sitting there watching them reminded me so much of me and Tahir I began to get physically sick. Well, she acted like he was her master so I guess that's why he felt that way. He then took her other hand in his, now holding both of her hands.

"...We had our ups and downs and I'm sorry for all that." She patted his hand.

"That's O.k. Kareem nobody is perfect." Sam was sitting across from me and damn near took my leg off when he kicked me underneath the table. Samir stared at me and I looked at my plate. Kareem kissed both of Starr's hands.

"Yo Starr, I love Kareemah and I want us to make her lots of brothers and sisters." Starr laughed a little.

"You better go 'head Kareem. You know I don't want no more." He smiled a bit but clenched his teeth in the process.

"We can talk about that later Starr." His voice had completely changed from that sweet syrupy voice to the vicious rattle snack that he was. Starr picked up on it and patted his hand again.

"O.k. Kareem." She was acting so stupid and I couldn't stand it. She grabbed his face in her hands.

"Please baby continue. I am so sorry for

interrupting." He faded back into his smooth, calm voice.

"Starr Angel will you marry me?" He went into his pocket and pulled out a rock (diamond) the size of Kareemah. Me and Sam just locked stares at each other. She jumped out of the chair causing it to fall back.

"Yes Kareem! Yes I will marry you!" He placed the ring on her narrow finger and they hugged and kissed. I almost lost my cookies for real that time. I didn't know what to do. Damn near 2 minutes before that he was making gestures that he wanted to fuck me and now he was trying to marry my best friend. She was so happy. I couldn't say anything but, "Congratulations." I kicked Sam under the table and he replied, "Yeah what D said." Samir was so ignorant at times. She was smiling from ear to ear like a damn Cheshire cat. She ran over to me and stuck her hand in my face.

"Look Diamond!" I took her hand an examined the ring knowing he had to pay at least $20,000 for it. At least, it could have been more. I got up and gave her a hug. I forced a smile on my face. She pulled back from me and had tears in her eyes.

"D, I'm getting everything I prayed for. My family back and my home right. I missed you Diamond." I hugged her again.

"Yeah I missed you too Starr." She grabbed my hands.

"Diamond let's not fight ever again O.k.?" I shook my head up and down.

"O.k. Starr." Samir got up and shook Kareem's hand.

"Yo man. You better treat my sister right!" Kareem gave Samir a firm hand shake.

"I will dog, I will take really good care of her." I never told Samir how Kareem used Starr as a punching bag. She asked me not to tell so the code of friendship is not to tell no matter what. Me and Starr cleared the table while Kareem and Samir went to watch TV. She stood and looked at her ring.

"So sis, what's new?" I shrugged,

"Nothing." She sighed.

"Me either girl but guess what?" I asked unenthused, "What?"

She exclaimed, "I'm going back to Howard next month!" I smiled.

"That's good Starr. Who's going to watch Kareemah?" She rinsed the dishes off getting them ready for the dishwasher.

"Either his mom, his sister or him. He is really trying Diamond. He has been staying home more and he takes good care of Kareemah." Samir walked in the kitchen.

"D, are you ready?" I walked over and hugged him around his neck.

"Yeah I guess." Starr wiped her hands off on the dishtowel.

"No y'all. Please stay! Samir where is Kareemah?"

"He went to get Kareemah. She was upstairs crying." He kissed me on my cheek.

"Come on babe, I'm tired. I have to work tomorrow unlike some of us." Me and Starr laughed because neither one of us did.

"Oh Samir you know I volunteer at the battered women's shelter so don't play me out." I turned to Starr and she looked down. I didn't have to work because my father wanted me to concentrate on my studies. As long as I got good grades, I could have the summers off on him. So, I got good grades.

"Starr we do have to go because it is getting late." I looked at my watch.

"Dag it is already 11. Starr, we gotta get going." We began to walk out of the kitchen towards the door. She followed us.

"D, do you want to do something tomorrow?" I shrugged.

"I don't know yet but I will call you." I just couldn't go on like everything was all good. I was really upset but put up a façade like everything was O.k. When we got home and in the bed Starr called.

"Diamond I do not feel like everything is O.k. between us, do you want to talk about something?" I lied.

"No Starr. I'm O.k." She sucked her teeth.

"Diamond we have been friends forever so who do you think you are lying too?" I sat up in the bed.

"Starr trust me. I'm fine. It will just take some time for our friendship to heal is all."

"O.k. D, but is there anything I can do to speed it up?" Now I know y'all know me by now, and you know what I was thinking, yeah dump his punk ass but I kept it cool.

"No Starr just be patient with me O.k.?"

"You got it D." I sighed.

"Goodnight Starr."

"Goodnight Diamond." At that time Samir walked into the bedroom from getting him a late night snack. He put his bowl of ice cream down and sat next to me.

"What's the matter boo?" I kept crying.

"Nothing Samir." I rolled over to not face him but he grabbed my shoulder and rolled me back.

"Don't tell me nothing D, and you sitting here crying." I cried out, "I don't know what is wrong with me Samir. I just miss Starr that's all. The old Starr. And now, that bastard is gonna marry her and really lock her in. I hate him Samir. I swear I do." Samir hugged me and kissed my forehead. He spoke to me in a calm, soothing tone.

"I do too D, but we gotta respect the fact that, that is what she wants." I calmed down a bit and then pouted.

"Well O.k. but I won't respect him." He smiled at me and pinched my cheek.

"O.k. cupcake don't respect him, but don't cry either." He kissed my tear stained face all over. He climbed on top of me. He blew in my ear.

"Lets get the extended version of what we started earlier." I didn't put up a fight. I just laid there and let my man slowly undress me. He licked my naked body up and down and all around and then ventured between my legs and let his tongue be like Calgon because it was surely taking me away. We made slow, sweet love and it was the best sex I can remember. Uh well one of the best times. (Smile) Then me and Samir cuddled all night long. Living together had its advantages because that was just what I needed at that time.

My summers were filled with volunteering at shelters for unwanted kids and battered women. I also was a housewife. I cooked and cleaned for my man.

The same deal my father gave me, Samir's father offered him but he could not turn down that internship. If Starr wasn't so grown and hot she would be living the life like me but she rather be with Kareem so I said, 'More power to her.' The next morning Starr called me bright and early.

"Hey Diamond, want to do breakfast." I rolled over and looked at the clock. That's when I noticed the ice cream from the night before. Samir had left it there and the condensation from the bowl stained my cherry wood nightstand.

"No Starr. I don't feel like." She begged and pleaded with me.

"O.k. Starr…let me get dressed and I will be there."

CHAPTER 48
IS THAT A BOOT PRINT?

When I got to Starr's house, her and Kareemah were almost ready to go. We sat in the living room while Starr put on Kareemah's sandals. While Starr fastened the left sandal Kareemah threw up all over Starr's jeans. Starr smiled.

"Oh Reemah look what you did to mommy." She cleaned Kareemah up then stood up.

"Hold her for me D while I change my jeans." Starr stood right there and unbuttoned the jeans to throw them in the laundry room, which was right off of the kitchen. As she walked passed me to go upstairs I noticed a humongous black and blue marks up and down her thighs and legs. I put Kareemah down in her playpen to examine Starr more closely.

"Starr what happened to your legs?" She stuttered while trying her best to cover them.

"Uh...uh oh that? It's nothing girl. Let me go upstairs and get another pair of jeans so we can go." I followed Starr up the stairs screaming at her.

"Starr what the fuck is that? Is that a boot print? Cause it looks like somebody had on some Timberlands and was stomping on you." She reached her bedroom and grabbed a pair of white Versace jeans out of the closet. She sighed.

"D, I'm O.k. please don't stress the issue." I grabbed her shoulders so she could face me. Her face grimaced because she had a bruise on her shoulder as well.

"What do you mean don't stress? Your standing here all bruised up from head to toe and your telling me don't stress? Tell me what happened Starr." She sat down on her California king size bed.

"Oh nothing. When y'all left Kareem went out and got drunk and high off weed and when he got in we got into it cause he brought up the fact that I said I don't want anymore kids. We got to fighting and he kicked me a few times. No big deal D, trust me I'm fine." I paced back in forth in front of her.

"Starr see that's the shit I'm talking about...you know what forget it, you're grown so I can't tell you shit. Let's just go because I'm hungry." I walked out of the room and down the stairs to get Kareemah. We got in the car and I listened to the radio. Once we sat down for breakfast at my favorite place, I.H.O.P., you could hear a pin drop. I just played with Kareemah trying not to even look at Starr. I couldn't believe that a guy, any guy, could hit on Starr like that. She was such a nice giving person and I know she deserved better. Starr begged me to keep the bruises to myself. I put my hand up in her direction.

"Listen Starr, that is your business not mine and I am at the point where I am just going to stop caring. I care about Kareemah because she is not able to leave but you on the other hand..." Starr rolled her eyes and her neck.

"Here you go again with the leaving thing. We just got engaged yesterday and you said you were happy for me. Was that a lie." I rolled my neck in her direction then raised my right eyebrow. I slapped my palms down on the table.

"What do you think Starr?" We engaged in a stare down. She didn't move and neither did I. The waitress came over and took our order and the stare was broken. After we ordered Starr continued to stare at me. I flicked my hand at her.

"Look Starr don't even answer that...I don't know why you keep asking me these silly questions and backing me in a corner to tell you how I feel. You know how I feel so just don't ask me any questions pertaining to that piece of shit O.k.? Cause no I don't like him, no I don't want you to be with him, no oh hell no I don't want you to marry him and I really, really hate that I hate him Starr but I do. He ain't shit and you could do better, so please don't cry, don't get mad or none of that cause that is just how I feel and by the way I won't be in attendance at your wedding." She had a few tears in her eyes but held them back like a trooper.

"O.k. Diamond I respect that. I won't say no more about my life or my relationship to you, and don't worry, you don't ever have to come to my wedding. I am going to marry him and be with him whether you're there or not. He will love me and his daughter and you just don't have to concern yourself with it." I gave her a sarcastic applause.

"Well good then! Let's eat!" The food came and we ate in silence. When I dropped her off she got out and didn't say anything. I felt sick thinking about them even getting married. When I got home I called Zak because I needed to talk to him and hear his soothing voice. I told him everything that happened. Zak sighed,

"I don't know what has gotten into Kareem. I am going to say..." I cut him off.

"No please don't say anything to him at all. Then he will know she told me and I told you and he will beat on her again."

"D, I think she needs to get out of there. That is my man and all but he is putting his hands on her too much lately. He brags on it at the shop saying stuff like 'Starr got out of line last night and I had to take off my belt.' Some of the guys laugh but I always pull him to the side and tell him to chill." I began to cry.

"What? A belt? Ooh my God, I am scared for her life." He chuckled.

"Come on D. My man is a lot of things but he ain't no killer. He would never take it that far." I sniffled.

"You promise Zak. You promise he will never kill my sister?"

"I promise D. I wont say anything about the boot

428

prints but I will just ask him what's going on with him hitting on her so much lately and that he needs to cut it out or cut her looses. Feel me Shawdy?" I wiped my eyes.

"Thanks Zak. I wish Starr was with you and not him." He laughed.

"That's sweet D but I wish you were with me and not Samir. Keep your head up. Everything will be O.k. I promise you that." I sighed.

"Thanks Zak! I love you! If this was another time and place I would have definitely been with you!" He laughed again.

"I still got hopes for that Diamond." I laughed with him. We talked a bit more about his son and then we hung up.

After that day me and Starr spoke briefly, very briefly sometimes but the conversations were always about Kareemah. I stayed seeing my baby. When school started Starr did go back. We happened to have a class together, not planned. Since we had grown so far apart I had new friends that I hung with and took classes with. On the first day of class, Starr sat next to me and 2 of my friends, Monique and Nicole. I introduced Starr to them but I could tell by her face she wasn't feeling them. Nicole was from Philly and Monique was from Ohio. Me and Nicole were talking 90 miles a minute and Monique would put her 2 cents in. Starr just sat there silent. The only thing me and Starr had in common was Kareemah. I knew that Kareem was still hitting on her because she was wearing heavy make up and sunglasses all the time. She wore long sleeve shirts and pants even in September when it was still warm. I know one specific date that stands out in my head and I will never forget it for as long as I live.

CHAPTER 49
I'M SENDING YOU A 4 PAGE LETTER

It was Friday, November 15th 1997. It was cold and raining real bad outside. Earlier that day Starr saw me in the library.

"Hey Diamond, I need to talk to you but I mailed you a letter and I rather you read it first and then we can talk." I was looking for a book so I cut our conversation short.

"Yeah, O.k. whatever Starr," and I walked away. That night me and Samir decided to go out to the 8:15 movie. We went to see Liar, Liar. Jim Carey is a mess, do you hear me. We left there and decided to go to T.G.I. Friday's. We left Friday's and headed home. We were riding down Georgia Ave and it was pouring down in bucketfuls of water. I was looking out the window and noticed Kareem's brand new white on white Benz (yeah he got a new one.) He was double parked with the temp in the window and the hazards on. Samir was still driving his civic. He slowed up so we could see. I saw Starr running and Kareem chasing after her. He caught her, grabbed her by the throat and smacked her down. My eyes looked like I had thyroid disease the way the bulged out of my head. I screamed, "Oh my God Samir pull over!"

He did and we both jumped out like we were the cops. I yelled, "Kareem get your mother fucking hands off my sister!" He turned and looked at me.

"Bitch mind your business! Your sister here thinks she's slick and I gotta teach her a lesson she will never forget." Samir yelled, "This is our business now let my sister go." Starr stood up and tried to hug Kareem but he pushed her back down.

"Samir, I will fuck your punk ass up!" Samir ran up on Kareem.

"What? Well bring it on!" Starr pulled herself up to her knees. Her make up was streaming down her face smudging on her full length cream colored cashmere coat. She grabbed the bottom of Kareem's pea coat.

"No Kareem. Please I'm sorry I lied. I had to do this project for class and if you knew I was going to the library with a guy you wouldn't have let me go. I had to do this project or I will fail the class." He pushed her back down while I held Samir back.

"A project my ass bitch, you were fucking him, weren't you? Weren't you?!" She stayed on her knees pleading with him.

"No I wasn't Kareem. I love you, I would never cheat on you." He grabbed her by her collar and pulled her up to her feet. Her dress pants had wholes in the knees from her kneeling.

"Whatever bitch! Get your ass up and in this car right now. I will deal with you when we get home." She looked down.

"Yes Kareem." She proceeded to walk to the car. Samir ran up to Kareem and hit him. They started fighting and I jumped in it. I jumped on Kareem's back and he threw me off and I fell into his car. I got back up and tried to scratch his eyes out. Starr jumped out. I screamed, "Starr good you got out...go in your brother's car. You can come home with us. Please Starr you don't need this shit." Starr jumped between Kareem and Samir and pushed Samir back.

"Samir get off of him. Kareem are you alright baby?" My jaw fell open and Samir froze. It felt like we were stuck in time. Kareem sucked the blood off his busted lip.

"Yo Starr, I am sick of this shit. Diamond you are always butting your nose into our business! You need to get a life and mind your own business." I yelled, "Fuck you Kareem!" Samir was still standing still. He stared at Starr not believing what was going on. Kareem demanded, "Starr you need to make a decision right here and right now. It's either me or your family. Now who is it going to be?" I flailed my arms around like a mad woman.

"Huh! Who are you, God? Tell him Starr, tell him bye and come home with us. We can figure it out. Come on sis let's go." Starr looked at Kareem and then looked at me. She looked back at Kareem, then at Samir, and then at me. Mascara stained her face while tears and blood mixed with the rain ran down her face.

"Well D, I'm letting someone go but it's not him...it's you." Now you know my jaw went back down to the ground. I couldn't believe what I was hearing so I said, "Huh? What did you say Starr?" She linked her arm in with Kareem's.

"You heard me Diamond. You sat and told me you didn't want to hear about my life or my business so butt out! He is my fiancé and my children's father and I need to stay with him." I rubbed my forehead.

"Children? I know you're not pregnant again?" She got up in my face and put her hands in my face.

"If I am? It is none of your business. Leave me alone Diamond. I never want to talk to or see your face again!" Kareem smiled and winked at me. She turned to him and took his hands in hers.

"Kareem baby, I'm sorry. Can we just go home and talk about this." He opened his arm and took her in for a hug. He kissed her forehead.

"Yeah boo we sure can. Come on." Samir came out of his trance.

"Starr you stupid bitch! After all you and Diamond have been through, you're gonna choose that nigga. If you're cutting Diamond off you're cutting me off too. Come on Diamond before I commit a double murder out here. I have had it up to here with her. She is stuck on stupid and just fuck her D." As she walked to the car to get in she yelled, "Forget you Samir! You are supposed to be my brother." He yelled back, "What? I am your brother and you letting this clown ass nigga come between you and your family!" Kareem snapped his fingers.

"Starr, car now!" She went to lift the car handle. She looked at Samir.

"No I'm not Samir. We can work this out. You guys are letting him come between me and my family not me." Samir yelled, "No we can't Starr and no we're not. It don't matter, it is finished. Diamond will be with me and if you don't speak to her then don't speak to me either! If we never see your ass again it won't be too soon!" She jumped up and down and screamed, "Forget both of y'all!"

Kareem cut in, "Starr what did I say?" As she sat in the Benz, before she closed the door she said, "I thought y'all loved me. Kareem is right. He is the only person that loves me. Y'all don't. I'm glad our friendship is over Diamond and Samir to me your dead! I don't have a twin. Do you hear me, you're dead! When you see me don't even speak!" I spit at the car.

"Oh yeah fuck you Starr! Don't come calling us when he beat or cheat on your ass again!" Kareem yelled from the driver seat, "She won't. Don't you worry about it!" He spun off into the rainy night. I stood there and cried. Samir wrapped his arms around me.

"Samir I never would have thought..." He hugged me.

"Diamond fuck her! She is gone! She has completely lost her mind. She is like a fiend for drugs, you know how they lose their minds? She might be getting high now. She acts crazy enough." I sniffled, "Samir what are we going to do?" He pulled me to get into the car.

"Grant her wishes and leave her alone and never call her again. She better not think about calling our house. That bitch! I can't believe her."

And you know what, Kareem was right cause she didn't think about calling us. She never did call us again. Once I got home that night and Samir jumped in the shower, I snuck and called Zak and told him what happened.

"D, I'm going over there now. I will call you when I leave there." I heard the water in the bathroom stop. I whispered, "Be careful Zak."

"I will be. O.k. I will talk to you in a while. Answer the phone when it rings. I don't want no problems with Samir." I laughed a little.

"You got it Zak."

CHAPTER 50
WHY OH WHY?

About 3 AM my phone rang. Me and Samir were asleep so I jumped up and snatched the cordless from the base, hit the talk button and ran down the stairs to the kitchen before Samir woke up. I put the phone to my ear out of breath, "Hello."

"Hello this is Howard Hospital calling may I speak to Diamond Staple or Samir Mitchell?" I cleared my throat. "Yes this is Diamond. How may I help you?"

"Ms. Staple, it has been an accident. Your sister Starr has you listed as next of kin on her medical records. She fell down the stairs and is listed in critical condition. You need to get down here right away." I dropped the phone and began to scream at the top of lungs non-stop. Samir ran down the stairs full steam ahead and came into the kitchen. He grabbed my shoulders and began to shake me.

"What's wrong Diamond? What happened?" I was comatose. He picked up the phone.

"Hello?...What?...We will be right there." He hung up the phone and dialed his parents to le them know what was going on. Samir yelled, "Diamond snap out of it, we gotta go." I just couldn't move. My best friend was in critical condition. I don't know how I got to the hospital but I remember the first person I saw was Kareem standing with the doctor. Kareem walked over to us with crocodile tears in his eyes.

"I don't know what happened? We were talking in the kitchen and she backed up from me playing, and the basement door was open and she fell down the stairs and hit her head on the concrete stairs." He then fell to his knees looking up at the ceiling screaming, "Oh God please don't let her die!" Samir lunged at Kareem's neck.

"You son of a bitch. I know you pushed her down the stairs." They started tussling and I jumped in it kicking Kareem in his back in the middle of the waiting room. The security guard came and broke it up. We knocked him down and continued to fight. He called for back up while he tried again to break us up. His back up boys came and broke us up. They put Kareem on one end of the waiting room and me and Samir on the other end. We were warned if there were any more outbreaks we would be put out. The doctor stood there in awe looking at us fight in the waiting room. I pulled on the doctor's white lab coat.

"Dr. Francis, can we please see her?" He was a young light skinned African American doctor with glasses. He pushed his glasses up on his face.

"Briefly she needs her rest." Me and Samir gripped our hands together and walked slowly into her room like we were walking the Green Mile. I peeped around the corner of her room. I pulled back from Samir after the quick peep that my eyes saw. I heard Beep! Beep! Beep! As the respirator machine caused my best friend, my sister's chest to rise and fall. Samir pulled my hand back.

"Come on Diamond. You can do it." We entered the room to see tubes coming from every hole on her body. Her face took on a grotesque appearance looking like she was Rocky from Mask. I stood there trembling, squeezing Samir's hand as if it were a stress ball. I slowly shook my head back and forth not believing what my eyes were seeing. I looked at Samir. He blinked and a tear landed on his eyelashes. Dr. Francis came in and touched our shoulders.

"O.k. I am going to have to ask you to step out. She needs her rest." Me and Samir looked at her and then at each other. We followed the doctor into the hallway. He was walking away but I had questions.

"Yo Doc, why is her face so swollen like that?" He looked down at the chart he was carrying.

"Well, she fell down concrete stairs. She broke 3 ribs and must have hit her face on the tumble down." I covered my face with my hands and wiped the tears away.

"Well it looks to me like somebody might have kicked her in the face." The doctor eyed me up and down over the top rim of his glasses.

"Miss, you're just upset." I smacked his clipboard out of his hand.

"Fuck that and fuck you! He did this to her, I know he did. The one that is out there crying all those fake tears, he did this, he did. Are you ruling out foul play? He needs to be locked up!" Samir picked up the clipboard and handed to the doctor. The doctor's face produced a scowling look towards me.

"Listen Miss, I know you are upset, but I will have to ask you to refrain from that type of language and behavior here. This is a hospital so I suggest you keep your voice down and attitude in check before you are asked to leave. Now I have seen this before. The steps are solid concrete and so is the floor she landed on. Mr. Blackwell has been very helpful in this situation and he is willing to go in for questioning, but in my professional opinion she took a nasty fall. It is raining outside bad and he said she slipped and fell and I believe him. Now we are doing all we can to help her. Your best bet is to pray and calm down. Now excuse me, I do have other patients." He walked down the hall and I yelled behind him, "Well that's not good enough! I need answers and I need them now!" The doctor turned around and began to walk back towards me. Samir wrapped his arm around my neck and put his hand over my mouth.

"D please calm down...Excuse her Dr. Francis she is just upset." He looked at me and then at Samir. I bit the inside of Samir's hand.

"Ouch D. What are you doing?" I pushed him off of me and grabbed the doctor's lab coat collar.

"Dr. Francis please, what about her baby? She is pregnant." He looked down and then up pushing his glasses up on his nose. He sighed, "Was pregnant. I am afraid she miscarried the baby when she fell down the stairs."

I ran out of the I.C.U and into the waiting room. Kareem was sitting there with this smug look on his face. I put my finger in his face as I rocked back and forth from my left foot to my right. My whole arm trembled as I spoke.

"Kareem I know you did this to her. I know you beat her up and pushed her down the stairs. You wanted her to lose that baby. I know you did and I'm gonna get you! It might not be today, it might not be tomorrow but I'm gonna get you!"

He stood up and security came over.

"Diamond I know you are upset but I love her. I would never lay a finger on her. She was having my first son." I tried to charge him.

"You lying ass bastard!" Security grabbed me up under my armpits.

"Miss I warned you. We don't tolerate this in here, I will have to ask you to leave." I struggled to get free.

"No please! I'm sorry please that is my sister I need to be here. I need to see my sister." Kareem tapped the security guard.

"Yo fam, she can stay. I know she is just upset." The security guard looked at me and warned me one more time. Once he let me go, I ran back into the doors of I.C.U. Samir followed me. I stood in front of her door and Samir took my hand in his. He kissed it.

"D listen, she is going to be O.k. she is a fighter. I need you to calm down though baby." I used my free hand to wipe away my tears.

"Your right Samir. Can I be alone with her for a minute please?" He let my hand go and found a seat down the hall in I.C.U. I walked back in her room with tears streaming down my face. I sat next to her bed and took her bruised hand in mine. The machine was still beeping. I closed my eyes to make sure I wasn't dreaming. I opened them. Nope I wasn't dreaming. I stroked her hand ever so softly.

"Starr, I'm so sorry I let this happen to you. I don't know exactly what happened to you but I know Kareem is behind this and believe me, I won't rest until he gets what he deserves. Starr please don't die, I need you, Kareemah needs you here. That's our daughter and she misses one of her mommies. You are a good mother Starr. I love you, always have and always will. You are my best friend, my sister. Get well Starr so we can be the way we were." I bought her hand to my face and rubbed it across my lips. Sam walked in. He took her other hand in his and kissed it.

"Come on Starr. You can pull through this. We are twins we need to be together not a part. Open your eyes Starr. We are here for you. Open your eyes." He looked at her and then at me.

"D, you O.k.?" I shook my head back and forth and dropped her hand softly on the bed. I leaned on the bedrail and cried softly. Samir came over, leaned down, and hugged me from behind. He kissed me on the back of my neck.

"She is a fighter D, she will be fine. You just have to believe." He stroked my hair while I struggled to stand up. I didn't know how he was being so strong in a situation like this. The nurse came in.

"Hey you 2, I know you are upset but she really needs her rest." She gave a squeeze to my hand and smiled.

"Pray for her. Lord knows I am." Samir helped me up and out of the room. I leaned on him because my body was dead weight to me. He got me out to the waiting room where I laid my head on his lap as we waited for his parents to arrive. Kareem sat on the other side of the waiting room with his head resting on the wall asleep. Who could sleep at a time like this? Me and Samir had dozed off ourselves.

It had to be close to the morning because the sun was up the last I remembered. Both our parents arrived at about 8 AM. Krystal rushed in first. Her eyes were puffy and she looked like she cried the whole ride down. She shook me to wake me.

"Diamond what's going on?" I sat up and Samir's eyes popped open. Dr. Francis was at the desk and I jumped up and introduced her and Mitch to him. I hugged my dad. His arms felt safe. I released myself from the hug. "Dad I tried to get her from that monster. I know he did this to her Daddy." Krystal and Mitch filed a complaint with the police so that Kareem could be questioned. Kareem had pulled a disappearing act. In the meantime, we took turns going in periodically to see Starr. There was no change. Samir went and got coffee from the cafeteria for our parents. He handed his mother her cup. She took a sip and looked at me.

"Diamond where is Kareemah?" I jumped up and paced around.

"Oh my God, Kareemah! I don't know." I dug in my bag and pulled out my cell phone. I ran out to the front of the hospital. You know there are no cell phones allowed in hospitals. I didn't want to mess with somebody's pacemaker or something. First I called Starr and Kareem's house. He answered regular as if his fiancé was not lying here in I.C.U.

"Hello."

"Kareem where is my baby?"

"Oh so now you want me to get you pregnant?" I screamed, "What?!...Why you fucking...(I then calmed myself down)...Look you're doing this shit to get under my skin, my sister is lying in the hospital in I.C.U. so this is no time for games. Where is Kareemah?" He chuckled,

"Oh don't be so uptight Diamond. She is going to be fine. Kareemah is with my mother."

"Don't be so up...Never mind. Starr's parents are here and they want to see her, but they don't want to see you."

"O.k. that is fine. The police are here now anyway asking me to go for questioning, but I don't care because I'm innocent. You hear me D, innocent. I didn't do anything."

"Whatever!" And I hung up on him. I looked through my phone at the M's. Ms. Chickie. I hit the call button.

"Praise God." I sucked my teeth.

"Ms. Chickie I need to come get Kareemah."

"Oh hello Diamond, I am sorry to hear about Starr. I am praying for her and called Pastor Carter from my church, New Hope Baptist Church, and he is praying for her as well."

"Yeah well thank you, I will be on my way shortly."

"Diamond, I hope she is O.k. I would like to come see her if I could." I got an instant attitude.

"Look, she is in I.C.U. and only family is allowed."

"O.k. sweetheart. I will pray for your family as well. I will see you when you get here."

"Yeah whatever." O.k. yeah I was getting smart with her and I know it wasn't her fault but it was her son's fault and she birthed that bastard so I had to take it out on somebody.

That Saturday afternoon I finally went and got Kareemah. When I bought her in the hospital lobby to see everyone, she brightened up things a bit. After a while, my mom and dad took her back to my place and me, Samir, and his parents stayed at the hospital. We continued to go in on our shifts to check on her.

CHAPTER 51
I'M SORRY...

Early Sunday morning, God called his child, Starr Angel Mitchell, home to be with him in Heaven. I will never forget sitting there in the room with her and the machine going from Beep! Beep! Beep! Beep! Beep! Beep! to Beeeeeeeeeeeeeeeeeeeeep! The nurses rushed in and told me and Krystal to leave out. Sam and Mitch were sleeping in the lobby. We ran out to tell them what was going on. Mitch stood up and fell to his knees. Tears ran down his cheeks and dripped to the floor, "Please God, let them save my baby!" Krystal hugged her husband and cried along with me. Me and Samir tried to help them up when Dr. Francis came out. He seemed to walking towards us in slow motion. He helped Mitch stand up and then helped him sit down. He looked up to stop his tears from falling.

"Mr. and Mrs. Mitchell, I'm sorry..." We all knew what that meant. It meant she was gone from this place forever. That day was the longest day of my life. All I remember is Mitch screaming, "No," while Samir punched a hole in the wall. Dr. Francis hugged Krystal while I slid out of the chair onto the floor like I was snack. I lay there for a while just looking at the patterns on the ceiling not wanting this to be real. The security guard came and helped me up. I sat in the chair with Samir holding me. We cried on each other's shoulders.

Krystal and Mitch had to fill out a lot of forms and

Krystal kept telling me, "Diamond go call your parents." I didn't move. By the time I stopped crying I just sat there like I was auditioning for that movie Awakenings with Robin Williams. The doctor revealed to Starr's parents that she was pregnant and miscarried the baby. Krystal began to cry hard knowing she was going to be a grandmother again. I just knew I was having a nightmare and if I screamed Samir would wake me up. Well I screamed, but he didn't wake me up. He just reached over and held my hand trying to gather his own composure. He went and called my parents from his cell phone and told them the news. They reached the hospital about 15 minutes after he called. They bought Kareemah into the hospital and she was reaching her arms out for me to take her. I didn't have any strength to hold her. I tried but almost dropped her. My dad caught her and I passed out. When I came to I didn't remember anything about passing out. I was only out for a few minutes but it felt like hours. My mom was holding my hand. I opened my eyes squinting to bring her into focus, "Mom, I don't want to live anymore. Please just let me die. It hurts Mommy, it hurts so bad." My mom cried and my dad reached for my other hand. He turned my face to his.

"Baby girl I know how you feel but dying won't solve anything." I pulled my hands from my parents and pulled myself into a ball, "Oh yes it will. I want to die!" At that moment Kareem walked in. The police had released him from their custody. He walked over to Samir, "How is she?" Before I knew it Samir hooked him and Mitch jumped in it too. My dad jumped up from my side but was stopped by Security. I struggled to sit up and rested my head in my moms lap sitting on the floor. Security broke up the fight and Kareem was escorted out. I watched him walk out and passed out again. The next time I woke up I was in a hospital bed. Dr. Francis said I was working myself up too much and I needed to calm down. I couldn't take the hurt. The hospital sent me home and gave my mom a prescription to help me sleep. Once home my mom gave me a pill and put me in the bed. They were downstairs trying to pull themselves together. I got up and took the whole bottle of pills. They weren't working fast enough so I hurled the TV remote at the mirror. The mirror shattered in a million pieces. I stumbled to the glass to pick up a piece. Everyone ran in and I lifted the piece of the glass to slit my wrist. Before I could drop the glass down my father tackled me on the floor. He grabbed my arm and shook it until I dropped the piece of glass I was holding. I whined, "Daddy let me go. I don't want to live anymore. Have a double funeral for me and Starr." Samir was standing over me crying. I had seen tears stream down his face but I had never seen him cry hysterically the way he was. I suddenly became confused.

"Where am I? What is this? What did I do? What happened to the mirror?" The overdose of the prescription had me bugging. Samir picked me up and shook me like a rag doll.

"Diamond please! What is the matter with you? Please D don't do this to me...Mamma Ann what is the matter with her, please help her, I don't want to lose her too!" I just flopped down on the bed and looked at Samir. My reflexes began to slow down and I even blinked slow. He sat down next to me, "Diamond please stop trying to hurt yourself! Why you want to leave me D?" At the time Kareemah started crying from downstairs. I jumped up and tried to run to her. I got down the stairs in slow motion into the living room, "What's wrong Kareemah? Your God mommy is here. Don't cry sweetie. I won't let nothing happen to you, I promise." Kareemah's cries had snapped me back into reality. My best friend was dead and I had to be a mother to her child. As I reached for Kareemah I passed out and they couldn't wake me up. My mother ran upstairs to read the side effects on the bottle and discovered I had taken all the pills. All I know is I woke up in the hospital once again with an I.V. in my arm. Samir was sitting next to me holding my hand. I woke up with a splitting headache. I opened one eye first then the other. Samir stood up and looked me in my face, "Hey Diamond."

I swallowed hard.

'What happened Samir?" He rubbed my hand.

"Nothing baby you just um took some pills by accident you will be fine." I looked around the room and at my arm with the I.V. in it.

"Diamond, you are in the hospital. You had your stomach pumped because of taking too many pills." I scrunched up my face.

"How did I take too many pills by accident?" He kissed my cheek.

"D please just rest O.k.?" I shrugged my shoulders and laid back. He sat back down. I looked at the ceiling. It all came rushing back to me. I flicked my neck towards Samir.

"Samir?" He stood up over me again, "Yes baby?"

"Starr is gone isn't she?" He sniffled, "Yes D she is. She is in a better place." I couldn't say anything. I tried not to cry or move. I felt like I felt when Tahir died but 1000 times worse. When you don't cry or move it is not real or at least it doesn't feel real. They released me from the hospital later that day. When I got home I didn't want to talk to anybody. People from school had found out and were blowing my cell phone up. I just turned off the ringers in my house and turned my cell phone to the off position. I had to get myself together and pack. We were headed back to Jersey to lay my best friend to rest.

CHAPTER 52
HOMEGOING

Starr's body was shipped to New Jersey to Drew's Funeral Home. Monday when I got back to Jersey it felt funny being back in my old room. I had Samir stay with me and I wouldn't let Kareemah out of my sight. The wake was set for Friday at Bethel A.M.E. Church and the funeral for Saturday at the church as well. On Wednesday, Thanksgiving Eve, I ventured across the street and went into Starr's old room. Krystal had kept everything the same. I crept in her room slowly. One by one I gradually opened her drawers and went through her things. I found old notes I had written her from junior and high school. There were pictures we had taken and phone numbers from numerous guys she met. I looked at each thing one by one and laughed and cried all at the same time. Sam came in her room as I sat on the floor looking at things. He sat down Indian style next to me, "Are you O.k. D?" I shrugged and closed my eyes.

"I guess, I'm just reminiscing." He put his arm around me and lifted my chin. I looked deeply into his eyes. I swear I could see his soul crying. I hugged him.

"Samir I miss her so much." I broke down into a massive ball of sobs. He hugged me tighter.

"Me too Diamond, me too." I fell downward into his lap and cried as I felt his warm tears fall into my scalp. At that moment Danny walked in. I had refused to see anybody since I had been home including him. He began to cry as well and joined in on a group hug with me and Samir. He kept repeating, "Why Diamond why?" He broke down bad. I had to muster up some strength to hold him. I sat up and let him lay in my lap.

"D, if I wouldn't have cheated on her this would have never happened. She would be right here with us." I stroked his hairline.

"Danny don't blame yourself, it wasn't your fault." He sat up pushing me back off him. He jumped up and towered over me and Samir.

"Yes it is! If I would have just did her right..." Sam stood up to calm him down.

"Danny it is not on you. Don't blame yourself man." He gave Danny a manly hug and they sat back down the floor with me. Us 3 looked at pictures saying things like, "Remember this?" and "Oh this was the day..." We talked about old times, fun times, bad times and glad times that we spent together.

When I got back across the street my voicemail box was full. I had messages from old friends that heard what happened and wanted to offer their condolences. Quan called and left a message saying he would be at the services and if I need a friend I knew the number. I sat and thought about Q. I am not gonna front, I did miss him. I always thought about what would have become of us if I didn't catch him out there.

Thursday was Thanksgiving and I couldn't think of one thing to be thankful for. I know y'all, I had a lot to be thankful for but at that specific time, I couldn't think of one thing. My mother cooked but I didn't eat anything.

Friday was the worst day of my life. I was shaking uncontrollably all day as if I was freezing cold. I regretted this day and prayed it would never come, but here it was, my best friend/sister's wake. We went to the church early to see Starr's body. She looked beautiful in her cream colored casket with gold trim. The swelling in her face had went down and the make up artist did an excellent job. She wore all white with a crown made of white flowers. Her hair laid perfectly with her make up matching her skin just right. Her lips had a skin tone lipstick on them making her look like she was lying there sleeping.

I approached the casket with Kareemah in my arms. I hugged her tight because I still couldn't believe it was real. When Kareemah saw Starr she got excited and tried to jump out of my arms to get Starr. I had to hold her tight because she wanted her mommy and so did I. Samir took Kareemah from me. I got close to her chest. It looked like she was still breathing. I touched her hand.

"Starr get up. Come on you can do it Starr. Get up. Get up Starr, right now. Stop playing this is not funny anymore Starr. Come on get up. Get up now!" I leaned into the casket and began to shake her. My father came and pried my fingers off of Starr and pulled me back. I was fighting and kicking and screaming, "Let me go Daddy! Let me go. She is still breathing. She is playing a horrible joke on us. STARR GET UP! GET UP NOW!" My father dragged me down the aisle to get me out of there. He took me down the stairs to get me some water.

"Daddy. Please believe me. She is alive she is not dead. She is alive now let me go." My father sighed.

"Please Diamond don't do this. She is gone baby. She...is...gone. I know you miss her. We all do D but I need you to calm down. I need you to be strong for Samir and for her parents and for Kareemah up there. No more outbreaks baby. She is gone. There is nothing you can do about it." I pushed my father.

"She is not gone! Don't ever say that. She is not gone. She did not leave me here Daddy. We made a pact. We couldn't die until we got old. We were supposed to grow old together Daddy. She wouldn't lie to me Daddy. She wouldn't. She wouldn't leave me here. She promised me." My dad hugged me through my struggles to get away. He held me tight in one place.

"Daddy get off of me. Get off of me Daddy. I have to go get my best friend up out of that casket. I don't want them to bury her by accident. She didn't leave me daddy.

She didn't that is my best friend and my sister. She is all I got. She didn't leave me. She didn't. All of you are wrong and I'm right. Now you were right about Tahir but Daddy you're not right about Starr. She just needs somebody to wake her up. That's all now let me go so I can wake her up." The harder I tried to get away the more my father held me. I punched him, kicked him and tried to bite him but he wouldn't let me go. I then began to scream. My mother came down to the lobby, her eyes filled with tears.

"Diamond baby please. Please stop. Stop baby." I struggled to still get away from my father.

"Stop what Mommy? Starr is still alive. I saw her breathing. She is not gone." My mother exhaled and shook her head. She pulled me into her bosom for a full hug. My dad went and got tissues for us both. My mother placed her hands on my shoulders and looked me square in my eyes.

"Listen to me baby. Starr is gone. She is in a better place. Do you hear me? Diamond do you hear me?" I just stood there and looked through her. I didn't want to hear such nonsense, how could Starr be gone? She began to shake me.

"Diamond? Get yourself together before you go back upstairs. Now I know you're upset baby but you are making everybody else more upset when you act like that." I had a long snot string from my nose to my chin. My mother licked the napkin and wiped my face. I was too distraught to get on her y'all, doing that nasty mess. She placed her arm through mine to keep me up. My dad did the same on the other side of me. My mom leaned into my ear.

"Now come on baby. I need you to be strong and come upstairs." I followed suit. Don't know how I climbed those stairs, but my mother sat me down and I stared into space. As the time rolled on the wake became packed. I was sitting next to Samir still in my own world. I came out of my trance when Q came in. It was him and his mother. Jackie rushed to me and I had my face buried in my hands. She put her arm around me and gave me a kiss on my cheek.

"Baby it is going to be O.k." I leaned on her shoulder. She went in her small clutch bag and pulled out a tissue and wiped my face. She hugged me tighter and I hugged her back. I glanced over at Q who was standing there with tears trickling down his cheeks. I pulled back from his mother and blew my nose. I whispered, "I'm O.k." Samir was holding Kareemah and Krystal came over and got her. Samir stood up and shook hands with Q. They hugged and Q said, "Yo, I'm sorry man." Samir was holding up good under this pressure. He pushed out a half of smile.

"Thanks man." Q handed him a card and me one too. Jackie moved down and let Q sit next to me.

"I'm so sorry D. You O.k.?" I slowly nodded. He put his arms around me and we hugged. I broke down again and began to hyperventilate like I had asthma. I needed some air. Q took me by my hand.

"D let me walk you outside so you can get some air." As me and Q were walking out, Kareem, Ms. Chickie (his mother), and Sheya (his sister) were walking in. I screamed,

"You murderer! How dare you show your face here! You have some nerve." Q grabbed me.

"D please calm down." He kept pulling me towards the doors. As he pulled me I yelled, "I'm going to get you Kareem, I swear it! I promised my sister that on her death bed!" Sheya turned around and looked me up and down. She got snotty.

"Look Diamond, I know you're upset but my brother didn't kill Starr so you needs to stop accusing him of it ight!" I screamed, "Bitch!..." The folks that were going up the stairs stopped and turned to see who was using obscenities in the Lord's house. I continued on just like the wretched sinner that I am.

"...Don't tell me who to accuse! Your brother used my sister as a punching bag everyday and now she is gone!" Q held me tighter and yanked me harder.

"Come on D, come on. Let's get you that air you

need." As he continued to pull me I was still in rare form.

"And don't get it twisted Sheya, you can get some too!" Their mother pulled their arms to go up the stairs into the viewing. She said, "Listen she is upset and has good reason to be, so don't start with her." Ms. Chickie walked over to me.

"Diamond I'm so sorry. If we are making you that upset we will leave." I put my hand in her face.

"BYE!" Kareem stormed over to me.

"Fuck that Ma! D, look I didn't do it, I told you I didn't, the cops told you I didn't, the doctor told you I didn't, I didn't do it! If I did then the cops wouldn't have let me go. I was interrogated for 18 hours and they decided that I didn't do it. I loved her for God' sake, that was my fiancé! We got a child together and my son was on the way. I wouldn't hurt her." He started with some fake crocodile tears. I scowled at him. Q dragged me out the door.

"D, come on let's get some air." I was standing outside when they came out. Actually, I was in the middle of puking my brains out, which is all that would come out considering I didn't eat anything. Ms. Chickie came up to me concerned. She touched my back.

"Diamond are you O.k.?" I shrugged my back upwards to get her hand off of me. Between burps I said, "Yes I am, please just leave me alone." Q was rubbing my back as I was hunched over the railing. I spit one last time and stood up. I wiped my mouth and nose with the sleeve of my shirt. Hey, I know that's nasty but I didn't have a tissue. I looked at Q.

"I think I'm O.k. now Q. Can you walk me back inside please?" I watched the Blackwell family walk and get into Kareem's car and pull off. At that moment I wondered where Zak was at. I hadn't seen or heard from him since the night that bastard killed my sister. I came back into the wake.

"Samir what happened?" He looked my in my eyes.

"Nothing Diamond. There is no energy left to fight. If he did this, he will get what is coming to him." I jumped up and down in front of Samir.

"If? If he did this? Oh he did it and he will get what is coming to him!" Samir grabbed my shirt to pull me down. I left it at that. The next day at the funeral our unofficial town singer, Mrs. Crawford sang, His eye is on the sparrow. Mrs. Crawford could sing and whoever died they wanted her to sing at their funeral. Shoot, I want her to sing at mine. When Reverend Fubler asked if anyone wanted to say something I stood up to read a poem. I almost got through it but broke down towards the end. One of my girl's Shannon came and finished it for me. Even growing up, she was the youngest of our group but she was the mother hen. I looked out into the audience and saw the Blackwell's. When I was done Kareem slowly walked up to the microphone. He had his Gucci shades on and a white suit with a white fur on. Enough already Kareem, he was in over kill mode. He cleared his throat.

"I um just wanted to say that I um love my um fiancé, She was an angel, a good mother, and a good listener." He walked to the casket and kissed Starr's forehead.

"Rest in peace Starr. I will never find another like you. I love you." I jumped up but Samir grabbed my before I could get to him. Samir slammed me down in my seat.

"Please Diamond not here, not now. Respect Starr please. I dropped my head backwards on the pew. I cried hard. Samir put his arm around me and wiped my tears away.

On the way to Hollywood Cemetery it was pouring down raining. We were all in the limo together and my mother reached and touched my hand.

"Starr just got her wings baby." I tried to smile but couldn't because I was too busy crying. At the cemetery Samir held my hand tight. I guess he knew I really wanted to throw myself in the hole but that is when him and Shareef couldn't take it anymore. They both were crying and hugging each other. Krystal fell out as they lowered her body in the ground. Mitch tried to pick his wife up but she was screaming, "My God, why have you taken my baby girl from me? Why didn't you take me God? Why God? Not my baby!" Reverend Fubler said the famous, "Ashes to ashes and dust to dust." 2 white doves were released from their cages.

Black, Samir's boys from back in the day, worked there and tried to be strong as he lowered the body but he broke down too. The casket fell side ways and the other workers had to catch the body. The casket was lopsided as the flowers that adorned the top of it fell over into the hole. My mom and dad were holding me up as this funeral turned into a cry fest. Our girls from back in the day were trying to hold each other up, while the guys did the same. Danny began to shadow box the air and the boys grabbed him. Reverend Fubler tried to say a prayer but it didn't work. People were screaming and falling out all over in the rain. It turned to pandemonium and chaos in a matter of minutes. Mitch dragged Krystal to the car as Samir and Shareef fell over each other near the muddy grave. Kareem and his family left with out a trace. I fell backwards on my butt and splashed in the mud.

"Why is she gone? I can't understand this; I want her back here with me. She is my only sister and I don't know how I am supposed to go on living with out her! I can't, I just can't." My dad pulled me up to my knees and I was limp like rag doll. He got me to my feet while my mother helped him. Kareemah screamed at the top of her lungs at the sight of people passing out around her. Everyone began to disperse back to their cars and I was frozen. Samir and Shareef leaned on each other to go back to the car. My father tugged on my arm, "Come on Diamond. It's time to go." I shook my head back and forth and pulled myself free from his grasp.

"No Daddy. I need to talk to Starr alone please before they cover her over completely with dirt." My father looked at my mother and my mother raised her eyebrows. I folded my hands together.

"Please I will be O.k. just go to the car I will be there

in a minute." They were weary of me being alone and walked slowly and watched me. I stood over the hole and looked in. Dirt was being tossed in while I spoke.

"Starr look, I love you with all my heart and all my soul. You are my best friend and my sister and no matter what happened at the end. And God as my witness, I will get Kareem for you. I don't know how and I don't know what I will do but I have to do something. Kareemah will be taken care of. Don't you worry about anything Starr. You rest in peace baby girl. Rest in Peace!" At that time lightning shot across the sky and thunder roared. I walked slowly to the limo soaked and wet but the rain couldn't hide my tears. My hair stuck to my forehead and my clothes felt 50 pounds heavier filled with water. I got in and laid on Samir's chest. My dad reached for my hand.

"Sweetie are you O.k.?" I yelled, "No Daddy I am not. She is my only friend how am I supposed to go on?" Samir put his arm around me.

"Diamond I am your friend too. Always and forever." I looked up at him and he smiled at me. I smiled back. My Goddaughter wined for me to take her. I took her from Krystal and hugged and kissed her. She was going to stay with Krystal and Mitch until May when me and Samir were set to graduate and then we would take over with their help. The next week Kareem called Krystal.

"Hello Mrs. Mitchell. How are you?"

"I'm fine Kareem. What do you want?"

"My daughter. I want custody of her." Luckily Starr had it in writing who she wanted her baby to be with and it didn't say Kareem on the paper. Since he didn't show up for Kareemah's birth he didn't sign the birth certificate so the courts didn't know he was the father. Kareemah did love her father and Krystal worked out a schedule for him to see her. He was happy with that because he didn't want to be a full time father anyway. Me, I didn't trust him. I let him take away my best friend but I wouldn't let him hurt me again. His visits would have to be supervised.

CHAPTER 53
FIRST NAME JACK LAST NAME DANIELS

That following week it was back to D.C. for me and Samir. Over the week we were gone our mailed piled up. The first letter I noticed was the handwritten one from Starr that she told me I would get. I cried and smelled the letter that had her scent. I opened it. I slowly unfolded the letter. When I saw her handwriting I instantly folded the letter back up and put it back in the envelope. I placed it in the bible next to my nightstand. I decided to read the letter later.

I found out upon my return that Zak had got locked up that night for speeding to Starr's rescue. He had 2 kilos of coke in the trunk and wouldn't see the outside for at least 3 years. I felt responsible for him getting locked up. I called inmate locator and got the address and his state number. I sat down and wrote him a heart felt letter asking for him to forgive me. I couldn't talk about Starr's death so I didn't write much.

He wrote me back saying he didn't blame me for what happened to him, but he wanted me to accept his apology because he felt in his bones Kareem would do something to Starr that night and tried his best to get there. When he got pulled over he explained to the cop that he needed to get somewhere and the cop told him to save it for the judge. So in the end, he felt responsible for Starr's death.

Kareem hadn't written him or came to see him or anything. He gave up his half of everything to his brother and told him to hold it down while he did his time. I told him no matter what I would be doing his 3 years with him. Little did I know it would be from jail to jail.

Over the next few weeks me and Samir went through a lot of pain, arguing, and suffering. We argued mostly because I missed Starr. We almost left each other because one day he got drunk and stepped out of line. He was throwing back shots of Jack Daniels and when the bottle was more than half gone he looked at me with utter disgust on his face.

"You know, you're the reason Starr is dead. It is all your fault." I pointed at myself.

"How is it my fault?" He threw back another shot and slammed the shot glass down on my living room glass table and cracked it.

"Why didn't you ever tell me that nigga was putting his hands on my sister? I should put mine on you and see if you like it." I began to cry.

"Samir she begged me not to tell you or anybody. I had to keep it a secret." He tried to stand up but lost his footing and fell back down on the couch. He slurred.

"Bullshit! You wanted him to kill her. You must have or you would have gotten her help. Don't you volunteer with battered women? You know they have to get out of the relationship but nooooo you couldn't help my sister. I hate you Diamond and I don't want to be with you no more!" He tried to lift the bottle to his lips but passed out instead. The liquor ran down on my couch and I grabbed the bottle and placed it on the floor. I looked at him and shook my head and then at my table. I tried endlessly to call his name to wake him up. I began to shake him but he was snoring hard. I couldn't let him stay like this. I ran upstairs and started a hot shower for him. I came back downstairs and Pow! I smacked the taste out of his mouth. His eyes popped open.

"Bitch you hit me? I am going to fuck you up." He went to grab me but I moved and he fell in the space between the couch and the table. I helped him up and put his arm over my neck and struggled to get him up the stairs. Once in the bedroom I pushed him back on the bed. I pulled his shirt off him. He didn't have any control of his limbs.

"Get off me whore. You fucking Zak ain't you? I just

ignored him and never told him that Zak was locked up. I took his pants and boxers down next. He mushed me in the head to push me away.

"Get off me. You not getting none of this thug dick ever again!" I just got teary eyed and ignored him. I stood him up and leaned him on the wall. I tried to get his boxers and pants from off his feet and when I lifted one leg her slid down the wall and fell and hit his head on the edge of the nightstand. I screamed because he was out cold and I thought he was dead. I called 911 and they were on their way. I pulled his pants and boxers up and tried to get his shirt back on. The ambulance came in less then 10 minutes. I rode in the ambulance with him to the emergency room. He had to get 13 stitches in the back of his head. When we got home from the emergency room he didn't remember anything but he had a banging headache. I got him in the bed and cleaned his blood off the nightstand and the carpet.

We were best friends again after that because I had to wait on him hand and foot. I never told him about the hurtful things he said to me that night.

Soon after that we went to New Jersey for Christmas break. This was going to be Kareemah's first Christmas. On Christmas Eve me and Sam got matching tattoos on our left shoulder blades in memory of Starr. We got a tattoo of a picture of Starr with wings that said Starr Angel R.I.P. 10/31/76-11/17/97. She had just turned 21 in October.

That night our families, including Aunt Michelle and Aunt Debra and their sons had dinner together and let Kareemah open some of her gifts. As I watched her tear open wrapping paper I plotted what I wanted to do to her father. Whatever it was going to be it wasn't going to be good. We gathered around the table and sat down to eat. Before my father prayed Samir raised his glass and clanked on it with his fork.

"Listen up everybody I got something to say."

457

CHAPTER 54
WOULD I EVER!

Samir was sitting next to me and turned towards me, "Diamond, we have been together all these years and basically I think we need space." I looked at him like he had 2 heads.

"What? What do you mean we need space? I have been..." He pulled out a velvet box and put it in my face. My mouth fell open.

"When I say we need space I mean we need space that we share together forever." He got down on one knee, opened the velvet box in one hand and took mine in his other. My mouth was still hanging open.

"Diamond I love you and I want to be with you for the rest of my life. There is no one else for me. What I'm trying to say is, Diamond Crescent Staple will you marry me?" I still was sitting there speechless. My father laughed and zoomed in on my face. Now I told you he was Spike Lee Jr. so you know he was taping.

"Oh my God Samir. I have never seen her speechless. Now I'm glad I'm taping this." The family chuckled but I still didn't answer. Samir squeezed my hand.

"Well Diamond? What will it be?" I bent down and hugged him.

"Yes Samir. Yes I will marry you." He took the ring from the box and placed it on my finger. I looked at It and then at him. I cocked my head to the side.

"Ooh Samir you remembered." You see it was the ring I had picked out the year before in the jewelry store at the Short Hills Mall. I remember walking past hand and hand and I stopped at the window display. I tapped on the glass excitedly.

"See this one Samir. This the ring I want when I get engaged." He looked over at it nonchalantly and laughed.

"Well call me and let me know when the wedding is and who you're getting engaged to." I pulled my hand from his and walked away. We hooked back up an hour later in the mall. I still had an attitude but let it go. We left and I never mentioned getting engaged to him again. He laughed remembering my attitude that day.

"You know that day as soon as you walked away I went in there to see about that ring." I gave him a hug.

"Aw Samir you're so sweet." I kissed him and then looked at my ring. Princess cut diamond with baguettes titivating the sides. I put my ring in Kareemah's face.

"Kareemah look. God daddy finally did the right thing." She started laughing like she knew what I was saying. She was so beautiful and she looked just like Starr so sometimes it was hard to look at her with out getting emotional.

So as time went on the new year came and soon after that Kareemah's first birthday, which of course she had a big blow out. Me and Samir stayed in school and burned 95 North up coming up on weekends to see Kareemah or Krystal would bring her down to us. By order of the court Kareem was able to see her every other weekend. I had to act like we were O.k. so I could put forth the master plan. Kareemah loved Kareem to death and she would be so happy to see him. It was sickening. His time to come see her was on Sundays while she went to see his mom on Saturdays.

Me and Samir graduated from Howard University in May and guess who else graduated? Q, from Georgetown. He was in the 5-year program. You know that program right? You can't finish in 4 years so you finish in 5. After Starr's death we remained friends and would sneak and meet for lunch. No no no! We weren't creeping but I know Samir wouldn't have been having that. At one of our many lunch dates we had a heart to heart talk about us. He reached across the table and held my hand.

"Diamond I will never find another girlfriend like you. I might end up staying single for life. Who knows? I'm saying, I won't front, I do hate that you and Samir lasted and I am definitely hating on the engagement. But let me tell you something, if Samir ever mess up I am getting back in that spot and never leaving again. " I pulled my hand back and laughed.

"Well I'm sorry Q. Me and Sam are in this to win this." He frowned up his face.

"I know and I'm happy for y'all but on the low I got hate in my blood." I laughed at him. Q was a good friend and a good man. I'm glad I met him and had him in my life.

Anyway after graduation me, Samir, and Q all got together and threw a big bash. It was a real nice gathering in my yard. Danny was still in college and his daughter was a little Aunt Debra. She cussed like her and everything. Danny and Gina were off and on and after all that shit she popped, Aunt Debra loved being a grandmother and had Dagina with her all the time. David had graduated a few years prior and worked as a financial advisor at Summit Bank. He had his bachelor's pad and was not thinking about marriage. Shareef? He was real bad off when Starr died and he had moved back home after living with his girl for years to be closer to Kareemah. I think he loved Kareemah more than anybody.

Well it was June and it was time for my master plan.

CHAPTER 55
WHOSE THE WO'MAN' WITH THE MASTER PLAN?

So look, Samir was on a business trip with the company he interned for in Boston. We both were moving back to New Jersey where I was going to look for a job in marketing and Samir got a transfer to the New York law firm he interned for. He was going to go to Columbia University for law school in New York as well.

That day in June I was home alone packing our things that we were taking back to New Jersey. It was Sunday afternoon nearing the evening and Kareem had called to come see Kareemah like he usually did. I told him he could come over to see her, but she wasn't even there. I went up to the bedroom to put the things in my dresser and nightstand in boxes. I cleared off the top of my nightstand first throwing my bible into the box. I was mad at God for letting Kareem take Starr from me and he was walking around fine. I never picked up that bible and I had stopped going to church and listening to gospel music. I didn't think of Christmas as the birth of Christ and Easter was out. I thought if God wasn't going to do anything about Kareem then I was. I gave him over 6 months to do something and he didn't so I was taking matters into my own hands.

One thing I have learned while here in jail is God does things on his own time. I had always heard people say, 'he may not come when you want him, but he'll be there right on time.' This statement speaks the truth, the whole truth, and nothing but the truth. We as humans think we can rush God and it doesn't work that way. He is our protector and our guidance and we have to obey him or our lives will be in shambles. You must put God first and all other things will fall into place. You must know that only through Jesus can you get to God.

Well enough with that sermon. Once I slammed the bible down into the box something fell out. It was the letter from Starr. I never read the letter because it was too hard in the beginning and I ended up forgetting about it. It was finally time to read it. I slowly opened it as tears filled my eyes. I exhaled and began to read the letter aloud.

Dear Diamond,

I hope this letter finds you in the best of health. Lord knows I am not. This is the hardest letter I ever had to write. I am pregnant again Diamond. The doctor said it's a boy. I can't believe I allowed myself to get tangled up into this mess. I would be excited but it gets worse. I took my H.I.V. test and it came back positive. Kareem gave me AIDS Diamond! I don't know what to do or who to turn to and I need you. Please don't tell anybody Diamond. I know if anyone can keep it to themselves then it is you.

I am going to die Diamond. Maybe not today or tomorrow but I am going to die. I know we all are going to die but I am going to die sooner than most. If the disease doesn't get me, then Kareem will. I wanted to kill myself and at first I was going to ask you to help me. I don't know what I am going to do D.

I am 4 months pregnant and if I pass this on to this baby, he won't have a chance at life because I am bringing him into the world with this horrible disease.

Diamond I am so sorry for all the things I have said and done to you. I didn't tell Kareem yet because I don't want him to think I gave it to him and he black out and kill me, the baby, and Kareemah. You know I have never cheated on Kareem Diamond. I have always been faithful and always been true. Why me?

Kareemah is fine so that means he got it after her and gave it to me some time after she was born. I never thought I would have this. I always thought it happened to other people, not me. I thought me and you would get married to the men of our dreams and live forever but there is no hope for me. I will not leave him now because if I do who will want me?

I am bitter and I will not tell any of these girls that call here anything. Let all of them end up like me. With a death wish that comes sooner then it should. All I know is all them chics that call here trying to play me out, they will all end up with it.

I have known for over a month and that is why in class I don't say much. It is not you or your new friends. I am happy you have new friends that can go out and o things and not be stuck in the house like me. It is me who has the problem. I am depressed and suicidal. I mean what was I thinking having a baby so young. I thought it would be a piece of cake but it is not and I believed Kareem when he said he would be there to help me. Ha, that's a joke. I do everything on my own all he does is support us financially and sometimes doesn't do that.

D I want you to raise Kareemah for me when I...well you know. I had it put in writing if I ever...you know, that you will take care of her. You and Samir.

D I am soooo sorry. I never wanted to let you down. You mean so much to me and so does Samir. I always wanted you to be proud of me and me to be proud of you. Well I am proud of you Diamond. I know Samir will be disappointed in me and want to kill Kareem and I don't need that on my conscience. I know how you are going to feel and what you are going to say but how do you think I feel about myself right now? I feel ashamed, disappointed, disgusted; soon I will look sick and then what? I know people are living longer and things like that but since our time is really limited now, please don't turn your back on me. Please forgive me for all my wrongdoing and love me like you always did. Find the kindness in your heart to love me.

I wonder how long I can keep this from Kareem? I will have to take a lot of medicine to try to keep from giving it to the baby but nothing is guaranteed. I can only imagine how many other girls will end up like me because Kareem doesn't like how a condom feels. He likes to feel a female. You always were so careful with making guys wear condoms. You didn't play that and I wish I would have listened when you said make him strap up. Now my days are numbered and my daughter won't have me to grow up with. Thank God she will have you. I give myself 10 years tops to live on this earth but I want to make it the best 10 years ever. I want us to travel and I want you to be in my wedding and I want to be in you and Samir's wedding. (Smile)

Diamond please, I'm begging you, I know I can't make you and you might not want to be around a H.I.V. positive person like me. Who knows, but I hope you still see me as Starr not sick Starr. I'm still the same loving person I was just with a little less time. I still will go upside a chics head if she steps to my sister. (Smile)

Well D, I hope this didn't bring you down or upset you. It wasn't meant to. I love you Diamond, always have and always will even when I'm gone. We never kept secrets and I don't want to start now. Luckily in Heaven there is no sickness and sadness. I will just get there first and hold a spot for you. But until that time let's just live for today.

I LOVE YOU DIAMOND
Starr Angel

I dropped the letter and grabbed my chest. I braced myself on the edge of the bed. This sorry ass nigga gave my best friend AIDS W.T.F. (what the fuck.) This disease doesn't have a name on it and it can happen to any of us. I looked down at the letter and ripped it up into tiny little pieces of paper. Nobody knew that she was sick when she died and nobody was going to know now. I got up and flushed the ripped up letter down the toilet. Then the doorbell rang. I looked in the mirror, splashed water on my face and said out loud,

"It's show time! That's all folks!" I ran down the stairs and flung the door open. Kareem stood in the door.

"What's up Diamond?" I ran my finger down chest

between my cleavage.

"Nothing much." He looked around me.

"Where is my baby girl?" I smacked my cheeks like I was an airhead.

"Oh I completely forgot to tell you she is not here because I need to finish packing."

"So why didn't you tell me that on the phone Diamond?" I smiled at him.

"Cause I wanted to talk to you." He furrowed his brow.

"About what?" I opened the door wide.

"Come over to the couch and have a seat." He looked at me puzzled. I showed him both of my hands.

"I don't have anything Kareem. I just want to talk to you. Now come on in. I don't bite unless you want me to." He took one step in the door still looking around my place.

"Huh?" I laughed.

"It was a joke Kareem, would you lighten up?" I had on the shortest shorts I could find and a low cut tank top. When I sat on the couch I leaned over so he could see down my top. I licked my lips. He was still a little nervous and came over by the couch but wouldn't sit. He looked around nervously.

"Where is Samir?" I crossed my legs.

"Away on business and he won't be back until next week." He then flopped down next to me.

"Oh well what's up Diamond?" I scooted over close to him and ran my fingers across the back of his shoulder blades.

"Look Kareem, I just wanted to apologize to you for always accusing you for what happened to Starr." He sat up straight.

"Look..." I took his hand in mine.

"Let me finish please Kareem. (I was acting coy and shy.) When I watch you with Kareemah I know you love her and you're so sweet so I know you wouldn't be capable of killing Starr. I can tell you don't have it in you." He sat back and relaxed.

"That is what I have been trying to tell you." I flung my hair back over my shoulders.

"I know and I hope you can forgive me." He put his hands behind his head.

"Yeah I guess." So I put my hand out to shake his and I took my index finger and rubbed the middle of his hand like he did me in the past and he pulled his hand back. I poked out my lips.

"Oh I'm sorry did that make you uncomfortable?" He eyed my cleavage.

"No I just wasn't expecting it." I smiled.

"Well I'm sorry." He stood up.

"Well I guess I will get going." I stood up too.

"What's your rush? Are you hungry?" He looked around again.

"A little." I took his hand in mine.

"Well I cooked and I don't like to eat alone. I have been packing all day so I need to eat." I switched real hard into the kitchen. I had made lasagna. I called him from the kitchen entrance.

"Come in here. Let's sit at the table and eat. Would you like a glass of wine?" He came in and sat down still looking uneasy.

"O.k." I know you guys are trying to think ahead and hell no I ain't poison this nigga. How could I carry him out of there, think O.k.? Anyway we sat down and he thought the same thing, that I was trying to kill him. I shook my head back and forth slowly grinning.

"Kareem your food is O.k. let me show you." I got up and sauntered over to his chair. I picked up his fork before he used it and I took some food onto it. I placed the fork in my mouth real slow and sensual. I chewed the food and then I licked the fork from top to bottom. I picked up his wine and took a swig. I gargled it in my throat and then swallowed. He was looking at me with his mouth open. I leaned over with my breasts on his shoulder.

"See it is fine." He pulled in his bottom lip and looked at me.

"Damn girl!" I went and sat back down. We ate our food and talked about Kareemah basically. After we ate he picked up the dishes.

"Let me help you with these." I smiled hard and winked at him.

"O.k." So we washed and dried the dishes and put the food away. I stretched.

"Well thank you Kareem. I need to finish packing." He followed me into the living room.

"Let me help." I had him packing up all my stuff. I had my dad's navigator. There were boxes piled up by the door.

"Could you put all those boxes in the back of truck please?"

"Sure I can." All the big stuff was going to good will like our furniture and kitchen set. I wanted all new stuff for our new start in New Jersey. Once we got back in from packing up the truck he polished off the rest of the wine and had 2 Corona's that were in the fridge. He slurred a bit.

"Yo D, you looking good in those shorts." I smiled at him.

"Thank you Kareem." By that time he only had on a wife beater cause he claimed he had gotten hot from moving. I sat on the couch next to him and moved a little closer to me. He leaned in.

"I gotta keep it real girl, you looking good as hell." I laughed like a little schoolgirl.

"So you want me?" He exclaimed.

"Do I?" We laughed and I playfully slapped his leg.

"You know you crazy Kareem, we trying to work on a friendship but maybe we could sneak that in." I laughed and he joined in and rubbed his hands together.

"Word. That's what's up." He looked at me and licked his lips and rubbed his manhood.

"Down boy!" He leaned over and put his arm around me.

"O.k. boo. I knew you were just upset when Starr died but now it is all good with your sexy ass." I shook my head up and down.

"I sure was Kareem and it sure is." He rubbed his chest.

"Samir is lucky as hell." I playfully smacked his arm.

"Oh stop it Kareem." I started giggling making my own damn self sick. He scooted over almost on my lap.

"No I'm serious Diamond." I looked at him and got a bit nervous. I moved back a little.

"Well Starr was lucky too." He smiled and threw his hands behind his head.

"Yeah she was!" We laughed in unison. I got serious and looked him dead in his eyes.

"So look Kareem, I'm not a little kid anymore. When I see something I want to take it. So what up with the bedroom? Are you down?" He rubbed his hands together and licked his lips.

"Hell yeah!" He jumped up and headed for the stairs. I jumped up and blocked him off.

"Wait! Before we do go upstairs you gotta promise me this will be our little secret." He grabbed my arm.

"I promise boo. Let's go." I pulled back my arm.

"You promise you won't tell a soul?" He crossed his heart.

"Cross my heart and hope to die, stick a needle in my eye." I giggled again.

"Oh Kareem." So I walked up the stairs first and my stomach began to hurt. Kareem reached out and touched my butt. I turned around giggling.

"Not yet Kareem, not yet. Be patient." I had already laid out a 2-piece Victoria Secret's lingerie set on my bed. We walked into the bedroom and I closed and locked the bedroom door. I pointed at the bed.

"Kareem get comfortable. Let me go in the bathroom and change into something more comfortable. You just get yourself together and get ready for me." I winked at him and entered the master bathroom. I walked in with the lingerie over my arm. My stomach was hurting like you wouldn't believe. I guess it was cramping up because I was nervous about what I was about to do, but I was wrong. I sat down on the toilet to pee and what was there? I know the females thought quick, that's right my damn period. I thought, ooh great and took off the period stained draws and threw them in the sink. I washed them out real quick and washed up even quicker. I put a tampon on. I slipped into the shorts of the outfit and looked in the mirror. Tears began to roll down my cheeks. I took off my top and turned around so I could look at Starr tattooed on me in the mirror. I winked at the tattoo.

"This is for you sis." I put the camisole top on. I pinned my hair up in a bun. I heard the phone start ringing. Dammit, I got to get it. It might be Samir. I ran out and looked at him. I put my finger up to my lip. I answered it.

"Hello."

"Hey D, you busy?" It was Q.

"Yeah kinda."

"Well I got something important to tell you call me back."

"I will."

"O.k. D don't forget." I sucked my teeth.

"I won't now I gotta go." Q knew Samir was out of town and that is why he felt free to call the house phone. I hung up the phone and looked over at Kareem. He had stripped down to his boxers.

"Almost ready for this?" He tried to pull me over on top of him.

"Hell yeah. Come here." I pulled back. I could have spit on him for infecting my sister. I winked at him.

"O.k. hold up. Let me put the finishing touches on." He grabbed his swelling manhood.

"Well hurry up cause you got my man rock hard." I went back to the bathroom and looked in the mirror. I took a deep breath. I opened the top drawer by the sink. I took out Samir's Roscoe, the 380. The glock was loaded. I opened the bathroom door slowly with the gun behind me. He stood up.

"Um, um, um you look so good. Good enough to

eat!" I was standing with the sexy pose with one hand behind my back and the other up on the side of my door.

"You like what you see?" He licked his drunken lips.

"Yes." He squinted his eyes.

"What's behind your back?"

"Oh this?" I pointed the gun at him. He began to tremble.

"What's this?" I clenched my teeth.

"It will be your last day on earth if you don't tell me what really happened that night." Tears were running down my face. He talked calm.

"I told you what happened now put that gun down." I yelled, "Fuck you Kareem! You better tell me the truth about that night or I swear to God I will blow your mother fucking brains out." He started to get mad and took a step towards me.

"Look I told you I didn't touch her!" So I shot him in his knee. He fell, his face grimaced and screamed out.

"You stupid bitch you shot me!" I cried.

"I know and I will again now tell me the truth." He held his leg.

"I swear to God you better fucking kill me or I promise I will kill your ass just like I did Starr!" That was my cue.

"This is for my sister. You took her life in 2 ways. You pushed her down those stairs and you gave her the H.I.V. virus. I guess I will see your soul in hell!"

His facial expressions went from in pain to shock as he repeated, "H.I.V.? What are you talking about?" I shot him again in his other leg.

"H.I.V. you dirty dick nigga. I didn't stu stu stutter you gave it to my sister and that is why I am giving these bullets to you." He then got angry screaming, "I didn't give that bitch shit. I don't have that shit. I ain't no homo." I shot him again for his ignorance.

"First of all you ignorant piece of dog shit that is not a gay disease, but why am I giving you a health lesson? It can't help you where you're going!" With that I let off 2 more shots to his chest. His facial expression changed from anger to regret. I could read his eyes and they were saying, "I regret ever coming here." I guess he wasn't a real nigga like Tupac because I shot him 5 times and he surely did die. I dropped the gun and started crying hysterically. He was blocking the path to get out. When I tried to step over him, he grabbed my leg. Fooled me, he wasn't dead.

"You bitch, I will see your soul in hell!" I spit on him. I then kicked him in his face.

"Don't bet on it." I yanked my leg from his fading grasp. I didn't want him or his blood to touch me. He then closed his eyes and his body went limp. I ran out of the room and down the stairs and dialed 911. The operator answered.

"What is your emergency?" I screamed,

"I just shot and killed an intruder!" I was crying and screaming at what I had just done. I sat on the living room couch shaking and trembling until the police and ambulance pulled up. I ran out of the house screaming. The cop grabbed me.

"Miss where is the suspect?" I shakily pointed to the house.

"Upstairs dead in my bedroom." He looked around at his partner. One opened the cop car door for me to sit down.

"O.k. miss you stay here." Then my worst nightmare came true. One cop ran back downstairs yelling at the paramedics.

"Come quick he is still breathing." My mouth fell open. They flew in there like bats out of hell. They wheeled him past me with the oxygen mask on his face. The cop came back over to me.

"Miss we need to ask you a few questions." One cop came out with the gun in a plastic baggie. The cop talking to me flipped his little black pad open.

"What happened this evening?" I rubbed my forehead.

"Well I was packing up the last things because I am

moving back to Jersey..." (Of course I was crying and shaking like a leaf.)" I swallowed then looked at the cop.

"He rang my bell.." The cop raised his hand to stop the story.

"So you know him?" I crossed my arms over my chest.

"Yes, he was my best friends fiancé...She passed away last November." The cop scratched his temple.

"Well why was he here ma'am?" I sighed.

"Well he always comes by here on weekends to see his daughter because I have custody of her...He can't leave with her so he has to stay here when he visits. I forgot to tell him that she wasn't going to be here this weekend and he came over as usual." The officer nodded his head.

"O.k. well what happened after that?" I sighed and cried.

"Well he asked me if I need any help and I said yes if you don't mind carrying the heavy boxes outside. After he was done I said thanks Kareem I'm tired and I am going to bed. I said could you lock the door on your way out and he said sure no problem, I thanked him and went upstairs. I changed into my nightclothes in the bathroom and when I came out he was standing in my bedroom in his boxers. I jumped and said Kareem what are you doing and he told me that he wanted to make love to me." I let my face drop into my hands. The officer stopped writing and looked at me.

"So your late best friends fiancé told you he wanted to have sexual intercourse with you?" I cried harder.

"Yes officer! Is that so hard to believe? He was a slime ball. He always said things like that!" The officer sighed.

"Continue." I shook my legs back and forth.

"O.k. once Kareem was in my room I told him to stop playing because he was tipsy and he was bugging." The officer cut me off again.

"So he had been drinking? Were you drinking too?" I yelled, "No! I said he was...Then Kareem said he wasn't leaving until her got what he wanted. I told him he was going to leave in a body bag if he touched me and his best bet was to just leave. He laughed and said I was feisty. He began to walk towards me. I was scared and I ran to my nightstand and pulled out my gun. I had no intentions of trying to kill him, just scare him a little. I pointed the gun at him and told him I was serious. He asked if I would shoot him. I told him please just leave. He called me a bitch and said he wasn't leaving with out some pussy. He rushed me and tried to grab the gun and I fired and hit him in his knee. He called me a stupid bitch and tried to attack me again and I fired some more shots. I started crying and yelling. He knew my fiancé was away on business and I was home alone...I'm scared and nervous I need to call my parents." The cop put his hand on my shoulder.

"O.k. Ms Staple. We will need you to stay in town." I cried.

"I'm scared to stay here. Can I go around the corner and check into the Howard hotel?" The cop looked at his partner.

"O.k. that is fine but you can't leave the state is that understood?" I shook my head yes.

"We will be in touch ma'am." They let me drive myself to the hotel. I checked in and called my mother.

"Mommy I got something to tell you." She cried out,

"Oh my God Diamond, what is it? Are you pregnant?" I cried, "No Mom, I shot Kareem." She dropped the phone and picked it back up.

"You what? What happened? Are you alright? Is he alright?" I balled, "I don't know." I started crying and sobbing uncontrollably. Between sobs I told her what happened and that I couldn't leave D.C.

"Diamond sit tight me and your dad are on our way." Q was still living in D.C. as well and I called him back. I called him crying and he didn't ask any questions, he just came. He waited for me to take a shower and until my parents came. He just held me like a man is supposed to. I kept my story the same with everyone. When my parents arrived less then 4 hours later Q left. I called Samir and told him what happened. He said, "I'm sorry D for leaving you there alone. I will be on the next flight out of here!"

"It's O.k. just hurry home." I hung up with him and about an hour after my parents arrived it was a knock on the door.

CHAPTER 56
RISKING MY FREEDOM

"Ms. Staple?" I opened the door and the cop flashed his badge at me. I exclaimed, "What is this?" He took out his cuffs.

"I'm officer Francis. You are under arrest for the murder of Kareem Blackwell, we will need you to come with us." I screamed, "Wait, there has been some sort of mistake. It was self defense not murder." Well let me tell you, apparently Kareem made a dying confession that I shot him because I thought he killed my best friend. He told them that I fooled him into coming upstairs and I killed him. As I was being cuffed and read my writes I screamed.

"Ma!" They were in the next room and came running out. I had tears running down my face. I pleaded with my dad with my eyes.

"Daddy help me." My dad stepped up to the cops.

"What is this? Where are you taking my daughter?" Officer Francis looked my dad up and down.

"We are taking her to the precinct for murder!" I cried, "Daddy please do something!" My dad exclaimed, "Don't worry baby girl we will get you out of this." When I got to the precinct they took my fingerprints, my mug shots, and strip-searched me. I was degraded like I was a criminal. Hell in my mind I wasn't a criminal. I sat in jail for a week before they set my bail at $250,000.00. My dad consulted a bail bonds man and got me out. I wasn't supposed to leave D.C. but bullshit I went to Jersey.

Kareem's service had been during the week I was locked down and I heard through the grapevine that it was so many girls coming out of the woodwork saying they were his girl and they were either pregnant or had his child. I went to Jersey spending all my free time with Samir and

Kareemah because I knew I was going down.

I pleaded not guilty and my trial was set for August 1st. I don't remember too much about my trial because I was in a fog. I had killed the man that killed my sister. I didn't take the stand because the lawyer thought I would incriminate myself. I sat and watched as 2 sides battled it out for my fate. On the day of my verdict my family was there and so was Kareem's. Jackie and Q were there as well. My family got to speak on my behalf and Kareem's family got to speak on his.

The court found me guilty of first-degree murder and sentenced me to 25 years to life. In less than an hour of deliberation the jury decided my fate. They thought I was guilty. My mother fainted. Kareem's family cheered and clapped. My dad grabbed my shoulder as I stood up to be shackled.

"D be strong we will appeal this." Samir turned his head as they cuffed me. I yelled out, "Samir please look at me." He wouldn't. I kept talking.

"Samir I love you but don't wait for me. Move on with life cause mine is all messed up now! Don't mess up your life waiting on me." He turned his head slow to face me. He had tears in his eyes.

"Diamond we are Bonnie and Clyde! Clyde would never leave Bonnie and I am not leaving you. I will be there for you until you get out. I asked you to marry me and I meant it. There is no other girl for me." I started tearing.

"Bye Kareemah, mommy loves you!" She blew me a kiss. I had to turn my head to keep from boo hoo crying. Q and his mom were in the courtroom watching me get shackled. Q was going overseas to Italy to play basketball in September. Him and his mother had tears rolling down their faces. I shouted to Q.

"Q I gotta ask you something. What did you have to tell me that day?" He smacked his forehead.

"Oh they found Tahir's killer. He was set up by..." The bailiff yanked me.

"Come on!" He pushed me to leave. I didn't get what

Q was saying. I had to toughen up because I was going to prison. The first day I got there I got into a fight. This girl named Sherry. It was Kareem's first cousin. The second day I was there Sherry and her crew, Eva, Lindsay, Erika, and Kesha jumped me. They beat me so bad I ended up in the hospital with a concussion. My lawyer who was working on my appeal asked that I be moved to another jail closer to my daughter. The court granted my move and here I am in Clinton's Women Facility. When I got here I thought it would be all peace but my second day here I got into a fight and got thrown in the hole. Some dike named Mek AKA Tameka tried me. She must think I am like her since I got a female tatted on my back but ain't nothing happening. Once I got out the hole that is where I started in the caf and now I am here again. This time for a month. I can't get mail in or send any mail out. I surely can't have any visitors so I haven't seen my family. This jail shit isn't for me.

My appeal is already under way so we will see. I hope I can get out here. I told my dad to call Johnny Cochran or somebody. I am not going to take it in here for 25 years to life. Yo, I want you to pray for me. I have been working on my relationship with God again and I thank him for being a forgiving God.

Right before I came to the hole Samir and Zak wrote me. I was waiting for Q's letter but didn't get it before I got in the hole. I am sure by the time I get out it will be there. Q will be in Italy for 4 or more years playing ball. Maybe when he comes home he can play pro ball.

I know Samir don't want to know about me and Q or me and Zak corresponding but I gotta do me until I come home, if I ever come home. I need all the support I can get. I missed Tahir, Starr and just everybody. It is almost lights out but I got one question for you, how blind is love...really?

People always say love is blind but if it makes you that blind that you can't see, maybe you should learn from Starr's mistakes and open your eyes a little wider. Please if not for your sake, do it for the people that care about you most, your family. Remember from my life that family is all the people that love you and will do anything for you. To many times our bloodline families don't love us but our street families do.

It is too late for Starr, but if you are reading this and you are a victim of domestic violence it is not too late for you. Don't end up like Starr. Don't make one of your best friends have to trade places with me and what I'm going through. In the famous words of Mob Deep, "Don't make him or her have to risk their freedom!" Cause I sure did. One love, I'll holla!

<>Diamond<>

Stay tuned....for "Me is Me" the story of Mek AKA Tameka.....

ATTENTION ORGANIZATIONS AND BOOK CLUBS
Quantity discounts are available on bulk purchases of this book. For more information contact My Father's Child Publishing, P.O. Box 364, Vauxhall, NJ, 07088 or contactkae@kaebrown.com.

Please e mail me with comments about the book and I will hit you back!
contactkae@kaebrown.com
OR
Write me a letter
Kae Brown
P.O. Box 364
Vauxhall, NJ, 07088

Either way I will get back. Make sure to check out my website at www.kaebrown.com for updates and events.

Thanks for the love
Kae

Kae Brown

ACKNOWLEDGMENTS

It is said that in life people come into your life for a reason, season, or lifetime. I would like to break my acknowledgments down in that category.

First I would like to give honor to God who is the head of my life and from whom all my blessings flow. The sooner you learn that, the better your life will be. I can never thank him nor repay him for all the situations and circumstances he has carried me through but I can try to live my life in a style that is pleasing to him.

Reason- to meet a need you have expressed.

Moe (M.J.G) You came into my life for the reason of being my first love. You were my first everything and to you I say thank you for teaching me what true love was all about. Even through all the drama and all the arguments we can still say we are friends and to that I say thank you and I love you. Shareef (S.K.C.) You came into my life as my second love and to you I say thank you for teaching me what true love was not about. We were young and you taught me a lot of things about cheating (smile). I love you for that because you taught me to always keep my eyes open. With out either one of you gentleman I would have not been able to write this book so to both of you I say thanks for the memories, love you and God Bless. Any other gentleman that came before or after these 2 is not worth mention but thanks as well. To my young heart breaker Ahmad aka Maddy (Thanks Amirah & Dell for having him) - Kay Kay still loves you and I will have to come see you real soon. Moody Holiday www.moodyholiday.com. Moody what can I say? Words can not begin to express the joy I feel when I think about all the help you have given me. You started me on this path and made sure I didn't give up even when the going got tough. I am forever in debt to you and what you have done for me. God will always bless his children and you are definitely one of his children. Kalico Jones www.kalicojones.com. Kal, thanks for being my big sis in times I got weak. You always had the positive words to make me feel better about anything. Thanks again. Debra Sawyer. www.newarkis.com/dsawyer.htm Deb we met and you just jumped in my corner. I appreciate such a strong bond between us. Thank you so much for all your love and support. With these 3 women we have formed the Jersey Connection. If you love me support them as well because you will not be disappointed. Mrs. Gilda Harris. What more can I say the name alone speaks for itself. When I was lost in my job and wanted to leave God sent you to me. You are my second mother and I love you immensely for the prayers I know you ask God to give me. You are an amazing woman with an amazing spirit and it shines through. I am truly blessed to even say that I knew you. No matter how far in this world you travel away, I will still be your daughter and you will still be my mother. Mr. Harris, thank you for marrying her and bringing her to New Jersey if only for a while. Thank you as well because you know you're my second dad. Genea Robinson Jett and Family (Donta and Kiana) Thank God we met at the bank and held each other down when the going got rough in that place. I am happy to see your spiritual growth and be a part of that process. You were always willing to help no matter what and to you I say thank you. Sister Scott, Sister Credelle, Sister Hux, and Sister Williams and the young women's Christian fellowship group of First Zion Hill in Newark, NJ, I love you all. Thank you so much for accepting me into your group and helping me grow spiritually. I asked God for my purpose and in your group I found it. Summit and Fleet bank- all my buddies from work and I had a lot, Luis, Cindy, and Mel- you were the 1st to buy my book from the bank, thank you so much for all the love and support through all the things I went through and you held me down with. For those of us that got let go with the Bank of America Merger hold your head up and for those of you still there, GOD BLESS YOU:) I love you all and you know that and there were some I didn't love but I am grown now so I love you too.

Season- to share grow and learn with a person. (It

is only for a season though!)

Chad Bailey, you are my brother and I love you thanks for being in my life for a season. May God continue to bless you and your future endeavors. Starrnissa Daniels you are my sister and I love you as well. Thanks for being in my life for a season. I learned things from you and to you I say thank you. When I didn't have you made sure I did and again I say thank you. May God bless you and Sultan and your future endeavors. Khaliq P. (Liq-money) you use to be my homey use to be my ace and I will always love you and pray for your safety. Circumstances and situations bring upon change and unfortunately people change as well but you will forever be in my heart. Bruce AKA Pop you use to be my homey use to be my ace and I will always love you as well and maybe one day we can be friends again but if that day never comes the season was nice.

Lifetime- solid emotional foundation.

Now hold on, this may take a while. First I would like to thank my family. (Father's side)The Brown's have been an inspirational force in my life since my father passed away in 1993. I love you all and thank you for your love and support. Aunt Jackie, I will never be able to thank you enough for being a blessing to me. (Mother's side) Mommy thank you for wanting to get your life focused and be closer to me. Thank you for all the things you have done, I love you and stay just the way you are. Grandma Winnie, what can I say, you know you're my biggest fan. Thank you for EVERYTHING. Words could not express the gratitude and the love I feel for you so I won't say anything but thank you and what color Cadillac do you want? Aunt Beth, Uncle Kevin, Philip, and Ashley representing Ohio. I know my book will sell out there because you love me. Thank you for always being there through the good and the bad. I love you all. Adopted Auntie Bev, Uncle Truman, and Whit- thank you for treating my family as your own when they made that move to Ohio. I worry about them but with you, I have no worries. Thanks and I love you. Ohio crew part 2-

Kae Brown

Aunt Karen, Uncle Steve, Bria and Sameer stay focused out there. I love you all very much. The Twins- Ooh Lord, the twins. Leonard and Leon or Roc and Kerm- I love yall with all my heart and all my soul and all my mind. You are my brothers from another mother always holding me down no matter what I did: Thank you so much for all the things you do for me. Words can not express the joy I feel even talking about you two. Let me tell you all like this, if Leonard needed my left arm and Leon needed my right arm I would write with my feet. I love y'all. And Leon I love Jayla your baby girl with her cute self, looking like your mother. Reef, thanks for being a friend when I needed one. Much love to you, your wife, Connie, Shakil and our new baby on the way next month! Ashley D. we met at the bank and you have been my boy ever since. Even when people at the bank, you know who you are, tried to make our friendship seem vile and dirty we still stayed friends to the end. Love yeah much and I wish you and Linda, hey Linda, the best in life. Charles Family- where do I start. Shannon everything we have is like, 'both of ours' so I know we will always have. I love you for always having my back and in most cases getting my front. Knocking me out the way to see what's going on. Thank you for being one of my biggest promoters. Shawn aka Hoody Hood, the man that needs no introduction. Hood you know you are my best friend and whatever I got its yours. Londa, his wife and my dog, thanks for all the love and support and I got that bootprint for yeah:) And your kids Kiev and Kiya- I love them too even though they are a mess like their parents. Aunt Niecy, thanks for making Mid Town Miller our home. We love you and you know you are Mother Mid Town for life. Keep cooking for us and getting us fat. We love you. Travis Charles you just came but thanks. Darnell aka Buddah there are no hard feelings you still a part of the family. Love you and hold your head. Mitchell's- Gordy aka Black- OOH MY GOD what can I say thanks for being my biggest promoter and always asking about the book even though you don't read nothing but the Star Ledger. Thank you for always making me feel welcomed and letting me know if you got it, then I got it. I love you for that cousin. Saji and Sejada be good and do your school work or I will get the belt. Toiya Veals fiancé of Gordy- next time I write a book I better be able to say Mr and Mrs Mitchell you heard? Naw, but I want to say thank you, lately you have been my rock in this storm called life and I want to say thank you. Thanks for hooking up outfits for me through Sesa's fashion. Teka, cousin thank you for working with me during a difficult time in your life. You have 3 lovely kids Camadi, Camri, and Camil, well I don't know about Camil he said I can't write and he is only 4 years old- HAHAHA But thank you and your family. Ok Laure I have to put you in Amil in here or I would get a beat down from Amil. Also Mimi and the rest of the Hortons, thanks. I love y'all and thanks for everything. Aunt Jean- you have always supported me no matter what and to you I say thank you and I love you so much. Words can not express how much I love you. Jada don't give Aunt Jean a hard time or me and Shannon will jump you- Sike do good in school. Kae loves the kids. To Uncle Bud, Londa, Danny, Teya, Breezy, Lil Dan, Guy, Melissa, Kayla, Lil Guy, Kier, Mia, Chelsea and the rest of the clan that hangs on Aunt Jeans porch I love you and see this summer right back on the porch. Kim Carter and her crew- keep doing your thing- nothing in life is unattainable. Andew aka Big Light- keep making us laugh and stop laughing on the drums at church. Tyree- thanks for wanting to read. You and Andrew cut it out life is to short. Mrs. Hutchins, another one of my mothers, thank you for the support and push the book down in Pennyville. The rest of Vauxhall AKA the Hall thank you for your love and support. I know I wasn't the nicest kid growing up but I know I've been changed! O.K. next, my girls- Shannon no more shout outs for you, Adrienne aka Shorty we have been friends a long time and I wish you all the best in your life. I love you. Tahitia aka Bookey. Girl you know I love you like a sister. Thanks for all the support and encouragement. You're a great mom to Elijah and Elijah stop telling me all you learn in school is

Kae Brown

ABC's and 123's ok- HAHAHA. God has something special in store for you and mommy just watch God work. Keisha Ray, thank God we grew up and put our silly differences behind us. No matter what you always loved me so to you and my God son Tahkwan with his smart mouth I say I love you and keep God first. Thank you for everything you have done and will do. Keep the competition going- it keeps my pockets growing. you know what I mean HAHAHA. The rest of the Ray family. I love you and thanks. Akira, my nucca- Kira I love you for always making me laugh even through the rough times you are one friend I can say I never ever had any type of falling out with. God blessed you with that loving spirit to let things roll off your back and to you I say thank you and I love you. You are a good mom to Demetri- hey Meet- and keep up the good work. Meet, stay in school don't be no fool and keep making us laugh like your mother. Kira he is stealing your shine. To the rest of Kira's fam- Aunt Shell, Rachel, Anothony, Kirk , Jesse Duke, Jamil, and Naomi- I love you all thanks for letting me in the family. Naomi (Na) I love you and miss you- be good in the dirty! Sharonda my sister aka Ron Ron- to you your family and your kids Mo and Me Me- I love yall. Hey Asia I know you saying Kay Kay didn't shoot me out- yes I did- I love all y'all- you invited me into your family and embraced me like your own. Kim aka KJ- I love you- you have always been there for me when times got rough. I will always love you know matter how much you don't call me. Lakesha thanks for the support from you and Kalani and may God continue to work in your life and help you to see things his way. I love you both. Brandy- Ooh Lord what can I say about my sister from another mother but let's me share her father- Hey Dad (Jimmy Scott and Mom Wanda) and kids Jacob and Jordan- thank you for being an inspiration to the fight scenes. Just joking thank you for always having my back and being down for whatever. I love your mean, crazy butt and thank you. Jimmy, hold your head. Helen you are like a mother to me and friend and you opened up your home and family and shared them with me and I love you for all that. Nicole B. Girl when are you and Damien getting hitched- Well whenever I will be there- we have been friends since 7th grade and you always check on me and hold me down and to that I say thank you and I love you. My little sis Blair thanks Pearl from 227 aka Nosey for editing and keeping my hair tight. Holla at her at hairbyblair@aol.com- she does the best buns in the world. To Lil Sis Tiff from NY you still my lil sis even if we don't speak much. Do your thing in college and thanks for the advice for book 2. I love you. Vicki, hubby and kids Lateef and Zaheer thanks for letting me share in that special day with you- we have been friends since Kindergarten and you still here: To my sister Shanda. Thank God that Al Kabir blessed this earth if only to get us to meet- I love you and Chanice baby girl Auntie loves you- keep your head in those books and keep loving to go to church- the only little girl I know that loves church- Danielle best of luck to you and Tarzan, love going out with you. Shanda may God bless you and your family and Rodney as well. To my sister Jamillah and her 7 kids- I love all yall- I haven't talked to you in a while but I would love to- holla at me. Gina my cousin, thanks for holding me down and not cutting me off like you did other folks- HAHA just jokes I love you. Tani- love you and Quinn too. To my big brother Malik, I love you and right now you not in the best place but God will see you through, he did it before. He will do it again. To my cousin Rodney who fixed Nelly- I told you I wouldn't forget to give you a shoot out to you and Millington Auto Body doing the best work in the world. To the folks that read my book when it was just a manuscript- here we go, PSEG part time crew- Tyra, Kito, Mariam, Karen, Alnisa, Monique, and full timer Walida- what can I say when you use to come in and fight over the chapters it did my heart good. To Tyra's mom and fam, thanks. To Isiah and Billy, do go. Kito, Mari, Amir and the twins, good luck. Alnisa and Aniya, good luck. When I saw Tyra get a tear in her eye from the book I knew she was crying because it was that bad or that it touched her and I vote for the second one: I love all you guys and even some are gone and some still there we still have our part timers bound. Rah aka Monster- Ok this is my dude. I love you for reading my book and finishing it at close to 3 AM and then calling me to talk about it like I was up HA- thank you for your support and saying it was THE TRUTH- I love you for that. Shoot outs to your family and specially Little Shotty. Then Monster gave it to Mrs. Bailey. O.k. Mrs. Bailey read it and didn't even know who wrote it so once she liked it I revealed myself to her. Thank you Mrs. Bailey. Nia, my dog, read my book while she use to be on the phone with us straight ignoring our conversation and reading and then going to book stores finding out how I could get it published- my girl thanks Nia I love you. Shannon, you again? Naw Shannon, baby girl even though we get on each others nerves so bad sometimes I love you- You read my book in 2 week and you don't read. This is from someone who started a book, Asata, in her freshman year of college and um...wait did you finish it yet and graduated 2 years ago- you get the most props for that. Then you passed it to Londa my other nucca- Londa I love you and your ability to be real. Thank you for liking my book and calling me when you got to is that a bootprint, you are so crazy! Kee-Kee (wife of Kenny and mother of Kennedy) thanks for reading and giving feed back. Aunt Chickie thanks for reading my book and liking it. Good looking out. To my Book Club One Mind Many voices, Iyesha, Kia, Keisha, LaKisha, LaTasha, LaToya, Leticia, Ms. Bailey, Shimese, Tahitia, Tammy, and Wydiah- I love you much and thanks for the support. We have so much fun at our meetings and have formed a bond that can't be broken. Leticia keep writing, Toiya keep sewing and Tammy keep on with S'more Desserts. Iyesha and Dewey - thanks for creating my boyfriend Jahni. Jahni I love you, now stop being so bad. Stephanie thanks to you and Jerome for creating my other boyfriend Justin- I love you too- Kay Kay love the kids- they don't call me KAY KELLY for nothing y'all- It's jokes. To my editing team, Walida, Keisha, and Blair thank you for doing that for me- and if there are errors in the book it is probably because I changed something and didn't fix it. These ladies did a phenomenal job and I want to say thank you and I love you. Deneen www.deesign.com come on now the work speaks for it self- thanks for the web page and making my cover tight and for the bond we have formed through this. You're a special person and May God continue to use you for his purpose. For those that kept asking me about the book, Shawn aka Red, Black, Jeneane, Jenn Lewis, Sheya my biggest fan and cousin, Kia (kids Raquel and Jasmin), Aunt Pat and Uncle Junior,Cousin Iceberg, Aunt Linda and Uncle Joe, Aunt Mae, Aunt Lee, Cousin Stacey, Cousin Cindy and Aleah, Cousin Deja, Cousin Nadine, Aneesah and Robin, Cousins Chelsea, Kalya, Anthony, Asia, Shayna, Isiah, and Mariah, Uncle Frank and Aunt Avaline, Uncle Ernest and Aunt Colleen, Rae can the book be in the store or can I sell it at you and Zak's wedding- love you too Zak, Cousin Mary Anne, Cousin Chante and Alyssa Leak, Cousin Shanda and Cyrstal and hubby Dewayne- D its finally here- ight?, and Lisa from MSU, Emerson and Aunt Mary you both stay asking for it and you both better push it at the airport, can't wait for you to read it cause you read more then me, Taryn finally after we been from Bahamas years ago, thank you all for asking, Cornell thanks for always asking. Michelle and Rishanna yall too. Uncle Corrie- you know you my peeps- thanks for making me laugh with your crazy stories and your fake horror flick. To your daughter Aliyah love you. Howard University- I was there in '94 and it was fun- Jarrod, Preston, Lindsay, Sheena, Anita and my twin sister Serita from Philly- get at me I miss you. Danielle we had fun at Howard. Lekan, Monique, and Femi my nucca's from MSU- shoot out to MSU aka Montclair State the best college in Jersey, right right-Then comes Willy P- to all my Willy P heads from Shannon people like Carl, Tahir, Mal, Stan, Mike, Al (wife Janeen), Taj, Hameen(don't get brolic) Deebo I mean John and the rest of yall- ooh the girls Judith, Allison, Crishawn, and Keyana- shoot outs to yall- positive brothers and sisters doing there thing. Epiphany Sole starring Isis- do y'all thing I want you to sing at the book release party. Keep pushing out the banging songs. For times and locations of where they will be singing, frequently check my web page because where they are, I will be. Rodney and Hass thank you for always asking and wanting me to have the best I love yall E town. My other Mother Deb- I love you thank you for opening up your home and family K Mart 1,2, and 3 to me. I love yall. May God continue to bless you. DJ Love and Ice keep spinning. I miss Packees. Lonnie or L- you thought I forgot- when does the album drop- told you I would shoot you out. Ok Pooh, Will and Sheed here's some love for yall and the rest of the crew. Pooh when are we going to Miami we're waiting. Hass please you know you and Buddah Blast up here and the rest of the crew. Dutney you know I love you big bro. Uncle E I still love you even though you came from Florida a year ago and just hollering at me. Lil Cuz Rah- hold your head baby boy- you should be home soon. The old Mid Town Miller, Black, Hood, Q-tip, Rollo, Mal, Ab, Wali, Buddah, and Kay Kay (the boy)- your wives kids and your families- I love you all. Rah Riches- you make me laugh had to shoot you out. Yero- I will cook for you whenever. Bass you too, you get a little love. Marcus, Corey, Tasha and the rest of the Mickens- do your thing. Uncle Mook, Cousin Markie and Peasy lets get it going. Corey aka C Murder, My favorite cousin Hak cutting hair at QBG's love you.To the youth of Vauxhall, Kae cares- if don't nobody else care. I love all of you and I want to thank Marla for opening my eyes to helping the youth. Marla keep writing. Youth you can do your thing-now you know it is to many of you to thank but I will say O Blokk I love yall-yall my little brothers and you know it- Oregon a part of O Blokk- Denisha and Dwight- be good stay out of trouble. Denisha I have a hug for you- I know you love that-: Lil Joey you have a talent that God blessed you with to rap and to design clothes- keep mesmerizing folks. Lil sis Tiara keep modeling. Avis see you in church...Kenny hold your head and use this as a reminder not to be back there. Curryville-all y'all I love you much. Shoot outs to my churches-Growing up Bethel A.M.E with Reverend Fubler and now New Hope Baptist Church with Reverend Carter. IF you want to hear the word, come to church with me all are welcome. Last shoot out to the CLASS OF 1994 from UNION HIGH SCHOOL and some of my teachers from UNION SCHOOL SYSTEM- I love you all- I can't begin to name the whole class but a few to mention, Eva, Nicole, Kim, Lindsay, Erika, Sherry, and Brandy, my girls from high school. Well I have said a lot and I know I missed a lot of yall but PLEASE CHARGE IT TO MY HEAD AND NOT MY HEART-and let me know you will be first up in the next book- I promise- For now Keep God first and all else will fall into place! I'll holla! Love KAE

20 LIFE LESSONS FROM KAE

1. Always put God first and everything will fall into place.
2. Nobody is perfect so remember that when you want to judge somebody.
3. Always respect your elders.
4. Treat people how you want to be treated. ALL PEOPLE.
5. Don't take life for granted. Live each day to the fullest. Remember for 100 of us that woke up, 100 didn't.
6. Do good for people and towards people, you will get it back.
7. Blood is not always thicker then water. Real friends are hard to find, cherish them even when they work your last nerve.
8. Stand up for what's right. Don't take a back seat to life and ride, get up there and drive!
9. Beauty is in the eye of the beholder.
10. Ladies if a man doesn't love you, bump him. That one took me a long time to learn. If he's not loving your right let him go, is it easy? Heck no but it can be done.
11. Ladies have some sort of class about yourself. Stop sleeping around and not knowing who your babies daddy is. It is 2005 and AIDS is alive and real. How can it be 10

men that can possibly be your babies daddy. Get your life together, START TODAY!

12. Guys- stop being dead beat baby daddies- yeah, if you are I'm talking to you. Get your self together and do for you child in most cases your children.

13. Ask for forgiveness for your sins. If you wrong somebody make it right not now…RIGHT NOW!

14. Tell people that you love them even if they don't say it back. If you say it and they don't say it back you still love them right? Well tell them. Life is to short to play guessing games. Don't let folks stand around at your funeral or you stand around at theirs and have to question how you felt or how they felt- Let them know.

15. Stay on top of your game. Handle your business. Don't let your bills get so far behind that you are sinking. AND DON'T PUT NOTHING IN YOUR NAME- DON'T LET FOLKS MESS UP YOUR CREDIT.

16. Be open minded to all people.

17. Be forgiving. Just because y'all use to beef back in the day doesn't mean y'all should always beef. What are you gonna do beef forever? I know some said yep out of that smart mouth and its cool, these are not laws just suggestions.

18. Ignorant people raise ignorant children and the bond is never broken. Break the bond. Raise your kids to respect others and their property. Stop saying, "Not my child" because yes it sometimes is your child. Realize your kids and nobody else's are angels. Stop approaching kids about your kids like you want to fight them. Approach the parents. Kids will be kids and they will argue, tease each other, and fight that is a part of growing up.

19. Teenagers- Stop being so grown. Enjoy your youth. Sneaking and creeping is a part of life but at 13 and 14 you should not be a mother. I don't care what you say, you're not ready! Mom's of these teenagers- make them raise them. Stop letting them of so easy and letting them still run the streets while you home raising their child. They wanted to be fast and grown now let them see it. Hold up, don't

jump to conclusions and get bent all out of shape. If your teen is doing her thing, going to school, and working O.k. but I'm talking about the girls that have a baby today and be back hanging on the block or wherever next week. They wanted to lay down and have that baby let them raise it. Tough love works!

20. Guys, you not getting off scott free. Stop all this cheating. It has spiralled out of control. If you want to run free then break up with your girl. Stop giving your girls hush rings. You know what that is, give her a ring to shut her up but never marry her. You be engaged for 20 years. Stop all this playing. Stop saying women can't handle the truth- we can handle the truth it is just that half of you lie so much that you wouldn't know the truth from a lie. Be a man. Get a job. Stop wanting to go into these companies and be the C.E.O. It doesn't work like that. Stop blaming the white man for all your problems, own up to some of them. Stop saying girls are money hungry. All my women who independent - throw your hands up at me! Us independent women are real women. Real women handle their handle with our with out you. That's why guys don't like to date a real woman because your scared. Real women don't need you for anything. We don't have to sit around and wait for you to bring us money to get our hair did! You can't treat a real woman any kind of way except for with respect. That's it but that is they way you should want to treat us.

Bottom Line is we are headed for self destruction. We need to love ourselves and love one another. Treat each other the right way. For anyone reading this that I ever wronged, offended, treated badly, teased, fought, hated, disrespected I'm apologizing because I will be the bigger person. We all know life is to short so lets enjoy it and each other. Like my cousin Black always says to me, "Kae, you trying to get to heaven?" The answer- you know thats right! Its dark and hell is out- I'm out ONE   Kae Brown

Kae Brown

Kae Brown

Printed in the United States
32276LVS00003B/43-135